WRITTEN IN BLOOD

A Bloodwritten Flames of Ruin Dark Romance

B Wills

Golden Light Publishing House

Cover Design: Get Covers

Formatting by: B Wills

Developmental Editing by: AY Hamilton & Charletta Benedict

ISBN: 979-8-9928401-6-2

ASIN: B0FW6JVZSW

Printed in the United States of America

"For those who remember that gods were lovers before they were deities. For those who understand that worship and ruin are the same prayer. Every love leaves scripture behind. Ours was carved into flesh, bound in blood, and read by those who mistook it for sin."

BOOK PLAYLIST

1. In the Shadows You'll Hear My Voice – KIRRA47

2. Play with Fire – Sam Tinnesz, Yacht Money

3. Killer – Valerie Broussard

Author's Note & Content Advisory

Written In Blood is a dark-romance gothic thriller woven with themes of obsession, sacrifice, and transcendence. This story contains explicit sexual content, violence, religious imagery, and psychological manipulation.

Readers should expect morally grey characters, power-laden relationships, and supernatural elements that blur the line between devotion and destruction.

Please read responsibly and at your own pace.

This is not a safe love story.

It is a study of how far we go when love demands a sacrifice.

Happy reading, and remember to take breaks as needed.

—B. Wills

Contents

CHAPTER 1

Octavia

Blackmoor University has been my home away from home for the past four years, its sprawling estate and 1800s architecture the very reason I chose it in the first place. The ivy-strangled stone, the echo of footsteps in vaulted halls—it felt like stepping into a Gothic novel I'd always wanted to write myself.

Now, as August wanes, I begin the program I've chased like a fever dream—my Master of Fine Arts. Getting here wasn't easy. I spent the first two years after high school working double shifts, saving every dollar until I could pay for tuition outright. The look on their faces when I walked in with cash for my first two years—*unforgettable*. That was the proudest moment of my life.

I pulled late nights at The Golden Dragon and Antonio's Pizza, then dragged myself to my day job at *The Rosemont Gazette*. Sleep was a luxury I couldn't afford, but sacrifice became second nature. And now, in my fifth year at Blackmoor, I'm ready—*hungry*—to learn everything I can in order to finish my degree.

Today is my first Creative Writing Seminar with Professor Adrian Marlowe, and I'd be lying if I said I wasn't nervous. His reputation precedes him, but seeing him in the flesh at the front of the lecture hall? The reality is far more unsettling.

The hall itself is sweeping, with arched ceilings stretching overhead, sunlight cutting in pale shafts through the tall windows at the back. Professor Marlowe stands with his hands clasped behind him, surveying us as we file in. Nothing escapes his gaze—sharp green eyes shot through with gold behind thick black frames. His appearance is as meticulous as his reputation: a tailored suit, golden cufflinks that catch the light, a plum tie he adjusts with deliberate ease. When he shrugs off his jacket, it's with the casual precision of a man who knows he commands the room.

Our eyes meet for the briefest moment, heat rushing to my face and prickling down my neck. I shift in my seat, unwilling and yet unable to look away. A shadow of a smirk touches his mouth before he turns to the stragglers bustling through the door.

"My class is scheduled to start—" he glances at the golden Armani watch on his wrist "—now. Do not make it a habit of coming late."

The students scatter into their seats like startled birds. I smooth the front of my tan corduroy skirt, and my cream colored sweater, forcing my hand to draw out my notebook and pen. I lift my head just as his voice fills the room again—low, commanding, and impossible to ignore.

"My name is Professor Adrian Marlowe. In this class, you will learn to understand the nuances of the written word."

Every eye clings to him, every body leaning forward as though tethered to his cadence. One does not squander the chance to learn from Professor Marlowe—the man rumored to make or break a writer's career before it even begins.

"I will not go easy on you. If you've taken this course expecting an elective with an easy grade, you're in the wrong room. I won't hold it against you if you leave now."

A few students exchange nervous glances before slipping out, shoulders hunched as though hoping to disappear.

"I see," Professor Marlowe mutters, shaking his head as he returns to the podium. His gaze sweeps the hall, precise, inevitable—and then it lands on me. Heat coils low in my stomach, toes curling inside my shoes before I can stop myself.

"You will follow a rigorous schedule," he continues, voice measured, resonant. "One designed to make you question everything you think you know about writing. It will be thought-provoking. Uncomfortable. And it will push your boundaries in ways you've never experienced before."

His eyes don't leave mine. It feels as if he's speaking only to me—*for me*. My chest tightens, breath slipping out in a silent rush. My throat constricts, The air seems thinner here, harder to draw in. I press my thighs together beneath the desk, hunch-ing over my notebook in a clumsy disguise of note-taking.

Still, the weight of his gaze lingers, hot against my skin, even as he shifts his attention back to the class. His voice cuts through the silence, steady and deliberate, as he assigns our first task. A short essay on fear, shame, or obsession—filtered through the veil of fiction, and due on Monday.

He isn't long-winded, dismissing us well before the bell. A small mercy, since I still have to make it to my evening shift at The Golden Dragon. With a low groan, I gather my things and shuffle down the stairs, each step heavier than the last.

Tomorrow's obituaries still need to be written and filed, and Jessica won't be thrilled if they land late. Which means tonight will bleed into morning, and sleep—if I get any at all—will be brief at best.

As I descend the steps toward the exit, Professor Marlowe moves into my path, briefcase in hand, suit jacket slung over his arm. The gesture looks casual, though his presence is anything but. He stops directly in front of me, and my gaze betrays me—catching on the lines of muscle shifting beneath his shirt.

God, Tavia. Get a grip.

"Miss Hartwell, might I have a word?" His voice is low, smooth as velvet.

My pulse stutters, palms damp as I clutch my notebook tight against my chest. What in the world could he possibly want with *me*? "Of course, Professor. How can I help you?"

"I couldn't help but notice you write for *The Rosemont Gazette*," he says, adjusting the briefcase strap in his hand. "Your last obituary—the Presgraves family—read a little flat."

My jaw nearly hits the floor, eyes going wide as fury coils sharp and hot inside me. "Excuse me?" The words snap out, incredulous, my glare searing with contempt.

He doesn't flinch. His gaze blazes with something perilous, a spark I can't quite name. "It was nothing like your earlier work. What happened to the fire?"

The question snaps me back to reality. "There's plenty of fire in my column. Maybe you're not paying attention."

A smirk flickers across his mouth, an expression sliding into place that does nothing but stoke the anger boiling my veins. "Oh, trust me—I'm paying attention. I stand by what I said. I look forward to your essay, Octavia."

He leaves without a backward glance, briefcase swinging at his side, and I'm rooted to the spot—fury roiling beneath the flush of humiliation burning across my cheeks. My pulse hammers, impossible to steady.

"What the actual fuck just happened?" I whisper into the empty air.

There's no answer. Nothing but deafening silence.

I shift my weight, adjusting the strap of my leather satchel as I mutter his name under my breath, fury quickening my steps down the length of Montgomery Hall. Never in my life have I been so insulted—brazenly, and to my face!

At the double doors, I shove harder than necessary. The wood groans as they swing wide, and my leaden feet drag me into the courtyard beyond. The late-summer air presses heavy against my skin, but it does nothing to cool the fire simmering inside me.

What stings more—that he actually reads *The Rosemont Gazette*? Or that he *dared* to call my writing flat? Who does that?

If what he wanted was a reaction, he has it.

Now?

I'll prove him wrong.

The Golden Dragon has been my favorite "odd job" since my first year in Rosemont. My relationship with my parents was never much to boast about. I spent most of my childhood and teens neglected, expected to work to earn my keep. So, when I met Auntie Susan, I was surprised to learn that some families are normal, and give out a lot of love. More than I was ever given or used to. That woman accepted me without a second thought, flaws and all. Even after all this time, I keep myself on the payroll just to have an excuse to stop in and help when I can. Like tonight. Mae's home with her sick children—Julie, Tobias, and Benji all down with the flu—and I can only pray the restaurant has been properly sanitized. I can't afford to get sick right now.

As soon as I cross the threshold, the scent of garlic and soy hits me, mingling with the sharp tang of grease from the kitchen. The lobby is overflowing, customers jammed into every section, servers weaving frantically between tables, their trays rattling as they pass. The kitchen clangs like a forge, pans slamming, voices rising over the hiss of oil.

No sign of Susan at the hostess stand—she's clearly been pulled into the fray.

I rush to the back, shedding my coat, scrubbing my hands raw with soap, and twisting my hair into a quick braid before pinning it in a bun at the nape of my neck.

"Where do you need me?" I call, already sliding stacks of dishes into the washer.

"Hell if I know," Nick grunts, eyes darting like he's cornered. "Go help Jamie in section three—she's drowning."

I finish what I'm doing and dart through the sections like my life depends on it. Jamie looks wrecked—her face flushed as she hurries another tray out, fiery red bun unraveling into strands plastered to her damp cheeks. A streak of mascara trails down her skin, the telltale mark of someone who's already cried more than once tonight.

Sliding behind the register, I scan her tickets: three orders of General Tso's, two plates of crab rangoon, and a scatter of dishes bound for different tables. I start building trays, arranging the plates the way I know she likes—first order set at noon, the rest circling clockwise. If she can squeeze in refills, she will, but tonight there's no space. Or time.

By the time she returns, the first two trays are ready, and I'm finishing the third. Her eyes widen, disbelief spilling into sudden tears. "You're a fucking saint!" Before I can answer, she pulls me into a crushing hug. "Thank you for coming in tonight. I don't know what we would do without you."

"It's nothing," I mutter, awkwardly prying myself loose. I've never been good with physical touch, never mind open displays of gratitude.

"It's everything, and you know it!" Jamie shoots back, shaking her head. "I'll take these out—thank you again. I'd kiss you if I swung that way."

I laugh. "No, you wouldn't. Now go. I've got this covered."

She winks and sashays off, leaving me chuckling as I turn back to the trays. The rhythm of organizing orders takes over, each plate lined in its place until the chaos finally feels under control. When I finish, I head to the hostess stand, letting my eyes trace the red walls, the gold lettering, and the Chinese décor crowding the lobby. Paper lanterns sway gently overhead, casting a soft glow that makes me grin—until I nearly barrel straight into Susan.

She steadies me, her almond-brown eyes crinkling with delight. "There you are," she says, beaming from ear to ear. "I knew the smile on Jamie's face had to be your doing."

I shrug and settle behind the counter, sliding menus and takeout boxes back into neat stacks.

"Bad day?" Susan asks, leaning on the counter. She's dressed casually—linen pants and a black tunic with the sleeves rolled up. Her silver-streaked ebony hair rests at her shoulders, tucked behind her ears the way she always does.

"No," I lie, keeping my eyes elsewhere.

"You only tidy the hostess station when you're stressed. Spill," she says, eyes narrowing at me until they becoming tiny slits. She isn't going to let it go.

I sigh. "My creative writing professor is an asshole."

A smirk tugs at one corner of her mouth—enough to make me want to throw something. "*Why* is he an asshole?" she asks.

I whirl toward her and the words snap out, putrid as acid. "He insulted my writing—to *my face*."

Her eyes flash, "What did he say exactly?"

Cringing, I think about the way he delivered the blow. So detached and cold. "He said it lacked the fire he was used to seeing in my previous pieces. However, I don't know how an obituary is supposed to be filled with fire."

Auntie Susan cackles, tossing her head back in absolute glee. "Seems like you've finally met your match," she barks between peaks of laughter.

"Auntie Susan, this isn't funny. It's actually kind of creepy. Who takes that kind of interest in a student?"

Her laughter dies as quickly as it sparked, her gaze pinning me with something sharper than amusement. "Octavia Adeline Hartwell," she says, voice clipped, "have you forgotten you use your real name when you write for the column? He lives here. Of course he's seen your work."

Heat creeps into my cheeks as I stack excuses in my mind and find none that hold. Begrudgingly, I murmur, "Fine. You've got a point. But did he have to be that rude?"

Her brow arches. "Octavia, darling, what did I tell you when you decided you wanted to be a writer?"

I sigh, repeating the familiar warning. "That if I wanted to be a writer, I'd better be prepared for the sharpest criticism of my life."

"Glad to know your memory hasn't dulled." She winks. "I was starting to worry."

I groan, turning away and heading for the kitchen. Her laughter trails after me, light and unbothered, while my thoughts snag on every word she's left behind.

Was she right?

Am I overreacting to his bluntness? Because God, it wasn't just blunt. It was brutal. Cutting.

And somehow, it lodged deeper than I care to admit.

CHAPTER 2

Adrian

Delilah White laughs like she's never had to mean it.

Bright. Effortless. The kind of sound that believes the world was built to echo back her joy. She paints in the afternoons, leaves her window cracked even when the air tastes of metal. I stand across the street, watching the brush move in her hand. She's humming something tuneless. It shouldn't matter. It does. Because when she tilts her head toward the light, I see her face—and for one small, cruel heartbeat, I see hers.

Octavia.

That's the problem. The resemblance. It's not exact, just close enough to scratch the same wound open again.

Delilah is not special. She's a body mistaken for meaning. But she's the next proof I need, and I'm nothing if not methodical.

I cross the street. The fog parts around me as if it remembers. Rosemont fog always does—it's obedient in the right hands. Her apartment sits on the second floor of a building that forgot what century it was built in. The light from her window bleeds down the wall like spilled milk. I don't knock. I never do. Doors are ornamental lies.

Inside, the room smells of turpentine and orange peel. A canvas waits on the easel, half-finished—something circular, intersected by a flame-colored line. The same pattern I've seen in the Society's oldest texts, hidden beneath layers of translation: the seal of the Thirteenth Flame. I shouldn't find it here. And yet I do.

Delilah turns. Her mouth opens, closes. "Professor Marlowe—"

"Adrian," I correct softly.

Her voice stumbles over the syllables. "What are you doing here?"

I study her, and the question falls away like loose thread. "You painted something you shouldn't have."

Her eyes flick to the canvas. "It's nothing—"

"It's always something." I take a step closer. The distance between us collapses into the hum that lives under my skin.

I don't raise my voice. I don't need to. Control is a language all its own. "*Sit.*"

Her body stills for a heartbeat too long, eyes flicking as if searching for another option, then she sits. Not like someone choosing, but like someone remembering an instruction they didn't know they'd learned. The obedience isn't surrender. It's disbelief, a reflex born when reality begins to tilt. People cling to the last delineation that resembles order—even when it's offered in a voice that doesn't ask.

I move through the space quietly, noticing the tiny details. A chipped mug, a stack of unpaid bills, and three brushes rinsed too quickly still linger in the sink. I pick up one of the smaller knives from her table, the kind meant for detail work. The blade is clean. It won't stay that way.

When I touch her, I do it with exactitude. No haste. No cruelty—it is *wasteful*. This is not about pain. It's about the process. I map her skin the way a scholar maps text, line by line, testing what holds and what gives. I avoid arteries. The trick is not to end her too quickly. The trick is to make the body remember every inch of its undoing.

She tries to speak once—my name again, almost a plea—but I shush her gently. "No, Delilah. This isn't about words."

Minutes stretch. Time slows. The blood smells different once fear thickens it. There's an art to this, the balance between restraint and inevitability. When it's over, the silence lands heavy and pure. I stand there and let it settle.

I clean the blade. I study her face, the stillness that replaces animation. I don't feel triumph. Just clarity. She was necessary. A proof for those that require it, not a prize.

When I step outside, the fog greets me like a familiar accomplice. The night is quiet enough to hear the faint hum that lives in my blood—a darker rhythm, steady and patient. It thrums louder when I think of her—Octavia. The one whose absence bends the air.

I walk the long way home, letting my thoughts unspool with the same accuracy I give every ritual. The Society calls what I do sacrifice. They're wrong. Sacrifice implies loss. I don't lose. I refine.

Delilah's painting follows me in memory—the circle cleaved by flame. She shouldn't have known it. The Society keeps its symbology buried deep. So *where* did she see it?

I arrive home before dawn. The house knows me by sound. The slow groan of the floorboards, the sigh of the old cedar beams, and the click of the lock sliding into place behind me. The air is colder inside than out. I hang my coat, wash my hands, and study the thin shadow pulsing under my wrist. The ink has risen again. Always after a kill. Always in rhythm with something older than the heart.

In the mirror, I catch my reflection. Green eyes, flecked with gold. Too bright, too steady. The monster wears me politely, like a borrowed suit.

I pour a drink. The ledger waits open on the desk, a line drawn neatly beneath the last name.

Delilah White. The ink dries dark and even. Beneath it, I write one word: *Proof.*

Because that's what she was. Evidence that the pattern repeats itself, even if her blood was diluted. That the bloodlines the Society calls myth still move among us. That the flame that should have gone out didn't.

I think of Octavia again. The way she listens when I speak, the way her silence feels deliberate, like prayer. There's something in her that answers to what's buried in me. A resonance. I've seen it before—in old texts, in ritual pairings meant to call back what the gods abandoned. But never like this. Never living.

When I close my eyes, I see her as she was in class that day—head tilted, pen hovering just above the page, hair catching light like something that remembers fire. She's already half-lost to her own thoughts, even awake. She doesn't know yet that she's standing at the threshold of something far larger, or that she called to me long before she ever spoke my name.

The Society would call her anomaly. I call her inevitability.

I sit back, fingers pressed to the ledger's edge. The darker rhythm at my wrist quickens, sensing her name in my thoughts though I haven't written it. I won't. Not yet. Names have weight. To write hers is to claim it.

The ink inside me moves. I can almost hear it whisper through the veins—an invitation, or a warning.

She is the question I haven't answered. The hunger I've mistaken for study. The spark that knows the shape of the fire before it burns.

I take another sip, let the wine stain my tongue, and whisper into the empty room, "Soon."

Because I will find her. Because I can't decide whether I want to possess her or let her ruin me.

And because I suspect that in the end, there's no difference.

Chapter 3

By the time I climb the stairs to my apartment, it's well after eleven and I'm running on fumes. Every muscle aches, my eyelids drag like lead, but quitting isn't an option. Not tonight.

I head straight for the kitchen, yank an energy drink from the fridge, and crack it open. The sweet strawberry tang floods my tongue, a jolt of sugar and vitamins that almost feels like relief. I drink deep, then set the can aside and drag my laptop onto the desk. Notes clutter the surface, notebooks stacked like a graveyard of unfinished thoughts—a burn book for the dead.

The computer hums awake, its desert-red dunes and endless blue sky filling the screen before it gives way to the blank, waiting document. My fingers fly, darting between the keys and the scribbled pages beside me. I've never typed so quickly, never fought so hard to pin down the tone. I'm a woman possessed, fueled by the refusal to let his words settle like a scar.

Time blurs. What feels like hours of battle with sentences collapses into the span of two. Three obituaries are finished, polished, and saved. When I pause to crack my fingers and stretch, the clock blinks back one a.m. Relief washes through me as I glance at my calendar. My morning class does not starting until ten. For once, fate doesn't feel like a cruel hand.

Closing the laptop, I peel myself away from the desk and head toward the bedroom. Gray sweats. Rose-colored tank. Something soft enough to comfort, light enough not to stifle in the night, warm enough to guard against Washington's bite. A fragile armor against the hours still ahead.

I slide beneath my burgundy comforter, my head sinking into the pillows, the faint trace of lavender clinging to the fabric like a lullaby. It's a ritual, the one small comfort I give myself each night.

Sleep takes me quickly. Darkness tugs at the edges of my consciousness, pulling me under until I'm caught in a dream that feels too vivid, too *real*, as if I never closed my eyes at all.

Shadows roll in, curling through the corners of my mind, and the scene reshapes itself into a mausoleum. The air chills, heavy with silence. The structure rises in front of me, stark and beautiful in its gloom—arched stone, intricate carvings, glass the color of blood and ash. Stained windows gleam in the doorframe, their designs macabre and mesmerizing, fragments of bone and angel wings stitched in crimson light.

I've never seen anything so haunting. Or so beautiful.

Something stirs inside me, a thread tugged loose, unraveling faster with every second I linger in this strange place.

Then, without warning, Adrian emerges. He descends the mausoleum steps like a figure conjured from shadow, his dark green eyes blazing with an emotion I can't name.

"What are you doing here, Octavia?" His voice cuts through the fog, low and steady, his head tilting as if he already knows the answer.

My breath hitches. He's dressed in black nightclothes, the thin T-shirt clinging to his chest, outlining muscle I shouldn't be noticing. "I—I don't know," I stammer, the words breaking against my lips.

Adrian's mouth curves, the hint of a smile deepening into something darker, almost predatory, sensual in its edge.

"Where is... *here*?" I ask, my gaze skimming the mausoleum, but the world refuses to sharpen. The fog has thickened, swallowing everything beyond him and the stone at his back. Endless night stretches around us, and yet he is the only thing in focus. Him—and the mausoleum that seems to pulse like a living heart.

He doesn't answer. Instead, he extends a hand, palm open, a silent invitation. A lure. Secrets wait behind those doors, and he knows it.

Part of me wants to turn, to vanish into the fog and leave him behind. But another part—a dangerous sliver buried so deep I almost deny it—aches to take his hand. To follow him. To learn what he isn't saying.

My fingers twitch toward him—and the world *shatters*.

I jolt awake to my phone shrieking on the night-stand, my heart pounding like a trapped hum-mingbird. The clock's red digits blur into focus: after three a.m. Two and a half hours of sleep, *if* that.

The phone won't stop. I snatch it up, my voice scratchy and foreign in my own throat. "Hello?"

"Octavia, you're going to want to get down to Bellflower Street. Someone's been murdered. I need you to help me cover it." Jessica's voice rushes through the line, fast and electric.

"What the fuck, Jess," I mutter, torn between exhaustion and disbelief.

"It's the story of a lifetime, Tavia. Get dressed and meet me there." And just like that, the line goes dead.

For a beat I just sit there, the echo of his hand outstretched still lingering in my chest. Then reality slams back in. Murder. Story. Deadline.

I'm up in seconds, dragging on black jeans, a long-sleeved shirt, my brown leather jacket. My brush snags through my messy braid, and I unravel it, re-plaiting with quick, practiced motions. Stray curls fall against my face, but I leave them. There's no time, I'm already late.

Notebook. Press badge. Recorder. The holy trinity of survival in this job. I shove them inside my bag, lock up behind me, and run.

I make it in ten minutes, breaking every traffic law I can get away with. The street is a wash of flashing blue and red when I pull up, sirens cutting through the night. Jess waits just beyond the yellow tape, two steaming cups in hand, her face ghosted by the strobe of emergency lights.

The scene is crawling with officers, their movements grim, their expressions worse. Horror hangs in the air, thick and unshakable. The way they glance at one another, the way they avoid looking too long at what waits beyond the tape—it twists my stomach, turns my nerves to water.

Something about this doesn't feel routine. It feels like the edge of a blade pressing against my world, ready to split it wide open.

Jess passes me a cup, perfectly sweet, exactly the way I take it. I wrap my fingers around the heat, sipping until it burns down into my bones. For a moment I let it anchor me, but my eyes keep sliding back to the chaos, my exhaustion sharpening into dread.

"...no, not hacked up—slashed. Specific. Like whoever did this knew their way around an anatomy book."

The words cut through the static hum of sirens and chatter, catching me like a hook. I flip open my notebook, scribbling them down fast, my pen dragging harder than it should. A female officer stands a few feet away, her back to me, voice pitched low as she leans toward a forensic photographer.

"Yeah," she murmurs again, her head bent close to his, "I'd say that's an appropriate assumption..."

Another quick line in my notebook. My pulse thrums. Whoever did this didn't just kill—they curated.

As luck would have it, she turns and heads in our direction. Her expression says stay out of it. I don't.

"Excuse me," I call, stepping forward before I can think better of it. "Octavia Hartwell, Rosemont Gazette. Could I get a quote from you?"

She stops short, her glare scorching, dark eyes lit with fury. "Someone was *murdered*. Isn't that obvious?"

The words crack like a whip. Her clipped tone should send me reeling, but instead it digs me in deeper. I steady my notebook, refusing to back off.

Jessica elbows me, a quick nudge at my ribs. Her expression says exactly what I'm already thinking... *press harder.*

"Yes, but no one is saying who or what happened," I press, voice heavy with exhaustion and caffeine. "The citizens of Rosemont deserve to know if there's something to be concerned over."

The officer's jaw ticks, her dark brown eyes narrowing. For a second, I think she'll walk off, leave me standing with nothing but scraps. Instead, she exhales hard through her nose, the kind of sound meant to shut a conversation down without actually closing it.

"What I can tell you," she says finally, tone flat and rehearsed, "is that the victim was discovered a little after two a.m. by a passerby. It's an active investigation, and at this time we do not believe there is any ongoing threat to the public."

Her words are polished—*official*. Exactly the kind of vague line that satisfies protocol but leaves the truth buried.

I jot it down anyway, frustration knotting in my gut. Do not believe there is any ongoing threat to the public. Which really means: *we don't know.*

Jessica leans in, whispering, "Better than nothing."

Maybe. But as I close my notebook, I can't shake the image of the mausoleum from my dream. The fog and shadows. The way Adrian's hand stretched toward me like he held the answers no one else would give.

The officer doesn't wait for a follow-up. She turns on her heel, already retreating into the blur of uniforms and flashing lights.

Jessica exhales, a low whistle under her breath. "Well. That's about as good as we're going to get tonight."

I nod, though the weight in my chest disagrees. My notebook feels heavier than it should, filled with scraps of words that don't add up to answers.

We stand there for another moment, the cold biting harder now, the air thick with exhaust and dread. Sirens fade into background noise. It's all motion around me—officers, cameras, whispered theories—yet I feel caught in stillness, as though the world has shifted and I'm the only one who notices.

Finally, Jessica nudges me toward the car. "Come on, Tavia. Time to write."

I follow, my coffee cooling in my hand, the mausoleum still lurking in the back of my mind. The outstretched hand. The secrets behind those doors.

I shake it off, but it clings anyway.

CHAPTER 4

The cool bite of fog strikes me square in the chest as I jog the final stretch toward home. Each breath burns sharp in my lungs, the mist damp against my skin, clinging like a second shirt. Ahead, the house waits—its black-painted wood against the early morning, tall panes set deep into their frames, lines spare and modern where the neighboring Victorians fret and flourish. People pass and call it severe or too much, as if restraint were flamboyance. They don't understand that restraint is a choice. Restraint is a taste.

It's barely six, and the town is already awake with whispers. Rosemont feeds on scandal the way a body feeds on oxygen, and nothing ignites faster than the word murder. A girl dead. Slashed, precise, meticulous.

Delilah White.

Twenty-three. Curvy frame. Green eyes too dark. Chestnut hair that caught none of the fire of the sun.

I catalog the details automatically, committing them to memory the way one might recall a line of poetry or the phrasing of an old argument. The town will remember her as a daughter, a friend, a tragedy. I remember her as a body. A necessary loss.

But not enough.

The itch remains. Restless. Gnawing. Death ignites hunger—it does not dull it.

I mount the steps, pausing at the door. The morning paper waits on the stoop, ink bleeding faintly through thin newsprint. For once, I bend and take it—not for the headline. For the byline.

Inside, the house receives me with the quiet I expect. The silence is not absence but order, the kind that holds. Shelves line the walls in disciplined ranks, books stacked with exacting symmetry, manuscripts waiting in their towers.

I carry the paper to the study and set it on the desk like a prize. The fold resists, so I smooth the creases with deliberate care, each line pressed flat before my eyes fall to what matters.

There it is.

Her name.

Octavia Adeline Hartwell.

I read greedily, eyes catching on every line, devouring her words as if they were meant for me.

"Bellflower Street woke to the metallic tang of something that should never be here. Neighbors spoke of candles and quiet prayers, of a life cut short beneath the indifferent fog. Delilah White was twenty-three; she laughed too loudly in portrait photos and moved through the world like a small, stubborn sun. Tonight, the town folds around her family, pretending ritual can stitch what violence has torn—a small, useless theatre of grief."

"We file our questions into corners, the ones we whisper about over coffee: who, why, and whether we are safe. The police have asked for patience, and for now that will have to be enough. But the questions remain."

Her voice lingers in every syllable—defiant, too bold, burning to make sense of what she cannot yet understand. She writes for them, for the fragile masses clutching their candles and whispering about safety. But I see what she cannot put on the page. She avoids the method—the rhythm. She calls it violence, not finesse. Chaos, not design.

She feels the edges but not the symmetry. Not yet.

I read the article again, slower this time, savoring the cadence, the way her words strain against the surface of truth. My lips curl before I realize it. She doesn't know she's already circling closer, already pressing on a door she shouldn't open.

I fold the paper with care and slide it into the stack of clippings I keep. Not trophies—no. Records. Proof that the world is watching, that her eyes are watching.

The town will call this morning monstrous. They will call it senseless. They will mourn.

But I know better.

This isn't an ending. This is the beginning.

By eight, the fog has thinned and Rosemont looks almost ordinary again. The campus hums with the usual rhythm—students trailing into lecture halls, the low thrum of conversation, the faint scrape of chairs across tile. Ordinary is the point. Appearances are everything.

I walk the stone path to my office as though nothing has shifted, nodding politely at the dean in passing, answering a colleague's half-hearted comment about last night's news with the same measured sympathy I've perfected. It is an easy role to play.

Order. Normalcy. The ritual of civility.

But then I see *her*.

She rounds the corner, dark circles shadowing her eyes, exhaustion written into the slope of her shoulders. Coffee in one hand, notebook in the other, she looks like she hasn't slept—and still, she burns. Her presence carries that same relentless fire as her writing, the same refusal to yield.

I should let her pass. I don't.

"Miss Hartwell." My voice cuts clean through the hum of morning chatter. She halts, just barely, and those pale green eyes snap to mine.

"I see your piece made the front page," I say, adjusting my glasses with deliberate calm. "Bold work. Heavy on sentiment. Light on accuracy."

Her jaw tightens, the muscle feathering as she inhales. "Forgive me if I chose compassion over dissection."

"Compassion makes readers feel," I reply smoothly, "but it doesn't make them think. Not deeply. Not enough."

She takes a step closer, close enough that I can see the freckles scattered across her tired skin, the faint tremor of her hand where it grips the coffee. "Some of us still believe people deserve more than to be turned into an anatomy lesson."

A smile edges across my lips—small, controlled, deliberate. "Some of us know the anatomy is the story."

For a moment, silence threads between us, taut as wire. Around us the campus moves on—students shuffling by, professors locked in their own conversations—yet it feels as though the world has stilled, leaving only her fire against my calm.

Her verdant gaze narrows. "You always have to have the last word, don't you?"

"Only when the first one isn't enough."

The corner of her mouth twitches—not a smile, not quite fury, but something caught in between.

I let her go. *For now.*

She brushes past me, the faintest trail of lavender clinging to the air, her coffee nearly spilling with the force of her stride, her hair catching briefly in the morning light before she disappears into the stream of students.

I watch her go, careful to keep my expression unreadable, my body language neutral. To anyone else, it's nothing. A professor and a student, a passing exchange. Polite. Forgettable even.

But I am not anyone else.

Her words linger, clashing against mine like steel, and I feel the echo of them under my skin. Tired as she is, she still bites. Still pushes back when silence would be easier. That defiance is what sets her apart. What makes her worth watching.

A colleague waves from across the quad, oblivious. I incline my head in acknowledgment, my mask firmly back in place. Appearances are important. Order must be maintained.

But beneath the surface, the itch festers. The hunger coils tighter. I've let her think she's escaped.

The truth? ... She's already *mine*.

CHAPTER 5

Octavia

By the time I clear the quad, my pulse is still ticking from that exchange. His voice lingers, crisp and cutting, as if he'd carved the words straight into me: *Compassion makes readers feel. But it doesn't make them think.*

It shouldn't matter. Professors make snide remarks all the time. Half of them think they're gods in tweed jackets, untouchable behind their tenure. But something about the way Adrian said it gnaws at me. Too exact. Too... *certain*. Like he'd been waiting for me to write it, waiting to pull it apart.

The journalist in me wants to dig until the bones of the truth are exposed. The student in me says I should've stopped before I started hallucinating ethics.

I shake my head, shoving the thought down as I push through the heavy doors of Montgomery Hall. I'm tired. That's all this is. No sleep, too much coffee, and a deadline that had me chasing shadows at three in the morning. My nerves are shot; no wonder I'm reading into things.

Still...

I can't help jotting his words into the margin of my notebook, the ink scratching deep. I tell myself it's for later, for fuel, for the column. But the truth is simpler...

I *want* to remember them. I want to know why they landed so hard.

I shake my head, tugging my jacket tighter as I check the time on my watch. Eight. Too early for class, too late to crawl back into bed. My first lecture isn't until ten, but the thought of wasting two hours when his essay is looming over me makes my stomach knot.

The library is quiet at this hour, the kind of quiet that feels rare, almost holy. I slip into my usual corner table and unpack my things—laptop, notebooks, the battered pen I always reach for when I need to think.

The assignment waits in the back of my mind, the words circling like a hawk. Obsession. Passion. The fine line between the two.

I pull a notebook closer, flipping it open to a fresh page. My pen hovers, the words I want to write tangled with the ones I can't admit. Because how do you write about obsession when the echo of your professor's voice is still lodged under your skin?

I scrawl a line anyway—something half-formed, raw. It looks like the start of a story, and feels like a confession.

Obsession, I write, is not love. It wears the mask of devotion, but underneath it is hunger sharpened into a blade. It does not ask. It *takes*. It does not release. It coils tighter. Passion is a flame that flares and dies. Obsession is the smoke that lingers, filling every breath, clinging to your skin until you no longer know the difference between wanting and needing.

The pen stills. I stare at the words, uneasy. This isn't an assignment anymore—it's me, bleeding onto the page in ink that looks too dark under the library's fractured morning light.

And yet... this is exactly what he asked for. Fiction that cuts too close, fiction that claws at the edge of truth. Fiction that dares me to step over a line.

I drag a hand through my hair, groaning. "God, I need sleep."

But instead of pushing the notebook aside, my hand moves again, faster now. Words spill, untethered. The story begins to take shape, pulling me deeper with every line. A nameless narrator stalks through my sentences, their voice clear, their desire darker. They watch someone from a distance—first in crowds, then in silence, until the two blur. I describe the sound of footsteps behind her, the weight of eyes lingering too long, the breath of someone close enough to touch but choosing not to.

It's not me, I tell myself. It's not real. It's fiction.

But the narrator's hunger pours through me anyway, restless and alive, and I can't stop. My wrist aches, but the pen doesn't falter. Page after page stacks into something darker than I meant to write. Something I almost don't recognize as mine.

By the time I pause, my coffee is cold, the library clock reads nine-forty-five, and my pulse is hammering like I've been running.

I lean back in my chair, staring at the mess of ink spread across my notebook. It looks less like homework and more like a secret I was never supposed to confess.

And for the first time in hours, I'm not tired at all.

My pen rolls off the page, clattering against the wood, the sound too loud in the hushed cavern of the library. I flinch, glancing around. Only a handful of students occupy the scattered tables, heads bent over laptops and textbooks. No one looks my way.

Still, I feel watched.

The sensation prickles across my skin, a ghost of the dream that clung to me earlier—the mausoleum, the fog, his eyes blazing in the dark. I shake it off, telling myself it's nothing more than exhaustion, nothing more than words bleeding into nerves.

But when I gather my papers, sliding the notebook into my bag, my hand lingers over the page. The story sits there like it's waiting to be read. Like it wants an audience.

And even as I shove it out of sight, even as I pack up and push to my feet, I can't escape the feeling that I've written something that doesn't belong to me anymore.

It belongs to him.

By the time I stumble across campus, the sun has clawed its way high into the sky, too bright against the slate-gray buildings. It glints sharp off the windows, stabbing my eyes until I have to squint. My head feels stuffed with cotton, every thought dragging like it's wading through tar.

9:59.

I push through the heavy wooden doors just before they close, sliding into the lecture hall as a wave of cool, recycled air greets me. The room is dimmer than the rest of campus, the tall windows half-covered by old curtains that mute the light into dusty stripes across the floor. Students are scattered across the sloping seats, some murmuring, others hunched over their laptops. I sink into the middle row, clutching my notebook like it might anchor me to the present.

God, I wish I had time for a nap. Even ten minutes would've been something. But if I close my eyes now, I'll be gone for hours.

The professor clears his throat at the front. He's a wiry man with thinning hair, his voice carrying surprisingly well for his frame. "This semester, we'll be tracing the evolution of power and mortality through art," he begins, gesturing to the projector. A painting flickers onto the screen—Caravaggio, Judith Beheading Holofernes.

The image is violent, almost alive in the darkness of the room. Blood arcs in a vivid red slash, Judith's expression carved in stone-cold resolve.

I blink hard, but my exhaustion twists the scene further. For a split second, it feels like the figure's eyes roll toward me, hollow and black, watching from the screen. My pen jerks in my hand, scraping a useless line across the margin.

The professor drones on about chiaroscuro, about the way artists layered shadow over light to force the viewer into discomfort. My head throbs with every word.

The next slide flickers—memento mori, still lifes with skulls balanced among rotting fruit and overturned glasses. Symbols of death, of decay—a reminder that time strips *everything* bare.

Something in my chest tightens. My thoughts stumble back to the murder scene, to the whispers carried on the cold air, to the way Rosemont seemed to hold its breath as if the town itself knew something had shifted.

I press the pen harder against the page, forcing my hand to write focus in the margin, but it looks more like a warning than a note.

The lecture continues, a blur of names and eras, paintings I can't hold in focus. My notes dissolve into half-formed words and crooked sketches that mean nothing. All I can feel is the room pressing in, the silence heavy between the professor's words, the shadows from the curtains creeping longer as if they're alive.

When the clock finally ticks toward the end of class, I can barely unclench my hands from around my pen.

And as the lights flicker brighter, chasing the shadows back into corners, a shiver races down my spine.

Art is supposed to reflect life. But today, it feels like it's reflecting me.

CHAPTER 6

Adrian

The fog greets me first. It softens the grid of streets into washed-out watercolor, mutes the hard edges of brick and eaves until Rosemont feels half-imagined. Footfalls count out the hour. *Four, four, four*—each strike absorbed by damp air and early silence. I run before the town wakes because discipline prefers an empty stage. It is cleanest to maintain control when nothing answers back.

I cut along the bakery's dark windows, the café's lights just beginning to warm behind their shades, steam ghosting against glass. The neighborhood shifts as the route climbs. Narrow porches and buckled fences giving way to hedges clipped with fastidious hands, freshly painted doors in patient, curated hues. Rosemont is a town that rehearses itself. It believes polish will absolve.

A final hill lifts beneath me, and the house comes into view.

The gate's iron scrollwork slides apart. The front doors open before I reach them. Alcott stands with hands loosely clasped, white gloves today. He does not always keep these hours—he rotates, as staff should—but when he is here, the morning behaves itself.

"Good morning, Dr. Marlowe," he says.

"Alcott." I incline my head and step over the threshold.

The marble breathes back a faint, clean chill. A runner deadens my steps as I cross the entry beneath a chandelier that hangs like a small, deliberate constellation. The air is scented with cedar and a memory of leather, never sweet. Paintings sit precisely where they should. A somber Dutch portrait poised between two narrow windows, and a bronze bust with a gaze that refuses fuss. Nothing shouts. Everything holds.

I take the stairs at an even pace. At the landing the eastern windows lay down a pale band of light. The damned fog eddies against the glass as if trying to peer in. I do not give it anymore concern. Routine beckons.

The shower scalds where it should. Linen yields where it should. The mirror returns the expected man in familiar lines. My dark hair, trimmed, jaw clean, spectacles set, and eyes a shade most call green yet always look darker in winter. Control is an ordinary art when you practice it without interruption.

When I enter the dining room, the table is already prepared. Porcelain, silver, crystal set without flourish. Today it is smoked salmon, ribboned beside pickled fennel, a soft-boiled egg in a small white pedestal, berries arranged in a quiet geometry, and toast cut on the bias as requested. Espresso, crema like silk.

"Chef mentioned the salmon is the new supplier," Alcott says. "Colder cure, milder smoke."

"We'll keep it," I answer, after the first bite. Salt, sugar, smoke—none push. The fennel's acid cuts then leaves. An arrangement that understands subtraction.

He retreats without sound. Staff are to do as told and nothing more. They have their days to themselves, as I instructed. They have their tasks when here. It is not kindness. It is order.

Breakfast, like every ritual, is a study in proportion. The plate is cleared. The day begins again.

The drive is short enough to be a prelude. The campus gathers itself in brick and stone, ivy drafting its green cursive across facades that would collapse under scrutiny if not for the centuries of sentiment bracing them. The quad breathes with morning ritual. Students drifting in loose currents, backpacks weighted, cups in hand, voices pressed low to one another in the easy tide of morning routine.

When I step from the car, conversation shifts. Not silence, not spectacle—just a fractional change in current. A pause smoothed over. The air notes me, then resumes.

The lecture hall smells of varnish and chalk dust ground too deep to be erased. Wood groans under the shifting of bodies, every cough and shuffle magnified against the space. The room is not grand, but it is old enough to have learned authority. The walls listen. The clock presides.

I set a folder on the lectern. It contains nothing I will use. But the act itself steadies the room. Students straighten. Pages open. The expectation of form is more useful than the form itself.

"Today," I say, and the word stills them further. "We consider obsession."

It is a quiet word. It does not need volume to command.

A few pens rise as if startled into service. Their owners hesitate, waiting for the shape of what should be captured. The better students remain still. They know the mind records more than the page, if it is trained to.

"Obsession is not appetite," I continue, my voice unhurried. "Appetite can be sated. Nor is it romance. Romance craves spectacle. It thrives on excess. Obsession is different. It is an architecture.

It builds. It narrows. At its end there is no choice, only result."

The sound of the clock gears is louder than the first response. No one dares be the first.

So I give them the familiar. Brontë, not for the storm but the scaffolding it concealed. Poe, not for the grotesque but for the control that shaped it. The way shadow insists on light, the way confinement forces the gaze. I leave gaps, let silence rest like a blade across the room.

Silence teaches more than speech. The intelligent step into it. The rest shift in their chairs, coughing, crossing legs, filling the air with the small sounds of unease.

Halfway down the rows, Octavia Hartwell sits with a notebook in her lap. Fatigue has drawn her mouth taut, her skin paler than it was yesterday. A braid trails down the line of her back, strands already loosening. Her fingers tighten on the pen until her knuckles whiten. But her gaze does not falter.

Tired, yes. Yielding, no.

Her stillness is not the stillness of comfort, but of someone refusing to lean. It is the stillness of defiance, of a body that will collapse only when no one is there to see it.

I note it. I do not remark on it. To call her name would fracture momentum. And momentum is the only fragile thing I do not waste.

I turn the page of the lecture, invisible though it is, and keep the rhythm exact.

By the final minutes, the room begins to breathe again. Hands twitch upward with small questions, careful ones. Metaphor, as if it were dangerous. Symbol, as if it might betray them. They edge toward ruin but do not name it. I answer only what merits answer.

The bell releases them and the hall uncoils all at once—bags slung, feet scraping, laughter bubbling too quickly, relief arriving like oxygen. They spill into the corridor, voices tangling into the bright clamor of the ordinary.

I cap the pen I did not use. Slide the empty folder beneath my arm. Stand long enough to watch the room empty itself to the last shuffle of shoes against wood.

Control abhors hurry.

My study is the house's true throat. Shelves rise floor to ceiling, and the ladder's brass slides without chatter. Books stand in quiet ranks—spines sober, gilt restrained, cloth unfrayed. A manuscript breathes old paper into the space like a muted cologne. The fireplace holds a steady ember that gives heat without theatrics.

On the desk sits the morning paper. I unfold it once more. The circle of my pen is a dark ring around a name. *Octavia.*

Her column reads with the urgency of someone who has learned that words must sometimes hold the weight of a town. She does not show the body—that is mercy—or ignorance. She attends to what people do when they don't know what else to do: light, gather, repeat other people's sentences about safety. She avoids the method, which is appropriate and also incomplete. She is still writing to the living.

I read it again. Not for what is there. For what is not.

Predictability leaves a profile when you do not name it. Pattern leaves a pressure when you think you are writing around it. She has begun to notice the pressure.

The clipping joins others in the drawer. This is not a reliquary. It is a ledger. Records belong with records.

The itch that lived under my morning run returns, keener now that silence has made room for it. I let it remain. There is no virtue in pretending appetite is not real. There is virtue in giving it no audible voice.

It's remarkable how charity begins with champagne. The university calls it *community engagement.* I call it theater with better lighting. The valet takes my coat but I keep the mask. Inside, heat and cloying perfume collide, the air thick with the scent of money pretending to be purpose.

Obligation wears a different jacket in the evening—velvet trimmed with after shave and ambition. The donor circle gathers beneath chandeliers tuned to flattery, their light falling soft across burnished wood. Faculty orbit patrons like planets pulled by invisible gravity, each eager to be named indispensable.

"Dr. Marlowe," the Dean greets, voice practiced by repetition, the pin on his suit blinding. "We were debating whether our collection could sustain a winter exhibition on power and restraint. Your thoughts?"

I accept the glass I will not drink. "Only if the title promises nothing. Exhibitions talk too much. The objects should argue, yes, but the room should listen."

The ripple of laughter arrives as expected—warm, satisfied with itself.

A donor leans near, silk scarf glinting with another pin that marks more than family. "Perhaps you'd prefer Winterveil's private collection. Our circle is considering a... *curated* gathering."

The word *circle* lands too carefully to be chance.

"Constraint is easiest," I reply, "when it governs no one but oneself." I let the words hang between us, his audacity burning at the back of my mind, each presumption a spark I refuse to let catch.

The Dean laughs too quickly, papering over edges. "What Dr. Marlowe means is provocation mustn't alienate."

Another donor, younger, hungrier, slides in. "And what of your current work?"

"A paper," I say, "on the immoral utility of constraint. In narrative. And in life."

The hush after is not fear, but appetite. They enjoy the proximity of jagged edges—so long as they are not the ones nicked.

Conversation fractures into safer fragments. Laughter swells again, echoing too loudly in the wood-paneled chamber—sound gilded to hide exhaustion. The clink of glass, the rustle of silk, the familiar choreography of people pretending not to scheme.

I finish the drink I never intended to finish and set the glass down, its ring staining the linen like punctuation. The Dean catches my eye, ready to draw me back into orbit, but I incline my head and slip free before courtesy can anchor me.

The corridor beyond hums with quieter ambitions—heels, whispers, a door held too long. The air cools by degrees, perfume giving way to rain and stone. By the time I cross the threshold, the city's warmth has burned off entirely.

Outside, the night meets me like reprieve. The air is colder, biting, but their voices cling like smoke in the folds of my coat. By the gate, fog has already threaded itself low through the hedges, damp and waiting. The motor sighs open, obedient.

The house receives me in silence—not absence, but correction. The lamps settle to a dim that clarifies rather than conceals. From the east window, Rosemont stretches itself small. Across town, the patrons still talk. Bellflower Street, candles guttering, explanations rushing to clothe what does not yet want clothes. They chatter as if chatter steadies the floor. They dress absence in fabric and call it truth.

I rest my hand on the mullion, glass cold beneath my palm, their words still caught in the seams of the evening. *Circle. Constraint. Test.* The language follows me even here, pressing against the quiet.

On the desk, the paper waits. I smooth its crease, and her name fixes itself at the bottom of the column: *By Octavia Adeline Hartwell.*

A byline is a contract. She signs it every time she writes. She has chosen to be seen.

The town believes today has ended. They mistake sentiment for truth.

Today was preface. Tomorrow belongs to the book.

CHAPTER 7

Octavia

The air has changed. September drags its cold fingers down the edges of Rosemont, tugging leaves to the pavement, staining the campus in rust and smoke. The chaos of August—the police tape, the whispers, the unanswered questions—has dulled into rumor, softened into something the town pretends it can swallow.

Classes have settled into their rhythm, too. Assignments, deadlines, lectures that blur together. I've learned the exact hour the library is quietest, the best vending machine for coffee that doesn't taste like regret, the hallways where no one bothers to look up.

And then, there's *him*.

When Professor Marlowe hands back our essays, he does it without ceremony. A stack pressed onto the table's edge, the students scrambling for their names like children grabbing at candy. His face gives nothing away. Mine is in the middle of the pile, unremarkable in its plain folder until I open it.

The first words scrawled in the margins cut deeper than the typed lines themselves: *Predictable opening. Don't linger in sentiment. Obsession is never sentimental.*

I blink, my pulse skipping. My essay had been raw, half-confession, half-fiction, the kind of story you hope a professor recognizes as bold rather than messy. Instead, his notes crawl down the page like scalpel cuts.

You rely on metaphor where anatomy would suffice. Blood does not arc that way. If the knife is angled low, it splatters against the baseboards first... Always.

I freeze, staring at the ink. A chill works its way through me. He isn't just criticizing style—he's describing mechanics. The kind of detail you don't find in lectures or textbooks.

Line after line, his handwriting needles me...

Your narrator hesitates where she should already know. Hesitation ruins tension.

Too much flourish. Violence is rarely theatrical. It is clean, quick, decisive.

This is better—note how you let silence do the work here. Never explain what the body already says.

I grip the edge of the paper, my knuckles blanching. Around me, students flip through their own essays, groaning, scribbling notes, muttering complaints. Ordinary reactions to ordinary critiques. None of them look shaken. None of them look like the ground just tilted beneath their feet.

But mine—mine feels different. His comments sting, yes, but they also confuse, burrowing under my skin until I'm not sure whether he's dismantling my words or showing me something I wasn't meant to see.

By the time I close the folder, my heartbeat is too loud in my ears. The weight of his pen lingers heavier than the grade inked at the top.

B.

Average. Forgettable. And yet his handwriting crawls under my skin, impossible to shut out with the folder.

The scrape of chairs breaks the spell. Students rise, voices low, shuffling bags, trading half-hearted complaints about grades and readings. I stay seated, clutching the folder against my lap as if loosening my grip might let his words spill louder into the room.

One by one, they file out, until only the echo of footsteps lingers in the hall. My throat is tight, my mouth dry, but I force myself up. The folder feels heavier than my bag.

"Professor Marlowe?"

He looks up from where he's stacking the remainder of the essays, his expression unreadable. Neither annoyed nor indulgent—merely patient, as though he already knew I'd ask.

"I—" My voice falters, but I steady it. "I was hoping we could talk about your notes."

A pause. Not long enough to be silence, not short enough to be casual. His gaze fixes on me the way glass holds a reflection—unblinking, without distortion, making me question whether I see myself clearly at all.

"Of course," he says, with a faint incline of his head.

The words land like a verdict. I grip the folder tighter, step forward until the desk edges into my hip. My mouth is dry, but anger pushes me past it.

"I don't understand your comments," I say, my voice sharper than I meant. "You wrote about blood—splatter, angles—as if you've..." My pulse trips. "As if you've seen it firsthand."

Professor Marlowe's eyes catch mine, an expression sliding into place that I don't quite understand. He doesn't blink. "And you haven't?"

"I'm not a coroner," I snap. "I'm a student. I'm supposed to be learning how to write, not how to reconstruct a crime scene."

His lips tilt, not quite a smile. "Then why write what you can't control? Nothing shatters immersion faster than ignorance disguised as authority. Your story failed not because it was weak, but because you presumed the reader wouldn't notice the cracks."

Heat burns up my neck. "I didn't presume anything. You asked us to push boundaries—I *did*. Maybe you just don't like being pushed back."

His gaze is incendiary. "Do you imagine you pushed me, Miss Hartwell?" His voice stays soft, but it slices all the same. "A shaky metaphor, a misplaced spatter, a narrator that flinches when she should cut—those are not pushes. They are stumbles. And stumbles *bore* me."

My chest rises too quickly. "You're impossible," I fire back. "You say be bold, but then you tear me apart for daring to try."

"I don't punish boldness." His chair creaks faintly as he leans closer, closing the space without standing. The air between us heats. "I punish carelessness. And you—" his gaze flickers to the folder still clutched in my hands "—you blur the line because you're afraid of what accuracy costs."

The words sting more than I want them to. My fingers ache from gripping the folder. "Afraid? You think I'm afraid of you?"

His gaze holds mine, unblinking, unyielding. "Not of me," he says. "Of yourself."

My stomach twists. My throat is tight, but something else thrums beneath it—adrenaline, nerves, the edge of exhilaration. I shouldn't enjoy this. I shouldn't feel alive in the shadow of his cutting words.

"Maybe you should be afraid of me," I throw back before I can stop myself.

The silence after hums like struck glass. His mouth curves—not a smile, not approval, but something more dangerous.

"At last," he murmurs, voice low, deliberate, meant for me alone. "A sentence *worth* keeping."

My throat tightens. The words shouldn't feel like praise, but they do. They sink into me like ink on skin, staining deeper than I can scrub.

He leans forward, elbows resting lightly on the desk, his gaze fixed and consuming. His dark green eyes burn hotter under the dim light, gold flecks sparking like embers at the center of a fire. It feels like he is dismantling me without moving a muscle, stripping me down with nothing but the weight of his stare.

The folder in my hands has become useless. Heavy. My pulse ricochets in my chest, louder than the tick of the clock on the wall. I should step back—should *leave*. Instead I hold my ground, my legs taut with the effort of not retreating.

"Why does it matter to you?" I hear myself ask, my voice quieter now, betraying too much. "What I write, how I write it. You could have ignored me like you do the rest."

His head tilts, just enough to make me feel pinned. "Because the rest don't matter," he says. No hesitation. No softness. "They write words that vanish the moment they're read. You write words that insist on being *remembered*—even when they are wrong."

The confession sets something trembling in me. Not fear. Not exactly. Something shrewder.

Something that coils low in my stomach and makes it hard to breathe.

I try to scoff, to break the spell. "You mean words worth tearing apart."

His gaze sharpens. "Words worth tearing apart," he echoes, and the repetition feels like a verdict. His voice lowers again, quieter than the hum of the lights. "Do you know how *rare* that is?"

The air between us thickens, charged, as if the room itself leans closer. My fingers twitch on the folder, desperate for a tether, for something to hold that isn't him.

I should walk away. I know that. But I don't.

And neither does he.

For one suspended breath, it feels like we are the only two people in the world. His eyes on mine, my heart battering itself against my ribs, the silence stretching taut, unbearable, intoxicating. Too intimate. Too much.

"Class is over, Miss Hartwell," he says at last, the faintest curl at the corner of his mouth. "You should go before you say something you can't take back."

The words snap like a thread, releasing me. I stumble a step backward, clutching the folder as though it might shield me from what just passed between us.

But when I reach the door, my pulse still won't settle. His eyes burn behind my eyelids when I blink, his voice threaded into the marrow of my bones.

I leave, but the echo of him follows.

By the time I reach my apartment, the air has cooled enough that my breath ghosts in front of me. The walk back feels shorter than it should, though my mind refuses to let go of the class-room—his voice, his stare, the weight of that last line. I press the folder tighter under my arm like it might contain a version of me I can't afford to look at again.

The apartment greets me with its mismatched warmth. Secondhand furniture in shades of rust and cream, thrifted art covering cracks in the plaster, stacks of books doubling as side tables. A half-burned candle sits on the windowsill, lavender wax pooled unevenly around the wick. The radiator clanks when I shut the door, groaning like an old man rising from bed.

I kick off my ankle boots, peel off the jacket that's been digging into my shoulders, and let my bag drop heavy to the floor. Today I'd dressed for comfort—black jeans, a gray knit sweater that's already soft from over-washing, the kind of outfit that blends in against the backdrop of a campus where everyone's too tired to care. I collapse onto the couch, tugging the sweater sleeves down over my hands, trying to anchor myself in its worn cotton.

But the silence presses close, broken only by the refrigerator's low hum and the occasional sigh of the pipes. I want to shut my eyes, to let the day drain out of me, but my pulse won't settle. His words keep circling, low and deliberate, filling every quiet space.

The phone's sharp ring slices through the stillness. I jolt upright, fumbling for it on the counter.

"Hello?" My voice comes out raw.

"Octavia." Jessica's tone is rushed, breathless. "You need to get down here. *Now.*"

I blink, shaking my head as if that might clear the fog. "Jess, it's late. What—?"

Another breath on the line, sharp enough to cut. "Another murder."

The words slam into me harder than I expect.

"Same neighborhood. Same M.O. Young, female. Chestnut hair. Curvy build." She pauses, lowering her voice, as though the phone line itself might be listening. "This one's worse—like they're trying to perfect it."

My fingers go numb around the phone. For a second, the room seems to tilt, shadows deepening at the edges. My mind flashes back to the essay, to his red pen bleeding across the margins. *Blood does not arc that way. If the knife is angled low, it splatters against the baseboards first. Always.*

"Octavia?" Jess pushes, her voice frantic. "Are you coming?"

I force myself off the couch, dropping the phone to speaker so my hands can move. I strip the sweater, tugging on a black leather jacket instead, its lining worn smooth from years of use. The jeans stay because they're practical, sturdy enough, and grounding. I trade socks for boots, shove my notebook and recorder into the satchel by the door, phone in the palm of my hand. The mirror catches me on the way out—braid messy, strands pulled loose around my face, eyes too wide, too restless.

"Yeah," I say at last, voice steadier than I feel. "Text me the address."

The line clicks dead.

I stand there in the dim light, the candle guttering on the sill, phone glowing cold in my palm. My reflection lingers in the window—pale, wide-eyed, framed by chestnut hair that looks too much like a description in someone else's notes.

Same build. Same hair.

Same shadow pulling tighter around Rosemont.

By the time I reach Bellflower Street, the night has soured into something metallic and thin, the kind of air that tastes like iron at the back of the throat. Blue and red lights pulse across the rows of houses, their reflections twitching across windows and manicured hedges. Neighbors gather in clusters at the ends of their driveways, whispering into their sleeves, faces pale under the wash of sirens.

Jess waits at the tape, clutching her press badge like a talisman. She waves me over, a cardboard cup of coffee already in her other hand. "Thought you'd need this," she says, pressing it into mine before I can argue. The steam curls into the night, bitter and sweet.

The scene itself is chaos ordered into grids. Lines of yellow tape, cones, and officers moving with deliberate pace. Photographers crouch low, their cameras flashing against the dark, while forensics kneel in the grass, their plastic bags glinting under the floodlights.

I edge closer, notebook ready, when a young officer turns toward us. His uniform looks too new, his jaw tight with the eagerness of someone still rehearsing authority. He lowers his voice, though not enough.

"Second one in three weeks," he mutters, eyes flicking toward the house. "Same type. Curves. Chestnut hair. The cut was—" he stops himself, but not fast enough. "Too clean. Like they'd done it before."

My pulse stutters. Jess shoots me a look, wide-eyed, already scribbling.

Before I can push, a heavier presence fills the air. Chief Mateo Thornwick strides into view, his bulk cutting a path through the floodlight haze. His voice is gravel worn sharp.

"Officer." One word, heavy as a hammer. The young man straightens, paling under Thornwick's stare. "You'll remember not to share details outside the circle of this department." His gaze flicks briefly to me and Jess, as if weighing how much we caught. I know instantly it's too much.

Jess tucks her pen behind her ear, playing innocent. I lower my notebook, though my hand itches to write.

Thornwick doesn't linger. He turns back to the cordoned path, barking orders low to the team already swarming the scene. But the damage is done. The words hang between me and Jess, sharper than the smell of blood that seems to cling to the air even from here.

I sip the coffee, its sweetness suddenly cloying, and press the cup harder against my lips to hide the tremor I can't suppress.

Jess sidles closer, her shoulder brushing mine, her blonde hair catching the swing of the floodlights like pale fire. Her gray eyes narrow in that calculating way of hers, lips pursed around thoughts she hasn't yet spoken. She's curvy, solid, the kind of presence that fills silence instead of shrinking from it.

"Too clean," she mutters under her breath, echoing the rookie's slip. "Like they've done it before. That's not a rookie observation. That's experience talking. Either he saw something he shouldn't have, or—"

"Or what?" I cut in, though I'm not sure I want her answer.

"Or *someone* fed him a line," Jess finishes, her gaze darting to the Chief's broad back as he directs another officer toward the taped perimeter.

"Thornwick doesn't let information bleed unless he wants it to. You know that as well as I do."

The night feels tighter, the sirens' pulse pressing against my temples. "Then why stop him so publicly?" I ask, voice low. "If it was controlled, he wouldn't need to make an example of him."

Jess exhales through her nose, a soft, humorless laugh. "That's the game, Tavia. Leak just enough to bait attention, slam the door hard enough to make you second-guess what you heard. Keeps reporters chasing their own tails."

Her words make sense, but my stomach twists anyway. My fingers itch for my notebook, but I don't lift it. Not yet.

"What about the pattern?" I whisper. "Same build. Same hair. Curvy, chestnut, young."

Jess finally looks at me, her gray eyes sharp in the wash of light. "Yeah. And if you haven't noticed..." Her gaze drags down my braid, the strands that have come loose around my face, the figure I can't disguise under jeans and leather. "You fit it, Tavia."

The coffee cools too quickly in my hands. I want to argue, to dismiss it, but the words won't form. Not when the reflection in the window of my apartment still lingers in the back of my mind. Not when I can feel the weight of Professor Marlowe's handwriting carved into my skin.

Jess nudges me, lighter this time, forcing a crooked grin. "Don't spiral yet. Just means we're closer to the story of the year. But..." She leans in, her voice lowering to a conspiratorial hush. "Keep your doors locked tonight, okay?"

Her grin doesn't reach her eyes.

And this time, I don't laugh.

CHAPTER 8

The air tastes of iron. Not the crude tang of fresh blood—that has already been tidied away, parceled into bags and labels—but the residual trace that clings to wet grass and raw wood, a suggestion of something that has already decided itself. Sirens wash the street in alternating color. The fog receives their light and gives it back blurred. Compliant.

I stand at the edge of the watchers, hidden in plain sight. A man in a good coat, attentive and unremarkable. The trick is always the same—allow your gaze to rest, not linger. Your shoulders to square, not tense. Your curiosity to look borrowed, never owned. To observe is to disappear.

Bellflower Street murmurs with layered voices. The thin-edged whisper of neighbors conferring, the flat cadence of officers exchanging procedure, the crisp notation of forensics calling numbers into the cold. A row of porch lights shines as if the houses themselves are trying to keep terror at a proper distance. The tape makes its yellow angles. Cones mark the geometry of what happened and where. Photographers kneel and rise, kneel and rise, patient as metronomes.

They have removed the body, of course. People confuse removal with absence. They think the moment is gone once it is carried away. But the scene still holds the pressure of it. The grass knows the weight, just like the gravel keeps the slide of a heel, and baseboards remember the error of a wrong angle better than any witness ever will.

This one was cleaner. Delilah taught me the price of hesitation—flourish where precision should have been, sentiment where silence would suffice. Now, the incision moved with the room's design, all function, no vanity. No indulgence. No signature. The society prizes discipline over art. They'll learn soon enough how little difference there is between the two.

At the tape, a journalist shifts her weight to keep the cold from burrowing into her calves. Another—the one whose name I keep in my pocket like a pressed flower—holds her notebook too tight. Octavia is in black denim and a leather jacket that has been made honest by use. Her braid has come loose; strands lift at her temples when the damp breeze moves. She should have gone home hours ago and yet she stands like a blade someone forgot to sheath. She does not gawk. She studies. Even fatigue cannot teach her to look away.

The young officer—the one who has not yet learned to be silent—speaks where he should not. "Too clean," he told them. "Like they'd done it before." Thornwick arrived with the gravity of an old star and shut him up with a single word, but words are water when the ground is ready. The leak has already soaked in. I watched the sentence land in Octavia's face, a tremor disguised as a chill.

She fits because I shaped the pattern to her measure. The rest were necessary illusions, proof of constancy, of precision held across time. But they were repetitions, not revelations. She is the origin and the ending—the text that renders all other work commentary.

I am not yet certain of its ending. To possess her alive would be a kind of authorship, a heat that chooses itself. To end her would be authorship of a different order: the austerity of ash, of form reduced to absolute decision. One is conflagration.

The other is design. Architecture ends where it must. Until then, you keep building.

"Back behind the markers," an officer calls, palms out, tone trained into politeness by consequence. The crowd obeys with relief disguised as irritation. I go with them, neither first nor last, the easier silhouette to forget. Jess, the blonde with the quick notes and gray eyes, touches Octavia's elbow and draws her away with a word that looks like concern and sounds like work. Octavia resists half a step, then yields. Duty is a harness she fits willingly.

The fog deepens as we disperse—Washington's way of offering discretion. The street regains its private dark in increments, a dimmer turning down. I take the long way to the corner, the route that lets me see the scene's edges from a new angle. Thornwick stands solid at the center, pointing once, twice, and everything reorients. He is a man who knows how to keep a circle tight. It will not be tight enough.

I pass two men speaking low in the lee of a parked van—neighbors who speak of locks now, of lights, of new routes for their wives to walk. They are building a ritual around fear. People are most themselves when they are afraid.

My car waits three blocks away, fog jeweled on the windshield, roof beading like the back of a sleeping animal. I do not drive immediately. The engine starts, and I let it idle until my breath returns to a usual rhythm. Until the scene at my back shrinks in the rearview to a scattering of color and movement. The itch under my skin stays. Proof can discipline hunger into shape. It cannot remove it.

At the first light, I imagine her already home—boots discarded, jacket hung by habit, the apartment small but curated to anchor her—then I erase the picture, not because it is untrue but because it is not my right to hold yet. Precision is knowing what not to trespass. The line moves later.

The streets between Bellflower and my door are the same. Four turns, a hill, a straightaway where the fog yawns wider, the cold threading the hedge tops with dull silver. My gate receives me with its mechanical courtesy. The house corrects the world at once—the scent of cedar returning, the lamps adjusted to a dim that clarifies, the order unbroken. Nothing here acts without permission.

Coat off. Gloves away. Shoes aligned. The paper removed from the inside pocket and placed where it belongs—on the desk, its crease smoothed with a thumb until the line disappears.

I sit without quite meaning to. The study absorbs noise and returns only what you deserve. Tonight it gives back the bare sound of the ember shifting in the grate and the thread of wind finding a seam in the eastern window. I prefer that the house tells me the weather honestly. Most houses lie to their owners. Most owners encourage it.

The drawer that keeps what matters slides open on felt. Notes from faculty I will answer tomorrow. A card bearing a crest of privilege that forgets itself: frost and serpent entwined, beauty doing nothing to blunt the threat. Three clippings with her name and one with none—because not everything that belongs in a ledger requires attribution.

I let my eyes close long enough to test whether the scene will replay if invited. It does, in fragments. The cone at the end of the walk, the damp trace where the grass remembers how weight left it, and the rookie's mouth opening on words the chief did not authorize. Above all, *her*—chin inclined as if listening to an argument only she can hear. The defiance in her posture tonight was different than the last time in my lecture hall—it found something to brace against. *Good*. Resistance builds muscle.

On the desk, a narrow notebook lies open to a page drawn with neat columns. It is not the choked scrawl of compulsion. It is tidy. Date. Time. Location. Variables. Outcome. The line under tonight's entry is simple: *clean*. The line beneath it: *insufficient.* The one after: *stable witnesses: Thornwick; incompetent youth; Hartwell present.* I do not add thrill or fear or regret. Those are assessments people use when they want to pretend they are not building a life on choices. I add only: *calibration achieved.*

I could sleep. The body has earned it. But the mind will not. I shower instead—water hot, time exact, the mirror returning the expected face with hair disordered and eyes still too awake. Dark green with gold at the center—someone once told me it looked like moss lit by fire. I did not correct them, not because they were right but because it is uninteresting to explain metaphor to people who will never study it. Towels return to the bar aligned. A robe replaces the shirt with the warmed weight of wool.

When I step back into the study, the fog has pressed itself more boldly against the glass, scudding in thin sheets the light turns to tarnish. Rosemont dissolves at the edges like a drawing submerged in water. Somewhere across it, a woman stands at a window not unlike mine, her phone screen bright in her palm, her hair a dark banner in the night. A friend tells her to lock her doors. She does. She checks them twice, then three times, and sleeps poorly. She is not Octavia. I do not know her name, though I used it earlier tonight because it mattered then to say it. I will not say it now because accuracy matters more. The ledger already holds it.

I take the paper up again, not to read the column—I could recite it—but to look at the way her name sits above the text. How a line of type can announce a kind of will. Her work has moved in the weeks since the first death. The sentiment trimmed, the structure tightened, the relief of outrage replaced with the slower discipline of inquiry. She is learning where to cut. She is learning what not to say. Silence is an instrument most writers never tune. She has found the pitch and is testing it. I do not acknowledge the pride that coils within me.

My hand moves before the thought arrives. I take out a sheet of thin paper, vellum that takes ink cleanly. The nib lays a line of black as disciplined as a seam. I do not address it to her. Nor do I write her name. I write a sentence that will live in my drawer until it is required to go elsewhere: *When the story refuses you, remove what flatters you most and ask again.* Under it: *There is a difference between revelation and relief.* These are not notes for her. They are notes for me, because design requires a plan even when the plan is to allow for the pressure of unplanned force.

The society remains a watermark at the edge of thought, present when paper is tilted to the light, invisible when laid flat. It has rituals and expectations and the kind of appetite that dresses itself as purpose. Its rooms are warm and its words are cooled on the tongue before they are spoken. It imagines it knows endings because it has money and history and doors that open only to certain keys. It forgets that structure is a tool, not a destination. I will let it forget a while longer. I will let it believe that control is the performance.

On the wall opposite the window hangs a small map of Rosemont drawn in pencil by a dead student with an eye for proportion. He left the streets correct and the distances slightly off in a way that pleases me. I stand before it and place my finger lightly where Bellflower crosses the older line—where the town was young and the road still a path. Two discreet pins already mark other points. A third pin rests on the desk, its head a dull black that does not wink when the light passes. I do not lift it. Not tonight. Accuracy is knowing when to fix a point and when to keep it fluid. The pattern is clarified enough. To complete it now would be to mistake impatience for mastery.

The itch—never scratched, only dulled—settles into the space beneath the ribs where purpose lives. I imagine for a moment the heat of her language again in the classroom, the moment today when her chin lifted and she reached anger cleanly instead of decoration. "Maybe you *should* be afraid of me," she said. The only sentence this week that deserved to stay in the world unedited. The corners of my mouth move. Not a smile. A recognition of line.

It is late enough now that even those who like their power performatively have gone to bed. Thornwick will step into his shower and relive the young officer's error as if it were his own. Tomorrow the youth will be transferred to a desk and told that paper is the safer weapon. The reporter will sleep with her phone on her chest, waking to check whether the alert she dreamed arrived. Two houses from Bellflower, a couple will argue again about whether to sell and never notice that the argument is not about the house.

And Octavia? She will not sleep early. She will read the same paragraph twice and not remember either reading. She will turn her lock, then turn it again, and tell herself it is the noise of sirens that makes her do it a third time. She will sit with the folder on her table and fight the impulse to open it because doing so would give me back my voice in her head. She will lose that fight. She always will when the choice is between silence and the sound that unsettles her into wakefulness.

I return the vellum to its place, fold the paper with her name once more along the line I have erased and smoothed twice tonight, and set it parallel with the edge of the desk. The study darkens by a faint degree as the ember collapses again. I draw the curtains not to keep the town out but to remind it that admission is granted, not assumed.

Upstairs, the bed is correct. Linen cool and ironed. Pillows that yield and then deny. I lie down without the fiction of television or the vulgarity of music. The body will sleep when the mind permits. The mind will permit when the plan has been set somewhere not visible to curiosity.

Tonight's plan is a negative. Do *not* press the next pin into the map. Do *not* fold anything into an envelope. Do *not* test the outer perimeter where error lives. Precision achieved what it needed to do. The ledger will not receive a line tomorrow. The book will.

I close my eyes and invite the house to quiet itself. It does, the way it always does, as if the beams respect me personally. The last sound is the wind's thin finger at the window seam, then a small settling as the temperature decides a degree.

When sleep takes me, it is not indulgence. It is calibration. The shape of the ending is nearer, and the space between the two possible conclusions narrows as the architecture climbs.

I do not yet know whether I will write her in fire... or in ash.

I know only this... When I decide, there will be no seam to pull, no stitch to unravel, no place for the world to say it disbelieves.

And she—my book, not my echo—will look at me and understand *why*.

CHAPTER 9

Two weeks. Fourteen days of headlines that faded, of whispers that dulled, of streets that returned to their rituals as if nothing had been disturbed.

The city of Rosemont carries its ghosts badly. People bury them under errands, church bells, grocery lists, the rhythm of a town too polite to admit it is afraid. I see it in the way neighbors step a little faster past the corner where the sirens once wailed, in the way the Gazette softens its tone with cautious optimism. *Stability restored. Investigation ongoing. Chief Thornwick assures citizens there is no immediate threat.*

But I know better.

My desk at home proves it—lined with spiral notebooks, sticky notes, scraps of newsprint. I've made a map across my wall with push pins and twine, red threads trailing between Bellflower Street and the block where the first body was found. My handwriting loops across the page in midnight bursts, obsessive and frantic:

- Victim #1: Delilah White, 23. Curvy. Chestnut hair. Green eyes (not light—dark).

- Victim #2: Kara Liddell, 22. Curvy. Chestnut hair. Green eyes.

- Both cuts precise. "Too clean" — rookie slip.

- Thornwick shut it down. *Why?*

The question sits at the heart of every page: *Why hide it? Why disguise skill as randomness?*

I stare at the notes too long at night, tracing patterns that may not exist. Sometimes I wake to find I've been scribbling phrases in the dark, the pen cutting trails I don't remember writing. Sometimes I think about Adrian's handwriting on my essay, exquisite and surgical, his red ink insisting: *blood does not arc that way* and *baseboards catch what walls do not.*

The comments shouldn't haunt me. They do.

I shove the notebook closed and check the time. **09:40**. My ten o'clock class waits, and if I don't leave now, I'll walk in late with ink still staining my fingers.

Montgomery Hall's building breathes chill stone and old varnish. The hallways echo with the shuffle of boots and the scrape of chairs. I slip into my seat three rows from the front, not too close, not too hidden, notebook already open. Around me, the air feels... brittle. Students settle in with the unease of animals who sense weather coming.

He enters without hurry, without spectacle. Adrian Marlowe doesn't need it. His presence shifts the room the way a sudden shadow shifts a landscape. He wears a gray suit today, tie loose, the lines of his shoulders clean. His gaze sweep the room once—precise, measuring, then gone.

He sets a folder on the desk. Unsnaps a fountain pen. The silence tightens.

"Today," he says, voice even, carrying easily across the room. "We speak of violence."

A murmur ripples, uneasy. Someone coughs. A pen clatters to the floor.

"Not spectacle," he continues. "Not the pulp you consume in film and television. Violence as construction. As a choice of art in writing."

His gaze drifts slowly across us, daring someone to look away.

"Writers often cheapen it. They imagine blood as cinema—spurting fountains, crimson arcs. But real violence is quiet. It obeys physics, not imagination. It stains in straight lines. It pools where gravity insists. Its terror lies in restraint."

My throat tightens. I feel his words like live wires across my skin. He hasn't looked directly at me—not once—but somehow the lecture folds itself toward me anyway.

A boy in the back raises his hand, hesitant. "Are you saying... we should write violence more—realistically?"

"No." Adrian tilts his head, the faintest curve of his mouth threatening something like amusement. "I am saying you should respect it. Violence in art is not decoration. It is consequence. If you cannot face consequence, you have no business writing it."

The room stills, heavy.

Another student shifts nervously, then blurts, "But that feels... extreme. We're here to learn, not—"

"Not to be comfortable," Adrian interrupts, his tone clipped but not cruel. "Comfort is not education. Comfort is sedation."

The student reddens, retreating into their chair. No one else speaks.

I glance around, and I see it—the collective unease, the way shoulders hunch, pens hover, eyes drop. He hasn't crossed a line, not really. His words aren't threats, and his tone isn't hostile. But the room vibrates with something excruciating, something that makes every student want to shrink smaller.

Except me.

I can't shrink, not when my pen is racing, not when my pulse beats with every phrase. His words cut, but they cut clean. I know I should resent it, should call it arrogance, cruelty. Instead, I feel that dangerous thrill again—the one that coils in my stomach every time his gaze almost finds me.

Almost.

He closes the folder with finality. "For next week: a short fiction. Choose an act of violence and render it with accuracy. Not indulgence. Not cowardice. Precision. You may discover it is harder than you imagine."

Chairs scrape. Bags thump. No one lingers.

I gather my things slowly, every nerve thrumming. When I glance up, his eyes are already on me. Green, lit with a disconcerting emotion. Not approval. Not disdain. Something else. Something that feels too close to recognition.

My breath tangles in my throat. I break the look first, forcing myself into motion, into the tide of students spilling from the room. The hallway feels colder, the buzz of voices dulled as if the building itself holds its breath. By the time I step outside, the air is damp with fog, the kind that clings to skin and hair, and still I feel those eyes on me—impossible, but unshakable.

I carry it home with me. The stare, the silence, the weight of unspoken words.

Later, at my desk, I write until my hands ache. Notes blur into fiction, fiction into confession. My wall map watches me, threads trailing like veins, the paper littered with questions that refuse to quiet.

Rosemont pretends it is safe again.

But the storm has only gone quiet to gain momentum.

And I—I am running straight into its teeth.

CHAPTER 10

By the third week of October, the air tastes sharper, edged with smoke from chimneys and the faint musk of fallen leaves beginning to rot. Rosemont wears autumn well—brick buildings framed by yellow maples, ivy turning crimson against stone. Students rush the quad with scarves and paper cups, cheeks flushed from the wind. The world looks deceptively normal.

I don't feel normal at all.

The weight of today coils tight in my chest. The short fiction assignment waits like a judgment in my bag—fourteen pages of violence written in a fever, sharpened by every red slash Adrian Marlowe carved into my last essay. I'd taken his notes to heart. He demanded accuracy. I gave him consequence. He told me not to dress violence in theater. So I stripped it to the bone.

The story is about a woman who kills men who do unspeakable things. Not strangers, not random victims. Men whose names curdled in police reports, whose sins festered in the margins of trials, who had slipped through the cracks of justice like grease through a sieve. The woman waits, studies, selects. And when she kills, it is not with rage or flourish but with deliberate skill.

When I sealed the last page in its folder, my hands trembled. Not from fear of the story itself—but from the quiet thrill of how right it felt to write it.

Now, as I push open the door to the lecture hall, nerves crawl my spine. Students murmur, flipping through their papers. I see the faint streaks of red ink here and there, sharp marks slashed into margins. The smell of chalk clings to the air, mingling with damp wool coats.

And then he enters.

Adrian Marlowe doesn't need to raise his voice to still a room. He wears a dark suit today, ink-black, the tie loosened just enough to look intentional. His eyes sweep the space once and the chatter falls into silence. He carries a stack of folders under one arm, and when he lays them on the desk, the sound is soft but final.

One by one, he hands them back. No flourish, no hesitation. Students' expressions twist as they scan the margins—grimaces, sighs, relief. He passes mine last. His fingers brush the folder for the briefest moment before releasing it into my hands. The air between us feels charged, though his expression is unreadable.

I slide the folder open with more care than I mean to. The first line makes my pulse lurch.

Better. Sharper. You are beginning to respect restraint.

No sweeping red slashes this time. No brutal dismissal. His ink laces the margins in smaller notes, surgical but almost approving.

Your protagonist kills with purpose. You did not indulge her. You did not pity her.

Violence without consequence is indulgence. You avoided this trap.

And at the very end, underlined once: *This is not cowardice. This is craft. Continue.*

The words shouldn't thrill me. They do.

My cheeks burn. I flip the folder closed too quickly, afraid someone might see the way my hands tremble. I press them flat against the desk, breathing slow, forcing control. It's just feedback. Just words. But his words are different. His approval ignites something low in my stomach, something I shouldn't feel.

The rest of class passes in fragments. His lecture—something about restraint in Brontë, about shadows and form—washes over me in pieces. I write notes, but my focus keeps slipping back to the folder in my bag, to the quiet weight of his final line. *Continue.*

When the clock releases us, chairs scrape, students scatter. Bags sling over shoulders, footsteps echo down the hall. I stay seated, gathering my things deliberately, too slowly. My heart hammers as if it knows what I'm about to do.

By the time the last student leaves, only the two of us remain.

Adrian closes a book, stacks it neatly. He doesn't look up when he speaks. "You linger, Ms. Hartwell."

The sound of my name in his voice pulls heat to my face. "I—wanted to ask about your notes."

Now he looks at me. His gaze is sharp, exact. "You understood them."

"I think so." My voice feels too small. "But I want to be sure."

He leans against the desk, folding his arms. "Then tell me. What did you learn?"

I swallow, words clumsy at first. "That violence isn't about shock. It's about consequence. That if I write it, I have to... own it. Respect it."

The corner of his mouth tilts, deliberate as a knife laid flat. "So you were listening after all."

The silence that follows hums like struck glass. I can't look away. My pulse drums so hard it feels reckless.

And then—barely, deliberately—he reaches out. His fingers graze my arm, the lightest touch, but it floods through me like current. An invitation without words. A door opening where no door should exist.

The contact is nothing. And it is everything.

My breath stutters. Panic collides with something darker and hungrier. I jerk back as if burned, the chair legs screeching against the floor.

"I—have to go." My voice breaks, too high, too fast. I fumble my bag over my shoulder, nearly dropping it, and bolt for the door.

The hallway air is cold, damp, carrying the scent of wet stone. I take it in greedily, like oxygen after drowning. My feet pound the tiles too loud, too frantic. Behind me, the door shuts with a soft, controlled click.

I don't look back.

But even as I flee, my arm burns where his hand brushed, as if the imprint refuses to fade. His words echo in my skull.

Continue.

And the worst part is—I want to.

CHAPTER 11

I wake before the clock decides I should and lie still long enough to listen to the house name the hour for me. The shy tick from the study grate, distant pipes clearing their throats. I do not reach for the lamp. The dark knows me well. We have an old agreement, after all. When I rise, the floor is cool beneath my feet and the window is a single pane of graphite, condensation drawn across it like charcoal smudged by a thumb. Rosemont keeps its secrets best in weather like this. I prefer it.

In the kitchen, the range light casts its small halo. Alcott has left order where order belongs—steel arranged edge-in, copper dried without a single watermark, fruit segmented with an anatomist's mercy. Breakfast is a quiet affair. A grapefruit emptied of bitterness, oats holding their line, an egg lifted without scar. I eat while the espresso gives its low animal sigh. Nothing in me wants abundance. Simplicity is appetite's only honest form.

I dress for the day without drama—charcoal suit, navy tie loosely knotted, hair combed once and correct. When I button the cuffs, I notice the thing I always notice and never name aloud. The place where the vein at my wrist beats, the skin shadows a fraction darker than it should. Not bruise. Not stain. A deeper ink that rises when the air is cold and the mind is occupied. I press a thumb to it. It answers back with a steadier rhythm than the heart's. It is not something the Inkbound Society taught me, though they would like to believe they did. It is older than their candles and older than their Latin.

Classes hold the morning in place. I speak less than my colleagues would like and more than some believe necessary. Undergraduates file out chastened and alert. A graduate student leaves with a page of notes she will mistake for permission. The day folds to afternoon and then to the hour I do not admit I keep. The hour I choose to walk without destination and always find myself pointed toward the library quad.

She is there before I arrive, moving through the pale light with a rhythm I can read now without effort. Octavia wears black jeans and a jacket softened by honest labor, her braid already loosening at the nape where damp collects. She keeps a pen tucked behind her ear in defiance of the satchel slung at her side. She dislikes rummaging for anything she might need to wield. As she crosses beneath the gargoyles, she thumbs the corner of a folded page—one, two, three taps—then tucks it deeper. A talisman against distraction. A habit I have seen enough times to count on. The air swallows voices, but I would know her silence from across any distance. It is the stillness of someone listening to herself.

I do not skulk. Skulking announces itself. I am a man in a good coat making the same turns as other men. If the fog chooses to hang thicker at my shoulder than at theirs, no one remarks on it. If the lamplight blinks once when I pass and steadies after, the human brain explains it kindly to itself. She glances back once where shadow pools beside the iron fence. Not at me—her gaze slides a finger's width to my left, to the longer version of her own outline. Correctly, she lifts her chin instead of quickening her pace. Fear makes noise. She prefers data.

The route has settled into its own sonnet, library steps, ivy, narrow street, and a third-floor walk-up with paint that curls from the eaves like fingernails. I keep the opposite pavement and study what deserves study. Her posture tonight is better than last week's. The fatigue that hollowed the socket under her left eye has eased, indicating she has slept, but not long enough to erase the bite marks of thought. A thread of ink stains the pad of her second finger. Her shoelace is double-knotted not in a bow but in a square knot. Seamen trust them. So do surgeons.

At the stoop, she knocks the wedge loose with her foot—one small thing she can control—and moves on without looking down. The light in her window arrives before I cross the intersection. I do not require the light to know she is there. No, that knowledge is the kind that hums under my ribs of its own accord. I have never trusted the language other men use for that sensation. Desire is too blunt a tool, instinct too feral, fate too theatrical. If I were forced to put it to words, I would choose a technical one: *resonance*. As if the darker ink in my blood notes a frequency outside of hearing and aligns itself to it.

I could go up. She would open the door when she saw me through the chain. She would be polite because she was raised to be and argumentative because she taught herself that politeness is not surrender. I could say I returned a book and mention her story and watch the color move in her throat when she speaks about consequence. It would be a mistake. Errors are often born from wanting to confirm what one already believes. The experiment must be designed to disprove. Only then can the result be trusted.

I turn away because the evening demands it of me. The Inkbound Society convenes tonight, and my presence steadies the room. Absence would be read as a move.

The entrance hides where it always has, a panel of stone that has forgotten its seam to everyone except those taught the pressure and the measure of silence. The stair goes down steep, air cooling with each turn until breath leaves the body in two narrow streams. The hall remembers every ceremony it has swallowed, as beeswax burns low in iron cages. Roses rest on a slab of oak darkened by centuries of oaths. Pentagrams are carved where ivy curls, though, the geometry never announces itself until you look too long. They gather masked to erase faces and names. I allow the masks, and I lead the binding.

"Constraint is virtue." I speak. The room answers in an appreciative hum. The blade bites the finger, the droplet of blood falls, and I receive each pledge as it comes. When the bowl has its proper weight, I let the thorn kiss my own skin last—tradition, not necessity—and watch the darker bead thread the silver a shade.

Debate flares and dims, moves from text to precedent to what they prefer to call art. A gray-hooded keeper I do not trust tips her mask toward me in greeting and arranges her tone as if it had cost them something to acquire. "Headmaster," she says carefully, "there is appetite among the ranks for demonstration. Your hand, not theory."

"Appetite requires a leash," I say. "You have one. Use it."

They want more. Everyone in this room wants more. Not because they doubt my discipline but because to witness is to believe themselves nearer to power. They ask without saying the name: who, where, when. They do not ask why. The Society pretends to have outgrown that question. A young initiate answers too eagerly on another topic and is corrected without malice. We drink something red that isn't just wine. I touch the bowl because that is what is expected and watch the surface move as if the air itself had weight.

If I give them Octavia's name, the room will tilt a degree. Gray cloaks will lean. Red will lower their lids in approval. Someone will say the word canon and someone else will open the book that records offerings and add a tidy new line in a hand trained to outlive its owner. If I keep the name and give them another one, they will call it prudence and wait for the door I prefer to open. Everything about the choice would therefore appear to be political, and only a fool makes politics the center of anything.

I leave before their voices can decide I should stay. The steps back to the street return the temperature to the useful edge between breath and fog. When I reach the gate, the motor takes its practiced breath and the iron goes where iron is told. Inside, the scent of parchment is the first truth the house offers and silence the second. I stand at the east window and look at Rosemont until the map of it returns to me. The crooked alleys that refuse the grid, the single sycamore that pulls the streetlights' cone to itself like a child claiming a blanket, the three blocks between her door and mine that I travel without thinking when I am not thinking at all.

I could go to the desk and square the stack and smooth the crease in the paper where her byline sits and read it again without moving my mouth. I could pin a map and push a third black-headed pin where it will belong when the pattern chooses to be complete. Instead I let the study keep its neatness and ask the house to give me a different kind of honest report. The ember answers with a soft collapse. A draft whispers through an old join. My shadow on the floor is wrong by a finger's width—wider than the lamp allows, as if something stood beside me that does not.

I blink and it returns to what a shadow should be. I do not look for it again. There is a difference between superstition and evidence. The first is an explanation when the mind is tired. The second insists you are awake when you would prefer not to be. I make a note on a slip of vellum without marking the date: *interference increases in proximity to subject*. It reads like the line from an experiment. I allow it that shape. The alternative is sentiment.

When I sleep, it is deliberate. Sheets cold, pillow correct, the mind invited to shut its ledger for the night and the body permitted a single concession to comfort. The thing that beats slower than the heart at my wrist takes longer to settle. I count backward from a hundred in a language the Society believes it owns. At forty-two, the house makes the sound it makes only when the fog decides to lay its weight against the windows. At thirty-one, a door in the neighborhood opens, then closes more carefully than usual, as if someone decided halfway through that the act required tenderness. At twenty, the darker rhythm eases.

Morning proves that nothing exploded while I slept. That is always a disappointment if I am honest with myself. Explosion is vulgar, but it announces itself decisively. The day instead returns with its ordinary grammar. Students ask questions and do not mean them, while colleagues phrase requests as collaborations. The Dean smiles the way men smile when they want the money to believe they love ideas. I walk the campus and the campus pretends to walk me. At noon the sun remembers itself and at four it forgets.

I see her again not because I engineered it but because the town does what towns do. It funnels, it repeats. Octavia emerges from the library an hour later than habit suggests she should, eyes bright in a way caffeine alone cannot achieve. She navigates a knot of undergraduates by stepping through their laughter as if it belonged to her. Her braid has been redone; the strands that escape are fewer. A smudge of ink has migrated from her finger to the inside of her wrist where pulse lives. The sight of it is unnecessary information that insists on being recorded.

I let her pass me with two yards of air between us. The shadow inside me—never a voice, not exactly, but the weight of one—presses outward like heat against glass. It is not hunger of the simple kind. It is claim. I reject the word because it reeks of men who mistake ownership for intimacy. The more difficult language is the accurate one—*bond*. I refuse the romance tied to that vocabulary and keep only the physics. Two bodies known to each other despite distance, despite silence. How it began is less interesting than whether it persists under test.

She stops at the kiosk by the quad to pin a notice for the Gazette's call for interns: clean tear from the pad, straight pin through the corner, attention to alignment. She returns the pushpin jar to its exact position on the ledge, turns, and in turning, her gaze finds me fully for the first time today. There is no reason for it to stay. It stays anyway. The moment is not long, but it is defined. Her chin does not lift and mine does not lower. Someone behind her laughs, and someone behind me calls a name that is not mine. We do nothing. The air between us answers for us—one degree colder, one degree nearer.

I release the breath first. Control is often the right to choose where a line breaks. She moves on. I do not follow within her sightline. There are rules even in obsession. There must be or obsession becomes performance. I prefer the honesty.

When the evening arrives, the Society will expect more evidence of loyalty than I provide. They will tell themselves a story about my distance today, perhaps even a noble one. That I practice silence as rigor, that I keep apart because I am above their hungers. Let them. They are not wrong about the rigor. They are simply ignorant of its cause. I do not feed the ignorance. I let it graze.

I go home by a street I do not usually choose and find that I have chosen it to see the river from the low bridge where it runs black and fast this time of year. The surface breaks as if a hand moved under it. There is no hand. The reflection that should display only one man shows two for a fraction of a heartbeat. My silhouette and a second nearer to me than my coat could account for. I watch without correction as the extra dark resolves to nothing. My pulse neither quickens nor drops. I leave a second note when I reach the study: *artifact observed in reflective surface; duration minimal; orientation inward, not external.*

If the Inkbound Society read those lines, they would ask me to deliver a lecture on mythology next term and congratulate me on my control. If the part of me that wears ink beneath the skin could read, it would sign its name where mine already sits. We have reached a point at which the experiment requires a live trial.

The live trial is not blood. Not yet.

I wait until the town's lamps are old and the house has performed each breath on its spectrum at least once. Then I walk without coat, without gloves, and find myself under her window again. Not because I failed to plan, but because the plan has always included this outcome at this hour. The light is on low, not bright enough to announce, not dim enough to deceive. She is at her desk, shoulders bent, hand moving. Her hair is down, and the braid has resigned to necessity. A cup sits to the left of the page. She is a right-handed writer who learned to slide the heel of her hand above wet ink to avoid smearing the last line of every paragraph. The trick has not saved her wrist tonight. That pleases me in a way I prefer not to name.

I could knock. I could speak through wood and chain and watch the shiver travel along her forearm when she recognizes my voice. Permission is a civilized word for what men take every day and call ordinary. I am not interested in taking anything she has not already moved toward. My mouth forms her name without instruction to do so. The pane does not fog with it. The darker rhythm at my wrist answers faster now, a matching set. Resonance, it would seem, is no longer theory.

The decision remains. Ash or fire. To consume or to crown. The Society would say there is dignity in either. They would be wrong. There is only accuracy. Which end writes the truer book? Which end is invention and which end is cowardice dressed as purity? If I am honest—and what other standard should a man choose when he imagines himself better than the room he leaves—I want *both*. To end and to keep. To own and to absolve. It is a child's desire threaded through a scholar's diction. The admission is not elegant. It is necessary.

Inside, she pauses and the pen stills. She raises her head and looks straight at the glass as if she felt a change in the pressure of the night. The skin at the base of my throat heats as if someone placed a hand there. I do not step back. Her face has the expression of a person who is about to discover what kind of story she is in and hopes it is the kind that permits her to win without losing anything that matters. No story worth reading ever has.

I leave first because I am the one with restraint, because a man who believes he chooses his appetites is easier to forgive than the one who admits they have always been choosing him. The gate breathes me in, the house sets my shadow back where it belongs, the ember in the grate gives up a last small ghost of orange. I sit at the desk and smooth the vellum and write a single line I will not give the Society and will not yet send her: *When architecture decides its own roofline, the builder's job is to keep the walls from lying.*

The ink dries without feathering. Outside, the fog finally loses interest in the windows and takes its business to the river. The darker pulse learns how to be quiet again. I go to bed without checking the mirror and sleep without dream, because dreams are theater and theater is nothing but insult.

Tomorrow I will teach a text that imagines desire as salvation and mark it with a pencil harder than the paper deserves. Tomorrow she will arrive in a sweater the color of smoke and pretend she is not waiting to be told what she already knows. Tomorrow the Society will invent a new reason to think themselves older than anyone else alive. These are all probable truths. The truth that matters is the one that does not need prediction...

The bond is real enough to test, and the test has begun.

I do not know yet whether my name will be written next to hers in a column under witnessed or under authored. I know only that no other line will do, and that whatever I choose will leave the world as neat on the surface as it always was while altering its underpinnings by a degree that cannot be undone. That is what men mean when they say fate and lack the language to confess they are engineers.

When the house settles for the last time, a faint draft moves across my wrist. If I were superstitious, I would call it a kiss. If I were kind, I would call it warning. I call it what it is... *confirmation*.

Chapter 12

Octavia

Antonio's is too bright at closing time. The fluorescent bulbs buzz, drowning the place in a kind of cheap daylight that makes every corner look bleached, hollow. My hoodie smells like oregano and fryer grease, my hair like the faint sweetness of burnt dough. I shouldn't even be here—Jessica begged me to cover, swore she had a lead on some councilman's aide and vanished before I could argue. Rent doesn't negotiate, and sadly, pizza shifts don't wait.

Marco slides the last box across the counter with a flourish, grease seeping through the cardboard. "One more run, Tavia. Then you can go home and dream about a better life."

I glance at the slip. My stomach dips. The address is too familiar. Black iron gate. Fog-strangled hedges. The house that seems to breathe when you walk past it.

Dr. Marlowe's.

Of course.

The drive out of Antonio's parking lot is all wet asphalt and neon reflections. My little car rattles over potholes as if protesting the errand. Every red light feels designed to stretch the anticipation thinner, until I'm taut as wire by the time I reach the street. The fog is already waiting, thick and white, curling across the pavement like it knows exactly where I'm going.

The gates recognize the code scrawled in looping black ink. His handwriting—neat enough to make you think of scalpels, not pens. The motor sighs, the iron mouth opening wide. I drive in, gravel crunching like bone beneath the tires.

The house rises from the fog, like something out of a horror movie. Not monstrous, but not welcoming either—simply inevitable. It rules the block without effort, sharp angles and windows glowing dimly like watchful eyes. One light, low and amber, burns from a room on the east side. The rest of the house waits in shadow.

I climb the steps with the pizza balanced in my hands. The cardboard feels heavier than it should. My knuckles rap once on the door. A second later, it opens.

"Miss Hartwell." His voice is a blade dulled by velvet, the kind that slices quietly. He fills the doorway in a charcoal shirt with sleeves rolled just enough to show his wrists. The gold fleck in his gaze catches the hall light like a secret.

"Dr. Marlowe." My name for him stumbles out, awkward against the weight of his. "I—uh—Antonio's Pizza. Large, extra cheese. Anchovies."

His mouth curves. Not smile. Not disdain. Something that slips between. "So it arrives unscathed. I was beginning to think delivery was an unreliable institution."

"Guess I should be flattered," I say, forcing a dry laugh. "Restoring your faith one greasy box at a time."

"Faith," he murmurs, taking the box from me, "is an indulgence. Accuracy is better." His fingers graze mine. Warm, deliberate. Too much. Too long.

I swallow, fumble for the receipt. "Need you to sign." My voice is thin, traitorous.

He doesn't reach for the pen immediately. Instead, he glances behind him, into the house. "It's cold. Come in."

The words are simple, polite. But when I step over the threshold, the air changes.

The house smells faintly of cedar and citrus. Not homey—*exact*. The kind of scent chosen, not lived in. The entryway is all clean lines. Black wood and marble polished to mirror, a hall runner that shows no wear, a coat rack holding one immaculate overcoat. Overhead hangs a small chandelier that looks like glittering stars. To my right, a glimpse of a study—books shelved like soldiers, pages stacked with a discipline that denies accident.

He leads me toward a small sitting room with a single low lamp glowing amber. The furniture is spare but deliberate. A leather chair angled toward the east window, paired with a table of dark oak without a single scratch. Even the rug looks curated, its pattern geometric, clean.

I stand awkwardly in the doorway, clutching the receipt like a talisman. "Nice place," I say, my voice too bright, too thin.

"Appearances are important," he answers, taking the pen and signing the slip with that same surgical precision. His hand brushes mine again as he passes it back. "But you already knew that."

There's an edge beneath his tone—something that hums like struck glass.

"I know writers don't usually live like this," I blurt, my eyes flicking over the room again. "Most of us are buried in clutter, stacks of paper, unpaid bills. The starving artist cliché."

He tilts his head. "You assume I'm an artist. I'm a critic, Miss Hartwell. I cut. I sharpen. I remove what does not belong. That leaves less clutter."

The words sting, though they shouldn't. His gaze holds mine until I feel pinned to the spot. "Funny," I say finally, "you don't look like you've ever starved a day in your life."

Something dangerous flickers across his mouth, then fades. "Starvation is not always measured by food."

The silence that follows is thick enough to smother. His eyes—green with that *impossible* fleck of gold—don't look away.

My pulse stumbles. "Well. Enjoy your anchovies."

He sets the box carefully on the table, then steps closer. Close enough that the lamp shadows the sharp line of his jaw, close enough that I smell faint coffee and cedar. He holds out his hand as if to steady me, though I haven't moved. When I hesitate, he lets his fingers brush the inside of my wrist—light, careful, deliberate.

Heat sparks there, rippling up my arm, down my spine. My breath catches. His gaze flicks to where his skin meets mine, then back to my face. For one heartbeat, I think he might close the distance entirely.

Then he releases me. The absence of his touch feels louder than the contact itself.

"Good night, Octavia." My name in his mouth is ruin and ritual all at once.

I nod, too fast. My throat is dry. "Good night."

The night air hits colder than it should as I step outside. The gate sighs open behind me. My car feels too small, too fragile for the weight in my chest.

By the time I collapse onto my bed, still in the hoodie that reeks of oregano and smoke, my hands won't stop trembling. Not from fear. Not exactly.

From something far more dangerous.

Because I can't stop replaying the curve of his mouth. The brush of his fingers on my wrist. The way his eyes refused to let me go.

And the way, God help me, I almost wanted to stay.

CHAPTER 13

Octavia

The last week of October drapes itself over Blackmoor like a velvet curtain—heavy, dramatic, and just a little damp at the hem. The trees have surrendered most of their leaves, so the wind tugs at bare branches that claw the sky. Pumpkins slump on stone steps. The bell tower tolls with a sound that always makes me think of a throat being cleared before confession. Every brick seems to hold cold. Every pathway remembers footsteps that don't belong to the living.

In my apartment, the heater clicks on with a grudging rattle. I stand in front of the long, antique mirror perched by my dresser and stare at the devil staring back. It's not subtle. The dress is red satin with a glossy sheen that drinks the lamplight, short enough to defy sense given the temperature, cut close enough to make my skin hum. The neckline dips in a V that could slice a man's attention in half. I had told myself I would choose something clever, literature-themed, dark academia with a wink. Instead, I let Jessica talk me into a ridiculous archetype. "It's *Halloween*, Tavia," she'd pleaded, tugging the hanger from the rack with victorious zeal. "No one is grading you. Except maybe the devil."

The horns are satin-wrapped and small, pinned into my hair where the chestnut and auburn curls spill loose and wild, making them look almost—*native*. I ring my eyes in black eyeliner and smudge the corners enough to look dangerous. I slide on the thin black choker that always makes me stand a little taller, as if the throat needs armor for certain nights. When I sweep my hair over one shoulder, freckles dust the top of my chest in constellations the red makes brighter. I am not used to seeing myself like this—edgier, *sexy*, demanding to be seen. I feel like a story about to become a rumor.

On the bed, my black coat waits in patient protest. I shrug into it and check the time—eight-thirty. The party started at eight. Jessica's text pings, and I dive for the phone.

JESS: angel is flight-ready. where's my favorite little demon?

ME: pinning my sins to my head. five minutes.

JESS: i expect you to corrupt the punch.

ME: sounds illegal.

JESS: so is that neckline. blessed be.

I laugh despite myself and pocket my phone, grab my small crossbody bag—the press badge tucked in, because the habit is a harness—and switch off the lamp. For a heartbeat I stand in the doorway, listening to the apartment hold its breath the way it always does when I leave after dark. The corkboard, threaded with red lines and clipped headlines, seems to lean closer in the low light, a map made of insistence. The second victim's smile still slices from a newsprint oval. The first's shoes are arranged straight at the photograph's edge, a detail I can't stop staring at. Straightened by whom? Why? I shut the door before the questions can climb onto my coat and ride along.

The air outside tastes of metal and rain. The walk to campus is a procession of little haunted moments that somehow stick out at the forefront of my mind. A paper bat caught in a shrub beating one wing, a porch skeleton that shifts in a windless moment, the soft give of leaves breaking under my heels like damp parchment. Blackmoor's main quad is alive—strings of orange bulbs loop from lamppost to lamppost, jack-o'-lanterns grin on the library steps, and someone's queued a playlist that slides from synth-pop to a song with a bass that feels like a second pulse.

The party—officially sanctioned, allegedly supervised—has colonized Memorial Hall. It's the prettiest building and the most deceptive. All high windows and carved cornices, columns pretending to be innocent of what has occurred in their shade. Inside, banners arch across a ceiling painted with the kind of angels that always look like they're judging you for breathing. Long tables hold bowls that steam faintly, dry ice fog feathering the rims. Costumes swarm—witches bargaining with astronauts, plague doctors offering gummy worms to fairies, a trio of classics majors dressed as Fates and cutting licorice strings with embroidery scissors.

Jessica finds me before I find the bar. She snaps into focus from across the room like a beacon—angel wings that glitter, halo on a thin wire, short white dress with a flounce that would be innocent if it didn't fit like a plan. Her blonde hair is curled into wide, soft waves that catch light the way a knife catches sun. Stormy eyes that miss nothing. She moves through the crowd like a queen who learned politics at ten and never forgot.

"Confess," she says, pressing a plastic cup into my hand. "You wore that for journalism. Investigative cleavage." Jess even waggles her brows at me to make her point.

I choke on a laugh. "You're going to *hell* for that rhyme."

She studies me with quick, affectionate skepticism, and when she sees something in my face that isn't joke-shaped, her grin softens. "Hey," she says. "Tonight is for pretending the world is nicer than it is. For one hour, at least."

"For *one* hour," I echo, and take a swallow from the cup. The punch tastes like an orchard fell in love with a pharmacy. I make a face and drink again. The bass thrums through my ribs. We dance because dancing is the oldest form of proof that we're still here. Jessica is good—hips that know exactly how to draw eyes without letting any of them win. She leans into me, we laugh, and she murmurs gossip in my ear, as if passing lit matches into my palm. I let the rhythm take me by the throat and shake.

An hour is elastic, stretching and snapping. I excuse myself to breathe and slip into the corridor that leads toward the cloisters, where the crowd thins to stray couples and a pirate dragging a spent ghost. The air is cooler here, with a smell of old stone and older dust. Through an open arch, the courtyard reveals itself under a tremulous moon, the hedges clipped into rectangles with an obe- dience that feels suspect. I step into the archway, grateful for the quiet.

And stop.

Adrian Marlowe stands at the far end of the cloister walk, exactly where the darkness becomes a decision. He is turned three-quarters away, speaking low to a man I don't recognize—older, heavyset, jacket that fits too well to be ready-made. A gloved hand passes something small and dark into Marlowe's palm, fast, like a trick. A flash of black against black, caught and closed. The other man touches two fingers to his forehead—the shape of a gesture that wants to be respect but stops at calculation—and peels away into shadow without looking back.

Adrian turns and sees me at once.

The collision of his gaze with mine is a physical thing. I feel it at my wrist, in the soft meat just below the thumb, where my pulse decides whether it will embarrass me tonight. He doesn't look surprised. He looks—covered. As if he pulled a lid down over everything a second before I arrived. He walks toward me with that unhurried economy I hate and crave.

"Miss Hartwell," he says, voice clean as a blade dipping through water. The devil horns must look ridiculous to him. The dress, a tactic. I square my shoulders anyway.

"Professor," I say. "You're far from your anchorites."

A flicker at the corner of his mouth. "You take your metaphors to parties. How earnest."

"It's a costume," I answer. "I left the footnotes at home."

His eyes move—once, down and up. Not leer. Survey. We stand inside a very small hemisphere of air in which everyone else stops existing.

"You were dancing," he says, not quite a question.

"Sometimes people do that at parties."

"I've heard." He glances past me, toward the hall. "You shouldn't be out alone in the cloisters tonight."

"Because it's drafty?" I tilt my head. "Or because you prefer your students where you can see them?"

He meets my provocation with indifference so precise it's an insult. "Because people drink, and edges are edges." He slips his hand into his coat pocket and I know—without reason, without proof—that the small dark thing he was given is in there, waiting like a held breath. "You should get back to your... *angel.*"

"*Jessica,*" I say, too quickly.

A half-beat of silence. "Of course," he says, and the two words manage to weigh the world. I watch him calculate a gentleness he doesn't believe in.

"I didn't know you went to parties," I say, because I have to ask something I can pretend is innocuous.

"I don't," he says, and his mouth makes the suggestion of something that isn't a smile. "I'm on my way to a meeting."

"At ten p.m. on a Wednesday?" The devil is useful for boldness. "Sounds like a cult."

He looks down, then up, composed. "It sounds like a faculty committee, which is worse." A pause. "Good night, Miss Hartwell."

I can feel suspicion unfurling inside me like a slow smile. "What do they discuss at this hour? Funding? Or the proper angle of a knife?"

For a moment, something sparks behind his eyes—surprise, pleasure, that wolfish recognition you catch when a predator remembers your scent. Then it's gone. He becomes the closed book I hand my name to twice a week.

"Shake it off," he says, so softly I almost don't hear it. He steps aside, leaving me the corridor like a gift he doesn't intend me to keep. And then he's gone, swallowed by the stair that descends into undercroft, each footfall placed with the patience of someone who has never once tripped without choosing to.

I stand in the archway longer than I should. The wind threads fingers through my hair and lifts the smallest curl at my temple where the horn is pinned. I want to pull my phone from my bag and text Jessica *you were right about the neckline* and also *he carries secrets like other men carry wallets.* I want to follow the steps and see where they go. I want too many contradictory things at once, and the wanting makes me angry.

Back in the hall the music is louder, the bodies closer. Jessica spots me from half a room away, reads my face in an instant, and cuts a clean path through fairy wings and fake swords until she's close enough to hook her fingers into my sleeve.

"You okay?" she asks, bright voice dipped in steel.

"Ran into Marlowe," I say. "In the cloister."

She rolls her eyes skyward like an angel receiving a message from a deity she finds tedious. "Of course you did. Did he critique your costume?"

Her gaze flicks over my shoulder, scanning. "What did he say?"

"That I should get back to my angel." I swallow. "He was... weird."

"He's always weird," she says, but the humor doesn't land. She studies me longer. "Weird how?"

"Closed," I say, searching for the word that will make this feel less like obsession. "Like he put a lid on something. And he was meeting someone but didn't want me to know who."

Jessica's smile returns, practiced and gentle. "Tavia. It's Halloween week. Everyone's meeting someone. You can't keep making a murder board out of passing glances."

I flinch. She squeezes my arm. "I'm not scolding you," she says. "I'm reminding you to be twenty-five at least twice a year."

"Once a year," I say, and manage to smile. "On Halloween."

She lifts her cup in a toast. "Exactly." Then she leans in, her halo bumping my horn, and stage-whispers, "Also, we spent thirty minutes taping me into this dress. If you disappear for detective work, I will haunt you."

I surrender to her, let the music insist. I dance. I let strangers' laughter slick the edges of my thoughts. I eat a cookie shaped like a tombstone and lick black icing from my finger and think about ink and blood and how easily they look the same when the light is wrong. Jessica does a spin that makes half the room clap. An economics major in a werewolf mask asks me to dance and I say no, kindly. A girl in a moth costume tells me she loves my obituaries and I say thank you and swallow the flinch the word *loves* puts in my spine.

The hall breathes. The hour loosens. For a moment I forget the shape of the map on my wall.

It's past eleven-thirty when the call comes. My phone shivers against my thigh like a startled animal. I step out of the crowd to answer. "Hartwell."

"You're on campus?" Jessica's voice in my ear, not the pulsing room beside me—no, not Jessica. I blink and look up. She's right there, halo askew, eyes on me. She checks her own phone and shakes her head. "Not me," she mouths. I frown, glance back at the screen.

Unknown Number.

"Who is this?" I ask.

A beat of breath. Then a male voice I recognize from a hundred official statements that always manage to sound like regret without apology. "Hartwell," says Chief Mateo Thornwick. "You need to come to Riverside. We found another one."

The words split the room. I realize later the music didn't actually stop. It only stepped aside inside me.

"Same MO?" I ask, walking toward the exit on legs that have remembered their purpose. "Same—"

"Enough," he says, and for the first time since I've known his voice, it sounds tired. "I shouldn't be calling, but I figured you'd rather hear it than trip over it. Don't bring a camera. You won't get close enough anyway."

The line clicks dead. He hates phones. They take your refusals and build a history out of them.

Jessica is at my shoulder in an instant. "What happened?"

"Riverside," I say. "Another one."

Her face shifts—party to press in a breath. She looks at me like she's measuring how much of me is left to spend. "We go."

"We go," I echo, and the echo is vow and surrender both.

We move fast because speed feels like purpose. Out into the cold again, the night peeled open by blue and red blooming faintly in the distance like a terrible flower. Jessica's wings glitter under the streetlights as she jogs. I take three fast steps to keep pace. She's already calling someone as she runs—her source at Dispatch, her voice low and quick, "Text me a grid, I owe you a week of coffees." I text Landon *on it*, our illustrious and mostly absent boss, then shove the phone into my pocket and dig for my press badge by muscle memory. It bites my palm with its little metal clip.

We cut through the quad. The decorations seem obscene now—the grinning pumpkins, the paper bats, the plastic tombstones stamped with names that mean nothing. Blackmoor's windows watch us pass like a hundred old women in shawls. In the cloister, the air is still cooler, touched with the undercroft's breath. I can feel, without seeing, the stair that goes down. If I had the nerve, I would take it. If I took it, I don't think I'd come back as the same girl.

"Hey," Jessica says, a soft warning. "Stay with me."

"I am." But my gaze drags toward the darkness at the edge of the arch as if a magnet were sewn into the hem of my dress. *What are you hiding,*

Professor? Where do you go when the night opens a door?

The sirens thicken as we reach the street. Riverside isn't far—a laced path treed with old sycamores that hang over the water like a row of judges, their branches still leafed with a stubborn handful of yellow. Police tape is already strung wide. Floodlights cut the dark into sections, turning fog into solid beams we have to step around. Officers move with choreographed efficiency, which is how you recognize shock—people cling to steps when they can't trust their feet.

Jessica slows us as we approach, posture friendly, open, harmless. She's done this dance enough to make it look like she's greeting old friends at a barbecue. "Evening, Davis," she says to a cop I dimly remember from a double-park ticket fight she had in June. "Pretty light show."

He snorts despite himself. "Press stays back," he says, but softer than he should. "Chief's not in the mood."

"When is he?" Jessica asks, smiling. She tilts her head toward the tape. "Give us a hint and we'll stay out of your hair."

He looks like a man who wants to be good and also likes us just enough to commit a misdemeanor. He leans in a fraction. "Down by the retaining wall," he says. "Off the path. Don't say I said it."

"Wouldn't dream," Jessica says. "You're an angel."

I don't look down at my dress, and I don't try to interpret the joke. The air is wrong. The river tugs at it, pulling cold through my coat like a thread. The floodlights make the water look like oil. If I turn my head just so, I can see a stretch of ground that gleams too dark where the earth has been disturbed. A forensic tech kneels, camera hunch-shouldered, as if praying to a machine. A shape under a tarp is the kind of shape you only mistake once. It is smaller than I want it to be.

My mouth tastes of copper and apples. I fish in my bag for the notebook that never leaves it, hands steady because familiar rituals steady hands. Notes make the world behave. I write: *Riverside. Retaining wall. Floodlights. Officer Davis—kind eyes, worry-smile. Tarp small.* My pen hovers over the date. The numbers look worse in ink. It feels like signing a ledger.

Beside me, Jessica murmurs, "We'll get what we can. We won't push." Her wings stir against her shoulders as if they have a mind of their own. She glances sidelong at me. "You okay?"

"Define okay," I say, and the steadiness of my own voice surprises me. My stomach twists, nerves tangling tighter with every sweep of the floodlights across the riverbank. Whatever waits under that tarp, I already know it's going to follow me home.

Jessica squeezes my hand once, warm and quick. "We're here, Tavia. We do the work in front of us."

The river hisses something low. A gust lifts the hair at the back of my neck. On the other side of the tape, Thornwick appears, shoulders squared to the work, face rubbed hard as if he could erase the last hour by making his skin ache. He sees us. Our eyes meet. For a breath, I think he might shake his head, send us home like children who found the wrong room. He doesn't. He gives the smallest nod in the world—permission, or resignation, or the acknowledgment that some animals always show up when there's blood in the air.

I write that down too. Not the blood. The nod.

The radio chatter clicks and murmurs. A tech calls a number. A detective gestures with two fingers, the shape of someone drawing a line in their head. My heart beats slow and heavy, the way it does before I jump from a high rock into water—commitment without permission. I look past the tape because I can't not. The tarp lifts for the briefest moment, just enough for the night to learn a new name.

Chestnut hair with auburn light trapped under flood. Green eyes closed by kindness someone paid for with a tremor in their hands. Curves that look like mine when I'm not wearing armor.

The world leans.

I think, stupidly, of my devil horns pinned neat into my hair and Jessica's halo tilting and the way Adrian said *shake it off* like a blessing and an order, and I understand something I had been pretending not to understand for weeks...

Whatever is hunting us is not finished. Whatever book is being written under Blackmoor's stones has not reached its final chapter. The ink isn't dry.

Jessica's hand is on my elbow, steadying me. "Breathe," she says.

"I'm trying." My voice sounds distant and precise. I write *same build* and the letters look like spiders. I draw a straight line from the word to the date and another line from the date to a blank space that waits like a dare.

I look up at the river, at the way the fog skims it like a veil. Somewhere on campus, wind rattles a line of paper ghosts. And somewhere deeper still—beneath the stones and ivy, in rooms people only whisper about—men may be moving pieces on a board and calling it tradition. Secrets pressed down so long they've learned to shape the ground itself. Not far from here, I can't help but imagine him—Professor Marlowe—walking away from one of those whispered meetings, something small and dark tucked into his pocket like a truth I'll never be allowed to see.

My phone vibrates again—a text from Landon *hold what you can / write what you must*—and I bite the inside of my cheek to keep focus. The taste of iron anchors me to my body.

Halloween is almost here. Costumes have a way of showing people who they are when they think they're pretending. Angels and devils don't need labels. They leave marks.

I cap my pen and slide it behind my ear the way I always do, so I don't have to rummage and lose time. Jessica catches the gesture and nods, simple and fierce. We edge closer to the tape, careful, professional, polite. We ask the questions you're allowed to ask. We don't demand the answers that would get us thrown back. We do the work in front of us.

But under the questions and the notes, under the assurance that we know how to be good citizens in the presence of a body, another truth hums and refuses to be shut off. It sounds like a bell behind a door. It tastes like ink on the tongue.

Something has decided it knows my outline.

And tonight, somewhere between the angel and the devil, I decided I'm going to learn its name.

CHAPTER 14

Adrian

The floodlights burn the fog into walls of white, the kind of light that doesn't illuminate so much as obliterate, flattening the world into stark contrasts of shadow and glare. They make the river look like oil poured over stone, slick and heavy, a black current sliding beneath the surface of the town like a secret no one is meant to name. The police tape trembles on its posts, yellow plastic pulled taut against the night, a barrier that pretends to separate grief from order. Officers hunch their shoulders against the damp, photographers kneel with the posture of supplicants, and detectives murmur to each other with the tense precision of men arranging dominoes they fear will fall too soon. It is choreography more than procedure, and I have seen it before, a hundred variations, each ending the same way—a body tagged, bagged, catalogued. An offering disguised as evidence.

And she is there.

Octavia stands just beyond the perimeter, notebook in hand, pen balanced between her fingers like a blade she's only begun to test. Jessica hovers at her side, wings still pinned from the party, glitter dulled by fog, halo knocked sideways by the night's damp. They are a matched pair tonight—angel and devil, but the truth is less symbolic, or simple. It is Octavia who holds the attention of the night. She stands against the floodlights like a figure painted onto the canvas of shadow, her hair wild from the damp, curls loosed by the October air, chestnut threaded with auburn where the lamps catch and splinter copper across the strands. The red dress glints under her coat where it parts, satin like fresh blood against the dark. She gazes past the tape, unflinching, as if she has chosen to look into the thing everyone else is trained to avert their eyes from, as if staring is an oath she has sworn.

And I feel it again.

The thrum beneath her skin. A vibration that does not belong to the merely human. The same resonance that answers under my own veins when the air thickens and the dark presses close. It is faint, buried, but alive. A thread of ink in her blood, dormant, waiting. It whispers with the same rhythm that coils beneath my wrist, a darker pulse than the heart can name. She doesn't even notice. She writes in her notebook, calm as rit-ual, unaware that every stroke of her pen hums in frequency with what lies beneath her ribs. The blindness is exquisite. The blindness is *dangerous*.

She leans closer to Jessica, murmurs something I cannot hear. Jessica squeezes her hand, the way angels are supposed to do. But the tremor is there anyway—the faint shake in Octavia's wrist, the quick press of her lips together as she steadies her-self before another line of ink. The body knows what the mind refuses. Her blood knows. It is speaking, even if she has not yet learned its lan-guage.

The tarp lifts at the far end of the scene. Cam-eras click with greedy urgency. A detective curses softly. The wind carries the smell. Iron, wet earth, the faint sweetness that lingers when blood has not yet decided whether to belong to earth or air. Octavia closes her eyes for one second, lashes trembling against her cheeks, then opens them again and writes. She is learning to metabolize horror into text, to siphon terror into sentences. It will cost her. Everything worth writing always does.

I stay until the hour folds itself into useless repetition—questions asked twice, evidence bags labeled and relabeled, officers moving on reflex rather than reason. When she finally pulls her coat tighter and lets Jessica steer her toward the street, I let the distance reclaim her. The fog clings to her hem, the floodlight glare whitens the side of her cheek, her shadow passes and the hum at my wrist stirs harder, answering hers across the space as if the river itself had decided to carry a message between us. The ink in her blood is not silence. It is a hymn she cannot hear.

The walk back is deliberate, my pace aligned to the measure of my thoughts. Fog collects at the hem of my coat, too. It threads into the wool, follows me like a hand unwilling to let go. Not normal Washington fog, the kind that follows the shadows of the society. By the time I step through my gate and the motor sighs its mechanical welcome, the sensation of her resonance has not faded but sharpened, like a frequency that refuses to die even when the instrument is at rest. The house greets me in silence, lamps dimmed to the exact hue I require. I remove my coat and gloves with order. The coat smoothed, the gloves aligned, the sleeve brushed where fog left its residue. Disorder is not permitted here. Disorder breeds chaos, and chaos is hunger ungoverned.

In the study, the fire is low but steady, amber embers collapsing with soft reports that sound like punctuation. I let it burn while I take the desk. The files are arranged not alphabetically but by frequency of need, each folder a ledger of observation. Her folder has grown thicker these past weeks, swollen with newspaper clippings, class assignments, marginalia in her hand and mine. I have written notes she will never see, drawn lines she would not think to connect, catalogued her words as if they were relics. Patterns, hints, small confessions that slip between the sentences she intends. Tonight I want *more*.

The university archives yield easily. Systems like these are built on the assumption of compliance, and I have never complied with anything except precision. Passwords are ornamental. Locks are symbols. A man who understands pressure and silence can walk through walls. Her student file unfolds on the screen in careful columns: name, age, address, prior schooling. Nothing I don't already know. Until the lower fields reveal themselves.

Adoption.

One word, tucked among sterile lines. Legal guardians: Hartwell. Parents: [Redacted.] I scroll again. No birth certificate. No medical record before her eighth year. Nothing before Hartwell. A gap that is louder than any entry could be.

She doesn't know. I am certain of it. She carries herself with the conviction of someone who believes her history is accounted for, her roots shallow but visible. She has no idea that her bloodline runs deeper, darker, threaded into rituals she has not yet glimpsed. Her blindness is not accident—it is design. The ledger of her life has been edited, the power coiling within her stifled. And now it is *my* hands turning the pages.

I study the record, and memory stirs like something long submerged rising to the surface. I recall a ceremony years ago, red roses pressed into palms, vows spoken in shadow. Two figures stepping forward, their voices low, their presence brief. They vanished soon after, their names only rumor in the years that followed. I had not thought of them in a decade, yet the surname flickers in the archive with the faint clarity of a half-burned photograph. Their absence had been recorded as tragedy. Perhaps it was instead.... *design*.

The fire cracks. A coal drops into ash. I lean back in the chair, fingers steepled, letting the silence carry the truth forward: *she is not what she believes.* She is not merely Octavia Hartwell, student, journalist, writer of obituaries and short fictions. She has been sewn into a story that began before she could spell her name. Her pulse carries the ink. Her blood hums in shadow. And she is walking blind into a history that wants her back.

The adoption record lies open before me, but the greater record is older, hidden beneath stone and oath. If I search deep enough, if I press the right fingers to the right seam, I will find the missing pages. And then I will know who she is meant to be.

The ember collapses again, a soft exhalation. I smooth the crease on the record with my palm. The ink beneath my skin stirs in answer, the darker rhythm at my wrist syncing with the confirmation before me. Blood knows blood. It has always known. She does not yet. But soon.

When she learns, the world will not remain what it is. And neither will I.

CHAPTER 15

The smell of the river still clings to me even though I've showered twice and changed clothes. Metallic, like pennies pressed into damp earth, like the echo of iron in the back of my throat. It's in my hair, my jacket, my notebook. When I lift the pen, my fingers hesitate because the smell feels like a residue on the page too. Writing usually helps me make sense of things, but tonight it feels like dragging words through mud.

Across from me, Jess nurses a paper cup of tea gone cold. She's curled sideways in the chair, knees up, glitter still caught in the crease of her collarbone from the party. The halo she wore is gone but I can still see where it pressed into her hair. She's looking at me like she's waiting for me to break, or maybe confess, and I'm not sure which one I'm closer to.

"Are you going to write it?" she asks, voice low. Not a challenge—more like someone checking if a wound still bleeds.

I look down at my notebook. The page is half full: location, time, the names of officers I overheard. Nothing about the tarp. Nothing about the body. Nothing about the way the smell curled under the tape like a hand. Nausea churns in my stomach and I want to vomit. "I don't know," I say instead.

She tilts her head, studying me. Her gray eyes always make me think of keys—like they could fit any lock if you hold them right. "That's not like you."

I want to tell her that nothing is like me right now. That I don't feel like me right now. Instead, I shrug and take a sip of cold coffee just so I have something to do with my hands. It tastes like burnt paper.

Jess sets her cup down with a soft clack. "You're pale. Paler than usual."

I smirk but it feels borrowed. "Thank you for that."

"I'm serious, Octavia. You're shaking."

I hadn't noticed until she said it, but my hand really is trembling. I shove it under the table. "It's just the night," I lie. "Long day."

Her mouth tightens but she lets it go. She's always been good at reading a room—even when the room is just me trying not to come apart. She switches tactics. "What do you think happened?"

I stare at the steam ghosting from my cup as if it has the answer. "Someone died," I say finally. "And someone else is going to decide what that means."

"That's not an answer," she says.

"I know."

For a moment neither of us speaks. The office smells of toner and old carpet, paper stacked on every surface like a forest trying to regrow itself indoors. The Gazette has always been our sanctuary—a place to be clever, relentless, a little self-righteous. Tonight it feels like a mausoleum, and I'm the exhibit.

Jess reaches across the table, touches my wrist. "You've been different lately," she says softly. "Secretive. Distracted."

I swallow. "Maybe I've just been busy."

"Busy with what?"

The answer coils in my throat but never makes it out. Not the late nights tracing patterns between case files. Not the spreadsheet of names hidden under "laundry." Not Adrian. Not the sense that something in this town is circling me. "It's complicated," I say finally.

Jess drums her fingers once on the table. "Complicated is my favorite kind of story."

I almost smile. "You'd lose your job if you printed this one."

"Try me."

I shake my head. "Not yet."

Her eyes narrow—not angry, just mapping a puzzle she can't solve yet. She leans back, arms crossing, bracelets clinking. "You're starting to scare me, Tavia."

I want to tell her I'm scaring myself too. That the fog at the river still clings to my clothes at night. Instead I flip my notebook shut and push air into my lungs. "You're not allowed to scare easy. That's my job."

She huffs a small laugh. "You know what you need?"

"A time machine?"

"A night out. Again."

I blink. "Seriously?"

"Yes, seriously. We went out once, you didn't die. So let's do it again. Landon's in Portland for that conference, so it'll just be us. Three nights from now. Halloween at the club."

I laugh without humor. "There's still only one club in this town."

"Exactly." She leans in, chin propped on her fist. "Costumes, bad DJ, overpriced drinks. Nobody cares who you are, nobody cares what you're writing. It's the only time this place actually feels alive."

"Jess—" I start, but she cuts me off.

"You need this. We both do. You've been acting like a ghost and I've been playing editor-slash-therapist. You're starting to freak people out. Come with me before you forget what normal feels like."

The way she's looking at me—bright, stubborn—makes my excuses wilt. "We'll see," I say finally.

"That's a yes."

"It's not."

"It's close enough." Her grin flashes, glitter catching the overhead light. For a heartbeat she looks like she did our first summer at the Gazette—barefoot, singing off-key, newsprint on her fingers.

I glance at my watch and realize we've burned an hour without a single usable line. Jess notices too. "Go home," she says. "Sleep. I'll cover the desk."

"You're already covering for me."

"I've been covering for you all week," she says pointedly, but softens it with a smile. "Don't make me drag you to Halloween in chains."

I can't help laughing. "You're *evil*."

"*Angel*," she says, flicking invisible wings. "You're the devil."

"Maybe," I murmur.

"You okay?" she asks, a little quieter.

I should tell her no. That the smell of iron hasn't left my throat. That I've started walking streets at night looking for something I'm not sure exists. Instead I give her the smallest smile I can manage. "I will be."

She studies me a second longer, then nods, saving the rest of her questions for later. "Halloween, then."

"Maybe," I say again, softer.

When I step outside, the night air slices clean through my coat. Streetlights halo in the mist, trembling on wet asphalt. I pause on the curb, notebook heavy in my bag, and inhale until my lungs ache. Through the Gazette's glass door, Jess is already at her desk again, hair slipping from its knot. She doesn't see me watching. For a second I feel like I'm back behind the tape—outside the perimeter, looking in at something I can't touch.

I start walking. Three days until Halloween. Three days to pretend I can be normal. Three days before whatever this is finds me again.

Above, clouds shift, swallowing the moon. My skin prickles. I tell myself it's just the cold.

I don't believe it.

The bass shudders up through the sidewalk long before we reach the door, a second pulse stitched into the street, the kind of beat you feel in your teeth. Halloween has peeled Blackmoor open at the seams. Lecture halls are dark, dorm windows flicker in strobe mimicry, and every path seems to tilt toward the same inevitable point—our one nightclub. A brick box of heat, fog, and appetite jammed into a lane that smells like rain and cigarette sugar.

Jessica slides her arm through mine and tugs me faster. She's ethereal tonight in a pale blue butterfly dress that floats when she walks, the fabric cut on some bias that turns her hips into light. Wings spring from her shoulder blades—veined panels of blue and yellow with a wash of green at the tips, iridescent under the streetlamps. Her face is its own constellation. Neon paint traced in tiny chevrons across her cheekbones, glitter dusting her lids in layered blues that shade from cornflower to midnight. She looks like a benevolent hallucination. People part for her without realizing why.

"Okay, *succubus*," she says, grinning, "you ready to ruin someone's life in there?"

"Just mine," I say, and her laugh sparks through the air—bright, defiant, like flint struck against the memory of the murders we're all trying to outrun.

The horns are satin-black and small, pinned into my curls neatly. The wings—black, sheer, ribbed with velvet—flutter when I breathe. The black velvet dress is heavier than it looks, the kind of fabric that drinks light. It dips low, clings tight, and leaves the air cool against too much skin. Each step is chosen. The dress moves, the chain warms, velvet sighs against my skin. I let the noise of the last few weeks fall away—the blood, the questions, his shadow—and walk like I'm trying to remember what freedom feels like.

Inside, the club swallows us whole. Fog spirals from vents just above head height. Strobes dice the darkness into bright, violent inches. Color strobes bruise the air—magenta, cyan, ultraviolet. Sweat and perfume bloom together. Someone's spilled cinnamon whiskey, and someone else has managed to atomize cheap champagne into a sugar haze that sticks to the back of my tongue when I breathe. The DJ's set climbs and dives like a hunt.

"Bar, then dance," Jessica says, towing me along, her blue wings brushing a shoulder here, a back there, leaving glitter in her wake. At the

counter she orders two drinks with quick, efficient motions that say she knows this place
like a second apartment. The bartender watches her neon-painted eyes and gives us a third
on the house. We sip the first—too sweet, too
strong—and I feel the heat loosen the tight string
inside my chest by half an inch.

That's when I see him.

Adrian Marlowe belongs nowhere and therefore belongs anywhere he chooses to stand. The
crowd reveals him the way a trick photograph reveals a hidden image—you look and then you *see*.
He's at the end of the bar, not drinking, watching
the room with a gaze that edits while it observes.
No costume. No mask. The suit is dark and correct, the shirt open one button more than the
daylight version of him would allow. The light
finds his eyes and kindles the gold that hides in
the green. It finds me—a collision disguised as a
glance. My breath forgets what to do with itself.

"Don't look now," Jessica says, which is a guarantee that I will, "but your dissertation topic is at three o'clock."

"My dissertation topic?"

"Obsession. *Architecture.* Men who collect verbs like knives." She leans in, glitter catching at my cheek. "If you want to leave—"

"I don't," I say, too fast, and realize that's the truest thing I've said all week.

His attention crosses the room in a straight line and lands. Not a search. Not an accident. A decision. He comes toward me with that exactness he carries like a private weather system, and the crowd flexes around him, people shifting half-steps without knowing they've moved. He stops close enough that the bass seems to come from inside his chest.

"Miss Hartwell," he says, voice pitched just under the music, so soft the name feels illicit. The look that travels the length of me is not crass and not kind. It's assessment caught on the lip of hunger. It marks the horns, the wings, the velvet that fits like a sentence I want to refuse and cannot. The corner of his mouth curves. There is no attempt to hide his desire. For once, he is careless with restraint, and the carelessness is a wound I want to press.

"Professor," I answer, my mouth dry. "I didn't think this was your habitat."

"*You* are in it," he says, and it sounds like explanation.

He lifts a hand, palm open, asking without asking. I give him mine because the part of me that would refuse is busy being reckless. His fingers close around me—warm, sure—and he draws me away from the bar and into the churn of bodies as if I have always been walking toward this.

The dance begins in proximity and becomes instruction. His hand settles at my hip—heat, weight, grip—and I feel the shape of it even through velvet. He guides, never shoves. The pressure of his palm telegraphs a turn, a step, a hinge and release, and my body answers before my mind can decide if I approve. His other hand finds mine and lifts it, our fingers lacing like ribbon through eyelets, pulling me toward his rhythm. The bass climbs. His knee brushes the outside of my thigh, and the friction turns language into uselessness.

"This is—" I start, then abandon the sentence. The dress drags heat up my spine. My hair keeps catching at his sleeve and releasing, catching and releasing, like it has an idea of its own.

"Efficient," he says, and his mouth is too close to my ear. "Dancing removes the need to pretend we are not already speaking."

"Is that what you call this? Speaking?" The retort is breathless and I hate that he can hear it.

"It *is* a kind of grammar," he replies. His hand slides higher, not much, just enough to claim a new country on the map of me. "You are fluent."

"Don't tell me what I am," I say, and the words come out low and bright, and he laughs once, startled, as if my mouth just solved a problem he was enjoying.

The song breaks and drops into a darker one, a sine-wave bass that sets the floor humming. He turns me and brings my back to his chest, the heat of him a wall. He knows where to place a hand so a woman forgets her own name. He knows how to keep it from being an order. I breathe and feel him breathe. My shoulder fits against his collarbone like we rehearsed this. I rock my hips and his fingers tighten fractionally, like a yes. The horns press light into my scalp, the wings itch where the straps sit just beneath the fold of my shoulder blades, and my heartbeat climbs until it's an ache in my throat.

"You're staring," I say, without turning my head.

"I'm studying," he answers, not bothering to deny the first truth for the sake of the second.

"I'm not an object."

"No," he says. "You're a force."

My laugh is small, angry, and pleased. "Say that like a hypothesis again and I'll fail your next assignment on principle."

"You already handed it in," he murmurs, and when I spin to face him, the motion pulls us closer than decency wants. We are saturating the same square foot of air. I cannot tell which heat is mine.

"What are you doing here?" I ask.

"Revising," he says, eyes on my mouth. "I had theories. I'm testing them."

"What theories?" A pulse of bodies knocks against us and he shifts, bracketing me with an arm on either side, sheltering or trapping. The scent of cedar and something darker—coffee, smoke—threads the sweat and sugar around us.

"That you prefer control when you can have it," he says, "and speed when you cannot. That you are not afraid of the edge, only of the quiet afterward. That someone taught you to survive by naming things, and tonight you would rather be the thing unnamed."

"I hate you," I say, and the lie tastes like honey.

"Good," he says. "It clarifies."

His hand finds the small of my back and I step into him because the alternative is to fall. We move, the two of us, in a loop that folds the crowd into static. I don't know how long we dance like that, only that time starts counting differently—song lengths instead of minutes, breaths instead of counts. A strand of my hair hooks behind his ear and stays there, insolent. He doesn't remove it. He doesn't stop looking at my mouth.

"I can feel you thinking," I say, half-dare, half-prayer.

"You should feel," he says, and then he takes my free hand and slides it to the inside of his wrist. The skin there is hotter than it should be, the pulse steadier, deeper—a second rhythm that shouldn't exist. Something answers under my own skin, a low thrumming—warning or welcome, and the shock makes the world tilt. He sees it register. Something hungry and satisfied moves behind his eyes. He turns, drawing me with him, and the crowd opens like a curtain, and suddenly we are in an alcove behind the bar where the noise blurs into a single pressure and the light gets shy.

He doesn't crowd me. He stands close enough to ruin me and gives me space to decide. My back meets the cool of old brick and the velvet catches, a soft drag, a reminder I could say no. His hand lifts, pauses a breath from my jaw, then settles—two fingers at the hinge, a thumb under the line of my ear, touch so light it registers as certainty. The heat there floods my neck, slides down, pools.

"Why do you write about blood the way you do?" he asks, and the softness of the question is a knife. "As if you've seen it under different light. As if you know how it moves when it wants to be witnessed."

"Maybe I do," I whisper, and I'm not sure if I'm bluffing.

"I think you do," he says, and the smile that follows is not kind and not cruel. It is recognition.

His other hand finds my hip again, and this time he lets his fingers disappear into the velvet's nap, a slow, deliberate press that could be guidance or claim. I lean forward the distance of a decision and stop, every nerve standing at attention, the space between our mouths a wire so tight I can hear it.

"Say please," I breathe, because I want to see what happens when he obeys.

He doesn't. He turns obedience into inevitability. His gaze drops, then lifts, and the permission between us is signed without paper. He bends, unhurried, the angle precise, and the room constricts to the single point where his mouth will meet mine—

"Octavia!"

Jessica's voice slices the air like glass. She stumbles into the alcove, hand pressed flat to her stomach, the other already reaching for me. The neon blues on her eyelids have smudged darker, and the glitter has migrated to her cheekbones in accidental galaxies. Her wings—blue, yellow, green—quiver once and then sag. She's too pale beneath the paint.

"Hey," I say, catching her, sliding an arm around her waist. "What happened?"

"Dizzy," she breathes. "Sudden. I—" She swallows hard. "Can you take me home? *Please*?"

"Yes," I say at once, the word snapping a taut thread inside me. I turn, already moving, and find Adrian exactly as I left him except his hand has fallen from my jaw and his mouth has folded back into composure like a blade sheathed. Only his eyes tell on him. They are brighter than they should be in a dark place.

"I have to—" I begin.

"Go," he says, and the softness is real enough to anger me. "Now."

There is no time to interpret the permission. I loop Jessica's arm over my shoulder and steer her out of the alcove. The club, so recently a universe of nothing but him, becomes geography again—bar, exit sign, stagger of stairs. The bass follows like a jealous thing. I do not look back, but I feel his gaze on the strip of skin the dress leaves bare, on the line where my wings attach, on the nape of my neck. The sensation moves with me like heat.

Outside, the cold is a mercy. Jessica breathes in ragged little pulls, the night air grabbing at the glitter and lifting it from her skin. I get her into the passenger seat and buckle her in with the tenderness you give a child and a bomb. On the drive, she leans her forehead to the cool window and mutters, "I'm sorry," three times like prayer beads.

"Don't be ridiculous," I say, keeping my voice level. "You saved me from terrible decisions."

"You looked like you were about to make a very good one," she mumbles, and even sick she can still aim low and land a hit.

Streetlights pass in regular beats. Fallen leaves scuff the asphalt like paper whispers. I keep the car steady and my breathing steadier. At her building, I walk her up two flights, blue wings folding and unfolding against my arm. Inside her apartment I coax her out of the dress, into a soft T-shirt, leave a glass of water on the nightstand. The neon paint leaves a faint comet trail on the pillowcase. She squeezes my fingers once, eyes already closing. "Text me when you're home," she says.

"I will," I lie, because home is not where my body will go next, not with heat still living under my skin like an afterimage.

Back on the street, the air has sharpened. The club's bass is a duller throb now, but the memory of it hasn't moved out of my blood. I walk because driving would feel like surrender. My wings creak at their straps. The horns press a ghost circle into my scalp. Every reflective surface tosses me back a woman I recognize and do not—succubus shaped by velvet and nerve, mouth still parted where a kiss did not land.

I tell myself I should go straight home. Instead my feet take me along the back lane that runs behind the club, where the smokers' door lets out a lungful of fog and laughter every minute, where the brick is warmer from the heat trapped inside. I slow without wanting to and see him where the lane curves—shadow folded into deeper shadow, head tilted in that way he has when he is listening to something no one else hears. He's on his phone for two breaths, then not. He tucks it away and lifts his face like he already knows I'm there.

We stop two body lengths apart. The world is suddenly, impossibly quiet—no cars, no voices, just the distant rub of bass and the soft whisper of leaves scudding. The intention that almost became a kiss returns as pressure in the space between us, like a storm that moved on but left its weight behind.

"Is she all right?" he asks.

"She will be." My voice comes out rough, like I've run. "Dehydration. Bad timing."

He nods once, hands in his pockets, and that posture should look casual but does not. It looks like a man putting knives somewhere polite. "You should sleep."

"You should stop telling me what to do."

"You enjoy it," he says, and I hate him for being right and for refusing to make it easy.

I could leave. I *should*. Instead I take one step toward him that feels like four and ask, "Why did you come tonight?"

The smallest tilt of his head, like he's listening for a pitch inside the question. "Because," he says, "I suspected there would be a moment when you stopped negotiating with yourself. I wanted to see the shape of it."

"And did you?"

"Yes." He doesn't adorn it.

"What shape is it?"

His eyes move, quick, to my mouth, then back to my eyes. "Mine," he says quietly, not a boast, not a claim—an observation that embarrasses the cold. "And yours."

I have nothing for that. The night takes the words and makes them larger. I should cut it with a joke. I should thread it with barbed wire. Instead I say, "If Jessica hadn't—" and stop.

"If Jessica hadn't," he says, and leaves the sentence on the jawbone of possibility where it belongs. Then he steps back, mercy disguised as distance. "Go home, Miss Hartwell."

"Make me," I say, because I am still the girl who makes dares when she should make plans.

He laughs once, the sound low and reluctant, and it hits me in some small, secret part of my chest that has been waiting to be chosen for anything. "Tomorrow," he says. "I don't bargain with tonight."

There is nothing left to do except obey or sin. I pick obedience because it will make sin brighter when it finally arrives. I turn and walk, and I do not ask if he watches me leave because I already know he does, because the heat lives between my shoulder blades like a lit match.

The apartment smells like perfume and street and the faint tang of fog that hitchhiked in my hair. I stand at the mirror and peel the horns away, then the wings. The elastic leaves dents in my skin that look like evidence. The velvet clings when I shimmy it down. The cold of the room raids each inch as it's uncovered. I wash glitter from my face and find more glitter hiding along the collarbone, like small, ridiculous stars. I should be ashamed that my hands shake. I am not. I am awake in a way I can use.

At the corkboard I pin a fresh index card and write nothing. I just stand there and feel the quiet rippling in the walls, the way the building settles, bones creak-tongued, the way the city breathes. Somewhere on campus, the bells will ring in nine minutes, a sound like a throat deciding to confess and failing. Somewhere under that sound, if I listen with the wrong part of me, I can hear a second rhythm answer—the one that lives under his skin, the one that made mine answer back when his fingers found my wrist. The echo reaches me like a rumor the blood carries. Not words, not yet. Just... *certainty*.

I climb into bed and the sheets hoard the cold. The ceiling is the color of unsaid. I close my eyes and the alcove comes back with obscene clarity: the cool of brick, his hand at my jaw, the tiny breath we shared, a fraction of a kiss suspended in the mouth of a dark room. Before sleep, I feel for the place under my ear where his thumb rested and press there, as if a bruise might bloom just because I want one.

When the heater kicks on, it sounds like a chorus inhaling. Halloween has a way of showing you the mask you've been wearing all along. I lie in the dark and admit something I have been pretending wasn't true.

I am not only afraid of what he is. I am afraid of what I am beside him.

Outside, a siren threads the night and unwinds. Somewhere, a door closes gently, the way you do it for someone sleeping. My phone buzzes—a text from Jessica, **alive. water. never drinking again.** I send back **succubus forgives you** and put the phone face down like that could dim the heat running its circuit under my skin.

When sleep comes, it feels less like surrender than a deal struck. Tomorrow I will wake and build sentences with sober hands. Tomorrow I will measure what happened and file it in the correct drawer. But the drawer will not stay shut. The club's bass is still in my bones. His hand is still on my jaw. The dress is a black shape on the chair, smelling of smoke, sugar, and decision.

And there, at the very edge of sleep, I realize the worst thing. I am no longer studying the story for

where it might end. I am studying it for where it
wants to begin.

CHAPTER 16

The club should have repelled me. It's engineered to—bass as blunt instrument, light as interrogation, bodies as weather. But the room learns my outline the moment I step inside. Pressure translates to space, and the crowd edits itself. Fog lifts off the vents and clings to the wool of my coat as if it recognizes a thing older than condensation, older than sound. I do not intend performance, but the room performs anyway. Then I see her, and intention becomes irrelevant.

Octavia is a black star in a turbulent sky—horns satin-dark and neatly curved into chestnut and auburn curls that refuse discipline, wings sheer and ribbed, and a velvet dress that turns shadow into heat. She leans against the mirror at the bar, a point of refusal around which lesser orbits scuff and burn. She does not look like a woman who writes the names of the dead and files them under grace. She looks like a decision the night has been waiting to make.

Her gaze finds me and fixes. Not accident, not plea. A line drawn between two points that have finally chosen to be locations. I cross the floor. The club moves around me as water moves around a stone, and the stone does not ask. The bass thunders, light fractures, and her breath lifts once, steadying itself against her own ribs.

"Miss Hartwell," I say, voice pitched just under the music, so soft her name feels illicit. The look I let travel the length of her is not crass nor kind. It's assessment balanced on the tip of hunger. It marks horns, wings, the velvet that fits like a sentence I want to refuse and cannot. The corner of my mouth curves. I do not attempt to hide desire. Carelessness is not my habit. Tonight, I let it happen and watch what it does to her.

"Professor," she says, mouth dry enough to betray her. "I didn't think this was your habitat."

"You are in it," I say, and that is explanation enough.

I lift my hand—palm open, a question phrased as a fact. She gives me hers because the part of her that would refuse is occupied elsewhere, making rules it does not intend to keep. Warm. Sure. I draw her away from the bar and into the churn of bodies as if I have always been walking toward this.

The dance begins in proximity and becomes instruction. My hand takes her hip—heat, weight, grip—and the velvet broadcasts the shape of her into my palm. I guide without shoving. Pressure telegraphs turn, step, hinge and release, and her body answers in a language it apparently speaks when her mind has not granted permission. My other hand finds hers and lifts. Our fingers lace like ribbon through eyelets, pulling her toward my rhythm. The bass climbs, my knee brushes the outside of her thigh, and friction renders language ornamental.

Heat coils between us, a current that doesn't need translation. Her breath catches, then evens, the rhythm of it syncing with the pulse at my wrist. Her spine arches slightly beneath my hand, dress warm where my palm settles, velvet shifting like breath made tangible. Her hair brushes my sleeve again—catch, release, catch—leaving behind faint traces of static and scent, proof written on skin instead of air.

We move as if the room itself has narrowed around us. The bass folds into bone, heartbeat disguised as percussion. Every small motion becomes a sentence. Her shoulder turning, my hand adjusting, the silent exchange of balance and pressure and control. There's no need for speech. The body has found its own grammar.

Her pulse trembles through the fabric, each beat threading into mine until movement replaces thought. She leans back just enough for surrender to register—an instinct, a fraction—before reclaiming herself, body and space folding back into defiance. The rhythm between us becomes its own quiet argument, a wordless exchange written in breath and skin, in the precise press and release of restraint.

The song drops low, bass rolling into a darker hum. I draw her in and turn her, her spine finding my chest as if our bodies already remember the shape of this. My hand settles where heat gathers, just above the place a woman forgets her own name, holding her there without command. Her hair brushes my jaw, her breath tangles with mine.

Every shift of her hips writes another line of a language we shouldn't know but somehow speak fluently. Horns press faint light against my chin. Feathers whisper against fabric, her pulse climbs, quick and reckless, until it trembles beneath her skin like a word she's not yet willing to say.

"You're staring," she says finally without turning.

"I'm studying," I answer. I will not waste denial on a less interesting truth.

"I'm not an object."

"No," I tell her. "You're a force."

She gives me a laugh that is small and angry and pleased at once. "Say that like a hypothesis again and I'll fail your assignment on principle."

"You already handed it in," I murmur, and when she spins to face me the motion pulls us closer than decency's margin of error. The same square foot of air saturates with us. I cannot tell which heat is mine.

"What are you doing here?" she asks.

"Revising," I say, eyes on her mouth because that is where honesty sits tonight. "I had theories. I'm testing them."

"What theories?" A body glances off my shoulder. I bracket her with my arms, not trapping, not shielding—replacing friction with intention. Cedar and darker notes—coffee, a hint of smoke—thread the sugar and sweat. She inhales, some part of her recognizing that smell now and files it under ache.

"That you prefer control when you can have it," I say, "and speed when you cannot. That the edge does not frighten you; the silence after does. That someone taught you to survive by naming things, and tonight you would rather be the thing unnamed."

"I hate you," she says, and the lie is sweet on her tongue.

"Good," I say, and I mean it. "It clarifies."

I find the small of her back again and she steps into me because gravity prefers precision to pride.

We move through a loop that folds the crowd into static. Time chooses different units: not minutes, but song-lengths; not counts, but breath. A strand of her hair hooks behind my ear and stays there with insolence I will reward later. I do not remove it. I do not stop looking at her mouth.

"I can feel you thinking," she says, half-dare, half-prayer.

"You should feel." I take her free hand and slide it to the inside of my wrist. The skin there is hotter than surface logic grants, the pulse steadier and deeper than the heart's. A second rhythm, older. The ink in my blood answers her touch with a thrum the body recognizes even when the mind refuses. Something under her skin stirs—warning or welcome—and she jolts, eyes wide in a way she cannot translate. I see the recognition cross her face and file it where it belongs: *proof*. I turn, drawing her with me, and the crowd opens like a curtain. We step into an alcove where noise compresses into a single pressure and light falls shy of names.

I do not crowd her. I stand at a distance that would be respectable if memory were not already staining the air. Her back meets cool brick. The velvet drags softly, I lift my hand and pause a breath from her jaw, then let my fingers set—two at the hinge, a thumb under the line of her ear. Contact like a verdict. Heat blooms under my touch and spills down into the throat I will not mark tonight.

"Why do you write about blood the way you do?" I ask, and keep the question soft enough to cut. "As if you've seen it under different light. As if you know how it moves when it wants to be witnessed."

"Maybe I do," she whispers, and I'm unsure whether she's bluffing or unwilling to lose.

"I think you do." The smile I allow is not kindness and not cruelty. It is recognition named aloud.

My other hand returns to her hip, fingers sinking into the nap as if velvet were permitted to confess. She leans forward the distance of a decision and arrests herself there, nerves at attention, breath a wire. "Say please," she breathes, testing whether I can be taught.

I do not. I convert obedience into inevitability. The gaze drops, then lifts. Permission signs itself. I begin to bend, angle precise, mouth close enough to feel the shape of hers—

"Octavia!"

The interruption is a thrown blade. Jessica arrives with the stumble of someone whose body made a choice without permission—hand pressed flat to her stomach, the other already reaching. Neon blues on her eyelids smudged into midnight; glitter migrated to cheekbones in accidental constellations; wings—blue, yellow, green—quivering once, then sagging. Her skin is too pale beneath paint.

Octavia catches her. "What happened?"

"Dizzy," Jessica breathes. "Sudden. I—can you take me home? Please?"

"Yes." The word fractures the wire between us and spares us the sound it would have made breaking. Octavia turns, already moving. I let my hand fall from her jaw and restore my mouth to the composure that keeps the world polite. Only my eyes tell. They always do.

"I have to—" she begins.

"Go," I say, and let softness exist where it has earned the right. "Now."

She loops Jessica's arm over her shoulder and steers her out. The club, which had been a small universe with a single law, resolves into bar, exit sign, stagger of stairs. I do not look away from the strip of skin the dress leaves bare, from the line where wing meets shoulder, from the nape. I know exactly where heat will live later when she lies about sleep.

The alcove cools by degrees, but not to neutral. The place where my thumb rested under her ear retains its ghost-warmth in my own hand. I stand still long enough for the pulse at my wrist to settle from insistence to information. Then the phone vibrates—a name that prefers alleys to doorways. Cael Navarre.

I step outside. Fog presses against brick as if trying to eavesdrop. The bass dulls to a felt phenomenon.

"You left the chamber waiting," Cael says by way of greeting. His voice is always a performance of leisure, as though nothing has ever forced him to hurry and he intends to keep that record intact.

"I did not promise to be there yet," I say. I have never mistaken an expectation for a vow.

A small laugh, all teeth and etiquette. "There's chatter. Your pattern has invited a shadow. The town doesn't see it, but the Society does."

"A copycat," I say, and the ink in my veins slows—not fear, not anger—calculation choosing a more careful instrument.

"Sloppier," Cael says, satisfied I arrive at the correct word. "No discipline at the finish, no patience at the start. Close enough for rumor, far enough to be insult. It stains if allowed to continue. And whispers have chosen a next configuration."

"Whispers," I repeat. The alley's light swings and steadies, a pendulum measuring patience.

"The journalist's orbit," he says. He does not know the names. The Society prefers archetypes until they require signatures. "The butterfly. Glitter, wings, too bright for this town. If she falls, it will look like you."

Jessica. I see blue, yellow, green shivering, and neon paint leaking into the soft lines around her eyes. I do not allow the image to become sentiment. I let it become problem. To wound Jessica is to strike Octavia's balance. To strike that balance is to send her into the dark without tether—and into my hands faster—or shatter her into something less useful than a writer. Architecture relies on load-bearing walls. Remove one too soon and the roof declares itself a catastrophe. I do not intend catastrophe. I intend design.

"Do you intend to intervene?" Cael asks, tasting the word to see if it sours. "Or permit the lesson to educate the town about disambiguation?"

"Clarity is a tool," I say. "Not a god."

He smiles into the phone as if I can see the small crease it makes where sincerity should live. "The Society will want ownership named. They have grown hungry for your ledger's next line."

"The Society values hunger more than meals," I snap, and end the call before indulgence becomes conversation. I slide the phone away. Fog threads the alley, a living filament.

When I turn, she is there again—returning along the back lane with the careful steps of someone who has been told to go home and has come to argue with the command. Her horns catch the sodium lamp; her wings creak once at the straps; in every reflection she passes the mouth still looks parted around a kiss that did not arrive. She sees me as though she knew I would be exactly at this corner of shadow listening to the thing the rest of the world calls silence.

We stop at a measured distance. The night clarifies. No cars ravage the street. Leaves scud and then lie down. Intention, interrupted inside, returns and stands between us like a third body.

"Is she all right?" I ask. Information before sentiment; the right order is its own mercy.

"She will be." Her voice is rough, as if she ran and then instructed herself not to admit it. "Dehydration. Bad timing."

I nod once and put my hands in my pockets, arranging posture like cutlery—everything in order, nothing threatening, every knife where knives belong. "You should sleep."

"You should stop telling me what to do."

"You enjoy it," I say, because I am not in the habit of letting useful truths starve. Her eyes harden at the pleasure of being known and at the insult of it arriving from me.

She should leave. She does not. She takes a single step that counts like four. "Why did you come tonight?"

Because the chamber's candlelight has begun to bore me with its own certainty. Because I wanted to know whether submission lives anywhere in your vocabulary and what happens to my own restraint if it does. Because I suspected my blood would hum when our heat touched within a legal distance. Because I have stopped believing in co-incidences where you are concerned.

"Because," I say, "I suspected there would be a moment when you stopped negotiating with yourself. I wanted to see the form of it."

"And did you?"

"Yes."

"What did you find?"

I let my eyes make the turn to her mouth and back, the shortest geometry in the world. "Mine," I say quietly—not boast, not claim, but the observation a scientist writes in a margin when the experiment resolves. "And yours."

The night hears the sentence and makes it larger. A lesser man would apologize to make it smaller again. I prefer accuracy. She has no weapon for accuracy yet. She reaches for a conditional instead. "If Jessica hadn't—"

"If Jessica hadn't," I say, and leave our mouths on the brink where the night abandoned them. There is no cleaner place to leave a truth than on the edge it prefers. I step back a measured degree and dress mercy as distance. "Go home, Miss Hartwell."

"Make me," she says, because she will always lay a match on a dry surface to see if it remembers fire.

I laugh once, low, reluctant, because the match pleases me and because I am not here to set the building alight tonight. "Tomorrow," I say. "I don't bargain with tonight."

She holds my eyes a beat longer than is safe, then turns. I feel her as she leaves. The heat traces up the bare strip of her back, the wings warble once like a hinge deciding to lie. The horns are small and certain as punctuation. When she is gone, the lane returns to brick and fog and the small etiquette of a town that believes Halloween ends with a sunrise.

I walk home without checking whether the Society's chamber still waits. The house answers cedar and dim, and I reward it by moving through it without disruption: coat on brass hook, gloves aligned, sleeve brushed where the alley's damp touched it. In the study the ember surrenders, then resumes its smaller work. I stand at the window and watch Blackmoor peel and flatten and fold. The night has given me three truths and a problem.

First: her blood is not silent. It speaks in a frequency the body hears before the mind grants vocabulary. She felt it when her fingers found the inside of my wrist. I saw the way the shock widened her eyes. She will search for the term. I will decide when she deserves it.

Second: my desire has ceased to be theoretical. Its carelessness in that first look was a wound I intend to keep open. Restraint remains a virtue because it disciplines. Abstinence is a theater because it starves.

Third: the town will not understand the copycat's work until it is forced to. Clarity is my task, but not for the Society's hunger. For the structure. Jessica cannot fall yet—not because I prefer her living, not because pity has found purchase, but because structure requires supports until the roof declares itself. If the mimic has chosen her, I will choose otherwise. Control is not a leash. It is a loaded calculation.

The problem: Cael will report patience as arrogance. The Society prefers theater when their candles burn low. They will want me to say the line that names ownership and removes doubt. They will ask for proof. I will give them neither until the book requires it. I am the head, not the choir.

On the desk, her byline waits where I left it. I place my hand over her name. Beneath the skin the darker pulse answers, slower than the heart, older than breath. I do not need a mirror to know my eyes have learned a new brightness in the dark. I remove my hand and the letters remain cool and flat, but the space above them holds heat like a mouth just left.

Tomorrow will be a day built from small obediences. Class at ten, email at one, and a committee at three that calls itself necessary. The town will borrow daylight to lie to itself. Jessica will text that she survived and intends to forgive sugar and liquor their sins eventually. Octavia will stand before a mirror and touch the place under her ear where my thumb rested and wonder why the skin answers as though remembering a word. Perhaps she will write. Perhaps she will not.

I will count streets between her door and mine and decide which distance means discipline and which means cowardice dressed as principle. I will choose the former because I am not interested in lesser calibrations.

The ember settles to a dull core and goes quiet. On the window, streetlight draws a thin blade of gold that narrows as the night deepens. The room pulls its shadows back into their proper corners. At the edge of sleep, a sound threads my wrist—not the clock, which obeys, nor the heart, which lies on command, but the other cadence, the ink-march. It answers the rhythm I met tonight and nearly tasted. It confirms what the doorway learned when the crowd made space, what my hand learned when velvet yielded without surrender, what her mouth almost wrote against mine.

The shape is decided. The proof will be arranged. And when the Society asks for clarity,

I will offer them a lesson instead. They can have their candles. I have the dark.

CHAPTER 17

The morning comes late, slower than it should, and it drags a headache behind it like chains across stone. Light needles through the blinds in brittle stripes, sharp enough to make my stomach protest. My tongue tastes like old sugar, like last night's drinks have curdled into something putrid, and my body aches as if the music never stopped. Halloween has passed but it left its hangover in me, stitched into my skin, clinging to my clothes in smoke and perfume.

Jessica's text hums the phone against my night-stand before I can will myself out of bed. ***Still alive. Just waterlogged. Meet for food?*** I rub at my eyes, focus on the tiny screen through grit. A relief unfurls in my chest like a muscle I'd for-gotten to stretch—she's better. Not collapsed on a bathroom floor. Just tired. Just hungover. I text back a quick ***yes***, fingers sluggish, and sit up slow enough to keep the room from rolling sideways.

Shower water is scalding, and I let it be. Steam fills the bathroom until the mirror drips. I scrub the glitter from my skin, streaks of red lipstick ghosting the towel until it looks like evidence. My hair falls heavy in damp waves across my shoul-ders. I dress without thinking too much—dark jeans, a burgundy sweater soft from too many washes, boots that make me feel planted. The costume is a memory folded in tissue paper, too close, too raw.

Antonio's is already humming when I arrive. The bell over the door gives its tired jangle, and warmth surges out, carrying with it the smell of melted cheese and tomato and basil ground between mortar and pestle. Jessica is at our usual booth by the window, hair scraped up into a messy bun, oversized sunglasses hiding the mess of her morning. Her wings and glitter are gone, but I swear the faint shimmer clings at her temples anyway, like the party hasn't let go.

"You look alive," I say as I slide in across from her, though her sunglasses tilt and the pale blue of her eyes says otherwise.

"Alive is relative." Her voice is rough with dehydration but she smirks, pulling her straw toward her lips. "I've been rehydrating since sunrise. I'm basically a water balloon at this point."

Pizza lands between us, steam lifting from its surface. I take a slice, let the burn scald my tongue because it feels like penance. Conversation drifts to safe places—class deadlines, work shifts, the way the whole campus is still buzzing with Halloween gossip. Yet beneath Jessica's words there's a drag, the memory of last night in the alcove of the club, his hands, his voice. I push the thought down with soda, fizz scratching at my throat.

Halfway through the second slice, Jessica leans across the table. "You okay? You look like you're somewhere else."

I laugh, too quickly. "Just tired."

"You're never just tired." She smirks again, though softer this time. "But I'll let it slide. For now."

Before I can answer, her phone buzzes against the table. Mine joins a second later. Notifications split the quiet. Both of us freeze, slices half-lifted. The subject line alone is enough: **Another body**. My pulse climbs into my throat.

"Where?" Jessica whispers, already reaching for her bag.

The message is vague—downtown, near the riverfront, an alley behind the old warehouse row. Male victim. That word blares louder than any siren—*male*. Until now, the deaths had drawn a pattern, all women, all variations of one figure repeated. This doesn't fit.

We don't say much on the walk out. The bell clangs again behind us, the warmth of the pizza shop closing like a lid. Outside, the air is brittle and sharp, the first true bite of November brushing at the edges of October. Leaves drag across the pavement in dry whispers. My boots find rhythm with Jessica's, the silence between us heavier than words.

The scene is already cordoned when we arrive. Tape stretches between poles, a trembling yellow line against brick. Floodlights slice the shadows open, painting the alley sterile white. Officers form their usual perimeter, the mix of fresh faces and seasoned ones blending into grim patience.

Chief Mateo Thornwick stands near the center, square-shouldered, his coat collar turned up against the wind. His dark hair is threaded with gray, his jaw perpetually tense, as if the job carved it sharper with every year. He looks up as we approach, his gray eyes sharp even in the artificial light.

"You shouldn't be here," he says, voice flat but not surprised.

"We got the call," Jessica replies. "Same as everyone else."

His gaze flicks between us, weighing. "This isn't like the others."

The words shiver down my spine before I see the shape on the ground. The victim is already sheeted, white fabric marred by the unmistakable bloom of blood. But the angles—the shoes protruding, the broad shoulders beneath the covering—it's different. Male. A break in the pattern.

"What do you mean?" Jessica asks, her tone gentler than mine would have been.

Mateo exhales once, a sound that frosts in the air. "Too much detail and you'll be writing the wrong story. But I'll say this... Whoever did this knew the earlier scenes. Knew them well enough to mimic and twist. The cuts, the arrangement—close, but not identical. Someone trying to speak a language they don't own."

A young officer, nervous, shifts nearby. His words slip before he can stop them. "Blood splatter's wrong too. Not radial. More... directional."

Mateo's glare snaps like a trap and the kid falls silent. But the words already live in me, clawing against my ribs. *Directional. Wrong.* Someone copying notes they don't understand.

Jessica catches my arm. "Don't," she murmurs, the single word layered with warning. But my eyes are already mapping the scene, tracing lines in the dark, imagining how a body moves when struck, how blood records its own history. I shouldn't know this. I shouldn't want to know this. And yet the questions arrive, insistent.

Mateo turns back to us, tone clipped. "Go home. Both of you. Let us do our job."

We don't argue, not out loud. Jessica tugs me back toward the tape, her grip firm. I glance once more over my shoulder, the alley yawning like a throat, the sheeted body a terrible punctuation. My skin hums with nerves I can't shake, and beneath them something colder, something whispering that the pattern hasn't broken at all. It's only widening.

Outside the perimeter, the world resumes its ordinary rhythm—cars passing, a dog barking down the block, the river carrying endless black currents. But every sound is muffled, as if the city itself is holding its breath.

Jessica exhales finally, a tremor hidden in the sound. "A man this time. That changes everything."

"Or nothing," I murmur. The words escape before I can stop them.

Her gray eyes cut toward me, startled. "What do you mean?"

I shake my head, though the thought persists, sharp as glass. "If it's someone copying, then the real hand—the *real* architect—still hasn't finished."

Jessica doesn't answer. Her hand squeezes mine once, warm and human, an anchor against the pull of darker currents. Together we walk into the waiting night, and the city feels smaller for all the shadows it cannot name.

CHAPTER 18

November takes the edges off everything and makes them ring. The air is thin and metallic, the kind that turns the bell tower's voice into a blade. Leaves have given up the pretense of holding fast. Instead, they skitter and collect where the wind decides they should be archived.

It has been a week since the man in the alley, a week of headlines that hedge and officials who articulate around the truth like dancers that won't touch. I have a notebook fat with notes I'm not supposed to have and a sleep schedule that looks like a stain. Every morning I tell myself today will be ordinary. Every night I prove myself a liar. Today, I tell myself, I will be ordinary for the length of one class. I will take my seat in Professor Marlowe's seminar, I will listen, I will keep my pulse to myself. I will not think about the alcove or the way he said *mine and yours* like the name of an element no one had bothered to discover. I will not think about the alley or the white sheet shaped like a man. I will do the work in front of me.

I arrive early enough that the hallway still carries its own echo and the seminar room smells faintly of dry paper and the chalk someone insists on using even though the boards are white now. The windows along the far wall make rectangles of cold light across the table. I set my notebook where I always do and arrange my pen as if its alignment matters. The copy of my most recent piece sits under my palm, too warm from my grip, the margins marked by his pencil—firm strokes, minimal, not the surgical dissection of the first weeks. I read again the line he underlined twice: *Mercy is a geometry. Incorrect angles collapse the room.* I don't know whether he means it as praise or as a dare.

Students filter in, chairs scrape, a whispering tide makes the room feel used and less like a stage. He steps in just before the hour, the room's temperature changing the way water changes when a stone is dropped in. He doesn't need to clear his throat to claim the quiet. The quiet recognizes him and delivers itself.

"Obsession," he says without preamble, as if finishing a thought we've all been thinking since September, "is a form of attention with a narrowed field of view and an expanded sense of consequence. It is not romance or hunger. It is an edifice that requires load-bearing choices. Today, we look at the ribcage—what holds, what fails, and why." He doesn't look at me when he says it. He doesn't need to. The line lands where it was aimed.

We move through the hour on rails he laid without our consent. He puts a paragraph on the screen and lets silence do the first pass of critique. Hands lift, voices try on confidence. He asks two questions that feel like he has been in our kitchens watching which cupboard we open first in the dark. He praises without warmth so praise becomes a measurement and not a cookie. Halfway through, he starts threading our work into the discussion—name, line, cut, return—and the room leans forward because we always pretend to dread it but secretly live for it. When he gets to mine, he reads a sentence I'd written past midnight with a heart that wouldn't slow down: *She cataloged his sins with the mercy of a ledger clerk and the accuracy of a blade.* He closes the folder as if he has closed a door, then says only, "We should talk." Not *good* or *better* or *you've learned to aim.* Just that. A neutral invitation that means everything.

When the hour releases us, chairs sigh back and backpacks hang from shoulders like fresh burdens. He doesn't look up as people file past his desk, which is how I know he is keeping the path clear. I pack deliberately, feigning slowness the way you do when you're already out of excuses. The last voice fades in the hallway, a door down the corridor bangs, and we are a room with two people.

He looks at me then, fully, the way he did in the club before he stopped pretending he wouldn't. "Miss Hartwell."

"Professor." My mouth decides on dryness as a defense, then abandons it.

He gestures for the chair nearest the corner of his desk. I sit and place my piece on the wood between us. He doesn't reach for it immediately. He studies my face as if my skin is an index to the text.

I resist the urge to touch my jaw where his thumb rested a week ago in a room that smelled like sugar and sweat and permission. He must know I'm thinking it. He lets that knowledge sit between us like a third participant that refuses to speak.

"You've stopped explaining your violence," he says at last. "It helps."

"Helps *who*?" I ask, more kniflike than necessary. "The story? Or the person who wants to believe it?"

"Both," he says, unfazed. "The story is a machine. The reader is a mechanism. Don't insult either with padding." He flips to a page I had marked and taps the margin lightly with his pencil. "Here, you let the consequence arrive without escort. The sentence steps aside. That's discipline."

"I don't feel disciplined," I say, and the admission is smaller than truth but larger than I intended.

"You will." He sets the pencil down. The sound it makes is quiet and final, like a pin placed exactly where it belongs. "Tell me why you chose to leave the last paragraph unsaid."

Because the only endings I believe in are the ones that are earned. Because I'm tired of men telling me what mercy looks like. Because I wanted the blade to be clean and the ledger to balance. Because the woman in the story knows a kind of math that doesn't use numbers. None of those are answers I am willing to make into air.

"It was better that way," I say. "The sentence wanted to stop."

"Good." A word like a coin handed over without looking. He leans back, folds his arms—a posture that reads as withdrawal until you notice how alert the body has to be to keep that much stillness. "There's a problem with your piece, though."

I feel it, in the soft under rib, where fear likes to hang its coat. "What problem?"

"You write about blood as if you've been in rooms you haven't." He doesn't blink. "As if you can smell iron on air in a way you haven't earned yet."

Anger flares before sense can grab it. "You told me to stop padding and now you want me to pad my ignorance?"

He lifts a hand, palm-out, not to shush but to pause. "Listen to what I said, not to what your nerves are afraid I'll say." He reaches for my pages then and slides them closer to his side of the desk, not possessively—precisely. "Your claims are accurate. Your vantage point is not. I'm asking you to notice the difference."

"What's the difference between accurate and earned?" It comes out too fast. "If the sentence is true, isn't the vantage point moot?"

"No." He says it like a mercy. "Truth requires a witness, not just a sentence. You're flirting with a language your body hasn't fully learned. It's working because you're talented. It will fail the moment talent tires."

I almost laugh, because talent tired weeks ago and something else has been carrying the weight. I think of the alley, the way the tableau cut itself into my eyes, the way my stomach lurched but my legs didn't. I think of the blood that does not behave the way poetry wants it to. I think of the heartbeat that isn't a heartbeat under the skin of his wrist and the way my own pulse answered like it knew the scale. My mouth reaches for a joke and doesn't find one.

"What do you want from me?" I ask instead.

"Less fear," he says. "Less performance. More precision." He lets the last word rest.

"I'm *not* afraid," I lie. He doesn't reward the lie. The room hears it die.

"Stand," he says.

"What?"

"Stand." He has already risen. The desk becomes neutral ground with both of us on our feet.

He comes around it, not close, not far, and the room recalibrates again, deciding where the edges of air should be. "Hold out your hand."

I do it without knowing if I'm obeying or proving something to myself. He doesn't take my hand. He holds his over mine, parallel, not touching, measuring the space. The air between our palms has the tension of paper just before it tears.

"You don't have to perform fearlessness for me," he says. "It's wasted material."

"Do I perform for you?" I ask, and hate the way the question sounds like an invitation.

"You perform for yourself. I'm an audience of convenience." He lowers his hand a fraction. The space gets crowded with something that isn't heat and isn't light. The line of hair on my forearm prickles up, one small field of grain reversing direction. I feel my pulse at my wrist double, not faster—deeper. It's the same second rhythm that sang up my bones in the alcove when he guided my fingers to the place under his cuff.

"I don't—" I start, and then my breath changes on its own. It gets quiet and wide, finding depth I don't aim it toward. He's watching my face with that clinical curiosity I should resent and can't. The air between our hands feels like the moment before a storm learns its own name.

"Good," he says softly, like he's speaking to a skittish animal and a co-conspirator at once. "Now tell me what your body does right before you write a line that works."

"This is ridiculous," I manage. "My body doesn't—"

"It does," he says. "You've just never watched it enough to earn the sentence."

I hate him, and I do as I'm told. I pay attention. The room drops away, the windows quit their rectangle of light, the clock stops pretending it has jurisdiction. There is the table, the grain, the paper, his hand above mine, and then there is something else. A pressure under the skin, low as the first ember in a grate when the log has only thought about catching. The skin at the base of my neck warms, then cools, then warms again, a wave on a tide table I didn't agree to. I can feel my shadow on the floor at my feet—not see it, *feel* it—as if it has leaned, as if it wants to detach and be bolder than I am. The hair along my nape lifts, ready to be counted. The air smells faintly sweet for a second, like a match right after it goes out.

He lowers his hand that last fraction until the heel of his palm hovers a sliver above my pulse. Not touching. Close enough that my blood decides to speak. It hums. A clear, thin note, barely a sound, more like the idea of a sound. I realize with a jolt that my mouth is open. I close it. The hum doesn't stop. It builds the smallest degree.

"Enough," he says, and the word unfurls as a release valve. He lifts his hand. Air rearranges. The shadow at my feet lies flat again as if it hadn't just moved. He watches me like I've performed a trick he hoped for but didn't dare to ask from a student. He doesn't smile. Something in him loosens anyway—his shoulders, a line at the corner of his mouth, a breath that previously had no right being held.

"What did you do?" I ask, and hear my voice do a thing I don't like, a falling off at the end.

"What did *you* do?" he counters. "Describe it."

"I—" The words are hard to pin. "I felt... pressure? Heat. Not heat. A... brightness without light. There was a sound I couldn't hear." I stop, because I sound unwell, and the second I stop the silence makes the description feel too accurate to be safe.

He nods once, as if I have answered a question on a test with no right key. "Good."

"That's it?" Some part of me wants him to give the thing a name. The rest of me is terrified he might.

"For now." He tilts his head, studying the inside of my wrist where the skin is thinner. "Does it frighten you?"

"No," I say, and this time the lie is small enough to pass.

"Then learn it," he says. "Don't dramatize it. You'll ruin it."

He steps back, the room exhaling with him, the windows returning to their rectangles, the clock remembering itself. He returns to the desk, picks up his pencil, and underlines a word in my piece I had stopped seeing. My heart discovers a slower setting and refuses to use it. The backs of my knees feel hollow, as if someone took out the simple bones and left string.

"I want a revision by next week," he says, not looking at me now because looking would be too much like admitting the last four minutes occurred. "Cut two paragraphs. Add one sentence you didn't dare. Do not make it pretty. Make it correct."

"Correct," I repeat, because I need a word that isn't *what the hell was that.*

He finally looks at me and the reaction I missed while it happened flickers across his face in retrospect—no theatrics, nothing so satisfying as a startle. The pupils are a degree too open for the light, the green cut with metal like a thing polished by a focused cloth. For a fraction of a second I think he's going to reach for my wrist again and then choose not to. He places his palms on the desk instead, flat, claiming the wood. "And, Miss Hartwell," he says, voice trimmed to its neatest edge, "do not go to crime scenes without sleep. Your sentences know when you've starved them."

"Don't keep telling me what to do," I say, because the script insists on being followed at least once per meeting. It breaks the tension into something I can pack in a bag and carry out of the room.

He allows the smallest ghost of a sound that might be a laugh if it weren't ashamed of itself. "Then don't tell me what to ask of your work," he says. "We'll call the ledger even."

I gather my pages. The air feels like it's choosing a side. When I move, the skin under my ear—the place where his thumb had hovered without touching—warm's for no reason. My nerves aren't willing to submit it as evidence. I say *thank you* in a tone that makes the phrase into a challenge, and he accepts it as if I had offered him a blade to weigh. When I reach the door, he adds nothing. That restraint makes my back straighten the rest of the way to the hallway.

Students in the corridor talk too loud about nothing. The ordinary world pretends it is unbroken. Posters curled at the corners, a janitor's cart left neat against a wall, a student laughing at a joke no one else will remember by the end of the day. I press the papers to my chest because my hands need a task that isn't reaching for a wrist that isn't mine. The walk back to my apartment is longer than it should be and shorter than I want. I pay attention the way you do after a near-miss. Street names, the order of houses, the familiar crack in the sidewalk that nobody fixes because it reminds them of a story they think they love.

Inside, the quiet feels like someone else's. I set the pages on the table and watch the top one lift at the corner from the heater's exhale. The room looks normal. Dishes drying, a jacket thrown over the back of a chair, the corkboard with its web of red lines pretending to be a map instead of evidence of a nervous system. I sit and press my fingers to the inside of my wrist as if my body left me a switch I can find twice. Nothing happens. Which is to say, nothing dramatic. My pulse goes about its domestic work. But if I listen there—past the regular thud, past the polite bodily noises—I can almost tease out the echo that started in the classroom. Not a second heartbeat. A thread. A held note. It isn't louder. It isn't even sound. It's the idea of heat where no heat is. It sits there, stubborn and patient as a candle that knows the room has more oxygen, waiting for a hand to cup it and insist.

I stand and cross to the mirror because I have done it since I was a child. Check the face, confirm the self, count the freckles to make sure none have escaped. I tip my head and see nothing dramatic—no light in the eyes that isn't always there, no mark on the skin where none has a right to be. But when I lift my hair, there, just under the angle of my jaw and back a finger's width, the skin shines as if something warm had rested there recently. Not flush. Not embarrassment. Not injury.

The shine fades while I stare, and the spot returns to ordinary skin. I raise my fingers and touch it. Cool. My hand smells faintly of graphite from the pencil I stole from the seminar table without noticing, and under that, something sweet. Not perfume or soap. The breath of a candle after a thumb and forefinger have deprived it of future.

A thought rises the way a bruise rises hours after you hit a door frame. In the room, when he lowered his hand that last fraction, he had inhaled—not a gasp, not surprise, a small, deliberate intake as if he were receiving a signal. His pupils widened just enough to read as hunger if I were the kind of woman who ran toward flattery. His hands flattened on the desk when he told me to learn it. A man choosing *not* to reach. And when I left, he didn't watch me with his mouth. He watched the place where my wrist disappeared into my sleeve, as if that inch of skin had taught him a word he needed to find again later with the door shut.

My phone buzzes with a text that I ignore for one, two, three pulses—Jessica, a link to an update about the man in the alley, a new line the paper thinks is revelation and the police think is a leak. I open it anyway, because discipline is not the same thing as refusal. The details have been arranged to sound like mercy. They almost succeed. I set the phone face down and sit on the edge of the bed the way you sit when you're not sure if you've been chosen or marked.

My shadow on the floor looks like all my other shadows. It lies there and takes up exactly the amount of space physics allows. I look away and look back quickly, the way you do when you think you've seen a stranger you know. It doesn't move. Or if it does, it does it in the part of reality that doesn't belong to light. A spark stirs under my sternum, not pain, not panic, a clear little flare that says *here* in a language my nerves are going to have to learn without the glossary.

I lie back without meaning to and stare at the ceiling until its paint stops being paint and returns to a surface that keeps weather out. The class, the desk, the inch of air between our hands, the hum—these arrange themselves like index cards on a table inside me. I know better than to push them into a story too soon. He told me not to dramatize it. He isn't always right, but he's right about this. If I name it too quickly, I'll make it into a costume and wear it until it resents me.

The heater clicks again and the page on the table lifts, falls. I get up and write a sentence on the back of my piece where he can't see unless I let him. *The room learned my outline and did not resent it.* I don't know if that's about the seminar or the city or the way my body feels less like a house and more like a wiring diagram someone left half-finished for me to complete. I set the pen down. My fingers smell like graphite and something extinguished. I should be afraid. Instead I am awake in a way I can use.

Night will come, and with it, the urge to find a crime scene like a dog finds a river. I will resist until I'm sure resistance is not just vanity. I will go to class again and let him tell me where my sentences are lying. I will learn to press my thumb to the spot under my ear and make nothing happen, and then I will learn to make something happen and pretend I didn't. I will do the work in front of me and the work beneath me and the work no one has given me permission to claim. And when he asks me again to stay after—and he *will*—I will hold out my hand before he can ask, and I will meet the hum instead of being met by it.

Outside, the city rearranges itself—doors closing, engines sighing, the usual noises pretending at peace. It doesn't matter that my blood has begun to hum a different tune. The world keeps its steady rhythm, too indifferent to notice. I turn off the lamp. In the dark, the pulse gathers just below my wrist, not frantic, not gentle—steady, waiting. It feels like being watched by something inside my own skin. I lie still, listening to it, wondering if this is what awareness sounds like before it becomes revelation. When sleep comes, it doesn't drag me under. It opens—a familiar door now lit from within—and this time, I step through without hesitation.

CHAPTER 19

The hunger begins with the hour. Not the blood-hunger—older, cleaner, obedient—but the kind that uncoils when knowledge refuses to stay quiet. It wakes before I do, slips between thought and breath like smoke under a door. The house feels it first. The walls hold their breath. The ember in the grate dies early. Even the cedar scent seems to lean inward, listening.

I rise before dawn, because restraint has always been the thing that keeps the world from burning. Cold water against the face, collar straight, cuffs buttoned with the same precision as every other day. But the mirror tells a different truth. There's a brightness behind the eyes that isn't human polish, it's the gleam of a creature starving for revelation. I press a thumb to the pulse in my wrist, that second rhythm that beats deeper than the heart, and the skin hums with faint heat. Her name threads through it—Octavia—and the syllables flare and fade like a match against oil.

The study smells of paper and night. I pull the ledger toward me, the one I promised myself I would not open again. Its spine groans as if it resents being disturbed. Inside, thin vellum pages hold the history of every lineage the Inkbound Society has ever claimed dominion over. Power mapped in calligraphy, bloodlines catalogued, sigils branded beside forgotten crests. I run my hand down the columns, past the families I already know too well: Varcarin, Ashmore, Noctevaris. My own line snarls in the margins, written in a darker ink than the rest. And then, half-buried, I find a single entry that has been rewritten more than once—ink layered over ink until the parchment itself seems scorched.

Embergrave.

A name older than the current tongue, tethered to a line that vanished before the wars ended, before the fires at Alpenshield's peak burned their last gods to ash. The note beside it is brief, but my pulse answers it anyway—*line corrupted by light; offspring unknown.*

Her name does not appear, but her blood already confessed itself to me. I felt it the night of the dance—the hum that found its twin inside my veins, the spark that made the air between us collapse. I thought it was attraction. It was recognition.

I turn the page. Beneath the entries of the known houses is a smaller ledger, handwritten, not by any archivist but by a prior head of the Society. The handwriting is ancient, elegant, and merciless. It lists only partial names, the ones who were hidden, shielded, or forbidden. Among them, a single phrase without date. *The phoenix does not forget what the flame burns. It only waits for the spark that names it again.*

I know what that means. I should stop reading.

I do *not* stop reading.

The sun rises by the time I close the book. Light climbs the glass, limping, half hearted. I am not fooled. The daylight does not belong to me. It never has. But I stand in it anyway, letting it touch the skin it cannot burn, because somewhere in my ancestry the fire learned to make a truce with the dark. The Noctevaris blood in me prefers shadow, but the other half—whatever survived of the first line that crawled out of the tomb of dawn—craves the heat she carries without knowing.

Her scent is already in the air of the classroom when I arrive. Ink, lilac shampoo, a trace of burnt sugar from the coffee she always forgets to finish. The students trickle in, notebooks snapping open, the low murmur of academic exhaustion filling the room. I hear none of it. When she enters, I feel the shift like a weather front crossing the threshold.

Her hair is unbound today. Bright where it catches the light, dark where it tangles. The pulse under her skin sings to the rhythm I have been listening for in every sound since that night at the club. The hum beneath my wrist finds it instantly and answers like a tuning fork.

She doesn't notice. She only frowns at her notes, lips parted slightly as she concentrates. The small, human movements that make her dangerous.

"Miss Hartwell," I say, because that is still the name she believes in. "Your latest submission."

Her head lifts. The room quiets as if it re-members it is temporary. She walks the aisle between desks, that particular defiance in the way she moves—as though she has decided to risk being seen, and therefore no longer flinches at it. She hands me the folder. Our fingers brush. The air tightens.

For a moment I think she must feel it too—the static, the small detonation that happens under the skin when two currents find each other. But she steps back, pretending she doesn't, and I let her keep the illusion.

The class begins. I talk about narrative tension, about how the best stories lie to tell the truth. I move through the discussion with precision, words sharp and deliberate, but the back of my mind is still circling her paper like a hawk. Her writing has changed. The restraint I demanded is gone. In its place is blood, fire, and something alive enough to watch me as I read it.

When the hour ends, I dismiss the others with a nod. They file out, muttering, laughing, scraping chairs. She lingers, waiting for the room to empty.

The sound of the door closing is softer than it should be, but it seals us into something neither of us can pretend to misunderstand.

"Stay," I say, and she does.

I circle to the edge of the desk, the folder in my hand. "Your work," I begin, and my voice sounds too calm to be safe. "It's *different*."

She crosses her arms, defensive by instinct. "Different good or different bad?"

"Different inevitable." I open the folder. Her story spills out in ink that looks almost red under the light. The title: *Inheritance.*

I read a line aloud. "'She woke with the scent of smoke in her mouth and the taste of memory behind her teeth.'" I lift my eyes. "You're not guessing anymore. You're remembering."

A flicker of confusion crosses her face, then something warier. "It's fiction."

"All fiction confesses."

She exhales sharply, eyes shrewdly pinned on me. "You think I wrote myself into this."

"I think you wrote something that doesn't belong entirely to you."

Her jaw tightens. "You sound like you're accusing me of plagiarism."

"No," I say, stepping closer. "I'm accusing you of honesty."

The words land between us like a match. The air seems to pulse. I can hear her heartbeat. It's too fast. The smell of ozone coils faintly, impossible but real. Her pupils dilate. The green of her eyes brightens to something nearer gold.

She looks down, presses her hands to the desk as if to anchor herself. "It's just a story," she whispers. But the air around her disagrees. A thin wisp of shadow curls from the edges of her fingertips, black shot through with faint red light, and dies as quickly as it forms.

I see it. I know it. I have seen it in mirrors when I was young and too careless to hide what my blood could do. She doesn't notice. Her breathing is shallow. The shadows vanish, but the scent of heat remains.

"Octavia," I say before I can stop myself, her name bare of title.

Her head snaps up, and for an instant, the gold in her eyes flares brighter—sunlight caught in a forge. Then she blinks, and it's gone.

"What?"

"Nothing." I force my voice steady. "You've done well. That will be all."

But she doesn't move. She stands there, watching me like she's waiting for the next instruction, or maybe for permission to leave. The instinct to reach for her overrides everything civilized.

I step forward. My hand finds her arm, not hard, not soft—contact measured like a question. Her skin is warm, too warm, the kind of warmth that means blood is remembering its other uses. She freezes, but she doesn't pull away. The hum beneath my wrist flares to meet hers, resonance so exact it makes the hairs on my neck rise. The scent of something burning edges the air—not smoke, only the ghost of it.

"Do you feel that?" I ask, low.

She shakes her head, but her pupils betray her. "I don't know what you're talking about."

"Then you will."

The words leave me before I know I've spoken them. My thumb moves—just slightly—tracing the line of her pulse. The shadows answer, faint and red, then vanish. She gasps, quiet but real, and the sound is enough to nearly undo the last thread of my control.

If I bite her now, she will burn. If I kiss her, she will ignite. Either way, the world changes shape.

I release her.

She steps back, unsteady, and the space between us swells with everything we haven't said. The silence stretches thin, ready to tear. I close the folder, slide it across the desk. "You've exceeded expectation," I say, and the understatement feels like blasphemy.

"Thank you," she answers, voice low, confused, too intimate for a classroom.

She leaves before I can say more, the door closing behind her like a line drawn in blood.

When she's gone, I stand still long enough for the air to reset. Then I move. The folder opens again. Her handwriting stares back at me, neat and firm, a script that knows itself too well for its age. The scent of her blood still clings to the paper, faint but undeniable, and it matches the signature I found in the Society's ledgers. The same resonance. The same mark.

Octavia Hartwell is the name the world believes. The ledger only whispers another—*Embergrave*—an Alpenshield descendant, ash threaded through the blood, a memory of flame that refuses to forget.

I should destroy the evidence. I should call the Society. Instead, I fold the page and slide it into my inner pocket, where the warmth of her presence lingers through the fabric.

By the time I reach home, night has settled clean and sharp over the city. I leave the lights off. The dark welcomes me back as one of its own. The pulse beneath my skin runs louder than it should, almost jubilant.

In the study, I open the drawer where the old sigil rests—a small iron emblem, shaped like a phoenix eating its own tail. The Society keeps copies, but this one is mine. When I touch it, the metal hums, faintly warm, as though it recognizes her blood on my fingertips. I could take this to the chamber tomorrow, present the lineage, name her as the lost heir they never expected to find.

But I won't.

They would consume her, as they consume everything they name.

The hunger that lives in me—the one that is not thirst and not power—doesn't want to destroy her. It wants to keep her. The difference is not moral. It's territorial.

She doesn't know yet what she is, and I don't know what she will become when she does. But I know this. The light in her blood sings the same key as the dark in mine. The song is older than both of us, and it has waited long enough.

I pour a glass of red that isn't wine and drink until the warmth settles. My reflection in the window is too pale, the eyes too green and gold to pass for entirely human. The vampire in me counts possibilities. The man in me counts the risks. The creature in between counts the heartbeats until I see her again.

Tonight the house breathes differently. The air feels like the moment before a confession. I press my palm to the glass, and in the reflection behind me, I almost see her standing there—the waves of her hair, the flare of her eyes, the faint shimmer of smoke at her shoulders. Not a ghost. A premonition.

My hand lowers to my wrist. The hum is steady now, synchronized to hers, a shared heartbeat across distance. The bond is unfinished, but real.

I could stop. I could leave her to her human life, her columns, her pretty fictions about the dead.

But I am past the point of stopping.

Obsession is a structure. Every structure reaches its final line of symmetry before it collapses into design. I built this one myself, and I will see it *burn*.

She is mine in every way that does not yet have a name. And when the time comes, I will not ask. I will not beg. I will claim what the blood already promised.

The ember on the desk flickers and dies. The room smells of smoke that isn't there. The pulse under my skin steadies, then answers itself, as if from far away—hers calling to mine.

The night smiles with all its teeth.

Tomorrow begins the ruin.

CHAPTER 20

Octavia

Under the stark morning light, Blackmoor looks scrubbed of its sins—brick rinsed clean, paths swept, trees pared back to the exact lines of their limbs. It's been a week of quiet glances that aren't quiet at all, a week of my nerves behaving like live wires, a week of Adrian Marlowe teaching as if nothing inside either of us is changing while everything is. The bell hasn't rung yet when I cross the quad, a strip of wind running down the center like a seam. I tell myself I dressed for armor, not provocation. The tight leather skirt that holds my figure like a promise, black tights patterned with tiny skulls and hearts that flash when I walk, a cropped knit that kisses the edge of my stomach, pretending innocence it doesn't have. Boots that announce each step, reaching just above my ankles. I left the bra in the drawer because the sweater is thick, heavy, and the morning is cold. But as I push open the seminar room door, I feel the choice like a confession under my ribs.

He's already there, back to the windows, hands braced lightly on the table, the posture of a man who knows the room has learned to orbit him. Students drift in with the usual theater of fatigue—mugs, yawns, anecdotes about printers. He looks up once, and the look is not a look. It's a hand placed—calm, deliberate—over the center of my chest from across twenty feet. Heat blooms at the sternum and spreads, not a blush exactly, not embarrassment. *Recognition.*

"Good morning," he says to the room. It lands like dusk anyway.

We take our places. The board stays blank. He prefers us to earn the right to write on it.

"Endings," he begins. "The difference between stopping and finishing. The difference between a door closing and the house choosing not to lie."

Pens lift. Eyes make the effort they were not considering making five minutes ago. His gaze passes over faces, over me, returns, leaves again. The rhythm is merciless and precise. He angles us through a story that isn't ours, and somehow it becomes ours. When he reads a paragraph down the table, I know before he says my name that it's mine. He doesn't praise. He doesn't cut. He holds a single line to the light and turns it until the image inside it surfaces. When the hour thins, he closes a folder with that small, surgical sound of his and says, "Miss Hartwell, stay."

The room exhales, scrapes chairs, sheds bodies. A student asks if something will be on the exam that doesn't exist. He answers in a sentence that manages to be both generous and unhelpful by design. The door opens and closes and we are the remainder.

I pretend to gather slowly. He pretends to write a note. The air between those pretenses thickens until my sweater feels warmer than wool should be. I go to the edge of the desk and set down my revised pages. He doesn't touch them yet. His eyes travel from the knot of my throat down to the hem of the knit as if measuring the space where the sweater ends and the rest of me begins. My breath falters, then chooses its pace with intention.

"Another good piece," he says. "Less decoration. More truth."

"Decoration is for trees," I say before I can stop myself. "Truth is for ledgers."

The corner of his mouth curves. "And sins."

I should deflect. I don't. I say, "You've been...
different."

"In what way?"

"Calculated," I answer. Then, "Worse."

He laughs once, a soft exhale that doesn't con-
cede anything and somehow concedes everything.
"I've been deciding."

"What?"

"Whether to continue pretending that whatever
is happening between us is merely pedagogical."

The floor seems to tilt. The room's far windows
turn their rectangles of light a degree brighter, as
if they, too, want to listen.

"You shouldn't say that," I manage.

"I should say exactly that." He steps around the
desk, close enough that I can see the thread where
his cuff meets the sleeve. "You are an adult, Miss
Hartwell. So am I. The rules are real, and I do
honor them. But there is another rule older than
the faculty handbook, and it began the moment

you stopped performing your fear and let your sentences tell me what your blood already knew."

"My blood knows nothing," I say, and the lie reaches up, touches my mouth, and melts.

He studies my face as if the truth were written there in a language only he reads. His expression is dangerous not because it is hungry but because it is certain.

"Look at me," he says, though I already am.

"I'm not looking away," I say, though I am beginning to understand why people do.

He lifts his hand, pauses just shy of my jaw, and for a moment the air is as taut as a wire. Then he rests his fingers there—feather-light, barely pressure at all—and the hum under my skin answers as if his touch is a struck note. It isn't a startle. It's recognition landing with both feet.

"Your sweater," he says, voice so low it belongs to a smaller room. "It lies."

"How?" My mouth is dry.

"It claims modesty." His gaze dips for one dangerous beat. "It is, in fact, a provocation. Very effective. Bravura."

I should laugh. I don't. "You noticed."

"I notice what is *mine* to notice." He doesn't push or pull. His thumb moves once, a quiet line along the hinge of my jaw, and the heat that has been living under my sternum finds air and becomes something else. I feel it—tiny, impossible. A *spark*. Not metaphor. Not poetry. A single, pinprick firefly of warmth that flares under the skin where his fingers rest and then darts along my collarbone like a shy animal choosing a path. I inhale. The ember answers. Horror and delight arrive as twins.

"Do you feel that?" he asks.

"I don't know," I whisper, because if I say *yes* I won't be able to pretend later that I didn't choose this.

"You do." He takes my hand—not the showy, public hold of the dance floor, but the quiet, private grip of a man proving a point—and turns it palm-up. My pulse shows itself without shame. He lowers his other hand until his wrist almost touches mine, the place where I felt the impossible beat that night. Skin doesn't meet skin. Air is enough. The hum leaps, bites delicately, and a scatter of heat shivers up my forearm, sunset under the skin.

"Adrian," I say before I've earned his name.

"Yes." Not a correction. A receipt.

"You said you were deciding."

"I decided." He steps a fraction closer, and the world compresses to sweater, leather, breath. "*I want you.*"

The words exist, then *live*. The room acquires their gravity. He doesn't say *only your mind* or *just your body* or any of the lies men use when they're afraid of their own appetite. He lets the triad be total. Mind. Body. Soul. The admission is not a performance. It is brutal honesty.

The next moment chooses itself. The kiss is not a soft rehearsal. It's shrewdness landing after a long flight, proof that the coordinates had always been true. His mouth finds mine like a door closing on weather. Heat isn't the right word—heat is too crude. This is a clean burn, a disciplined flame. My hands go up without permission—one in his hair, one fisting the front of his shirt as if I could pull all those weeks of controlled conversation into this single point and make them answer for themselves. He makes a quiet sound that lives in the back of his throat, and I feel it in my hands, in my stomach, in the place under my ear where his thumb rested last week and taught my nerves a new alphabet.

When he angles my face to deepen the kiss, the hum under my skin stops pretending to be theory. Sparks answer his mouth—minuscule flares, a scatter of ember-bright sensations running along my lower lip, then the edge of my teeth, then the inside of my cheek. I gasp into him. He stills for a heartbeat, not pulling away, only calibrating, then answers with care that feels like ownership without theft. The world beyond the desk erases itself. There is only breath and the astute way his hand brackets the back of my neck, not forcing, guiding. My body decides to belong in the space he leaves for it.

"Say it," he murmurs against my mouth, and the words are a vibration I swallow.

"What?"

"That you want me."

I've said many things to many men. I have never said the true version aloud. It sits in my throat like a coin I've been saving for the wrong toll. The sweater is too warm, the room is too small, and my name sits inside his mouth like rearranged my bones. The decision takes no time and a century. "I want you," I say, and the *you* lands like a spark on tinder that was not dry until this moment and is now a forest.

He inhales, not theatrical—primed. The hand at my jaw slides to the base of my throat and rests there with a weight that makes my knees wonder whether they have ever had another job. He doesn't squeeze. He doesn't test. He holds the place where my voice lives as if he's learned a new instrument and intends to play without breaking it. "Again," he says.

"I want you." Not breathy. Not coy. Clear.

He kisses me like a man who believes clarity should be rewarded. The spark answers again, brighter this time. It touches skin beneath the sweater, flashes along my ribs in the suggestion of a line. He draws back half an inch, eyes on my mouth, and I feel the place he is not touching as fiercely as the places where he is. His gaze drops to the sweaters' edge. When his palm skims lower along the knit, stopping at the hem, the fine hairs along my stomach lift in greeting. He doesn't push beneath it. He drags his fingertips across the wool in a slow arc that recognizes the shape beneath without making a spectacle of it, and the sensation arrows through me so clean I could weep. My body answers by leaning in. My mouth answers by parting. My pulse answers by becoming a drum I cannot pretend I don't hear.

"You chose deliberately this morning," he says. It isn't a question.

"Yes," I say, and the word is lightheaded and also anchored.

"I approve."

"Is that necessary?"

"No," he says, mouth curving, "but it is the truth."

I want his hands everywhere. I want them to memorize the coordinates the way my sentences have been trying to learn the shape of a crime scene they weren't supposed to see. I want to climb him and forget the names of days. I want—God, I want. He seems to feel the escalation in me before I admit it to myself. He deepens the kiss once, a low voltage pushed across a wire, then eases back until our mouths barely graze.

"Careful," he says softly, his breath shaping the word on my lower lip. "You're sparking."

I look down, disbelieving, and see it—almost nothing, a glimmer that could be a trick of light or a flake of sun on water. Except it moves where his thumb has just moved, and when I exhale, it brightens. A brief, delicate constellation skates along my skin under the sweater's hem and vanishes.

"Don't be afraid," he says.

"I'm not," I answer, and the miracle is that it's true. "I'm furious."

"At?" He sounds pleased.

"At the time we wasted. At rules that make sense until they don't. At you for not kissing me a week ago in an alcove that has been living in my mouth ever since."

He closes his eyes like the confession is a taste. When they open, the green is edged with something metallic, and I remember, the way a body remembers a fall after the bruise, that he is not like other men in ways that go beyond vocabulary. The knowledge should cut. It doesn't. It clarifies.

"Tell me to stop," he says, and means it. "Or stand still."

I stand very still.

He bends and places his mouth at the corner of mine the way you set a seal on a document you intend to keep. He slides along the edge of my jaw, the place where the pulse comes closest to the surface. When he reaches the spot under my ear that has been waking up since November began, he breathes there and the spark becomes a line of contained fire, bright and small and sure. I make a sound I have never made. He makes the mistake of answering, and that is when my hands find the knot of his tie and pull, once, a small correction. He laughs into my skin. The laugh is not kind and not cruel. It is *delighted*.

"Greedy," he says.

"You asked me to be correct," I say. "This is correct."

He withdraws before I can choose otherwise. It's not abrupt, it's masterful. He leaves heat behind like a signature. The room looks exactly as it did fifteen minutes ago, and I will never be the same again. I can feel the glimmer under my sweater, the ghost of it licking along my ribs where his hand hovered. It is both a warning and a benediction.

"I want…" I begin, but the sentence breaks.

"You'll have," he says. "All of it. Not here."

It takes longer than it should to put the room back in focus. He smooths a page that does not require smoothing. I straighten a hem that didn't move. Somewhere a clock resumes being a clock.

"Tonight," he says, not question, not request. "There's a gathering."

"Faculty?" I ask, and the word tastes wrong.

"Something older." He considers me for one beat, decides, and leans closer. "You will see a version of me that the university does not hire and does not fire. You will also see something you already suspect—about yourself."

My breath waits suspended in the space between us. "Where?"

He tells me in a way that is not telling at all, half an address and half a path, and somehow I know the rest. The place beyond the place. A door in the stone where doors don't grow. He watches my face while I translate.

"You came back for me that night," I say. "After Jessica."

"Yes."

"Why?"

"Because I prefer design to chance." He lifts my hand again and, without kissing it, turns it so my pulse faces the ceiling, like he is reading a map. "And because you were already walking toward me. It is courteous to meet someone halfway."

What I want to say is reckless. I say it anyway. "If I come tonight, I want more than your courtesy."

"You'll have more," he says, and the promise does not feel like a seduction. It feels like an oath. He releases my hand. "But you will also have honesty."

"About what?"

"About the parts of me that require night," he says simply. "And the parts of you that have been pretending to be daylight."

I swallow, throat suddenly and inexplicably tender. "What should I wear?" It is a coward's question. It is also a necessity.

"Wear the truth," he says. His eyes dip, then return to mine. "And if you bring that sweater, I will forgive the lie built into it."

The class period has bled into an hour that doesn't belong to anyone. Students will arrive for another course soon and inherit the air we have rearranged. I gather my things with hands that have decided to be steady. At the door, I stop. He is watching me, not possessive, not patient—present. Something in me, the part that always looks over its shoulder for danger, goes still for the first time in months.

"Adrian," I say.

"Yes," he answers, and the ease with which he wears my use of his name tells me everything I need to know about tonight.

"Don't make me wait forever."

"I'm not a cruel man," he says. "Just a careful one."

I leave with heat tucked under my skin and a path written in my mouth. The hallway noise rushes up—rattled lockers, a cough, a laugh, a crumpled flyer stuffed deeper into a corkboard—and none of it can find purchase on me. Outside, the day exists in that sharp, honest way November days have before the early dark claims them. I cross the quad, boots talking to brick, nerves tuned to a pitch I have never carried this far into afternoon. Every door I pass looks like it could open to a stairwell I've never taken. Every window feels like it's watching me on behalf of an older architecture.

In my apartment, I stand very still and do nothing for a full minute. The air settles around me like fabric. Then I move, not quickly, not theatrically—deliberately. I lay out the sweater, laugh despite myself, fold it and set it aside. I choose another truth. The mirror does its familiar work. A stranger looks back and tilts her chin until she recognizes the angle of her own want. On the table, my notebook waits with its web of red thread and names and lines that have stopped wanting to be stories and started wanting to be warnings. I add one line. I do not label it. Labels are invitations to limits.

Dusk tilts across the windows, trimming the buildings to silhouettes. I feel the hum at my wrist settle into a steady tempo, as if someone in another room has begun to drum their fingers on wood in perfect time with me. I think of his mouth at the hinge of my jaw. I think of fireflies under my skin. I think of the word *tonight* and how some words don't know how to share.

I pick up my bag. I turn out the lamp. The door clicks behind me, neat and final, and the corridor's silence accepts the fact of me. Outside, the campus arranges its lights and waits. He told me to wear the truth. I do not know yet what that looks like. I know where to find it.

And I know whose hands will teach it to me.

Chapter 21

Octavia

The courtyard is not just quiet at midnight—it's suspended. Even the ivy seems to have stopped breathing. My heels strike the flagstones louder than they should, each step echoing back like a dare. The black velvet dress from Halloween clings to me under my coat, a choice that feels less like clothing and more like a declaration written in my own skin. Tonight is not costume. Tonight is truth, or the edge of it.

I don't know what waits beyond this meeting. Only that for the first time the wanting—the *need* for answers, for him, for myself—outweighs the fear. My breath ghosts into the air, thin white threads that dissolve before I can follow them. I pull the wool coat closer, the gloves a small mercy against the cold, but they do nothing for the nerves crawling in my stomach like ants returning to a nest.

Then I round the corner and stop.

Adrian stands exactly where I've imagined him—by the old stone well at the center of the courtyard, the one spot on campus rumored to cover more than a forgotten cistern. He's dressed in black from collar to cuff, the suit absorbing what little light there is. Even his tie is a shadow. His posture is stillness sharpened to an edge, but his eyes—green cut with gold—find me and heat begins where they land.

He holds out his hand, waiting. Not a question, not a demand. An inevitability. I slide my gloved fingers into his, the leather whispering against his palm, and feel the current between us hum like a struck string. His gaze drifts down, catches on the glimpse of velvet beneath my coat. A flicker of something—approval, hunger, claim—moves across his face.

"I see you chose your truth," he says, his voice low enough to seem meant for the stone.

I nod because my throat has forgotten how to hold words.

He doesn't speak again. He turns, guiding me across the courtyard with a surety that makes the shadows lean back, and leads me to the stone steps spiraling into the earth. Each one is worn smooth, carved deeper than the stories say. We descend together into a tunnel lit by sconces, the flames steady and old, as if they've been burning here longer than the university itself.

I tighten my grip on his hand, the only warm thing in this narrowing passage. Symbols crawl across the walls—patterns I almost recognize but can't quite read, like a language whispered through a dream. At the tunnel's end, an obsidian door waits, its arch etched with silver-thin inscriptions that glint and shift when I try to focus on them.

Adrian stops, turning toward me. In the dim light his features look carved, but his eyes are alive—lit from within by something that isn't just firelight.

"Are you ready," he asks quietly, "to learn what you are?"

"Yes."

He presses his palm flat against the obsidian door, and a string of words spills from his mouth—syllables like fragments of iron striking water. They aren't a language I know. They're older than language. The carvings flare from silver to white, a vein of light running outward from the center. For a heartbeat it's blinding—pure, merciless brightness—and then the door unseams itself and Adrian draws me through before I can think to resist.

Darkness folds back over us like a curtain, and for an instant I'm grateful. Then I lift my eyes and my breath snags hard.

The mausoleum from my dreams stands before me exactly as I saw it—arched and grave and beautiful, its stained-glass windows glinting like jeweled eyes in the night. My throat works but no sound comes out.

"It wasn't a dream," Adrian says quietly, answering the question clawing up through my panic.

I don't speak. I can't. My pulse is a fist hammering against the cage of my ribs. He shifts his hand to the small of my back—just enough pressure to guide, not enough to push—and walks me forward. The glass doors open beneath his fingers as if they've been waiting.

Inside, the space opens wide. The ceiling climbs into shadow. Red candles gutter in iron brackets. And across the marble floor, arranged in a slow circle like a living clock, stand dozens of figures in crimson robes and masks, their faces erased into anonymity. The scent of wax and rose petals cuts through the cold like a blade.

Adrian bends his head, his mouth at my ear. "Welcome," he murmurs, voice low enough to vibrate my spine, "to the Inkbound Society."

My throat is too tight to speak. Confusion scatters through my thoughts like blown ash. He draws me toward the center of the room, positioning my hand in the crook of his arm as though this is some formal procession and not whatever ritual this is. My mouth tastes like metal and dust.

"You asked for proof," he says, his voice carrying now, turning me so the masked faces can see. He slips my coat from my shoulders with a single motion. My curls tumble free, brushing the bare skin the velvet leaves exposed. "Here is my proof."

Something shivers through the space—a collective murmur, a ripple of sound like a book being opened in unison. I feel it before I see it, the tether between us drawn taut, humming in the hollow behind my sternum. He hasn't touched me, not really, but the thread thrums like a struck wire.

Then light blooms.

At first it's only warmth on my collarbone, a blush beneath the skin. Then the glow pushes outward, gold spilling from the hollow just below my ear, tracing the line where neck meets shoulder. I look down at myself, at the glow brightening with each breath, and the panic becomes something else—something fierce, electric.

"She is *mine*," Adrian says, and the growl in his throat is not entirely human.

The room answers like a single body, murmured congratulations and phrases I can't catch, the name of something—*soul-bond?*—spoken and repeated like an oath. Masks dip, hands clasp, a ritual I don't understand performed around me like a crown being woven in air.

I stand in the center of it all, trembling—velvet clinging to my knees, my heart a hammer inside a cage of light—and realize I've stepped over a line I never knew existed. The air hums between us, charged and waiting. When he asks, "Do you consent?" the question coils through me, molten and certain.

"Yes."

He draws me against his chest, his breath ghosting the shell of my ear. "Now the fun really begins," he murmurs, the low purr in his voice thrumming down my spine until every inch of me is awake.

His hands find me—roaming, deliberate, claiming without hurry. My breath catches, my pulse quickens, knees weakening as his warmth presses close. He blows lightly against my ear, and my control splinters.

"What fun would that be?" I ask, my voice unsteady, breathy, betraying me.

He doesn't answer with words. His lips brush the curve of my neck, a ghost of a kiss that deepens until I forget how to breathe. His teeth graze the spot, a sharp promise, a warning, before his fingers trace the edge of my thigh through the velvet hem. I part for him without thought, lost in the heat, the hum of the crowd fading until there's only this—his touch, his scent, the dangerous rhythm that binds us.

"Do you see," he asks the crowd, voice velvet over steel, "how prettily she comes unraveled for me?" His fingers slide higher—never quite where I ache for them to be, skimming, denying, promising. Heat blooms under my skin, rises to my cheeks until I can feel the color like a second pulse. I dip my head, instinctive, seeking somewhere to hide, and the reprimand lands sharp across the curve of my ass. A sound escapes my throat before I can bite it back.

"Do not lower your head again, my wicked ruin." His hand lingers at the place of the sting, a caress masquerading as punishment. "Let them see you. Let them want what they cannot claim. You are *mine*. Say it."

"I'm yours," I whisper, breath catching but voice steady enough to hold.

"Good girl." The words are low, warm, dangerous, the kind of praise that sinks claws in deep. The slickness between my thighs becomes its own confession, rising, scenting the air between us with something no one here can pretend not to feel. His fingers climb higher, ghosting across the edge of my sensitive flesh without yet trespassing, his mouth finding the hollow of my neck again, tongue moving in slow, lazy circles that promise ruin.

It's too much. The heat of the crowd's gaze, the sting fading to warmth where his hand struck. The way his presence eats every sensible thought from my head until there's nothing left but him—the weight, the heat, the impossible intimacy of being watched and claimed at once.

I'm unraveling, heat blooming in my body at a dangerous pace. I'm burning from the inside out and his fingers are fanning the flames, precise and relentless. He works quickly, gliding over the sensitive bundle of nerves at the apex of my thighs with the control of a man who understands exactly what fire can do.

But I don't want control.

My eyes widen, vision spilling past him into the room. The air has thickened—dark, perfumed, humming. Energy coils through the chamber like smoke. Members shed their crimson robes in slow cascades, fabric pooling at their feet, revealing bodies of every shape and beauty. The ritual is as old as breath: women and men pairing, touching, mouths and hands mapping flesh as if it were scripture. The collective sound—moans, whispers, a susurrus of skin on skin—rolls over me in waves.

I'm fascinated, enthralled, wholly entranced. My gaze refuses to look away even as my body trembles under Adrian's touch. Every nerve fires. Every breath is a gasp pulled between my teeth.

"Release it," Adrian murmurs against my ear. His mouth moves lower, teeth grazing the curve of my neck sharper now, a promise and a threat. My skin stings, and a thin ribbon of blood slides down my collarbone. I barely notice it over the rising tide inside me.

"Come," he commands, the single word vibrating through me like an invocation. Pleasure surges—a vortex that turns my spine molten and lifts me toward something I've never felt. The flames inside me flare higher than they've ever dared, tendrils of golden light spilling into the air, weaving between the bodies, between the pillars, curling like incense smoke but brighter, alive.

I blink, sure my mind is breaking, until I feel it shift under my own skin—a ripple, a purr rolling out of my chest that doesn't sound human at all.

Adrian shifts behind me, but his fingers never stop their slow circles. "There you are," he says, voice low and triumphant, like he's been waiting for this exact moment.

"What am I?" I whisper, still aware of all the eyes on me, still aware of Adrian's presence—his hand sliding inside the top of my dress, his tongue catching the blood at my throat in one deliberate stroke. I should recoil. I should be repulsed. But I'm not.

"Something *new*," Adrian says. His words brush my ear like a brand.

The thing inside me is delighted by his words, and I feel myself shedding a barrier I didn't even know I'd been holding up. It slips away like old skin, leaving everything raw and bright. Around us, the room climbs toward a fever pitch—bodies moving, murmuring, the collective sound of ritual turning into a single thrum that rattles the stained glass. Adrian's fingers pick up speed, perfectly matching the room's pulse, each glide of his hand an echo of its rising tempo.

"I want you to unravel for me again," he murmurs, voice pitched low enough to feel like it lives under my skin. His breath strokes my ear, his teeth graze the edge of my neck. "Let them hear you this time. Quit holding back."

It's the exact thing I need to push me over the edge for a second time. The command lands like a match struck against dry tinder. I don't hide the sound that tears from my throat, a cry that splits the heavy air, or the way my knees shake violently under the weight of it. Energy—gold, molten—leaps from my skin again, invisible to everyone else or maybe not, curling upward like smoke lit from within.

"Such a good girl you are," Adrian growls against the curve of my ear, the praise almost a snarl, "my wicked ruin."

The words shudder through me, a vibration that makes my blood feel like it's caught fire. My body arches against his, answering his rhythm without permission. The crowd's noise fades to a dull roar as the only thing I can hear clearly is him—his voice, his breath, his fingers fanning the flames higher.

Then he bites me—teeth sinking into my skin with a sharp, deliberate cruelty that jolts every nerve awake. The pain is electric, bright enough to tear a scream from my throat, raw and unrestrained. It echoes against the vaulted chamber until the sound itself shatters into something else. *Pleasure.*

It floods in like a fever, curling hot through every inch of me until the ache turns liquid. My body arches instinctively, meeting him, grinding against him in a rhythm older than reason. The taste of iron lingers on the air; the world narrows to the pulse between us. I can't breathe for the way it feels—too much and not enough, every nerve begging for more even as they tremble under the strain.

A low chuckle rolls from his chest, dark and sensual, the sound vibrating through me like a secret promise he hasn't yet put a name to. It's not laughter—it's a vow in disguise, the kind of sound that says *he knows exactly what he's done.*

The room tilts, spins—its edges fraying like wet paper. Blackness flits at the corners of my vision, darting in and out like a predator circling. I claw at the moment, refusing to surrender, my pulse a drumbeat of panic and defiance. I don't want to sleep. I don't want to go under. I want to stay awake, to stay here, to keep feeling every nerve he's woken.

But my body has turned traitor—weightless now, numb. My legs no longer belong to me and my hands can't find the floor. It's as if Adrian alone is holding me upright, his arms the only gravity I have left, his will the only anchor keeping me from slipping away entirely.

Darkness creeps closer, spilling across my sight like ink in water. I fight it. I fight harder, the panic in my veins sharpens until it tastes like metal in my mouth. Some deep, primal certainty grips me—that if I let my eyes close, if I lose this battle, I may not wake to see the morning.

Still, inevitability is patient. It wears me down like tide against stone. In the end, the darkness swallows everything.

CHAPTER 22

When I wake, it feels like surfacing through tar. Every breath drags, sticky with something that doesn't belong to air. The ceiling above me is white, but not sterile—an ivory touched by candlelight, shadowed by the faint motion of flame. The scent that threads through the room is unmistakable. Cedar, smoke, and ink, the same scent that clings to Adrian Marlowe like a signature.

Sheets rasp against my skin when I move—too soft, too fine to be mine. I'm still in the velvet dress, though it's torn near the hem, the sleeve half slid from my shoulder. My pulse flickers at the edge of my throat, raw and fragile, and I press my fingers there as if I could quiet it back into rhythm.

The realization comes slowly, like shadows taking shape onto walls. I am in *his* home.

The thought should frighten me. It almost does. Instead, I lie still for a moment longer, listening. Somewhere below, a clock chimes twice. There's no traffic noise, no students laughing their way home from the bars—only the deep hush of a house that's always been awake longer than anyone living in it.

When I finally sit up, the world sways, edges blurring before they sharpen again. A faint ache lingers in the side of my neck, the memory of teeth and heat. My hand drifts there before I can stop it. The skin isn't broken, but it feels marked all the same—an invisible brand that hums with the same strange rhythm that's lived under my skin since I met him.

The door opens before I can decide whether to flee or stay.

And there he is... *Adrian*.

Not the man who lectured behind the safety of a podium, nor the one who cornered me in the dark like a prayer that had forgotten its god. This version of him is stripped of his armor. The black suit jacket is gone; his shirtsleeves are rolled to his elbows; the top button undone. The lamplight paints him in shadows and gold, the faint gleam of his tie pin the only bright thing about him.

"Good," he says quietly. "You're awake."

His voice is the same, but something beneath it has changed—lower, less *human*.

"What happened?" My throat burns, the words scrape down my throat like shards of glass. "How did I get here?"

"You collapsed," he says simply. "Your pulse was erratic. The transition—" He stops himself, considers. "It was too much."

"The transition?"

A pause. "You'll understand soon enough."

I swing my legs off the bed, testing the floor. My boots are gone, but my tights are still on. The carpet beneath my feet is dense, almost silken. The room itself is austere but deliberate—dark wood, shelves lined with books older than the house, a painting that looks like smoke frozen mid-breath. Everything here has purpose. Everything here knows how to wait.

"You brought me here," I say slowly. "You carried me."

"Yes," he answers. No deflection. Just the naked truth.

"Why?"

His eyes lift to mine. They're darker than green now—richer, molten at the center. "Because you stopped breathing for eight seconds."

I should feel the horror of that. Instead, I feel a tremor low in my stomach, something electric and traitorous. "You should have taken me to a hospital."

"I could have," he agrees. "But you wouldn't have survived it."

The room tilts again, but this time it's not from weakness. "What do you mean?"

He studies me like a man trying to decide if he should tell the truth or build a softer lie. "What happened last night wasn't *chance*, Octavia. The Society does not deal in accident. You were claimed, and in claiming, something in you woke that doesn't belong to their making—or mine."

"I didn't agree to any of it."

"No," he says softly. "You didn't. That's what makes you dangerous."

I take a step back, my hands curling into fists. "Dangerous?"

He moves closer, slow enough that I could leave if I wanted. "You *burned*, Octavia. Not metaphorically. Not poetically. You burned. Every instrument in that room responded to you as if it had been waiting centuries for that particular frequency. You are the first thing in a long time that reminded them the old myths weren't myths."

"I don't understand," I whisper.

"You will."

The fire in the hearth catches with a low pop, casting gold across his face. He looks older suddenly, not in years but in weight, as though the act of explaining himself costs something he doesn't often pay.

"What are you?" I ask.

He doesn't smile. "Old. Wrong. And perhaps not the one you should be asking that question of."

He turns away before I can answer, crossing to a side table where a tray waits—crystal decanter, two glasses, an untouched plate of bread and fruit. "Eat something," he says without looking at me. "You've lost too much energy."

I hesitate, then take the glass of water instead. The first swallow burns like liquor. When I set it down, his gaze meets mine again.

"You're angry."

"I'm confused."

"Confusion is just curiosity without enough data," he says. "You'll have it soon."

"That's not an answer."

"No," he says, his voice quieter now. "It isn't."

He circles the room slowly, coming to stand before the window where the fog presses soft against the glass. I half expect him to fade into it. "Do you remember what I told you about obsession?"

"That it's an architecture," I say before I can stop myself. "That it builds and narrows until there's no choice left—only result."

He turns, and the look in his eyes steals the breath from my chest. "Then understand this, what binds us now is not romance, nor the Society's ritual. It's design. A bond. Two halves of something ancient that decided, without our consent, to recognize itself."

The air in the room feels thicker, charged, as if something unseen leans closer to listen. "A bond?"

He nods once. "Soul-bound, if you prefer the older term. It's the simplest language for something that isn't simple."

The words hang there, enormous and quiet. "You make it sound like a choice."

"It isn't," he says, stepping closer. "But what you do with it is."

I want to laugh. I want to scream. "You're telling me that whatever this is—" I gesture between us, the air crackling faintly in response—"I didn't choose it, but now I get to decide what to do about it?"

"That's what choice has always been," he murmurs. "After the fact."

He's close enough now that the scent of cedar and smoke wraps around me again, dizzying. My pulse stumbles, and the hum under my skin rises to a pitch that borders on pain. "Why me?"

"I could tell you you were chosen," he says. "That fate wove us together, that it's sacred. You'd hate that answer."

"Try me."

He exhales, eyes tracing the line of my throat as if measuring truth. "Because the moment I saw you, something in me recognized its reflection. The same flaw. The same hunger. The same shadow. I wanted to understand it. Now I think I never stood a chance."

My heart slams against my ribs. "So what now? You keep me? Like a—what—some kind of relic?"

He steps closer still. "No. I offer."

"Offer what?"

"Everything," he says simply. "Power. Knowledge. The truth about what you are and why you were never meant to fit into the world you keep trying to live in."

"And if I say no?"

"Then you leave," he says. "And I will not stop you."

He means it. I see it in the stillness of his stance, in the way he holds his hands loosely at his sides like he's forcing himself not to reach for me. But something deeper than reason anchors me in place. My curiosity has teeth.

"What does being soul-bound mean?" I ask.

He tilts his head slightly, as if deciding how much to tell me. "It means our energies mirror and feed one another. My strength can sustain you when yours falters. Your power—what's waking in you—can heal what's long been fractured in me. It's... symbiosis, not subjugation."

"That's your simplest explanation?"

He almost smiles. "You wanted honesty."

I cross my arms, though the gesture feels flimsy under his gaze. "Why does it feel like my blood hums when you're near?"

"Because it knows what the rest of you hasn't accepted yet."

"Which is?"

"That you are not ordinary, and neither am I."

The admission feels like a key turning in a lock somewhere deep inside me. "You're telling me I'm—what—magical?"

"Not in the childish sense," he says. "But yes. You are made of what the rest of us forgot to name."

I sink back against the edge of the bed, dizzy all over again. "This is insane."

"Perhaps," he says. "But insanity and revelation share a border."

The silence stretches, heavy with everything I can't ask yet. I trace the seam of my dress absently, feeling the faint heat still radiating from my skin. "What if I don't want this?"

He watches me for a long moment. "Then I will find a way to sever the bond."

I look up sharply. "Can you do that?"

"No," he admits. "But I would try."

The honesty in that undoes something in me I didn't realize was still holding. "You're dangerous."

"So are you."

He moves closer again, slow enough that I don't flinch. When his hand lifts, I expect contact, but he stops a breath away from my cheek. "I won't touch you again. Not unless you ask," he says. "Not until you decide."

The restraint in his voice is a kind of violence—too deliberate, too controlled. It makes me ache more than any command could.

"Why do I feel like you're offering me more than power?" I ask softly.

"Because you already know what I want."

He says it without lust, without plea—just fact, terrible in its simplicity.

The hearth crackles once. My heart answers.

"What happens if I say yes?"

"Then I show you the rest," he says, his gaze flicking to the window where the fog curls like breath. "The part of yourself you've been afraid to meet."

"And if I say no?"

"Then I'll teach you how to forget me."

He means that too, and for some reason that terrifies me more than the alternative.

The firelight flickers across the side of his face, carving him into something mythic, something older than the walls that hold us. My pulse thrums louder, answering the quiet vibration in my wrist—the one that feels less like a heartbeat and more like a summons.

I swallow hard. "You said I burned. That I woke something. What happens now?"

"Now," he says softly, "you learn how not to be consumed by it."

He reaches behind him, takes a folded paper from the table, and sets it beside me on the bed. The seal is wax, deep red, stamped with a sigil that glows faintly even in shadow. "The Society meets again in three nights. This is your invitation. Not as a witness. As initiate."

I stare at it, then at him. "You're giving me a choice again."

"I told you," he murmurs. "Everything on a silver platter."

"And what's the price?"

His mouth curves, faint, indistinguishable. "Everything worth taking asks the same question."

He turns then, crossing to the door. At the threshold, he pauses, glancing back over his shoulder. "Rest, Octavia. You'll need your strength."

"For what?"

"For deciding whether you want to walk through the same door you opened last night."

He leaves before I can answer. The latch clicks soft behind him, final as a heartbeat.

I sit there long after the fire sinks to embers, staring at the wax seal. The hum under my skin hasn't faded. It's louder now, as if it's singing to the same rhythm the flames keep—rise, fall, breathe, burn.

When I press a finger to the mark on my collarbone, the glow flares again, faint but real.

I should be terrified. I should run.

Instead, I whisper to the empty room, "Maybe I'm tired of pretending I'm ordinary."

The mark warms under my touch, answering like a promise.

And somewhere beyond the walls, in the night thick with fog and ink, I swear I feel him smile.

Chapter 23

I begin the day with intention. Awake before the hour chooses me, still as a drawn bow, listening to the house name its small truths—the stretch in the beams, the shy tick in the flue, the far-off settling that means the night has given its ledger back to morning. I dress without ornament. Restraint is a uniform. When I button the cuff, the deeper pulse at my wrist answers once and then goes quiet, as if it has agreed to wait with me. Waiting is the work today. I will do it properly.

Blackmoor keeps its composure in November. Brick looks honest, paths admit their edges, trees show the mechanics of their reach. I place myself where a man like me disappears, among the purposeful, against stone. She crosses the quad at eight-forty with a paper cup and a face that has learned to carry two stories at once. The cropped knit has been traded for something sterner. The leather has become dark denim, the boots have kept their argument with the pavement. The mark at her collarbone stays veiled, but the air knows it. So do I. When she passes the statue, she checks the time without breaking stride. When a flyer lifts its corner in the wind, she smooths it with two fingers and aligns the pushpin by instinct. I record the data that matters. She still hates crooked things she did not choose, she still prefers precision to luck, and her blood hums harder when she moves toward a threshold.

At nine she takes a seat in a room that is not mine. I linger in the doorway long enough to be just another faculty shadow and watch her note-taking learn a new economy. She no longer pads a thought to make it safer to carry. She writes the thing, and when the hand wants to apologize, she denies it the word. Twice, her attention slips sideways to some calculation not on the board. Both times she returns with a sentence that has the clean weight of a sharpened tool. The hum at my wrist answers her concentration as if sound had a geometry.

Midday finds her at Antonio's with Jessica, the friend who arrived with wings and neon once and hasn't stopped making light since. I take a window across the street where glass makes me an abstraction and watch them split a pie like a pact. Laughter. Then quiet. The quiet is where the marrow sits. Octavia leans forward, forearms on the table, and speaks in the tone of someone choosing the angle of a blade, not the blade itself. Jessica shakes her head, then nods like concession tastes better than sermon. When Octavia rises, she pockets a folded note the way a person pockets a match—casual, careful, aware it can change a room.

After lunch she folds herself back into the library's hushed machinery. I keep to the stacks that have learned loyalty to my shadow and let her show me, without knowing she does, the shelves she considers kin. Crime scene reconstruction manuals, a nineteenth-century bestiary shelved by a librarian with a sense of humor, and a slim, anonymous chapbook that has survived because its cover pretends to be dull. She reads quickly and rereads only what argues back. She copies nothing verbatim. The hand writes in a script that refuses apology. Twice she pauses and presses two fingers to the hinge of her jaw, where a bruise should be and is not. The mark is under the skin. The glow is memory now, not performance. Good. I want her to learn it without theater.

Waiting does not mean idling. While she studies the living stacks, I visit the dead ones. The chamber three levels below the old archives smells of vellum and iron and a patience that could be mistaken for piety. The catalog answers me now without requiring my name. Embergrave has always been the kind of word that does what it wants. Today it opens a door it has been pretending is a wall.

Hartwell—adoption decree, transformed twice by bureaucratic hand to erase the heat of the original act. The seal is municipal, and the ink? Routine. The date matches the year a small girl with chestnut-and-ember hair would have been taught to count to ten. The adoptive mother's signature is neat and unembellished. The space for the adoptive father is blank. The line for the birth mother carries no name at all—only a mark that is not a mark, the sour little infinity loop I have seen in three other places. A marginalia in a ledger the Society pretends does not exist. A token sewn into the hem of an Alpenshield banner that should have burned. The inside corner of a page that lists offerings no one now alive remembers making. Whoever bore her hid in plain sight and used the symbol all cowards use when they want to vanish without telling the truth about leaving. Or perhaps it is not cowardice. Perhaps it is a wall a living woman built to keep a dead machine from recognizing her face.

Octavia Embergrave. Adopted into Hartwell because the world prefers its names with dull edges, her mother equally afraid of what she might become. When the time comes, I will tell her this much and not more. It is enough to know which lock she carries in the blood. The key will be hers to forge.

Afternoon arrives and the campus admits the length of its own shadows. She works at the

Gazette office until the light thins, editing copy other hands believe finished, returning phrases without cruelty and without lenience. A boy with a quick mouth tries to charm a concession out of her. She declines with a sentence that leaves him grateful. It is a rare skill to be exact and kind. The Society would call it a weakness. I know it for what it is—control.

When she leaves, I follow at a distance that can be explained by coincidence twice and fate never. Her apartment door receives her with the small sigh all doors make when the person they have been built to open for returns. She moves through the rooms as if listing them to herself: table, lamp, bed, map, thread. The threads lead to a wall she has taught to hold a nervous system in red. She adds a line. She does not write the name. Names are invitations, and she has learned to hold her invitations behind gritted teeth until the room deserves them.

I leave her there and return to the study because the part of me that belongs to offices and lectures has finished its shift, and the part that answers to older structures has work that cannot be watched. The thirteen flames are not superstition, they are memory disguised as ritual so the world will forgive them for enduring. Every house learned them in a different order, swore by a different candle, wrote a different maxim in smoke. Noctevaris—the old darkness that learned lamp-light well enough to sit at a table with it—keeps the first and the last. Origin and return. Alpenshield, if one believes the last accurate transcript, keeps what they call the beacon—fire that shows where you already meant to go. Embergrave is the bridge some scholars insisted never existed, the flare at the moment of decision that turns the body into a proof. I light the sixth—temperance—and let it refuse to glow until it decides I have earned the hour. Then I light the ninth—fluence—and the wick takes with the stubborn efficiency I have always envied. The thirteenth stays cold. It will until *she* names it.

On the desk, the research waits in clean stacks. I have the dates, the signatures, the absence where her mother's name should live. I have the sigil that repeats. A loop meant to be infinity and failing at it, the way all human signs do. I have a map that shows three houses that no longer exist and five that have idiot heirs who will sell what they do not understand for compliments and clapping. Tomorrow is initiation. Tonight is the last night aloud to hope without instruction.

At dusk I walk the perimeter of town the way a surgeon runs a hand along a body before a cut—feeling for heat, for swell, for the small betrayal that tells you where to begin. The river keeps its black, the bridge keeps its lie of safety, and the mausoleum keeps its promise because stone is better at remembering than any book I have been paid to care for. I do not go down. The chamber will be busy with men whose hunger makes a noise I prefer not to name. They will call it fervor. They will mistake her for a prize. I will not.

Later, from the boundary of shadow across the street, I watch her window until the light inside lowers and her outline becomes a study in patience. She works long past the hour the campus will admit as respectable. She stands once with her hands braced on the table and looks at nothing until the room gives her back a decision. When she sits again, she writes a sentence that makes her stop after the period and touch the place beneath her ear as if someone had said her true name in another room. The urge to cross the street and let the glass decide whether it is barrier or veil is a hunger I have taught myself to starve. I starve it now. Discipline is a form of worship when the thing you want could destroy what you claim to love. The word love does not sit easily in my mouth. I will not use it. But the structure it points to is one I have been building for longer than the Society would like to believe I am capable of.

I return to the house and let it take my weight the way it always has—without complaint, with a patience that borders on contempt. The ember in the grate lowers to a core and holds. On the desk, the ledger I should burn opens of its own accord to the page I shouldn't look at and do—*Embergrave*. Written twice, struck once, rewritten in a smaller hand that belonged to a woman who hid in a library in 2000 while a city pretended not to be on fire. Beside it, a note I found today in a folder that had learned how to be misfiled: *child hidden under salt and ash, father unknown, mother unnamed, sigil left, flame uncalled.* The archivist who wrote it preferred nouns to poetry. I thank him for that. Clarity is a mercy even when it fails to soothe.

There are things I will tell Octavia when she asks and things I will not. I will tell her Hartwell is a shelter she outgrew the second she learned to write a line that told the truth. I will tell her Embergrave is a door and not a sentence. I will tell her that every system that pretends to keep order has a room under it where the real work was always done, and that the Society has mistaken the room for god. I will not tell her yet that the first time I tasted her blood in air I heard the river hesitate and then continue as if it had decided to believe in itself again. I will not tell her yet that the hunger the bite woke was not the hunger I have disciplined for a century, but something stranger, older, cleaner. The desire to build a world inside which the worst parts of me do not need to be heroic to be harmless. The word bond sits easier than love. I will use it until she teaches me a better one.

Near midnight, the phone vibrates once with a message no one should be able to send because no one has the right to the number they used. *She will come,* it reads. The sender has chosen the name of a man who is dead and has used it before because he enjoys playing with stories he did not earn. Marcus knows how to make his tone sound helpful. It will not help him if he decides to test the line he keeps pretending he does not see.

I do not answer. I do not sleep. I practice old breath, and even older stillness. At three, when the town gives up pretending that anything holy happens at that hour and the day shrinks to its furnace core, I go to the east window and let the glass offer me the city in its true proportion. Small. Ambitious. Capable of kindness without applause. I touch the wrist where the darker pulse lives and count the beats until the other rhythm arrives in answer—soft, far, exact. She is awake. Or I am. The distinction becomes academic near the event horizon.

Dawn begins as a rumor and then proves itself. The house accepts it, my study refusing to flinch. Today will be full of duties performed by men who enjoy being seen performing them. I will let them have their performance. They mistake spectacle for proof—a fools mistake.

I will follow her at a distance that keeps my promise to let her decide. I will arrange the conditions so that decision can be made without the wrong eyes turning it into theater. I will stand where she can find me and not be ambushed by gratitude. I will tell her what I have and hold back what will only burn for the sake of burning. I will teach the old ways if she asks and keep my mouth shut if she does not. I will show her the candles that matter and let her light the one that bears her name. I will put the adoption letter on the table where she can touch it and not touch me, and I will say the word Embergrave once and then refuse to say it again until she says it back without flinching. I will show her the blank where her mother's name should be and not offer to fill it with story. I will tell her I have looked and failed and will continue to look and hope to fail better. I will not call that love. I will call it accuracy.

If she does not come, the thirteenth will remain cold and the Society will congratulate itself on keeping the world safe from a truth it cannot even locate. If she comes, the room below the stone will learn what it means to be useful instead of hungry. If she runs, I will know that I have misread the ledger and that the hum under my skin means nothing I can use without lying.

The sun clears the rough edge of the far buildings and throws a thin stripe across the desk. The stripe lands on the seal she broke and left on my table like a small wound. Wax remembers the shape of pressure after the hand has gone. So does a throat. So does a city.

I step away from the window because waiting does not keep itself. The day has begun to guage me. I intend to meet it with the clean arithmetic of someone who has chosen his variables well. I will watch, as I *always* have, and I will not make a sound that pretends to be a summons. If she is the thing I believe her to be... Then, summons are an insult.

The old books have this much right—*flame arrives when the air is correct. The work is to build the room that does not lie about its oxygen.*

I leave the house and it lets me go. The street accepts the weight of my stride without commentary. The campus is already awake enough to pretend it was never asleep. She will cross it soon with a face that has learned it can hold two stories at once without breaking. I will be where the two stories meet. If she looks up, she will see a man in a good coat who has learned how to be mistaken for scenery. If she does not look up, I will continue to be correct until the hour that requires me to be otherwise.

Tomorrow has an altar. Tonight is the last rehearsal that admits honesty. I am very good at honesty when it is quiet. I intend to be better at it when it is loud.

Chapter 24

The morning is colorless, washed out like parchment left too long in the sun. I wake before the alarm, body already tense, and lie still for a while listening to the city breathe beyond the window. The sounds are ordinary—delivery trucks, a radio somewhere, a door closing two floors down—but my pulse insists there's meaning hidden in each one. Since that night under the mausoleum ceiling, everything ordinary has felt amplified, as if the world's edges have been filed while I wasn't looking.

I push myself upright, the sheet slipping to my waist. My hands tremble slightly when I knot my robe. It's not fear. Not exactly. More like the feeling you get before opening a letter you know will change your life. In the mirror over the sink my face looks the same but not—the same green eyes under chestnut and auburn hair, but a new tension in the corners of my mouth, a faint glow at my collarbone if the light hits right. A mark I can't explain and can't stop touching.

Shower. Coffee. Lip balm. Small anchors. They help until I step outside and the November air meets me like a question. The sky is low and white, holding the promise of snow without delivering it. Campus smells of wet stone and fallen leaves.

Students move past in clusters, bright coats and bright voices, and for a moment I can almost believe I belong to them. Almost.

At the library doors I stop, fingers pressing against the cool metal handle. The memory arrives without invitation. Adrian's voice, a low murmur at my ear—*Here is my proof.* His hand at the small of my back as he guides me toward the dias. The crowd in crimson robes parting as if I were a lit fuse. The glow from my skin. The sound of his claim—*she is mine.* I remember the way it echoed in the chamber, how everyone's eyes fixed on me, how heat and panic braided until I couldn't tell one from the other. I told myself I wanted truth. I hadn't imagined it would feel like being unveiled.

Inside the library, I breathe deep and walk to my usual table. Books scatter the surface, pages with knowledge that will hopefully help me to begin to understand who I am. There's folklore of fire, obscure lineages, fragments of untranslated rituals. My own notes sprawl across a legal pad in cramped handwriting. I flip through them mechanically, but the words blur. *Soul-bond. Inkbound. Claim.* Words whispered in that stone room, clinging to me still. I don't know if they were threat or promise.

My phone vibrates.

Jessica: Lunch? Antonio's?

Relief. Normalcy. I text back, *yes*, and gather my things.

The pizza shop smells of oregano and melted cheese, a smell so rooted in my college years it's almost medicinal. Jessica is already at a booth, scrolling her phone with one hand and holding a soda in the other. Her pale blue sweater makes her skin look warmer. A week of rest has brought color back to her cheeks. She waves me over.

"Hey," she says, eyes crinkling. "You look... *not* terrible."

"High praise."

"I mean it." She studies me. "After the other night, I wasn't sure."

I slide into the booth. "I'm fine."

"You're lying."

"Probably," I admit.

Jessica pushes a paper plate toward me. "Eat. Tell me what's wrong without telling me what's wrong."

I pick up a slice, the grease warm against my fingers, and search for words that won't betray me. "He makes me feel things I shouldn't."

"'He'?" she says, eyebrows up.

I look at the pizza, not her. "It's complicated."

"Professor complicated?"

The blush climbs my throat before I can stop it. Jessica's smile turns wicked. "Oh my god. You're actually *serious*."

"It's not—what you think," I manage. "I don't even know what it is."

"Do you want him?"

The question lodges under my ribs like a thorn. I think of Adrian's mouth at my ear, his hand guiding mine, his whisper—*Now the fun really begins.* The glow under my skin answering his touch. "Yes," I whisper, before I can lie.

Jessica's grin softens into something more like concern. "*Tavia*... be careful."

"I'm always careful."

"No. You're curious. That's not the same thing."

I take a bite of pizza to avoid answering. Cheese and salt, familiar and grounding. Outside the window, a gust lifts dead leaves into a spiral. The sight pulls me back to the mausoleum again. I remember the robes, the murmurs, the word *soul-bond* rolling like a drumbeat through the crowd. I don't tell Jessica that part. I *can't.*

She sips her soda. "You look like you're somewhere else."

"I am," I say before I can stop myself.

By the time we part, the sun has shifted behind a veil of thin clouds, the world gone that pale gray that makes everything look half-imagined. I tuck my hands into my jacket and start back toward campus, letting the motion disguise the restlessness still buzzing under my skin. The wind carries the faint scent of ink and rain from the library steps—a reminder that there are safer obsessions than the ones with green-gold eyes.

The afternoon slips into a thinner light as I cut back across the quad, the stone brightening under a brief break in the cloud cover. I don't look for him. I refuse to. Instead I fix my gaze on the Humanities façade and the class I can handle—historical art, the sort that keeps its violence framed and labeled. The lecture hall smells like chalk and old projector bulbs, slides thudding from one to the next with a mechanical patience that steadies my breathing. Frescoes. Gilding. The lecturer's voice moves through patronage and piety, and I let the cadence wash me clean of pizza grease and dangerous thoughts.

It almost works. Almost.

When the lights dim for a final slide—saints ringed in gold leaf, their halos bright as new coins—heat thrums under my collarbone in a single low answer. I press my fingers there and pretend I'm checking a necklace I'm not wearing. No one notices. Everyone's too busy copying dates.

Class breaks, chairs scraping along the floor in a screech that vibrates through me. The corridor outside is a river of bodies and hurried plans. I move with it, then slip free and angle toward the library, where the day narrows to the kind of work that doesn't look like work from the outside. In the bright, open floors, students clatter and whisper. I don't stop there. I thread through map cases and periodicals and down the back stairs, where the air cools and the carpet thickens, where the half-burnt bulb at the landing leaves a soft bruise of light on the wall.

Lower stacks. The quiet that lives here wears shoes.

I dump my bag on a study table scarred with the initials of past obsessives and build my fortress: notebooks open, pen uncapped, a square of chocolate as bribe. Then I start pulling the shelves apart—not literally, but in the ways only a patient mind can. University ephemera first. The bound campus newspapers in their cracked leather jackets, spines stamped with dates that line up like vertebrae. I drag the 1890s down and heave the weight onto the table. That decade carries a mania for ceremony—groundbreakings, dedications, Latin mottos stitched on banners—and sometimes mania leaves its glove prints where righteousness thinks it's wiping the table.

Page after page, I let the ink tell me what it thinks it remembers. Students petitioned for a debate society, then a literary circle, then a "rotunda for moral instruction." There's a fair, a masquerade, a winter ball held in a hall no one uses anymore. Here and there a phrase glints where the rest goes matte: *private convocation, founders' vigil, candlelit procession*. Photographs show faces arranged in tidy rows and eyes that have not learned to smile for cameras. On the margins, a tiny symbol appears twice—an infinity loop that doesn't quite meet, lines written that don't make sense. The same wrong curve from the morning book. I copy it into my notebook, hand steady, jaw tight.

Next, the catalogue of donated collections. Blackmoor has always loved its donors. A roster of names trails their gifts like a bridal train—portraits, manuscripts, a ruined altar piece rescued from a chapel in the countryside. The donors who gave loudly are easy to spot. They insist on plaques. I skim their brass-burnished vanity and hunt quieter lines. "Anonymous bequest," "private patron," "in perpetuity." Three entries link to a benefactor with a name that reads like a rumor—House Inkbound. I can't tell if it's an affectation or a misfiled label the clerk didn't understand. The call numbers point down again.

I go where they point me.

Special Collections technically isn't open this late, but the glass doors are attended by a grad

assistant I've seen before—a man with a generous nose and a sweater that has carried too many
winters. He glances up, recognizes me as a regular, and raises one finger, the universal sign for
"don't do anything that makes me lose this job."
I nod, equally universal. "I won't." He buzzes me
through.

The room is climate-controlled and proud of it.
It smells of linen and gum arabic and concentrated
time. I fill out a slip for local histories and a slim
black ledger that only has a number for a title. The
assistant vanishes into the back and returns with
two gray boxes. He sets them down like offerings
and retreats to his desk, where his headphones
gleam.

I peel the lid from the first box. Handwritten
minutes from student organizations: *script leaning right, ink faded to tea.* I skim the pages that
praise fundraising and rush to the ones that do
not. *Meeting moved to old chapel due to weather.
Seconded. Motion passed. Circle affirmed—flame*

witnessed. There it is again, that ritual language that pretends to be administrative. My skin prickles.

The old ledger is worse. Better? I'm not sure. It's a book that forgot its name, filled in multiple hands over decades. Lists of attendees, references to "threshold," to "keepers," to "binding by witness." In the corners of three pages, the under-closed infinity loop. Beside one entry, the word Marlowe appears in a tidy script that refuses ornament. My throat goes dry.

I trace the name with one finger without touching the page. It could be coincidence. It could be a different man entirely. It could be my mind wanting to see him everywhere because if I can pin him to a page, perhaps I can understand him. But the dates align with a truth I feel in my bones: he belongs to rooms under rooms. He did not arrive at this version of himself by accident.

I copy the line exactly—date, name, the phrase that follows (*circle present, proof offered, thirteenth withheld*)—and sit back, dizzy with the amount of what I don't know. I flex my hand and realize I've been gripping the pen too hard. It stings, and a crescent of ink lives now in the crease of my middle finger.

When I close my eyes to rest them, it isn't darkness that greets me. It's a memory sharpened into a cut. Stained glass, the red robe of a woman with no face, the rise of my breath when a mouth touched the place beneath my ear. *She is mine.* The heat that answered that sentence flares for a breath and recedes, leaving me cold. I stack the books carefully, as if any sudden motion might crack whatever thin shell is holding me together.

Time takes on archive-speed here. Errand slow, oxygen building even slower. The grad assistant dims the lights to their evening setting without apologizing to the clocks. I ride the quiet into the next vein of research—microfilmed local papers, each sheet humming under the machine like a captive insect. Crisp headlines about donors and alumni births give way to lower-profile notices. A fire at the edge of campus, with no injuries reported. A faculty resignation that reads like a covered wound— "freak candle accident" blamed for damage to a chapel door. In a photograph of the door, burned tracery curls outward like a signature. I copy the pattern. It matches the arch etched on the obsidian door in the tunnel where I said yes.

When my eyes ache, I switch to the digital terminal and drop the pretense entirely. I search Inkbound Society, Blackmoor, knowing I'll get nothing worth trusting, and I'm right. Message boards full of bored bravado, a blog post about "secret rites" that reads like a dare. I search thirteen flames and fall down a hole lined with conspiracy and poor typography. I search the names of legacies and for some reason, *Embergrave* strikes a chord deep within my soul. I search Marlowe, Blackmoor society, and get a series of references that could belong to any Marlowe—donor acknowledgments, faculty citations—all except for *one*. A century-old paper by an Adrian J. Marlowe with a title that makes something under my skin rise to meet it. *On Constraint and the Architecture of Obsession*. The abstract is two sentences long and perfect. The byline dates to a year that makes no sense if the man who taught my class today is the same one who wrote it.

I print it before the system can forget me. The paper spits from the machine with a small victorious sigh. The grad assistant glances up and then away, conspiracy averted by mutual disinterest.

I don't stop. I can't. The pull now is a physical thing, a gravity in my ribs. I search for Embergrave without knowing why and get a handful of results that are not results at all—fantasy novels, a goth band, a genealogical footnote that dead-ends. Still, the word looks right in the search bar, like a door I haven't learned how to open yet.

Hours pass measured by the click of keys and the scratch of my pen. I fill pages with fragments. Dates that recur, names that vanish, a list of rooms on campus that share an architectural quirk—arched thresholds whose carvings almost meet. Twice I think I hear someone breathe behind me and look up, only to find my own reflection ghosted on the window. I laugh at myself and the sound startles the quiet, dying instantly, a candle pinched out with two fingers.

I push back from the table and stand to stretch. The room tilts for a heartbeat, a slow unmooring, like the floor remembered another life as water. I grip the chair back and breathe until the world remembers itself. Hunger hits then, late and sharp. I unearth the square of chocolate from my pocket and let it dissolve on my tongue like a bribe paid to my better sense.

When I sit again, I trade the ledger for a thin folder labeled only Chapel—maintenance. Boring, but useful. Work orders, signatures, the invisible handwriting of a campus keeping itself intact. In three different decades, the same anomaly. Service called for "lamp failures" that aren't electrical, "soot on mullions" with no source, "scent of roses" noted in a hand that's trying not to sound superstitious. My mouth goes dry at that—roses in a room with no flowers—and I write the dates in a column. They make their own rhythm. The column looks like a metronome keeping time for a song I haven't learned.

I check the clock and jolt. Closing time slipped by half an hour ago. The grad assistant does the polite hovering of a man who needs to lock up but has learned not to rush the desperate. "Ten minutes?" he mouths. I nod, grateful, and gather what I can into order that will make sense to me tomorrow. The printed abstract, my notes, the symbol copied three times in three different pens as if I could force it to confess by repetition.

On the way out I pause at the glass case near the exit—the one I always ignore because it wears its museum voice so proudly. Tonight the display is local "oddities". A silver candleholder engraved with vinework that almost hides the tiny pentagram tucked among roses, a photo of the old chapels' interior before renovations, a scrap of ribbon in a faded crimson that could be any ceremonial color from any decade. The placard lists donors in a sober column. Halfway down I find the line I didn't know I was looking for. *Anonymous*, by way of the Marlowe Collection. My reflection in the glass looks tired and older than the hour should make me. I force myself to turn away.

Up in the lobby the lights are brighter than they need to be. Students cluster around vending machines, a girl laughing too loudly at nothing. I shrink from it, step into the mild dark outside and breathe air that hasn't been filtered. The night carries the metallic promise of snow again. The lamps along the path throw steady halos on the walk. I tell myself not to check windows. Not to scan doorways. Not to wonder which shadow has the right height to be a man who knows how to stand still. I don't look. I keep moving.

My apartment receives me with the same small permission as always, hinges polite. I dump my bag and head straight for the corkboard on the wall. Red thread maps the city, pushpins mark dates and names that don't belong together until they do. I add three new lines—Inkbound—chapel, Marlowe—collection, flame—thirteenth withheld—and step back. The pattern is still wrong but less wrong than yesterday. A good sign or a dangerous one… I cannot tell.

I shower too hot and dress in the softest crime I own—old T-shirt, socks that would embarrass me if anyone were here. I brew tea I won't drink and sit at the table with the abstract from 19—whatever year that paper insists it came from. Constraint and the Architecture of Obsession. The voice inside the paragraph is the same as the one that lectured this morning, pared to bone, unwilling to pretend the world is anything but geometry and will. A line near the end makes me sit very still: *To make a clean result, remove theater from the equation and let the structure choose its end.*

I don't know if I agree. I don't know if I'm the equation or the error term he keeps circling.

A breeze presses against the window—not enough to rattle it, just enough to say I was here. The hum under my skin answers, smaller now, steady. I touch the place beneath my ear and feel warmth bloom under the skin, shy and certain. I don't think it's only memory anymore. I think it's a mechanism, and it's learning me.

Jessica texts: Make it home?

Me: Yes.

Jess: Sleep. Promise?

Me: I'll try.

Jess: Liar. Be safe.

Me: You too.

I put my phone face down and stare at the invitation I've refused to acknowledge all day—the memory of wax and sigil, the promise of tomorrow's hour. I am not naïve enough to believe a meeting can explain a life. But I am also not naive enough to pretend the life I've been living fits anymore.

The tea has gone cold. My notes blur into nonsense, the words Inkbound, truth, fire repeating until they lose shape. Outside, a siren passes and fades, and the quiet that follows feels like the city holding its breath.

I should sleep. I should stop turning the same thought over until it sparks. But when I close my eyes, I see his hand against the obsidian door, the light spilling from the cracks like blood turned gold. I see the mark below my collarbone, the way it answered him before I even knew the question.

Every sensible part of me says to stay away. To run. But sense has never burned like this.

I move to the window and look out across the campus. The bell tower is a silhouette against a bruised sky, its windows dim, its stones older than memory. Somewhere beneath it, a door waits. A truth waits.

The hum in my wrist syncs to my pulse—slow, steady, certain. Not asking. Calling.

I whisper into the glass, "Fine. Tomorrow."

The word lands like a match on dry paper. The hum steadies, satisfied.

I don't pack. I don't plan. I just stand there a moment longer, watching the city settle into its night, knowing that when morning comes, everything ordinary will end.

Chapter 25

The stairs remember me. Each echo finds its twin in memory—the first night, the terror, the light that wasn't light. Now? It's different. The fear has shifted its weight into something crisp, a kind of hunger dressed as resolve. I know what waits below, or think I do, and that's worse.

Adrian walks half a step ahead, the hem of his black coat brushing the old stone. His lantern burns blue-white tonight instead of gold, the flame bending in ways that defy breath and wind. I match my pace to his, though the air is thicker here, viscous almost, like wading through someone else's dream. The deeper we go, the more the pulse in my wrist syncs with the faint vibration of the walls. The Society calls this the descent. The name *fits*.

When we reach the obsidian door, there is no hesitation. I've seen it before, felt its weight in my bones. The runes shimmer faintly as Adrian presses his palm to the surface. His lips shape words that twist and bite the air—ancient, guttural, not meant for human throats. The symbols bloom in response, gold laced with red, like veins catching fire. The door yields with a groan older than language.

The chamber beyond isn't as shocking the second time, but it's no less overwhelming. The same vaulted ribs of black stone stretch overhead, lit by thousands of candles whose flames refuse to flicker. The air is heavy with incense—sandalwood, myrrh, iron. The smell of ritual. Crimson-robed figures line the perimeter, their masks carved to mimic beasts and angels, eyes hollow. The murmuring quiets when we enter.

Adrian's hand finds the small of my back, steady, possessive in its restraint. "Tonight," he murmurs, voice roughened by something more than smoke, "you stop being a guest."

He leads me to the dais. A goblet rests on an altar of volcanic glass, its surface catching the light in fractured crimson and gold. Inside, the liquid shifts too slowly to be wine—thicker, darker, glinting with faint veins of light that seem to move when I don't. The scent rising from it is metallic, electric, threaded with something sweet enough to make my teeth ache.

"The binding draught," Adrian says quietly. His tone carries the weight of ritual, every syllable deliberate. "You will drink, and you will offer blood in return. Afterward, the bond will recognize you."

My throat tightens. "Bond?"

His gaze meets mine, unreadable, those green eyes flickering like they're lit from somewhere behind. "Between the life you've known," he says, "and the one waiting for you beyond this night."

The words land heavy, cold, wrong in a way that makes my pulse stumble. I stare at the goblet, then back at him. "You make it sound like crossing a line I can't uncross."

"That's because it is."

My stomach knots. "And if I don't?"

"Then you'll go on as you have," he says simply. "As if none of this ever existed. But understand, Octavia—some doors, once seen, never close again."

I reach for the goblet, fingers trembling despite myself. The liquid clings to the sides, darker than ink, thicker than blood. I pause for a moment, deliberating, warring with myself. In the end, I choose knowledge. When it touches my lips, it tastes of copper and stormwater, of something ancient enough to recognize me before I recognize it. Heat rushes down my throat, spilling through me like wildfire.

Adrian catches my wrist before I sway. "Now," he whispers, "the offering."

One of the masked figures steps forward, handing him a blade slender as a quill. The hilt gleams bone-white. He turns my palm upward, eyes never leaving mine. "Do you trust me?"

"I don't know."

"Good. Trust is for children." His thumb strokes once across my wrist before the blade kisses my skin. The cut is clean, bright pain blooming into heat. Blood wells up—dark, almost black in this light—and when it hits the altar's surface, the glass drinks it. The room hums.

A low chant begins, rhythmic and slow, each syllable a vibration through the soles of my feet. The symbols carved into the altar ignite, racing outward until the entire floor pulses with light. My vision wavers. I see smoke twisting into shapes—wings, flame, a crown suspended in ash. My pulse beats with the rhythm of the chant.

"Breathe," Adrian says, voice close to my ear. His hand settles over mine, fingers slick with both our blood. "This is the point of no return, Octavia. After this, nothing you touch will ever remain ordinary."

The heat rises until my skin feels too tight. Sparks scatter from my fingertips, gold and crimson threading the air. My hair lifts as if caught in a current. Somewhere deep inside, something breaks—no, unfolds. The energy rushes through me, down my spine, curling low in my belly until I'm sure I'll combust.

Then, silence.

The candles steady. The chant stops. The air tastes of rain on metal.

When I open my eyes, the room is wrong. The faces of the Society—masks of bone and crimson cloth—are angled toward me in a silence so dense it feels like a hand on my throat. Their stillness isn't passive. It's waiting. Adrian releases my hand slowly, as if unhooking me from something sharp. The cut across my palm has already sealed, leaving only a thin crescent mark glowing faintly like a coal.

"What did you do to me?" My voice breaks on the question.

"What you asked for," he says, but his tone isn't calm—it's low, taut, like a wire drawn too tight. "You let it in."

The hum under my skin is no hum at all now. It's a pulse, a whispering vibration at the base of my spine, a heat coiling up my ribs as if something were crawling free. My breath turns shallow. "Let what in?"

He steps closer. His shadow folds over mine, and his breath ghosts my cheek like smoke. "Not what," he says softly. "Who."

My heart stumbles. A flicker of gold sparks across my vision and dies. I clutch my stomach. "This isn't—this isn't normal—"

"No," he agrees. "It's not."

My knees want to buckle but I don't let them. The thing inside me—hot, slick, and hungry—stirs as if it's been listening for this moment all along. "I want the truth."

He leans closer, his voice a pressure against my skin. "Your blood isn't empty. It carries fire older than this place, older than *me*. That what you thought was hunger is *inheritance*."

"I don't understand—" My voice scrapes out as a hiss. "You're talking like I was made for this."

"Not made," he murmurs, a flicker of something almost like hunger behind his eyes. "*Unbound.*"

His fingers lift and brush the hollow of my throat where light still lingers faintly beneath the skin. The touch is light but it's like pressing a switch. My pulse jumps, and the glow spreads a fraction farther. Panic claws at my ribs. "Stop—just—stop—what does this mean?"

He doesn't answer right away. His gaze drops to my mouth, and the crowd begins to murmur again—soft, reverent, a sound like ritual breath. The blood on the altar still gleams wet and red, the air metallic and sweet. The thing in me stretches, arching against my skin, and for a heartbeat I swear my shadow moves without me.

Adrian takes my face in his hands, and the gesture is both command and confession. "It means," he says finally, voice pitched so low I almost miss it, "that what's waking in you isn't something I can cage. It means you're standing on the edge of a truth that will burn everything you've used to hold yourself together. And it means—" His thumb drags once against my jaw, a tremor he doesn't quite disguise. "It means I will be the one standing closest when it happens. Whether that makes me your shield or your undoing..." He lets the words hang, dangerous, unfinished.

The mark on my palm pulses hot, the light at my throat flaring in response. My breath comes fast. I don't know if I'm shaking from fear or from the thing inside me pressing against my skin like a second heartbeat. All I know is that I'm not the girl who walked down the stairs anymore—and I don't know what will rise in her place.

Before I can speak, the candles flare all at once, flooding the chamber in gold so bright it hurts. For an instant I see everything—the runes beneath the floor pulsing like a heartbeat, the masks watching, the threads of light connecting every person in the room like veins in a living thing.

Then it fades, leaving only the sound of my pulse echoing in my ears.

Adrian steps back. "It is done."

The others bow deeper, whispering words I don't know but somehow understand: *welcome, flamebound.*

My knees threaten to give, but he's already there, steadying me. "Easy," he murmurs. "The first awakening burns the hardest."

"What happens now?"

He studies me for a long moment. "Now," he says, "you learn control. Or the fire controls *you.*"

I look at him, at the faint trace of blood still staining his hand, and realize I've already crossed whatever line there was. The girl who hesitated at the door is gone. What remains is something new—something lit from within.

As he leads me back up the stone steps toward the night air, the hum inside me doesn't fade. It grows, steady and sure, like the beginning of a song I already know the words to.

Chapter 26

Adrian

The night takes us back in one deep breath, cold enough to salt the tongue. Stone sweats where the catacomb mouth exhales, a square of dark recessed under the cloister arch. She steps out first and the air touches her like a shock—hair lifting, breath making a small white signature before the wind edits it away. The wool of her coat has kept the velvet's heat. I can smell it when she moves—clean fiber, a thread of smoke from the candles below, the metallic after-scent of ritual. The campus is pared down by November. Lawns crisped to a dull gleam, bare trees showing their intentions, lamps making islands on the paths. Somewhere a maintenance cart hums, invisible, practical, enough to remind the world it is still itself.

She says nothing. That is best. Words this soon would force her to choose shape before sensation. I walk beside her, half a pace offset, so the shadow of my coat never quite folds over hers. The stone steps hold the night's thin frost, deadly glittering jewels that beguile you with their beauty. She takes them carefully, attention careful even now. The hand that touched the altar stays curled inside her pocket. I know the mark the cut left—a crescent so faint you'd miss it unless you were looking for the places where a body changes its name.

"Cold?" I ask, not because I need the answer—her shoulders already said it—but because sound eases altitude changes.

"A little." Her voice is quiet, worn down at the edges, but it holds. She does not tremble. She does not lean.

The car unlocks with a blink of white and a courtesy glow, mundane as a kitchen light and therefore comforting. I open the door, and she slides in with small care, coat settling around the black velvet like dark water. The cabin's heat rises at once—engine low, leather warming, the faint ionized scent of the cabin filter scrubbing the night out of the air. I take the driver's seat and do not look at her until the gate's iron has shut behind us and the tires have decided to trust the road. A student crosses two blocks away with a pizza box held like an offering, a street light hums, a bus sighs. Blackmoor's late hour has always been civilized about its ghosts.

She watches the campus fall away in the mirror—quadrangle, library, the chapel's small steeple that pretends it belongs to an older country. "How long have you known?" She asks.

"Long enough to be certain," I say. "Not long enough to be careless."

Her head tips against the window for two seconds. The glass fogs, then clears. "You make certainty sound like a sin."

"In rooms like the one we left," I say, "it can be."

Silence. The city adjusts itself to our passing. Storefronts stacked in tasteful brick, their displays dark. A laundry open late, a man smoking with his shoulder to the wind, a crosswalk sign counting down to nobody. Her shadow on the dash is steady. Twice her hand flexes inside the coat pocket as if testing the cut's memory. When she turns, the gold at her throat is gone, the skin unlit. Good. The power has decided to rest. If it unravels too quickly that it can answer to anger or fear, it will adopt their grammar.

"Where are we going?" she asks.

"To my home," I say. "You wanted proof. I prefer to show it with paper."

"Paper can be forged."

"Yes." The light changes. We obey. "But it stains when it lies."

She exhales in a small sound that might be misconstrued as assent. When I park, her gaze climbs the front of the house the way climbers study a face. Not for decoration but for holds. No adjectives from her mouth—monstrous, imposing, beautiful—only the mechanics of appraisal, the way a person trained to survive looks for corners. I unlock the door and let the cedar answer first. The house always offers its oldest truth before any others. She pauses inside the threshold and inhales as if to test whether the air will accept her. It does. Houses that have kept too long a silence sometimes resist—hinges catch, floorboards complain, the old fire sulks. Tonight everything obeys because it knows what I bring in.

"Shoes?" she asks, glancing at the entry bench.

"Leave them," I say. "The floors won't mind." It sounds domestic and therefore wrong. I do not correct it. Wrong things can be useful if the mind is tired of beauty.

I take her to the study because that is where the myth and the math share a table. The room makes its argument in old wood and order. Books shelved by a logic that has earned its labels, vellum boxes stacked with their edges true, a worktable with a blotter that has never had to apologize for ink. The fire sits low, efficient, a heart that understands cadence. On the desk, arranged the way a surgeon sets his tray—what she came to see.

She stops a pace from the edge and does not touch anything. Her restraint is not submission. No, it is respect for the tool. Good.

"Octavia," I say, and when she looks up, I nod to the chair. "Sit."

She chooses the left-hand seat. Not the one guests take, not the one thieves take—the one that keeps the window in sight while putting her back to a wall. She could have been trained for this or born to it. The bond always blurs those distinctions.

I lay the first box in the pool of lamplight and lift the lid. The scent climbs—linen, dust, a thread of oil. I remove the adoption decree last because it should not greet her first. People mistake beginnings for causes.

"Start here," I say, and set down a sheet of onion-skin so thin the light almost erases it. The crest there is older than any municipal symbol pretends to be. A stylized flame inside a torc, the metal worked to look like plaited wire, two small marks at the base the color of rust until you notice they are not rust and not drawn—pressed into the paper while it was still wet, as if the emblem remembered heat. EMBERGRAVE, the caption says, in a house hand that knew how to be handsome without flirting.

She leans forward. The lamplight finds the auburn threads in her hair and writes them in copper. "This is... eighteenth century? Earlier?"

"Late eighteenth. The owner cataloged his life twice: once as inventory, once as wager. The wager is the set with nicer paper."

"Wager?"

"You'll meet better stories. The useful part is the shape." I set a second sheet beside the first—a later crest, the same core image but simplified by a hand that disliked ornament. The caption is clipped: EMBERGRAVE—NORTHERN LINE—HOLD OF FLAME. Below it, smaller: *thirteen kept*; *one carried*. If she asks which, I will not answer. Not yet.

Her mouth makes the shape of a question and decides not to spend it. She looks instead, eyes moving from line to line, teaching the brain to see what the eyes already have. "Why show me crests?"

"Because they persist when laws change. Families burn, sell, flee. The mark survives because it is easier to carry by accident."

She sits back. The line between her brows says she is filing the remark where she keeps the sentences that will argue with her at three in the morning.

The second box holds the ledger. Not the one the Society maintains, the one that pretends to be a church account book. I open to a ribboned page—2000. Three lines, the middle one faint, the right margin carrying a note in a small clean hand that wastes nothing. *Child hidden under salt and ash. Father unrecorded. Mother— a loop instead of a name, the same cramped figure of infinity that refuses to close. Token left: ember sign. Flame unnamed. Relocated per instruction.*

She reads it twice. The first pass teaches her shock, the second teaches her grammar. "Salt and ash."

"Old protections. Older than spite."

"And the mother? Why the loop?"

"Because names bring people to your door. A mark keeps the door but confuses the visitor."

Her hand finds the edge of the paper without touching ink. "Relocated per instruction... Whose?"

"People who were very good at speaking as if they worked for benevolence. They were not always wrong. They were rarely right."

She looks up. I can see the shape of the next thought arrive and choose to live. "This is mine."

"Yes."

"Not metaphorically."

"No."

She doesn't tremble now either. The color drains, returns. She steadies on breath alone. "Show me all of it."

I do. The municipal forms first. A name erased, a name written, a date moved from one line to another because a clerk preferred neat columns to truth. Then the university record that the library never meant to keep—notes on the Embergrave fund, quietly dormant, a donor list that ends abruptly in the same year the ledger offers its ash. Then the parish notation in the back of a family Bible, made by a hand that wrote names as prayers and nicknames as tenderness: *Octavia—found, not lost*. It is not her adoptive family's book. It belonged to someone who loved the act of writing as much as the content. The letters are too careful to be casual, their care says grief learned how to make itself useful.

She reads that one three times. When she looks at me, her eyes are darker, not from tears—she does not afford herself their blur—but from the way light behaves when it hits iron. "How long," she says again, and the repetition now is not for information but for the nervous system.

"Not from the beginning," I say. "I knew of you then, but not why you'd matter. I didn't start looking until later—when the pattern began surfacing, when your name appeared where it shouldn't have. After that, the paper behaved."

"And you didn't tell me."

"You weren't initiated."

"I'm not a dog you house-train." No heat in it, only bite.

"No," I say. "You're a room that writes its own map. I waited until the door belonged to you."

Her mouth tilts as if she means to kick me and decides to count instead. "The Society."

"What about it."

"You're its head."

"Tonight made that clear to some who needed reminding."

"And you want me in it."

"I want you *above* it."

Her laugh is small and sincere in its disbelief. "You expect me to believe that *you*—Adrian Marlowe, collector of rules—want *me* above the club that crowns you."

"I expect you to read what I put in front of you and notice that none of it says club." I set the last piece down—thin vellum, edges crisp, the ink browned by time but not ashamed of it. A diagram of flame as a sequence, not a picture. Thirteen circles arranged in a pattern that does not please the eye until you give it your breath. The key at the bottom is tiny and accurate. I touch one circle with a finger. "These are not gods."

"What are they?"

"Memoranda. How the first people who didn't die wrote down what they remembered. The Society mistakes liturgy for law. Your line did not. It kept the candles as reminders. It kept the thirteenth out of reach because it knew better than to light it in a room full of men who liked spectacle."

She leans in. Her hair catches the lamplight again. The velvet of her dress, now warm from the car, has learned the house's temperature and sits close to her skin. She holds still because stillness serves clarity. "Which one is mine."

"None," I say. She looks at me and for a second the disappointment flares because she thinks I am playing a game. I am not. "You do not get to be owned by a circle on a dead man's page. You are of a line that carried knowledge about the circles, yes. You are flamebound in the sense that flame has decided you are a vessel that will not insult it. But the power is not the diagram. It is the accuracy with which you choose" —I tap the space between the ninth and the thirteenth— "to proceed."

"Explain." She keeps her voice quiet. The quiet makes the request more dangerous. She is done being performed at.

"The world likes categories. It keeps them in glass because glass is easier to worship than correction. Your family preserved a set of corrections. They lived long enough to discover that what most people call a miracle—is *method*. They wrote the methods as flame because early minds learned better by picture than by algebra. Your adoption severed you from the vocabulary, not the phenomenon. Tonight returned the vocabulary to the body. Your mind will hate that for a time."

She exhales. The breath is almost a laugh—almost. "And Embergrave means what, exactly. That I'm—what was the phrase downstairs—*flamebound*."

"It means your body is more honest about cause and effect than most. It also means there are people who will decide what to call that honesty for you if you let them."

"You."

"If I wanted to name you," I say, "I would have done it years ago."

"You didn't know me years ago."

My mouth curves, almost a smile but not quite. "No," I say softly. "But something in me did—the part that remembers before memory, the pulse that's older than my own. It knew your shape in the dark, long before I ever saw your face."

I stack the papers back into the order I pre-fer—crest, ledger, decree, diagram. I leave the parish line on top because it did not ask to be helpful and therefore deserves to be. "The short version, because your blood is still louder than your mind. Yes, you are Embergrave by origin, Hartwell by love, flamebound by right, initiate by choice. You can walk away and the city will continue to be itself. The bond will not starve you for that. It will only wait."

She studies me. The room helps her. Pine grip under her fingers, the delicate scratch of the fire making its own minutes, the light off the glass giving back what it steals. The velvet at her knee reflects a thread of ember from the grate, and for a beat I want to touch it purely to know if the heat on my knuckle would come from cloth or her. I do not.

"You said 'by origin.' You mean I was adopted."

"Yes."

"That ledger. And the municipal erasures."

"Yes."

"My mother." The word stumbles like a child, then learns its feet. "You don't have her name."

"No." The admission does not cost me pride, it costs me patience. "She left a mark instead of a signature."

"The loop."

"The loop," I agree. "A way to say 'do not follow' in a room where men with stamps mistake curiosity for care."

"Do you think she's alive."

"I think the right question is whether she is a person who can be found by the methods the world honors. The answer is different than yes or no."

She looks back to the parish line. Her thumb rests near the words found, not lost. She doesn't touch them. "You want to show me a door and then let me decide if it opens."

"Yes."

"You're very good at making your control look like mercy."

"Mercy is another word for control," I say. "I try to be accurate about my aims."

She sits with that. The house counts three breaths, and the study counts the flame's collapse from small cone to low bell. When she finally stands, it is not abrupt. The velvet releases the chair and remembers itself. She does not sway. Her color is back. She smooths her coat sleeve as if the fabric had been listening and she wants it to know she is still in command of her hands.

"What happens if I say no," she asks.

"I take you home," I say. "I give you copies of what you read, not originals. I teach you three things that will keep you from bleeding out if you light yourself by accident. I attend your next seminar and behave as if I am another man. I do not come to your door unless you invite me."

"And if I say yes."

"Then you sleep *here*, without being watched, and in the morning we teach your body the quiet versions of the words it learned to shout tonight. We go to the library after it opens and you read the pieces I couldn't take from rooms that like to be seen guarding their treasures. You hold fire in a cup that does not burn. You learn to tell the difference between hunger and utility. You decide which parts of the Society deserve oxygen and which deserve a roof that collapses at midnight."

Her mouth does that almost laugh again. "You never say too little."

"I am trying to say enough."

She looks around the room as if expecting it to contradict me. It does not. The house is good at keeping its opinions to itself. Outside, a car passes. Its headlights rake the east window and leave. The road remembers us. The city continues.

"Keep the ledger page out," she says. "Not because I want to look at it. Because it makes me angry, and anger will be useful if I'm tired."

"You will be tired."

"I am now."

"Guest room," I say, and gesture. "You can lock the door from the inside. The hinges are honest."

She snorts. The sound is small and human and therefore significant. She takes the copy I have already made of the decree, not the original. The parish line, photocopied clean. The diagram, traced by my own hand because I do not permit scanners to teach secrets to machines. The crest, printed on cheap paper on purpose so she will not mistake gloss for proof. She tucks the pages into the inner pocket of her coat the way one tucks a narrow knife. She does not thank me. Good. Gratitude would cheapen the accuracy of the hour.

At the doorway, she hesitates. Not for effect. For engineering. She is deciding what sentence keeps tomorrow from lying.

"Adrian," she says without turning, "if I walk away later—if I decide this was you showing me a museum and I prefer the sidewalk—will you try to stop me."

"I will try to make sure you are not harmed by the parts of this that do not respect sidewalks," I say. "If that looks like stopping, you may call it what you like."

"And if I walk toward it."

"I will make sure the room you enter does not lie about its oxygen."

She nods once, which is an agreement with herself, not with me, and goes down the corridor the way a person who is not afraid of sleeping in a stranger's house goes down a corridor. Her shoulders square, head level, all the small muscles in the back awake. The guest room door closes. The latch behaves. The house registers the new pattern of breath and adjusts without complaint.

I return to the study, replace the documents in their boxes in the order I never deviate from, set the adoption decree one layer down so that I cannot be tempted to lift it again before there is someone on the other side of the table who has earned the next line. I watch the ember in the grate settle to a core that will hold until morning and feel, not for the first time, the other rhythm thread under the wrist—older than my heart, stubborn as a metronome that refuses to accept the room's tempo. It answers something across the hall, slowing when hers slows.

The window shows the street in its exact proportions. Two maples, one poor decision by a developer, a length of curb paint no one respects, and a faint sheen where the road has learned to be honest about winter. The sky has bleached to a paler dark. Snow is a rumor whispering in the wind. The city does not care whether the eldest house of flame remembers how to name itself. That is our work. The study agrees. The Society will learn to agree or remember how to be quiet. The thirteenth stays cold until its room is true.

I turn out the lamp because the hour deserves dark. In the doorway, I pause, listening for my own tendency to invent mercy where there is only appetite. The house gives me back the plain report: breath, heat, weight, paper, ash. The small sound a coat makes when it is set carefully over a chair so it will not crease. The soft agreement of linen when a body decides sleep is a tool, not a theater.

I allow myself one sentence, silent, without ceremony. It is not a vow. It is an engineering note.

Build the oxygen first. Then light what must be lit.

CHAPTER 27

The house wakes before I do.

Not loudly—no clatter, no sunlight shouting through glass—but with the quiet rearrangement of air that means something ancient has decided to keep breathing. I hear the soft click of pipes expanding, the low exhale of the heating system, the faint hiss of coffee blooming somewhere down the hall. The smell hits next. A dark roast, cedar smoke, the clean metallic tang of rain against stone. For a long moment I lie still and listen to the morning decide what kind of day it wants to be.

My body feels heavy, used in ways that don't bruise but still remember. The last thing I recall before sleep was the sound of Adrian's footsteps leaving the hall—the careful cadence of a man who trusts walls more than silence. Now the weight of everything that happened presses behind my ribs. The altar, the bond, the blood. I should be panicking. Instead, there's only a strange, measured calm. The kind that comes after a storm, when everything broken is too wet to catch fire again.

I swing my legs over the side of the bed. The guest room is spare but elegant, its palette almost monastic—slate, white, the deep brown of polished wood. A single window overlooks the street, blurred by a thin veil of frost. My coat hangs over the chair, the black velvet dress beneath it like a secret half-remembered dream. On the dresser rests a folded set of clothes that aren't mine—dark leggings, a long-sleeved top, both smelling faintly of clean laundry and cedar. A note lies on top, written in his unmistakable hand.

For the morning. Coffee. Training after breakfast.

— A.

The audacity of him makes me laugh under my breath, though it comes out more like disbelief. He plans my mornings now. I dress anyway. The fabric is soft and fitted, moving with me like something meant to learn my shape. When I catch my reflection, I hardly recognize the woman staring back. There's a faint shimmer under my skin, a warmth that wasn't there before. My eyes look brighter—not color, but light. As if someone has replaced me with a version that remembers too much.

The corridor outside is hushed. I follow the smell of coffee to the kitchen. It's all clean lines and dark counters, the only ornament a vase of dying chrysanthemums near the window. Adrian stands by the stove, sleeves pushed up, dark athletic clothes fitting his frame with infuriating precision. He looks more human like this—no tie, no armor of professorly restraint—but the ease is a deception. Even now, every motion feels deliberate, a choreography of control.

"Morning," he says without turning. His voice is lower than usual, gravel rubbed with silk. "You sleep?"

"Some." I hesitate in the doorway, then add, "You?"

He pours coffee into two mugs, slides one toward me across the counter. "I don't require much."

That's not an answer, but it's exactly the kind he gives. I take a sip, grateful for the heat. The flavor is sharp and grounding, a bitterness that anchors the room.

He studies me over the rim of his own cup. "How do you feel?"

"Like I've been rewritten," I say. "Half in a language I don't speak."

"That's accurate." He sets his mug down. "Your body's adapting to the bond. To itself."

"That's supposed to make sense?"

"It will," he says, and gestures to the table. "Sit. There's something you should hear before we start."

I obey more easily than I want to admit. The chair is cool beneath my palms. Adrian moves around the kitchen with the quiet assurance of someone who's been awake for hours. When he finally sits across from me, a folder materializes between his hands—thin, gray, anonymous. He slides it across.

Inside are photographs. Not glossy prints but archival copies—yellowed, grainy, the kind that smell faintly of toner and time. Each one bears a different woman. Different eras. The common thread is the same. Always dark eyes, sharp cheekbones, something bright and dangerous coiled just behind the gaze.

"These were taken over the last two centuries," he says. "Members of the Embergrave line, or what's left of it."

I glance up. "And you think I'm one of them."

"I know you are. What I don't know," he continues, "is why the blood didn't show itself until now."

I trace the edge of one photograph with my thumb. "Maybe it was waiting."

"For what?"

"For a reason," I say, and meet his eyes. "For you."

Something flickers there—something unguarded—but it's gone before I can name it. He leans back, fingers steepled beneath his chin. "When you drank last night, the bond accepted you. That much we knew would happen. But it also... reacted differently than any initiation I've seen. The energy wasn't purely flamebound. There was something else—something that resisted control."

"What does that mean?"

"It means your blood carries a dual signature." His voice slows, careful. "Part of you behaves like a succubus—the charm, the hunger, the ability to draw power through desire. But the rest doesn't match any succubi lineage I've recorded. It's older. Hotter. And far more volatile."

I laugh, short and brittle. "So I'm a walking contradiction."

"More like a forgotten equation," he says. "One that refuses to balance."

The tension between us sharpens. I can feel the air shifting, charged in that subtle way that precedes lightning. "You said it reacted. How?"

He studies me a moment too long. "When your power surfaced, the temperature in the chamber rose twelve degrees. The candles burned white. Every masked member felt it."

"That's impossible."

"Tell that to the wax that melted through the altar." His mouth twitches—a humorless almost-smile. "You carry fire, Octavia. The kind that remembers creation."

The words settle under my skin like an electrical current. I don't want to believe them, but denial feels like pretending gravity is optional. "So what now?"

"Now we teach you control." He rises, draining the last of his coffee. "Finish that. We'll start outside."

The air hits like baptism—cold, clean, unsparing. Frost still powders the grass, catching the early light in silver threads. The house backs onto a walled garden, spacious enough to pass for a private courtyard. A training mat has been laid out near a line of leafless trees. The rest of the space hums with quiet expectancy.

Adrian moves across the yard with the kind of grace that belongs to predators and old gods. The dark fabric of his shirt clings to his shoulders, the morning light catching in his hair. I hate the way my eyes track him, the way my pulse misbehaves in his presence. "You look like someone who plans to spar," I say, because talking feels safer than watching.

"Observation is part of the lesson," he replies. "But yes. I intend to see what the bond awakened."

He steps closer until the heat of him brushes against my front. "Hold out your hand."

I do. He takes it in both of his, turning it palm-up. "You remember the cut?"

The skin is smooth now, faintly luminous. "It healed overnight."

"As it should. Try to focus there. Breathe. Think of the moment before you drank."

"I'd rather not."

His tone softens. "It's not punishment. Just recall the sensation."

I inhale slowly, letting memory unfurl. The hum, the heat, the pull. Something stirs beneath my skin, small but insistent. My palm warms, and a flicker of gold races along my wrist, threads to my fingertips, then winks out.

Adrian's breath catches almost imperceptibly. "Good. Again."

"I didn't do anything."

"You allowed it. That's the point."

We repeat the motion. Each time, the flicker lasts longer, burning brighter before vanishing. The third attempt leaves a faint scorch mark on the air, a filament of light suspended between us. I stare, stunned.

"What is that?" I whisper.

"Evidence." He releases my hand reluctantly. "You're not imagining it."

The line of light fades, leaving only the ghost of warmth between our palms. I flex my fingers, breath shaky. "It feels like something's alive under my skin."

"It is," he murmurs. "And it wants a language."

He steps behind me, close enough that I can feel the low hum of his voice against my spine. "Your power feeds on focus. It will answer impulse first, but intention directs it. Try again, but this time—don't think of the ritual. Think of me."

My throat goes dry. "That sounds dangerous."

"It is." He moves closer still, his breath a whisper at the curve of my neck. "Do it anyway."

I close my eyes. The memory of his mouth, his hands, the way his voice darkened when he said mine—it floods back too easily. The hum erupts, this time fierce and bright. Heat rushes up my arms, my hair lifting with static. Adrian's hands settle lightly at my hips, steadying me as golden sparks spiral outward, fading before they reach the ground.

"Beautiful," he says quietly. "See what honesty looks like."

I open my eyes, heart racing. "That's not control."

"It's the beginning of it." He releases me, though the air still trembles where he stood. "We'll work on restraint later."

I turn to face him. "You said part succubus. What's the other part?"

His gaze meets mine, undecipherable. "I have theories. But I want proof before I hand you a name. Names carry weight."

"That's not an answer."

"It's the only one that won't harm you yet." He nods toward the house. "Come. You should eat something. Power burns through fuel faster than fear."

We walk back in silence, though the silence hums, heavy with unspoken questions. The cold nips at my cheeks, but there's warmth under my skin that doesn't fade with distance. Inside, the fire has climbed higher in the hearth, throwing amber light across the walls. He pours more coffee, this time without asking, and stands near the window, watching frost dissolve from the glass.

"I sent word to the dean," he says finally. "He won't expect you in class this week. I also called the Gazette. They won't be expecting you either."

I blink. "You can just do that?"

"I wrote the letter. He signed it." A pause. "He's one of us. As for the Gazette... The enchantment will hold."

Of course he is. I should have guessed that the Society threads deeper than I can see. Though... I don't know how I feel about him enchanting the employees of the paper. "So I'm your student and your... what, exactly?"

His eyes find mine. "My responsibility."

"That's not what it feels like."

"No," he admits. "It feels like recognition."

The word lands like a touch. *Recognition.* I think of the spark, the warmth, the way my body answered his—like a language I never studied. "And if you're wrong?"

He steps closer until the space between us is the width of a breath. "Then the world has made a very dangerous mistake."

His scent—cedar, smoke, the faint metallic sweetness of blood—wraps around me. For a heartbeat, the bond hums again, soft but insistent, and the air seems to tilt toward him. I should move. I don't.

"Why do I trust you?" I whisper.

"Because your blood remembers me," he says simply. "Even if your mind doesn't."

I look up, and for an instant the room blurs—the fire, the walls, the morning—all dissolving into a single point of heat where his gaze meets mine. Then he steps back, as if he's drawn an invisible line neither of us can yet cross.

"Rest for now," he says. "We'll continue tonight."

When he leaves the room, the air cools too quickly. I stare into my coffee and see my reflection shimmer, faint threads of gold running through the dark surface like veins of light. My hands tremble, not from fear, but from knowing he's right.

Something in me remembers him.

And whatever that something is—it's *waking*.

CHAPTER 28

As afternoon bleeds into evening, Adrian tests me three more times before dinner. By the time the grandfather clock chimes seven, I'm spent—every nerve drawn thin, every muscle trembling from use.

I feel like I'm barely hanging on, but Adrian insists I eat before bed. In truth, I've focused as much as I could today. Being in such close proximity to him makes me lose my head. His scent—cedar, smoke, and something darker—pulls at me like an invisible thread I can't name or sever.

Succubus.

The word tastes like ash on my tongue. Ironic, considering I wore that costume for Halloween. I wonder if Adrian thought of it too—the cruel symmetry of the joke. I don't ask aloud.

We eat in silence, the only sounds the faint clink of cutlery and the low hum of the fire in the next room. I want to speak, to ask what he sees when he looks at me now, but the air between us is too charged, every glance and movement its own language.

Whatever is beneath my skin stirs restlessly, an ache building low in my belly that food cannot touch. It's hunger of another kind—raw, electric, consuming.

Adrian doesn't miss a thing. His nostrils flare, eyes darkening, golden flecks burning like embers in the green. His attention is tangible, a living thing threading the space between us.

"Eat," he murmurs, voice low, the sound almost a vibration beneath my ribs.

I obey, though each bite turns to ash on my tongue. My pulse beats too fast, my breath shallow. The air feels heavy, and I swear he can hear the rhythm of my blood calling to whatever answers in him.

When he finishes, he stands, pushing the chair back in one smooth motion. "You've done enough for today," he says quietly. "Rest. The body remembers best when it isn't at war with itself."

I nod, grateful and frustrated all at once. My limbs feel molten, my mind still humming with the echo of his voice, the shape of his gaze.

He walks me down the hall, past the muted glow of sconces, until my door stands waiting like a beacon, calling me back to bed. Adrian stops just short of it and catches my hand, halting me before I can reach the knob. His fingers are warm, deliberate. His eyes catch mine and hold them, and I freeze—caught, utterly enthralled.

A slow smirk ghosts across his mouth. He lifts my hand, eyes never breaking from mine, and presses his lips to the back of it. The kiss is light but laced with power, a heat that seems to brand rather than soothe. My breath catches, my fingers tightening around his without meaning to.

"You could always..." His voice dips lower, rough silk. "Invite me in."

It's a dangerous suggestion.

The air between us stretches thin. I know what lives there—a flame so bright it feels like it might burn me hollow from the inside out. I want to touch it, to see how far it will go, to see how far I'll go. But even as my pulse trips over itself, the question coils tight. Am I ready to trade teacher for something else? Or is this balance his to keep—an edge he's meant never to cross?

"You decide, Octavia."

His words ring like a chord struck true, and something inside me unclenches. The thing within me screams to let him in, and I do. I open the door without loosening my hold on his hand, tugging him with me. "I've decided."

We cross the threshold—and it isn't like the books. There's no tearing at each other, no frantic ripping of clothes.

This is control at its finest. Patience at its highest virtue.

Golden threads of energy pulse from me now, weaving through my dark bedroom, illuminating it with a dim glow. My light.

He watches me, lowering himself onto the bed with an agonizing slowness that sets my whole body aflame. Sparks dance across my skin—not burning, not setting the room alight, only shimmering, alive.

I undress slowly, swaying my hips with each deliberate removal. My shirt first, then my leggings, socks, and shoes. All that remains is my bare chest and the pair of lacy underwear he'd laid out for me earlier.

I don't hide from his gaze. I let him drink me in.

He beckons me toward him, and I move without hesitation, crossing the space with slow, deliberate steps before settling astride him. My hips begin to move of their own accord, rolling against the hardness I feel at the apex of my thighs.

His hands find my hips, gripping, guiding—pulling me tighter against him until the friction becomes a pulse of its own. "I love it when you don't hide," he murmurs, his mouth finding my neck. "I can feel your heartbeat... it thumps deliciously—for me."

This time, when he bites, I know what to expect. I know what name to give it—*vampire*. I don't shy away. I tilt my head back, offering more, letting him drink. His groan vibrates against my skin, and that same dizzying rush floods through me—ecstasy laced with heat, unraveling thought and language until all that's left is want.

I feel it—the instant he loses control. His grip on me tightens, a tremor of restraint shattering, then he moves with inhuman speed, tossing me onto the bed before covering me with his body like a storm breaking.

His hands are everywhere and still not enough. He strips the last barrier from me, mouth circling the sensitive peak of my nipple, hot and wet, while his fingers slip lower, finding the heat between my legs. "You. Are. *Mine*," he growls, each word a low vibration against my skin as he strokes the slickness there, fingers moving at a punishing, relentless pace. He slides one inside me, curling it in a wickedly sinful way that has me seeing stars. "*Say it.*"

"Yours," I whisper, breathless, toes curling, my whole body strung tight under every stroke of his fingers.

"Again."

"I'm yours—only yours."

He withdraws his fingers and jerks me upward, his strength effortless, until the weight of my body rests on my shoulders. Before I can register the shift, his face is buried between my thighs and I cry out, the sound breaking free. "Adrian!"

His tongue flicks exactly where his fingers had been, devouring me like I'm the last meal he'll ever taste. He groans against me, a low growl that sends shivers up my spine, and drives his tongue inside my heat, licking up every drop as if it belongs to him. My legs quake, my body screaming for release, but still—he doesn't let up.

When I finally come, I scream his name again and again, the golden threads of energy snapping back into my body in a massive wave, pulsing through me. I feel the thing inside me seize it, greedy and wild, drinking it down. My skin glows faintly in the dim light, and Adrian eases me back onto the bed, sliding up beside me, his presence a dark warmth at my edge.

"I want—"

"*Sleep*, my wicked ruin," he murmurs.

Despite myself, my eyes grow heavy, the pull of exhaustion soft and absolute. My body relaxes beside him, sinking into the warmth of his skin, the steady rise and fall of his chest. His arms wrap around me, a cage and a comfort all at once, the heat of him pulling me toward the dark.

The last thing I hear is his voice, low and reverent against my hair—

"So beautiful, my wicked ruin... my sacred flame."

Chapter 29

The morning arrives like an apology it doesn't quite mean. Soft light filters through gauze curtains, too soft for the violence of what came before. I wake tangled in black sheets that still smell like him—cedar and heat and something older, faintly metallic, faintly wrong. My body remembers before my mind does. The delicious ache behind my knees, the phantom press of his hands, the echo of his voice whispering sacred flame against my throat. I lie still, unsure if I'm allowed to move, if the wrong movement will undo whatever fragile truce the night left behind.

Then I feel him. Adrian sits propped against the headboard beside me, half-dressed, the open collar of his black shirt exposing the pale line of his throat. The sight pulls a memory from the dark—a flash of teeth, heat, and the sound of my own name breaking apart on his tongue. My neck still tingles where he bit me, a dull throb that hums in rhythm with my heartbeat. His mark burns faintly beneath my skin, not a wound but a tether.

He's reading something, a leather-bound book balanced on his knee, a mug in one hand, eyes tracing the page as though the night hadn't shattered everything between us. As though this were any ordinary morning.

"Good morning," he murmurs without looking up. His voice is quiet, velvet against the bones of the room. "You were dreaming."

I push myself up slowly, sheets whispering against my skin. "I don't remember."

He glances over, that almost-smile curving his mouth. "You said a name."

"What name?"

"Liora."

The word sits between us, strange and heavy. It doesn't belong to me, not yet—but the sound of it vibrates through my chest like something half-remembered. I shake my head, brushing a hand through my hair. "I don't know anyone by that name."

"You will," he says, and closes the book. "Eat first. Then I'll tell you why the world burned for her."

He rises in one fluid motion, crossing the room to a low table where breakfast waits—steel tray, covered dishes, the silver gleam of utensils that look too refined for this kind of intimacy. I catch the faint trace of cinnamon and coffee before I see the food. Delicious fruit sliced thin enough to be ornamental, bread still warm, a bowl of something golden that glows faintly in the light.

He brings the tray to me and sets it across my lap, the scent of warmth spilling into the air between us. "You need strength," he says. "The binding takes from the body first."

I glance at him. "And then what?"

"Then it starts to give back."

The way he says it makes my pulse trip, but I take the spoon and taste what he's given me. It's sweeter than I expect, laced with spice that blooms behind my teeth. Honey and fire. My throat tightens around the swallow. "What is this?"

"Something from before language learned to name hunger," he says. "Ember Root. The Embergrave line used it during their early rites. It wakes the blood."

"It tastes like it's already awake."

He laughs once—low, pleased, dangerous. "It is now."

We eat in silence for a while, though I feel his gaze flicker toward me more than once. The air hums faintly, alive with something I can't see but can feel in my fingertips, the same golden pulse that had filled the mausoleum. When I finish, he sets the tray aside and leans against the headboard again, watching me.

"You said you'd tell me about her," I remind him. "Liora."

He nods. "And Nytherion. The first two flames. Before the Thirteen, before the world learned to divide creation from desire."

The way he speaks changes when he says their names. His tone slows, deepens. I realize I'm not hearing a story so much as a confession.

"Nytherion was the god of the void," he begins. "He ruled what existed before light—soundless, endless, and alive in its own silence. His was the hunger that shaped the first spark. And Liora... she was the spark. Born of his longing, made of everything he couldn't name. They were not lovers in the mortal sense. They were cause and consequence, mirrored flames."

I listen, drawn in despite myself. His voice becomes rhythm, almost chant.

"When she first opened her eyes, the void flinched," he says softly. "She burned so brightly that Nytherion believed he'd made something perfect. But light is never content to stay still. She wanted to know what lay beyond him. So she tore herself apart to become everything he was not. Stars. Fire. Breath. She created the world and left him behind."

"And he followed?" I ask.

"In his way," Adrian says. "Every shadow you see, every quiet between heartbeats—that is his pursuit. But he never meant to destroy her. He only wanted to be close again. The tragedy of the first flame is not in the burning—it's in the longing that survived it."

His words sink into me like warmth through bone. I can almost see it—the goddess of light, the god of shadow, circling each other through eternity. "You make it sound romantic," I whisper.

He shakes his head. "Romance is too small a word. They were law and disobedience, origin and exile. Without them, there would be no flame, no hunger, no need. Every bond since then—every soul that burns and every one that's consumed—is their echo."

I stare at him, trying to piece together what any of this has to do with me. "Why tell me this now?"

"Because you carry what they left behind," he says simply. "And because you need to understand what you've agreed to."

His gaze slides to the faint mark still visible along my collarbone, where the light had pulsed during the ceremony. "Your blood hums because it remembers her. Liora's fire. But that's not all of you."

I shift under the covers, uneasy. "You think I'm like her."

"I think you're the answer to a question she asked when the stars were still cooling." His eyes meet mine, steady and unreadable. "You're of the Embergrave line. Flameborn, yes—but your power... it bends differently. The Society whispers about the thirteenth flame. Some believe you're proof of it—a new manifestation. I don't know if they're right. Not yet."

The room feels smaller suddenly, the walls drawing in. "And what does that mean, exactly? If I am?"

"It means the world may start changing its shape to accommodate you," he says quietly. "It means the balance that kept Nytherion and Liora apart may not hold. It means every order that pretends to understand divinity will want a piece of your blood."

I can't breathe for a second. "And you?"

His expression doesn't falter, but something flickers behind it—longing, guilt, awe. "I want you alive to decide what to do with it."

Silence stretches between us again, thick as honey. I look down at my hands, flexing my fingers. The faint shimmer beneath the skin glows when I move—gold threads tracing veins like molten script. "You said my blood hums because of her. But there's more, isn't there?"

"There always is," he admits.

"Tell me."

He hesitates. For the first time since I've known him, Adrian Marlowe—the man who could turn knowledge into weapon and silence into art—looks uncertain. "You're not fully... changed," he says finally. "Not yet. The initiation woke part of what's inside you, but not all. The other half of your blood still sleeps."

"And you still don't know what it is."

His jaw tightens. "I told you, I have theories."

"Tell me one."

"I believe," he says slowly, "that the second line in you doesn't come from darkness, but from something rarer. Something that shouldn't exist anymore." His voice drops lower, reverent. "When I touch you, when your power rises—it's not only heat I feel. It's renewal. The kind of energy that doesn't devour, but rebirths. It's... celestial, and yet it burns. That combination shouldn't be possible."

I stare at him, pulse hammering. "What are you saying?"

He meets my eyes. "I think the other half of you might be phoenix-born."

The words fall into me like a spark into oil. I can't speak at first; the concept is too big, too unreal. A phoenix—those were myths buried inside myths, stories used to soften the edges of war and loss. And yet... I remember the fire that never burned me, the light that came from inside.

I shake my head slowly. "You don't know that."

"No," he says. "Not yet."

"Then stop saying it like it's written somewhere."

"I don't need it written." He leans closer, the gold in his eyes brightening to something molten. "I feel it every time your power wakes. Flame answers flame—but what lives in you answers differently. It sings. And when it sings, the air listens."

The room hums faintly, and I realize too late that my pulse is racing again, the same heat coiling beneath my skin. He notices. He always notices. His voice softens, gentles like he's speaking to something fragile.

"Breathe, Octavia."

"I am," I lie.

"You're not," he murmurs, and his hand finds mine where it grips the sheet. His thumb strokes along my knuckles, grounding, electric. "You think fire only destroys because that's all anyone ever let you see it do. But fire remembers creation. It remembers how to build warmth. That's what makes you different."

I don't pull away. I can't. His words sink into me, rewriting the shape of my fear. "Why do you care so much what I am?"

He studies me for a long moment. Then, softly, "Because I've spent a very long time watching flames die out. I want to see what happens when one refuses."

The air between us changes—thickens, darkens. My chest feels too tight. "You make it sound like I'm supposed to save something."

"Not save," he says. "Correct."

"And if I don't want that?"

His gaze flicks briefly to my mouth, then back to my eyes. "Then you'll burn beautifully anyway."

The tension is unbearable. I shift, meaning to move away, but his hand stills me, fingers firm at my wrist. The touch isn't force—it's gravity. "You should rest," he says. "The body always wants to overcompensate after revelation."

"Revelation?"

"That's what last night was," he says. "Your blood remembered itself. The rest will follow."

I pull in a breath, trying to steady myself. "What about you? What do you remember?"

He smiles faintly, and for once, it looks almost human. "Enough to know that I've spent too long in the dark to stop chasing the light when it finds me."

There's something in his tone that feels like both confession and warning, but I'm too tired to separate them. I sink back against the pillows, the fire still whispering beneath my skin. He reaches over, tucks a stray lock of hair behind my ear, and lets his hand linger just long enough to make me forget every reason I should be afraid.

Outside, the day has faded to ash-blue. The fire in the grate sighs and renews itself. Adrian picks up the book he'd been reading earlier and sets it on the table beside me. The title, in fading script, reads The Sacred Flames.

I trace the letters with one finger. "Is this about them?"

He nods once. "About all of us."

My throat feels tight again. "And how does it end?"

He glances at me, then at the window where the last light dies against the glass. "It doesn't," he says softly. "That's the tragedy—and the promise."

I don't answer. I watch the fire instead, the way it bends without breaking, the way it eats its own shadows. My reflection shimmers in the glass above the mantle—gold-threaded eyes, pulse glowing faintly beneath the skin. Something inside me stirs, recognition threaded with dread.

Adrian watches me watch it. "You're afraid," he says quietly.

"Shouldn't I be?"

"Yes," he says. "But not of what you are. Be afraid of what you'll do when you finally believe me."

The words root deep, somewhere I can't reach. I turn from the window and look at him, really look—his collar open, his eyes still catching light that shouldn't exist, his hand resting near mine like an invitation he already knows I'll take eventually.

The silence holds until the fire sighs again. My pulse finds its rhythm against his. The hum answers.

And for the first time, I understand what he meant when he said revelation. It's not knowledge that undoes you. It's the way truth looks back and waits for you to name it.

I don't. Not yet. But I will.

CHAPTER 30

The field behind Adrian's house holds the cold like a vow. Frost films the grass in pale needles, the ground rigid beneath it, and our breaths unspool in white threads that hang and vanish as if the morning is deciding whether to keep us. We've both dressed in darker colors—black leggings and a charcoal top for me, his long-sleeved shirt the same deep shade as his eyes in shadow.

He sets the mat near the old stone wall where ivy has browned to paper. Beyond it, the trees stand bare, their branches drawn like ink bones against a sky that refuses to warm. The air smells of cedar and iron and the faint smoke that always seems to keep company with him. He watches me take my place, quiet as reading. My heartbeat goes bright in my throat, too fast for rest, too eager for battle.

"Same drill," he says, voice low enough not to shatter the surface of the hour. "Breathe, then listen."

"To what?"

"The hum before the heat."

I make a fist and open it, just to remind my body it belongs to me. Between my ribs, the bond answers like a plucked wire. I draw the air in, cold and sharp, and let it go slowly until I can hear what lives beneath my pulse. The warmth rises—not a flare, not yet, but a steady climb, as if a hand is lighting each vertebra like a wick. He steps in close enough that I can feel the clarity of his attention along my skin.

"Better," he murmurs. His fingers hover just above my wrist, not touching. "Again."

We work in small increments. I pull the hum up my arms and let it settle at my palms, then withdraw it before it makes a spectacle. He corrects without humiliating, moves my stance a degree here, a degree there, angles my shoulder, quiets a tilt in my chin with one knuckle and a look that makes my breath forget its plan. If a spark jumps, he nods once. If my control wavers, he says my name in that scholar's cadence that turns command into grammar. I find the border between wanting and wielding.

"Enough," he says at last. "Take the heat down."

I obey. The warmth sinks, coin by coin, into a place that feels newly excavated and newly mine. The frost breathes again. The world widens.

We're about to start a second set when the morning changes its mind.

No sound announces them. Only a shift in pressure, an absence of birdsong, and the precise crunch of boots across the far edge of the lawn. I know before I turn that it will anger him. I know before I see them that whoever has decided to arrive unannounced believes in the kinds of rules that look like mercy until you get close.

Three figures step out of the treeline without hurry. Their coats are dark and severe, cut to flatter and remind.

The woman at the center moves first—her scarf a deep garnet that catches each weak ray of winter light like spilled wine. Her hair, pale as powdered frost, is pinned in an intricate coil that speaks of calculation rather than vanity. Her eyes—steel-gray, cold and keen—skim everything and linger on nothing. Power lives in the stillness of her hands, gloved in soft black leather that has never known a day of labor.

To her right walks a tall man whose elegance is a weapon. His coat gleams faintly under the gray sky, every seam aligned with military perfection. His face is all edges and restraint, mouth drawn in a line that never quite becomes displeasure, never quite allows warmth. The scent that precedes him is faintly metallic, like silver cut clean in the forge.

The last carries no ornament at all. He's lean, almost gaunt, with eyes too dark to place their color and a presence that feels like the air before lightning strikes. His silence presses rather than waits. The kind of silence that knows how to kill a sound before it's born.

Adrian's jaw goes still. He doesn't step in front of me, but the air between us thickens. The field learns a new shape.

"Lord Corin Shadebriar," Adrian says after the proper number of heartbeats, nodding in deference to each of them. "Lady Selene Ashvale. Warden Tareth Duskmere. To what do we owe the discourtesy?"

Selene's smile is thin, the kind that pretends to be graceful but tastes like polished ice. "Head of Council," she says, inclining her head a fraction. "Forgive the intrusion. We received notice—*belated* notice—that a claimant in your care survived the initial rite. Custom requires confirmation."

"Custom requires petition." His voice doesn't lift. "Consider this your first denial."

Shadebriar's mouth twitches, not quite in humor. "We could debate procedure until the frost thaws, Marlowe, but the charter speaks plain. Before a figure of potential significance is presented to the world, the council has the right to verify. We ask only for a demonstration. Brief. Controlled."

Tareth says nothing. His gaze measures me with a soldier's economy, assessing not for beauty but for danger.

Adrian doesn't look at me. "The claimant has a name," he says.

Selene's smile sharpens. "Of course. Miss Hartwell. We've come to see if your... *emergence...* is as our reports describe."

"What do your reports describe?" I ask.

"Atypical intensity," Shadebriar answers before she can. "Anomalous coloration. Resonance beyond customary flamebound responses."

"And the test?" I ask.

"Necessary," Selene answers.

Adrian's patience tightens like skin over a fist. "You have thirty seconds," he says. "She will not be surrounded. I will conduct the attempt. You will observe from the wall."

Selene inclines her head, conceding the point. "As you wish."

They take their places along the stone. Adrian steps until his shoulder brushes mine. He doesn't touch my hand. He speaks so softly the cold has to lean in to hear.

"We can refuse," he says.

"You already did."

"Their kind collects denials like charms," he says. "It helps them believe themselves as temperate."

"Do we give them what they want?"

"We give them what helps you," he says. "No more."

I nod. The anger helps. I draw in the air and let it scratch the back of my throat, then find the hum again, the real one, under emotion and under fear. It crawls to my palms as if called by name. He watches, eyes intent, posture apparently loose and actually prepared to reinterpret the world.

"Slow," he says. "Do not perform. Build."

I build. Heat braids with breath, each exhale a thread laid over another until they make a small, strong cord. Light gathers at my fingers, not gold at first but a thinner, paler shade, the color of straw catching sideways sun. The council watches. Shadebriar's expression does an elegant thing meant to communicate nothing but attention. Selene's knuckles whiten. Tareth's chin lowers a fraction.

The cord thickens. The light grows steadier. Too easy. Too pretty. I don't trust it.

"Octavia," Adrian says. "Stay with it."

I stay until the first tremor arrives, the one that means choice. I could let the heat spill and please them with spectacle, or kill the light and anger them with restraint, or look past both and find what had woken me in the mausoleum and would not sleep afterward.

I let politeness die.

The light collapses, not outward but inward, a star learning itself again. For a second the field goes ordinary. Selene breathes, audible from the wall. Then the hum beneath the hum rises from my bones with a sound I feel and taste, a note that rings the air like struck glass. Heat climbs my arms not as fire but as flight. The color returns, but not as gold. White bleeds into it until it is both: white-gold, feather-bright.

The frost hisses. Steam steps away from the grass. The smell changes—ash and something clean, like rain after a kiln. The light does not burn the skin it touches. It crowns it.

Selene flinches. Shadebriar's elegance falters. Tareth shifts forward, a reflex that betrays his curiosity.

I feel something behind the light, a rhythm more than mine, a heartbeat that has set its metronome inside my ribs and now wishes to be counted. When I breathe, it steadies. When I doubt, it presses harder, as if to remind me that doubt is only a cloud.

A single white-gold feather—if feather is the word when light pretends at matter—spirals from my wrist and hovers. It dims to nothing, flares once, and is gone. Where it nearly touches the grass, vapor moves like a patient animal.

Selene says quietly, "Ancestral convergence. Impossible."

Shadebriar's voice arrives later. "It cannot be a phoenix line. We burned the last—"

Tareth lifts a hand, warning without looking away from me. "*Enough*. We have seen."

Adrian steps slightly forward, placing his body between their questions and my breath. He doesn't look at them. He looks at me. His eyes are lit with gold fire and something older than both.

"Pull it down, Octavia," he says. No panic. No pride. Only the clean gravity I trust. "Come back."

The world feels too loud when the light goes out.

My body trembles, heat seeping from my skin in small invisible threads until I'm shivering in its absence. The frost returns to the field as though it had only paused to watch. My breath hitches. The hum fades to a quiet pulse somewhere deep in my sternum. I flex my hands and find no burns—only the faint ache of having held too much.

Selene speaks first, her voice tight enough to splinter. "A trick of alchemy. Surely."

"Alchemy doesn't sing," Tareth says. His eyes flick from me to Adrian and back again. "You heard it."

Shadebriar smooths his gloves, but the movement trembles just slightly. "If that was what it appeared to be, then the records were... inaccurate."

Adrian straightens to his full height, which is its own kind of blade. "The records were written by men who preferred erasure to humility."

Selene bristles. "You've hidden this from us."

"I've protected her from you," he corrects, voice even, quiet, lethal. "There's a difference."

Tareth's gaze remains fixed on me. I can feel it like static against my skin. "Phoenix blood hasn't manifested in centuries. If this is true, if she's carrying that lineage—"

"She's not carrying anything," Adrian snaps, cutting him off. "She is herself. You don't get to dissect her into prophecies."

Selene's lips tighten. "The council will need to reconvene."

"Do that," Adrian says. "Far from here."

They exchange glances—the kind that happens when old power tastes its own fear—and then Selene gathers the hem of her long coat with practiced grace, turning toward the treeline. Shadebriar lingers a fraction longer, his voice smooth again but his eyes too bright.

"You've invited a storm you cannot control, Marlowe. You always did mistake rebellion for guardianship."

Adrian doesn't move, doesn't blink. "And you always mistook cowardice for caution."

The silence that follows feels electric. Finally, Tareth gives a curt nod, and the three of them retreat toward the edge of the estate. The air shifts as soon as they cross the boundary—like the frost sighs in relief.

I'm left staring after them, heart hammering, skin still buzzing from what just moved through me. When I turn back to Adrian, his jaw is locked tight, and his hands—those careful, measured hands—are curled into fists.

"What the *hell* just happened?" I manage.

He exhales through his nose, long and deliberate, like a man counting the seconds between detonations. "Exactly what I didn't want."

"What does that mean?" I step closer. "They said phoenix line... They burned the last one. What does that *mean*, Adrian?"

His eyes find mine, but the fury behind them isn't directed at me—it's the kind born from restraint, from being forced to hold a truth too dangerous to name. "It means the council has very short memory and very long knives."

"That's not an answer."

"It's the only one that keeps you breathing right now."

I fold my arms, the cold biting through my sleeves. "You can't keep doing that."

"Doing what?"

"Talking in riddles. Deciding what I can or can't handle." The words come sharper than I expect, fueled by leftover adrenaline and something rawer. "You brought me into this. You said you'd show me the truth. So show me."

The muscle in his jaw flexes. "You think I wanted them here?"

"You knew this was going to happen."

"I knew they'd want to test you," he says tightly. "I didn't think they'd come uninvited, or that you'd—" He stops himself, pinching the bridge of his nose. "That you'd ignite like that."

"Sorry for existing wrong," I bite out.

That gets his attention. His gaze snaps to mine, sharp as the frost. "Don't ever apologize for that," he says, low, dangerous. "You have no idea what you are capable of, Octavia. And they just saw a glimpse of it. That alone is enough to make them either worship you or burn you."

The words hang between us like smoke. The fire in his eyes could melt glaciers, but underneath it there's something else—fear, maybe. Or grief wearing its best disguise.

"Why would they burn me?" I ask, softer now. "You said phoenix blood hasn't manifested in centuries. If they killed the last line—"

"They didn't kill it," he says, but his voice fractures around the edge. "They contained it. The Society made sure the ember never found air again. They called it mercy."

I stare at him. "And you think I'm that ember."

"I don't think," he murmurs. "I know."

The world tilts a little, and I steady myself against the stone wall, the cold biting through my palm. "Then what am I supposed to do with that? With all of this?"

"Learn fast." He runs a hand through his hair, frustration bleeding into the motion. "Train harder. And stop doubting the fire inside you."

I laugh, bitter and unsteady. "That's easy for you to say—you're not the one who almost turned a field into a furnace."

His mouth twitches, but it's not humor—it's tension trying to escape. "You didn't burn anything."

"Yet."

He steps closer, close enough that I can feel the heat radiating off him again, steady and maddening. "You think I'd let you destroy yourself?"

"I think you might not be able to stop me."

The wind cuts between us, lifting the edge of my coat, scattering frost from the wall like a warning. His expression hardens.

"That," he says quietly, "is exactly what they'll be afraid of."

"Then maybe they should be," I snap. "Because if they think they can decide what happens to me—"

"They can," he interrupts, the words rough. "And they will, unless I keep them from it."

My pulse stutters. "By protecting me or by controlling me?"

He flinches like I struck him. "You think there's a difference anymore?"

"Don't do that," I say, voice rising. "Don't turn everything into riddles and philosophy when all I'm asking for is the truth."

He exhales, long, slow, the kind that sounds like surrender. "The truth is this, Octavia. The Society has rules older than most nations and were made to keep people like you from existing. And now that you do, they'll want to decide what use you serve. I'm the only thing standing between you and their definition of purpose."

"And what's yours?"

He doesn't answer right away. The wind tugs at his hair, at the collar of his coat, like it's trying to steal the words before they can escape. When he finally speaks, it's low enough that I have to lean in.

"My purpose," he says, "is keeping you alive long enough to decide what kind of *god* they make of you."

Something in me goes still at that.

We stand in the silence that follows, the frost reforming around our boots, the air heavy with unsaid things. Somewhere in the trees, a raven calls once—harsh, singular—and the echo drifts through the clearing.

Finally, I take a step back, crossing my arms as if I can hold myself together. "You can't keep doing this alone."

"I've been doing it longer than you've been breathing," he says.

"Maybe that's the problem."

His eyes flash—a flicker of something between warning and reluctant admiration. "Careful, my wicked ruin."

"Don't call me that," I snap, the words slipping out before I can catch them. "Not when you won't tell me what it means."

He opens his mouth, then closes it again. For a heartbeat he looks like he might turn away, but instead he exhales and says, quieter, "Some things can't be told. They have to be remembered. When you're ready, you will—and you'll understand why names are the last thing we give and the first thing we lose."

The answer lands in me like a dropped stone. Too big for language, too old for comfort.

I search his face for the man behind the mystery—the one who kissed my hand last night, who whispered my wicked ruin into the dark as if it were both a vow and a warning.

"Adrian," I say finally, my voice thin with questions I can't even form properly, "if what they saw today means... whatever it means—"

He cuts me off, voice gone to steel. "Then let them learn what it means to play with fire."

Something moves between us then—not light exactly, but a glow, a pulse, as if the air itself recognized what we haven't dared name. It fades as quickly as it came, leaving only the cold night, the silence, and the faint echo of his heartbeat that somehow keeps finding its way to mine.

CHAPTER 31

Snow cleans the world too easily. It fell in the night without bothering to announce itself—thin, steady, deliberate—until the garden wore a new grammar and the black stone path recited a different poem under the weight. I stand at the east window with a cup that has forgotten how to cool and watch the flakes hang and decide and land. The house approves of the quiet the way old buildings approve of laws they can outlive. Somewhere down the corridor, the boiler makes its patient confession to metal. The fire gives its consent in small bone-cracks that pretend to be incidental. I did not sleep. I rehearsed. Memory wanted spectacle, but discipline insisted on architecture. I gave the morning a version of my face that would not frighten her.

She arrives without ceremony, barefoot, hair pulled to one side by a hasty elastic, the wool of my sweater oversized against her body as if she had conquered it rather than borrowed it. The snow turns the light thin and precise around her, and the thinness makes the heat under her skin more visible. She sees me at the window and doesn't hide the calculation—how close to stand, how near to the radiator, how much to pretend last night was simply a page turn and not a chapter tear. That is what I like most about her. That stubborn refusal to sell herself a story she cannot cite.

"You didn't sleep," she says. Not a question.

"No." The answer pleases the air. It means the hour will not be asked to lie.

She comes closer and folds herself onto the chaise with the blanket thrown across it, legs tucked, bare feet hiding in wool. The sweater's sleeves swallow her hands. A curl frees itself to lie like punctuation against her throat, and my bite—two pale crescents, nearly healed—beats there once in memory and then behaves. If she notices the way my gaze returns to that mark, she chooses not to punish me with it. Her eyes go instead to the snow and narrow the way a reader narrows at a paragraph that flatters itself.

"Tell me how they work," she says.

She means the council. She means the machine. She means the hands that clean themselves with language. I swallow the first answer the mind offers—poetry that would not serve—and turn toward the desk because paper helps men behave.

"Twelve ruling Houses," I say. "Each performs age as if it were virtue. Each names itself after something it's convinced it can't be destroyed by—stone, ash, winter, bloom. They pretend to balance each other. They do not. They keep score in favors and oaths and marriages. They vote when they want to bless an outcome they've already engineered."

"Engineered how?" She draws the blanket higher, but not for cold. Curiosity overheats the body if it's honest.

"Persuasion," I say. "You won't find decrees. You'll find invitations so carefully written that the recipient believes they were the author. Protocols that arrive wearing the voice of a grandmother. Genealogies that look like history and function like leash. They prefer to make you think the door you walk through was your idea."

"So they don't force."

"They rarely need to," I say. "When they do, they call it remedy. Old words prevent riot while they do things that should require fire."

She watches the snow, but the questions sharpen. "The Twelve rule the magical families."

"Rule, steward, guide—choose a verb that flatters the speaker," I say. "They appoint judges who have no courts, just rooms where agreements are made to sound like justice. They ration access to archives. They 'bless' unions—Houses intermarry—and label it *culture*."

"How deep does that go?"

"First teeth," I say. "Before a child learns their letters, the House has taught them a hymn they'll mistake for grammar. By the time they are told they are allowed to choose, they have already chosen on command so many times that consent looks like a mirror."

The blanket creases under her fingers. "And you sit at the head of that."

"I sit where the knives meet," I say. "Because someone should. Because the man at the head can choose when the vote accidentally fails. Because if a ledger has to be kept, I prefer to know which ink is used."

She turns to me then, slow enough to keep the motion from being a flinch. "That sounds like the kind of sentence a good man uses to justify bad things."

"It is," I say. "And it is also the only sentence that kept them from pulling you underground when you lit the field."

Snow thickens. The lawn stops pretending it has edges. The house settles—one beam relaxing, a floorboard offering its small second language. She lets the silence work. I love that about her too. People who like to be convinced rush the quiet. She lets it reproduce.

"Do they always come uninvited?" she asks.

"Only when they've convinced themselves they are the invitation."

"And they control marriages." No tremor in the word. She's presenting a bone for identification.

"They advise," I say. "They gather two families in a room and tell a story about security. They show ledgers with columns that guess at futures and use the language of blood the way bankers use the language of interest. A young woman says yes because the no is built to sound like treason. A young man says yes because the no has been dressed in the face of his father's disappointment."

"And if someone refuses?"

"They are adored in theory." I allow myself the smallest smile. "In practice they discover how quickly a calendar can fill with opportunities elsewhere. They discover that their House cannot find the specific page in the archive that proves the ritual they want is theirs to request. They discover the difference between being uninvited and being forgotten."

Her voice drops. "Did you ever forget anyone?"

"On purpose?" I look at the snow until its honesty can bleed into my sentence. "No."

"By design."

"Yes."

She doesn't look away. "Why?"

"To buy time," I say. "For someone who needed it. For outcomes that needed to develop enough spine that the council could not pretend to claim them."

"And for you?"

"No," I say again, because the truth has a better chance of working if it repeats itself without decoration. "Not for me."

She studies me the way a surgeon studies a body—looking for the problem that hides. "They're afraid. I could smell it."

"Yes."

"Of what I am."

"Yes."

"And of *you*."

"That is their hobby," I say. "Fearing me in public gives them permission to arrange their desire in private."

"And what do they desire from you?"

"The thing I do well," I say. "Restraint. Sacrifice. The Ledger. They confuse it with loyalty."

"And what do you desire from them?"

"Silence," I say. "Failing that—predictability."

She moves the blanket. The sweater slips higher on one thigh where she hadn't intended it to. The temptation to look is a primitive thing— to pretend not to look is worse. I choose accuracy, let my gaze record what it wants, let her see that it does, and return it to her eyes. The bond between us climbs one rung and waits.

"You make violence sound like a thesis," she says.

"I make it sound like a tool," I say. "Because that is the only way to keep it from making itself your god."

"Did you—" The sentence arrives like a man running and loses its shoes on the stairs. "The murders."

There it is. The name of the heat that has lived under the house since the first siren, the way the newspapers love the photographs it makes. She holds the word steady, reluctantly impressed by it, repulsed by it in the shape she needs to preserve. She wants me to laugh and deny. She wants me to refuse to dignify the assumption. She wants to see what my face does when I'm given the opportunity to prove myself ordinary.

I let the question find itself an outline in the air between us and leave it there. Denial is a blanket. Refusal is a knife. I am not a blanket.

"I think," she says carefully, "that if I had asked you that a month ago, the taste in my mouth would have been ash. Now it's—" She makes a helpless motion with her hand, a curl of the fingers that indicates hunger and apology. "I don't know what's wrong with me."

"You are not wrong," I say. "You are awake."

"And you're not going to answer."

"I am." I put the cup down. The porcelain gives back a small clean sound like a line closing. "I will tell you which corridors lead to rooms you do not want to see yet. I will teach you how men who learned the wrong kind of Latin talk to themselves before they do things the language will not house. I will give you the ledger and let you decide what belongs in the black ink and what gets written in pencil so it can be erased if you change your mind. I will not give you absolution. I will not pretend absolution is not a coin men offer women when they want to make the woman responsible for their comfort."

"Which answer is that?" she asks.

"The only one that doesn't lie to either of us," I say.

She doesn't say: "You killed them." She doesn't say: "You didn't." Her shoulders lower a degree, and the sweater moves again, and the fire remembers it's supposed to be audible.

"Tell me about the Houses," she says. "All twelve."

I do. I name them and their pretensions, their colors and their cathedrals. Shadebriar believes elegance is a science and breeds its children to do math in mirrors. Ashvale praises ash because it has learned how to brand erasure as rebirth. Duskmere favors silence the way some men favor wine and despises lights left burning in rooms that are not occupied. Thornehaven—the one that calls itself a standard-bearer—collects old weapons and new scapegoats. Ignisfold preaches discipline and mistakes anemia for virtue. Nightbloom funds poets when it wants to smell like culture and poisons them with appointments. Winterveil records everything and forgets the bodies that carried the pens. I write the rest on the air for her and watch her mouth shape the names with the care she gives any word that might later belong to her.

"And you," she says into the end of it. "Where are you in that?" A simple question with teeth, smiling.

"On the threshold," I say. "Because thresholds hate men who try to own them."

"And at the head of the table."

"Because the chair allows me to move the table."

"And because you prefer knives to hymns."

"That too," I say.

Snow learns how to be silent on the windowsill. The day turns that color the afternoon takes on when it has decided to become evening but won't admit it in front of guests. She stares a long time at the garden and the wall and whatever version of herself the glass returns to her. The mark at her throat steadies, and the hum at my wrist answers.

"Explain the marriages," she says at last, and the word marriages lands like a dropped tool.

"They begin with a letter written in the hand of a woman everyone trusts," I say. "That is important. If a man writes it, it smells like a transaction. The letter tells a story in which one House protects another house from a storm that has been renamed climate, which is to say, inevitability. It lists a lineage and a dowry and then does a clever thing. It uses adjectives that could plausibly be mistyped—honor for hunger, fealty for fear."

"And if the letter is declined?" She asks, arching a brow.

"Another arrives, only it does not mention the first. It is filled with praise and an invitation to winter in a place where the guard at the door knows which compliment he is required to pay you in order for you to say thank you instead of stop."

"And then?"

"If the second letter is declined, a man who read at the right schools meets the father of the bride in a club he already belonged to before any of us were born and tells him a story about legacy."

"And then?"

"By the third letter," I say, "the bride believes she composed it."

She watches me until the anger finishes knitting its scarf. "You hate it."

"It is poorly written," I say.

"Adrian," she says in admonishment.

"Yes," I say. "I hate it."

She breathes out, a sound that decides not to be a laugh because the body remembers the field and the bright feather that wasn't a feather. "Then why do you stay on their council."

"Because I am better at breaking their sentences than the men who would take my chair," I say. "Because sometimes the difference between captivity and control is the speed at which the door can be opened when the person inside stops pretending it is a room built for them."

Her eyes stay on me, dark and sharp as a verdict. "You talk like the world bends for you. But maybe it just rots slower where you stand."

It lands harder than she means it to. I feel it hit, low and clean—because it's true. Power doesn't purify. It only curdles at a different pace.

"I don't make the rot," I say quietly. "I *name* it."

"Do you?" she snaps, voice trembling—not from fear, but from the pressure of everything she's been forced to swallow. "Because it sounds like you catalogue it—file it away next to your justifications."

I let the words find me. I don't dodge them. "If that's what it takes to keep you breathing, yes."

Her mouth parts—shock, disbelief, fury threading together like the first fire through dry kindling. "So I should *thank* you for protecting me? For playing their game and pretending it's noble?"

"I never said noble."

"Then *what*, Adrian?!" She rises suddenly, blanket sliding to the floor, sweater hanging half-open over the curve of her shoulder. The light catches her throat, her pulse fluttering rapidly. "What am I supposed to be in all this? Your apprentice? Your experiment? Your—" She stops herself, breathing hard. "You think you can leash what you don't understand."

I stand too, slow enough to remind the room who it belongs to. "You mistake understanding for control. They're not the same."

"Then what's the difference?"

"Understanding asks questions," I say. "Control answers them before you have the chance."

"Sounds like the council, and *you*," she bites.

That lands too. The truth always does. I move past her, toward the hall. "Get dressed. We're training."

"I'm not—"

"You are," I say, not looking back. "Better you burn here than somewhere unprepared."

She doesn't argue again. I hear the hiss of breath behind me, the shuffle of movement, the low click of her boots on wood. When she follows me into the corridor, the air between us hums—like static before lightning remembers what it is.

The yard greets us with silence and the slow descent of snow, unbroken except for two sets of prints that end at the mat. The sky is a bruise-colored wound that refuses to close.

"Containment," I tell her. "You don't fight it. You let it build until it recognizes you."

"I'm not your weapon," she mutters.

"No," I say. "You're worse."

That earns me a glare that would've frozen gods if they'd been polite enough to look. She stands in the snow, breath visible, eyes molten with something sharp enough to wound and warm enough to resurrect. "You act like you know me."

"I do."

"Then you know I don't take orders."

"Yes," I say. "But you take results."

Her hands flex. I see the shimmer before she feels it—the pulse beneath the skin, the spark that lives between surrender and defiance. "You said control was different from understanding," she says. "So which one is this?"

"Instinct," I say. "The thing before both."

She lifts her hands, palms open. The gold threads flare bright and wrong. Uncontrolled. They spin wild and vicious, catching the air and twisting it into heat. The snow around her melts in a perfect circle. The earth hisses.

"Octavia," I warn.

"No," she says, voice cracking. "No more warnings. You tell me they rule everything, that you stand above them, that I'm supposed to bow and learn and pretend not to see the putrid foundation—and then you tell me I'm *dangerous*? That I'm something they should fear?"

I take a step forward. "They should."

"Then what about you?!"

The power flares. My control slips. I feel the answering surge in me—old, dark, too inhuman to name. The air buckles between us. Her light reaches for mine, uninvited, greedy. The snow turns to steam.

"Stop," I say.

"Make me."

Her challenge is pure ruin. The kind that tastes like worship disguised as war.

So I do. I move—fast enough the air whips, slow enough to let her see me coming. My hand catches her wrist, and the moment I touch her, the world detonates.

The threads blaze gold-white, searing through both of us. Heat, power, memory, rage—all of it folds and merges. I smell rain that hasn't fallen in centuries. I see wings—her wings—half fire, half ash, spanning a horizon that doesn't exist yet.

The Phoenix blood.

Her body arches against mine, eyes glowing with something older than the Houses, older than gods. The sound that leaves her throat isn't a cry—it's a call.

Then silence. Snow. The air trembles, singed. I don't release her. She's trembling, breathing hard, sweat slick against the wool. Her pupils are blown wide, her lips parted. For a moment, the entire world narrows to the echo of her pulse against my palm.

I can still taste her power on my tongue. And I just know the world hasn't decided whether to forgive her for existing.

"What—" she breathes, shaking her head. "What was that?"

"The part of you they'll never control."

Her gaze lifts to mine, wet, furious, bright. "You knew?"

"Yes."

"And you didn't tell me when you found out?"

Octavia is breathtaking, radiant with fury. "You weren't ready."

She laughs, sharp and raw. "You're just like them."

"I'm worse," I admit. "Because I tell myself I'm not."

The admission hangs between us like smoke. For a moment, neither of us moves. Then the Phoenix inside her stirs again—less fire this time, more grief.

The snow resumes falling, gentle, cautious, as if afraid to touch her. The steam cools to mist. Her shoulders shake once before she catches herself. "So what now? Will they come back to decide I'm useful?"

"They'll come," I say. "They'll pretend it's to honor you. It'll be fear in a nicer dress."

"And you'll let them."

"No," I say. "I'll let them try."

Her chin lifts. "And me?"

"You'll learn to burn without apology."

Her breath hitches. "And if I burn you too?"

I take her chin in my hand, thumb brushing the faint shimmer that still clings to her jaw. "Then I'll deserve it."

She doesn't flinch. "You already do."

That's when I realize control isn't something I lost. It's something she took—and the worst part is, I wanted her to.

She is the first to look away. Not to surrender—to *choose*. The gold recedes under her skin like a tide deciding it has made its point. She pulls her wrist from my hand, and the shock of absence is louder than the steam still lifting from the snow.

"Teach me," she says, voice rough. "But don't you dare lie to me again." She pauses, tilting her head in a calculating sort of way. "And don't think for a second I'm staying because of you."

I nod once. Agreement, not absolution.

She turns. The snow accepts her weight and then tries, politely, to erase it. Where she walks, a faint crescent of thaw follows and re-freezes—small glass moons set into the white.

The sweater is too large on her, looking suddenly like armor that learned softness by accident. At the steps she hesitates, not for effect, for aim—then goes inside without looking back.

The yard exhales. The house listens for her and adjusts its heat. I stand where the circle of melted snow holds, palms open to air that still tastes of copper and citrus and storm. The discipline returns the way it always does—late, unrepentant, useful. I gather it like a coat and put it on.

On the mat, a single filament of ash twists, bright as a hair in sunlight. Phoenix, yes—and something else that refuses to name itself in front of witnesses. The council will hear rumor and call it proof. They will arrive with their silk-threat smiles and their measurable concern. Let them. Doors close differently when fire has learned the hinges.

I go inside and leave the prints where they are. Evidence is sometimes a promise. In the corridor, the boiler speaks its low catechism to the pipes.

The stair counts my ascent and does not complain, and at her door I do not pause. Truces aren't guarded in hallways.

In the study, I smooth a blank sheet onto the desk and write nothing. The room approves. Not every hour deserves ink.

Outside, snow keeps doing its holy, useless work—cleaning what cannot be cleaned. Inside, heat gathers its patience. When the next chapter of this decides it wants a witness, it will not ask. It will arrive like she did—unannounced, correct, impossible to refuse.

I let her walk.

That is the only control that matters.

CHAPTER 32

Dinner passes like a negotiation neither of us agreed to hold. The house hums with its usual patience, pretending not to hear the argument that still burns at the edges of my thoughts. The clink of silver against porcelain feels too sharp, too exact, like punctuation in the wrong place. Adrian moves through the motions of civility, measured and deliberate, pouring wine, cutting bread, setting the fire to the precise level of comfort. But beneath it all, I can taste restraint—his, mine, the house's. Everything holds its breath.

I push food around my plate until it looks like I've eaten. My pulse still remembers the echo of his voice, the way control cracked through it earlier when the council's words hit the air like acid. My chest still aches from swallowing my anger instead of throwing it at him. He doesn't look at me. Not directly. His gaze skims past—over the glass, over the hearth, over me—as if proximity itself might reignite whatever we almost said. The silence between us isn't peace. It's glass stretched thin enough to shatter if either of us speaks too loudly.

When the clock in the hall strikes eight, I can't stand it any longer.

"I'm done," I say softly, setting my fork down.

His knife stops mid-motion. "You've barely—"

"I said I'm done."

It's quiet, not defiant. I'm too tired for defiance. But something in my tone makes his hand still. For a heartbeat, I think he'll follow. He doesn't. He watches me rise, eyes shuttered, and nods once.

"As you wish."

I leave before I can regret it. The corridor swallows me whole, its familiar shadows strangely intimate. My footsteps sound wrong—too loud, too alive. The house sighs when I pass, old wood shifting in its bones, firelight flickering down to embers. Everything feels like it's watching, waiting for something to give.

My room is colder than I expect. I close the door behind me and lean against it, pressing my palms flat to the wood as if it might stop the world from spinning. The reflection in the mirror across the room is a stranger. My skin looks fevered, almost luminescent, the veins beneath it glimmering faintly gold. I catch my breath and blink, but the shimmer remains.

Not again.

I move to the wardrobe and pull out what I can find that feels solid—thick leggings, a wool sweater, the long charcoal coat he bought me after our first lesson in the snow. My boots sit by the hearth, their leather stiff from yesterday's cold. I lace them with trembling fingers, not from fear but from the electric pulse building under my skin, the same pulse that once set the world on fire without permission.

By the time I step into the hall again, the house feels smaller, tighter—almost claustrophobic. Every lamp flame seems to bend toward me, drawn by something it recognizes. I ignore it, moving through the quiet with my hands shoved into my coat pockets, head down like a thief. Maybe that's what I am—a thief stealing one moment of solitude from a man who seems to own them all.

Outside, the night is a cathedral of snow. The air bites in clean lines, sharp and cold enough to taste. The world is silver and silent. My breath rises in pale ribbons that vanish too quickly. Each step leaves a mark in the perfect surface of the garden path, black boots breaking purity into confession. The trees stand in quiet judgment, their branches skeletal, their crowns heavy with frost.

I walk until the house is a faint shape behind me, until the lamps dissolve into fog and the field opens wide—an untouched expanse beneath a sky full of frozen stars. The cold cuts deep, but the thing beneath my skin welcomes it. It hums, restless. Hungry. Alive. I wrap my arms around myself and stare out at the horizon where snow meets dark. There's peace here, somewhere beneath the ache.

But peace doesn't last.

The moment hits like a pulse too large for my veins. Heat spikes through my chest, racing down my arms. My breath catches—half gasp, half warning—and golden light flickers at my fingertips. I grit my teeth.

"Not now," I whisper. "Not here."

The light answers anyway, shimmering through the air around me, thin threads weaving between my fingers. It's beautiful, if I didn't know better. It's ruin dressed as radiance. I press my hands together, trying to smother it, but the glow only brightens, pulsing with my heartbeat. Panic tries to claw up my throat, but I swallow it down hard. Adrian isn't here. No one is coming to pull me back this time.

So I breathe.

The first inhale is sharp, slicing down to the bone. The second steadier. The third opens something inside me that I didn't know could open. The heat stops fighting. It waits.

I remember his words—the ones meant for instruction, not salvation. Containment. Resonance. Refusal.

Fine. I'll try it his way.

I open my palms. The flames crawl up my arms in slow spirals, not consuming, only clinging. They move like living things—like wings trying to remember how to unfold. The snow at my feet steams but doesn't melt. The air crackles. My pulse slows. I stop fighting and start listening. The fire isn't separate. It's not punishment or gift—it's memory. It's bloodline. It's mine.

Light unfurls around me, blinding and soft at once. Golden feathers bloom where sparks fall, evaporating before they touch the ground. The world goes quiet except for the sound of my heart, beating in time with something older than sound. I lift a hand and the fire moves with me, answering thought before gesture, instinct before intent. The fear that used to live in its shadow is gone.

I don't feel human. I feel true. And then it happens—the shift.

It doesn't hurt. It feels like exhaling after years of holding my breath. My body lifts, weightless, bones rewriting themselves into something ancient. Flame ripples through my hair, spreading across my shoulders, down my back, until I see the edges of wings made from light and ash. The snow beneath me glows, a circle of molten gold etched into frost. The heat should destroy the fabric I wear, but it doesn't. The flames slide around the coat, the wool, the leather—accepting them as part of me. They burn, but they don't consume.

I open my eyes, and the field burns without burning. The snow around me has turned to glass, smooth and dark as obsidian. Above, the stars blur into streaks of gold. I feel their gaze. I feel everything.

This—this is what he saw in me before I could name it. The thing the council feared. The thing buried under blood and ink and too many quiet lies.

I move forward. The fire moves with me, leaving faint scorch marks on the glass that fade before I can look back. My wings stretch once—testing, learning, remembering—and then fold in close again. For once, I understand what he meant. The flame doesn't need to rage to prove its strength. It only needs to exist without apology.

I close my eyes and call it back.

The light resists, but I insist. It takes patience, a strange kind of surrender. I picture water, steady and sure, washing through me. I picture the sound of my own breathing, the rhythm of my heart, the way the snow felt before the fire. Slowly, the glow dims. The wings retract. The gold threads sink beneath my skin, humming like embers that refuse to die out completely.

When I open my eyes again, the night has returned to its natural shape. The world is dark and silver once more, the glass beneath my feet cooling to frost. I'm trembling—not from fear, not even from exhaustion, but from awe. I stare down at my hands, expecting burns, but there are none. Only warmth. Only proof.

The air feels different now. Lighter. Thinner. It's as though the world itself adjusted its breathing to match mine. The stars above pulse faintly, as if acknowledging the transaction. I take one step, then another. The snow crunches softly, almost reluctant to accept me again.

I walk to the edge of the field where the old stone wall divides the estate from the woods. Frost covers every surface, the stones glinting like fractured mirrors. I run my fingers along them, tracing old sigils barely visible beneath the ice. They hum faintly, recognizing me. The mark on my palm—the crescent left by the first cut, the one that began all of this—burns faintly in response. My breath fogs the air. I whisper without meaning to.

"Embergrave."

The word feels like a door opening. Not in sound, but in the shift of everything around me. The wind rises suddenly, spiraling through the field, scattering snow into whirling halos. My hair lifts with it. Something in the storm's voice sounds almost familiar—a rhythm I've heard before in dreams. Flame and feather. Birth and un-doing. I close my eyes and listen.

It isn't calling for help. It's calling for recognition.

I don't know how long I stand there, breathing in the cold, the warmth still humming faintly beneath my skin. The world holds its distance but watches all the same. The fire inside me has learned a new word—*patience*.

When I finally turn back toward the house, the lights in the windows glow faintly through the haze. Adrian hasn't moved them. He's probably still in the study, reading something old enough to smell like dust and faith. Maybe he's rehearsing what he'll say when he realizes I've gone. Maybe he already knows. He always seems to know.

I make it halfway up the garden path before I stop. The melted glass trail behind me catches what little moonlight there is, turning it gold. Proof. I wonder what he'll think when he sees it—if he'll call it progress or disaster. Maybe both.

My breath trembles out in a laugh I don't quite feel.

Inside, the hall lights flicker as I pass. The house senses me differently now. The doors don't creak when I touch them. Instead, they open as if they've been waiting. My reflection in the dark glass of the corridor looks otherworldly—pale face haloed in the faintest glow, eyes too bright, hair kissed with static. I look like I belong to the flame and the cold at once.

When I reach my room, I pause. My hands hover over the door handle. The air smells faintly of cedar and smoke—Adrian's scent still clinging to the fibers of my coat, my hair, my skin. I should feel safer for it. I don't. I feel seen.

I push the door open and step inside. The room feels smaller than before, its edges defined by memory instead of architecture. My boots track faint snow onto the rug, dark wet prints fading behind me. I shrug out of the coat and hang it by the hearth. The sweater sticks to my skin where the heat still lingers, soft and heavy with the scent of smoke. I sink onto the bed, elbows on my knees, and stare into the low fire that waits there, half alive.

For a long time, I do nothing. I just breathe.

Then the guilt starts whispering—low, persistent, shaped like his voice. Containment. Control. Discipline. The words that were supposed to save me now feel like chains. My fists clench in my lap. I can still feel the council's eyes, their fear dressed up as reverence, their judgment pretending to be protection. I can still hear Adrian's tone when he spoke for me instead of with me, like he could claim me by proximity.

But he didn't light my fire.

I did.

The thought steadies something inside me. For the first time since arriving at this house, the fear doesn't follow. It lingers at the edges, impotent. I stare at the flames in the hearth—smaller, weaker versions of what I carried into the field—and lift my hand. A single thread of gold rises from my palm, curling like smoke, then vanishes. Contained... *Mine.*

A slow smile tugs at my mouth. Not victory. Recognition.

The wind outside shifts. A window hums softly in its frame, the snow tapping like fingertips against the glass. Somewhere down the hall, a floorboard groans—the sound of a man moving, perhaps, or maybe just the house settling. I don't care. I don't rise. I lie back on the bed, boots still on, staring at the ceiling where shadows flicker with each pass of the firelight.

The ceiling patterns blur into wings. My eyelids grow heavy. Sleep teases the edges of thought. I'm not sure what tomorrow will bring—more lessons, more lies, more sparks—but tonight I know one truth that no council, no society, no man can rewrite.

I am not their weapon.

I am not his secret.

I am the flame that remembers itself.

The wind answers with a low moan, pressing against the walls, slipping through cracks in the stone. The fire stirs once, flaring high as if in agreement, then settles again. I reach for the edge of the blanket, drag it over my body, and close my eyes.

In the darkness behind them, the light remains—a faint, golden pulse that hums in time with my heart. When sleep comes, it carries the scent of ash and snow, and the promise of something still waiting to be born.

CHAPTER 33

Morning drapes itself over the world like forgiveness I don't trust. The snow has softened overnight, its cruel edges blurred by sunlight that filters through the frost-glazed windows in slow ribbons of gold. The house smells like cedar and the ghosts of last night's fire, sweetened faintly by the coffee Adrian must've brewed before I woke. I lie there for a while, pretending the ceiling above me is just plaster and not history, pretending I'm just a girl who fell asleep after a long walk instead of someone who burned a field into glass.

When I finally push the blankets back, my skin still hums faintly. The glow beneath my ribs—quiet now—feels less like power and more like breath. I can live with that.

The floorboards are cold under my bare feet as I pad toward the window. Outside, the sky is pale and forgiving, streaked with soft cloud, the kind of morning that makes you think of cinnamon and bakeries and people smiling without knowing what's breaking in someone else's chest. Thanksgiving is in a few days, and for the first time since everything started, I want—no, I *ache*—for normalcy. For laughter that doesn't end in blood, for something human enough to remind me that I was one once.

The mirror catches my reflection when I turn back. My hair is loose and wild, curls tumbling over my shoulders, threaded through with faint streaks of copper from the light. I look... different. Softer. The same girl who kissed a monster and didn't flinch. I run a hand through the curls, tug them into something like order, and decide I'll leave it down. Let the world see what it made of me.

When I open the wardrobe, my fingers hover over the dark tones I usually wear before stopping on something unexpected. A black mini skirt and a cream ribbed turtleneck that still smells faintly of Adrian. I pull them out and lay them on the bed. The tights are sheer black, just thick enough to tame the cold and covered in skulls. I tug them on slowly, then slide into the skirt and sweater, feeling the fabric settle like armor disguised as softness.

A pair of ankle boots, black leather with silver zippers, finish the look.

When I pass the mirror again, I almost don't recognize myself. The girl staring back looks like she belongs to the world beyond the gates. Not the council's world. Not Adrian's. Mine.

The hallway smells faintly of roasted coffee and the bitter tang of ink—Adrian must already be in the study. The scent of him finds me before I find him: bergamot, ash, the sharp sweetness of something that doesn't belong to mortals. My heart stumbles once and then steadies, traitorous thing that it is.

He's by the window when I enter, still in black but softer today—slacks, a dark sweater that fits too well, sleeves pushed up to his forearms. His hair is a little messy, like he's been running a hand through it while thinking. The sight is so achingly normal it almost hurts.

"You're awake," he says, setting his mug down. His voice is the same low warmth that haunts my dreams. "How do you feel?"

"Human," I say before I can stop myself. Then, softer, "Better."

He studies me for a beat longer than necessary. "You look different."

"Do I?" I feign indifference, crossing to pour myself coffee. The cup warms instantly between my fingers, the heat like a heartbeat I didn't ask for.

"Yes." His gaze lingers. "More alive."

I smirk over the rim of the mug. "Maybe because I didn't have to hide it this time."

That earns me the faintest smile. "You managed to sleep?"

"Eventually." I take a sip, letting the bitter bite ground me. "You didn't."

He shrugs, crossing his arms. "I wanted to give you space."

"Or you didn't want to see what I'd become."

"Octavia." The way he says my name is warning and prayer. "I've always seen it."

My chest tightens. "Then you should see this too."

Before he can ask, I set the cup down, lift my palms, and summon it.

The light blooms instantly, golden and precise, curling through my fingers like silk smoke. The air warms around us. His pupils dilate, drinking it in. I feel no fear this time, no loss of control. The flame listens. It shapes itself to my will, not the other way around. I turn one hand slowly, watching the threads coil and shift, then close my fingers into a fist. The light disappears.

"Containment," I say quietly. "Resonance. Refusal. Right?"

His expression softens into something almost reverent. "You learned."

"I listened," I correct. "And I want more. I want to understand this, to train properly. But on my terms."

He tilts his head. "Meaning?"

"I'm not hiding anymore. I'm not some secret to keep locked away until the council decides I'm safe enough to show off. I'm done being handled."

Something dangerous flickers behind his eyes. "They won't like that."

"Good," I say. "Let them choke on it."

The edge of his mouth twitches. "I might enjoy watching that."

"Then you'll love what comes next." I take my phone from the counter and scroll until I find Jess's contact.

He stiffens instantly. "Octavia."

"She deserves to see I'm alive. She's my friend."

"She's *human.*"

"Exactly." I meet his gaze head-on. "And I'm not hiding from that either."

He exhales slowly, the sound caught between amusement and despair. "You're inviting her here."

"I already did."

There's a long pause. Then, "Of course you did."

When Jess arrives, she brings the smell of city air and too many questions. Her car crunches up the snowy drive, and for a moment, everything feels normal again—just a friend visiting, laughter waiting at the door. Adrian stands by the entryway like a storm pretending to sleep, jaw tight, shoulders drawn taut beneath his black sweater. He doesn't know why he's on edge—neither of us do—but the air feels charged, brittle, as if the world is holding its breath. I elbow him lightly. "Behave."

"I'm considering it."

"Try harder."

Jess bursts in like sunlight—blonde curls, plaid coat, and a grin that dissolves the gloom. "Oh my god, you weren't kidding when you said mansion. Is this where you've been hiding?"

"Not hiding," I say, hugging her. "Just... learning."

Her perfume—orange blossom and vanilla—wraps around me, achingly human. I didn't realize how much I missed the scent of ordinary life until now. She pulls back and studies me. "You look incredible. Like you swallowed the sun."

I laugh nervously. "Something like that."

Adrian clears his throat. Jess jumps slightly, finally noticing him. "Uh, hi."

He nods politely, the model of restraint. "Adrian Marlowe."

"Of course you are," she says, eyes widening. "The *professor*."

I suppress a groan. "Jess—"

"Oh please," she whispers. "Now I understand why you disappeared. He's—"

"—standing right here," Adrian interjects dryly.

Jess blushes scarlet, and I shoot her a glare that promises violence later. "Coffee?"

"Please," she mutters.

The morning feels almost normal for a while. We sit in the kitchen, the table crowded with cups and croissants Adrian somehow acquired. Jess talks about her job, her boyfriend, the Thanksgiving party she's planning, how weird it is not hearing from me for two weeks. I listen, soaking up every trivial detail like sunlight. Adrian stays mostly silent, leaning against the counter with his sleeves rolled, eyes sharp but distant. Every so often I catch him watching me—not possessive, just watchful, like he's cataloging every human thing I still cling to.

And then the air changes.

It's subtle at first—a ripple beneath the quiet, the way pressure shifts before a storm. The flames in the hearth shudder. My stomach drops.

Adrian's head lifts instantly. "They're here."

Before I can ask, the doorbell chimes. Once. Twice. The sound echoes like judgment.

Jess frowns. "You expecting someone?"

Adrian moves before I can answer. "Stay here."

"Like hell." I push my chair back and follow him to the foyer. The cold outside leaks in through the crack as he opens the door.

Three figures stand on the steps, wrapped in dark coats that make the snow look ashamed. Lord Corin of House Shadebriar. Lady Selene of Ashvale. And behind them, Warden Tareth of Duskmere. The air bends around them, thick with power and perfume and disapproval.

"Lord Marlowe," Selene purrs, her tone sweet as poison, her lips dripping in crimson. "We didn't receive an invitation, so we thought we'd deliver our concerns in person."

Adrian's jaw tightens. "How gracious of you."

Shadebriar's gaze slides past him, landing on me. "The prodigy herself." His eyes flicker gold for a moment. "And *glowing*, I see."

"Don't," Adrian warns.

"Oh, but we must." Selene steps forward, her perfume—something floral and decayed—wrapping around me. "You brought a *human* into your

home, Adrian. Into our sanctum. How very…
reckless."

Jess's voice cuts from behind me. "Excuse me?"

Every head turns. She's standing in the hall, coffee cup in hand, eyes wide but unafraid. "Who the *fuck* are you people?"

Shadebriar's expression curdles. "Unacceptable."

"She's my friend," I snap. "You don't get to speak about her like she's dirt under your boots."

Selene's smile sharpens. "Careful, *Embergrave.* You're not yet in a position to dictate tone."

I step forward, heat flickering along my fingertips. "Try me."

The air shifts instantly. The snow outside hisses. Adrian's hand shoots out, catching my wrist, grounding me. "Octavia," he murmurs low enough that only I can hear. "Not like this."

"Like what?!" I whisper back. "Am I supposed to take this silently? Lying down—like a *good* girl?"

Selene's eyes narrow. "Do you see, Lord Marlowe? This is precisely why we advised caution. She's unstable."

"Unstable?" I laugh, the sound breaking like lightning. "Because I won't bow?"

Tareth finally speaks, his voice thin and cold. "You forget your station, child."

"No," I say, stepping closer until the gold in my veins gleams. "You forget that I don't have one."

For a heartbeat, no one breathes. The fire behind us flares in quiet agreement. Selene's composure wavers. Corin takes a step back, disgust twisting his mouth. "She'll burn us all."

Adrian's voice is steel wrapped in calm. "Then perhaps the world needs a little burning."

That does it. They retreat—not in haste, but in insult. Selene's final glare slides over me like venom. "The council will not forgive this breach."

"Good," I say. "I'm not asking them to."

The door slams behind us. The silence that follows feels heavier than sound.

Jess stands frozen near the wall, coffee forgotten, eyes wide. "Okay," she says finally, voice shaking. "What the hell was that?"

I open my mouth, but no words come. How do you explain an entire world made of secrets and bloodlines and divine fire to someone who still believes in traffic lights and coffee breaks? Adrian turns away, rubbing a hand over his face.

"Jess," he says quietly. "You should go."

"Excuse me?"

"It's not safe for you here."

She looks between us, betrayal and confusion warring in her eyes. "Tavia?"

"I'll call you later," I manage. My voice sounds foreign. "Please."

She hesitates, then nods, backing toward the door like someone leaving a church they don't belong in. The car engine starts moments later. When the sound fades, the quiet returns, thick as fog.

I round on Adrian. "You could've warned me!"

"I didn't know they'd come today," he says evenly.

"You always know."

"Not this time."

"Bullshit." The word cracks like a whip. "You said you'd talk to them! Make them wait. You said they'd respect—"

"They don't respect anyone's wishes," he snaps, finally losing that cold restraint. "You think defiance earns mercy? You *humiliated* them. In their eyes, you're not a woman. You're a weapon they can't control. Do you understand what that means?"

"I understand that I'm done living by their rules," I shoot back. "If they think they can scare me, they're wrong. I'm not the girl they burned out of the archives. I'm not a whisper in someone else's ledger."

He steps closer, anger flickering bright and brief. "You think I don't know what they're capable of? You think I haven't buried—" He stops, breath harsh. "You don't get it yet."

"Then explain it," I demand. "Stop hiding behind your riddles and tell me the truth!"

His silence says more than words ever could. I shake my head. "That's what I thought."

When I turn to leave, he catches my wrist again, gentler this time. "Octavia."

I pull free. "Don't. You can't protect me from this."

The flames in the hearth answer me, a single spark leaping high before dimming. The mark on my palm glows faintly through the fabric of my sleeve. I meet his gaze one last time. "You wanted me contained. Congratulations, you got your wish."

Then I walk out before he can follow, boots crunching against the snow that's already melting under my heat.

Behind me, I hear the house sigh—a long, low sound like resignation. The wind rises, carrying the scent of cedar and smoke, and somewhere in it, faintly, the echo of his voice.

My wicked ruin.

But for the first time, it doesn't feel like a curse.

It feels like a challenge.

And I intend to win.

CHAPTER 34

Snow stings my cheeks as I cross the yard. The garden wall looks skeletal in winter, vines brittle against stone. Beyond it, the trees stand like silent jurors, their branches scribbling black lines into the white sky. I shove my hands into my jacket pockets, but the heat inside me makes the wool unnecessary. I want distance. I want air that hasn't been breathed by the council, air that hasn't been owned by Adrian's discipline.

Every step sends up a hiss of steam where my heat touches the snow. My anger coils tighter with each footprint. I wanted Jess there. I wanted to explain. Instead the council came like vultures, polite and poisonous, staring at me as if I were a weapon they'd ordered but hadn't paid for yet. And Adrian—Adrian stood there like marble, no hint of the fury I felt. He controlled *everything*. The timing, the narrative, even my absence from the story.

"Octavia." His voice cuts across the yard, low and sharp.

I don't stop.

"Octavia." Closer now.

I reach the edge of the garden path when his hand closes around my arm. It isn't rough, but it's immovable. Heat meets heat where he touches me. Then, the snow under our feet sizzles and dies.

"Let me go," I snap, spinning on him.

He's bare-handed, coat unbuttoned, hair wind-tossed—no longer the professor at the lectern but something darker, the man who runs a society built on secrets. "You shouldn't storm off like this."

"Like what? Like someone whose life you've taken over?" I jerk at my arm. He doesn't release it. "Like someone who's sick of being handled, hidden, paraded out when it suits you?"

His jaw flexes. "You're exhausted—"

"No," I bite back. "I'm *furious*. And you don't get to call my fury exhaustion just because it's inconvenient!"

His grip tightens just enough to anchor me. "You're going to burn out if you keep walking away."

"Maybe I want to." My voice rises, the heat under my skin answering it. "Maybe burning is the only thing left that's actually *mine*."

He exhales, snow smoking where it hits his breath. "You think I don't want to tell them to stay away? You think I wanted Jess anywhere near that room?"

"I think you wanted control," I throw at him. "And you got it. You always get it."

For a heartbeat neither of us moves. The world shrinks to the pressure of his hand on my arm, the gold light pulsing under my skin, the smell of cedar and cold iron from his coat. The snow falls harder, muffling everything except our breathing.

Then his control breaks. He yanks me toward him, and the impact knocks the breath from my lungs. His mouth finds mine—no prelude, no soft testing—just heat and salt and teeth. It's not a kiss built for tenderness. It's a collision, a warning, a question he can't stop asking.

I push back, palms flat against his chest. "You don't get to—"

He cuts me off with another kiss, deeper, rougher. His hand slides from my arm to my waist, fingers digging into the small of my back. "Say you hate me," he murmurs against my mouth. "Say it."

"I do," I breathe, but the sound trembles, traitorous.

"Liar." His other hand fists in my hair, dragging my head back just enough for his eyes to catch mine. They're molten now, flecks of gold like embers caught in green. "Say it again."

"I—" The word dissolves when his thumb brushes the inside of my thigh through the fabric of my tights. My whole body arches into him. "I hate—"

"You hate how much you *want* this," he growls. His lips find my jaw, my throat, the bite he left there. "You hate that I see you."

I shove at him again, but he barely sways. "You took over my life, Adrian. You didn't even want me to call Jess."

He answers with a low sound, half-groan, half-snarl. "You think they would have spared her just because she was outside on the steps? They already scented her." His mouth grazes my ear. "You think I haven't already burned for that decision?"

The words slam into me harder than his grip. My heat flares, but not outward. It coils inside me, trembling, waiting. "You could have told me. You could have trusted me."

"I did." His hand slides under my jacket, palm against my back. His touch is scorching, but it's his voice that scorches more. "I do. But I will not let them circle you. Not Jess. Not anyone."

I hate how my body reacts to him even now—how the bond hums at the edge of my anger, how his scent threads through my pulse like a command. I hate that his control feels like safety at the same moment it feels like a cage.

"Let me go," I whisper again.

He doesn't. He kisses me instead, slower now but deeper, like claiming territory. His tongue traces the seam of my lips until I open, and the taste of him floods in—coffee, cold air, something darker, like metal warmed in a fire. My hands rise to his shoulders, meaning to push, but they end up clutching instead.

The snow drifts around us, blurring the garden into a white haze. I feel his heartbeat against mine, hard and fast. His fingers slide up my sides, under my sweater, calloused thumbs skimming skin. The cold should sting, but the heat between us devours it.

"This isn't training," I manage, breathless.

"No," he says against my mouth. "This is what happens when you light a fuse and walk away."

His teeth graze my lower lip, and I gasp. He takes advantage of it, deepening the kiss until my knees nearly buckle. I hook my fingers in the collar of his coat, pulling him closer, hating him, wanting him, unable to separate the two.

"You don't own me," I say when I break the kiss, panting.

"No," he agrees softly, eyes dark, voice rough. "But you burn like you want me to."

I shake my head, curls brushing snowflakes off my cheeks. "I don't even know what I am anymore."

His forehead rests against mine for a heartbeat, his breath hot in the cold air. "Then stop running. Stop guessing. Let me help you find out for sure."

For a moment the world tilts—the snow, the sky, his hands on me, everything sliding into one bright, dangerous point. I could step into it. I could step away.

I pull back instead, shoving at his chest until his grip breaks. "No," I say, louder this time. "Not like this."

His hands drop. The space between us feels like a wound. "Octavia—"

I turn, walking toward the trees. "You want my trust? Then stop taking everything else first."

Behind me, I hear him exhale, a sound like something cracking. I don't look back. The snow swallows my footprints as fast as I make them, but the heat in me stays, pulsing, waiting—mine again, for now.

The air is sharp enough to hurt when I breathe it in. It tastes like smoke and iron and him. I make it halfway to the gate before the pull hits—an ache low in my chest that feels like gravity remembering my name. I tell myself not to turn, not to give him the satisfaction, but the storm behind me moves like a living thing, and when his voice finally cuts through it, I stop.

"Octavia."

Just that. My name, spoken like a warning and a plea.

I shouldn't. But I do. I turn.

He's standing in the snow, coat half-buttoned, hair disheveled from his hands, his breath visible in the cold. The distance between us feels both impossible and meaningless. His eyes catch the faint light spilling from the house—gold burning through green—and I swear I see the moment restraint dies in them.

"Don't," I say, even as he starts toward me.

He doesn't listen. He never does when I tell him no like that—like I want him to hear the word but not obey it.

The snow crunches beneath his boots, steady, deliberate, until he's in front of me. His hand catches my wrist, and heat bursts through my veins like the ground itself flaring open.

"Let me go," I manage, though my pulse betrays me.

He steps closer. *"I can't."*

The words are quiet, but they strike like a spark to dry tinder. My breath catches. I hate that my body knows him this way—how it softens when he's near, how it remembers every place he's touched with reverent devotion.

"Adrian—"

He cuts me off with his mouth, and the world shatters. The kiss is rough, furious, more confession than comfort. His hands slide into my hair, pulling me closer until I can't tell where my heat ends and his begins. My jacket creaks under his grip, melting snow soaking the sleeves, the taste of him salt and winter and something darker.

I shove him back once, hard enough to make him stumble, but he only laughs—low, raw, ruined. "You're still angry," he murmurs.

"You think?"

His smile fades. He steps forward again, voice lower. "Then show me."

So I do. I crash into him, kissing him like a weapon, biting his lip until I taste blood and he growls into my mouth. His hands find my waist, lifting me off the ground, pressing me against the nearest tree. The bark digs into my back; the heat between us flares so hot the snow at our feet begins to hiss.

He breaks the kiss just long enough to drag in a breath. "Every time you walk away, I feel it burn." His mouth finds my jaw, my throat, the place his teeth marked before. "Don't make me prove it."

"Then stop trying to own me." My voice shakes, not from fear, but fury tangled with want.

He pulls back just enough to look at me, eyes bright, voice trembling on a dangerous edge. "If I could, I would." His hand slides beneath my coat, fingers splayed against my ribs. "But I don't know how anymore."

The truth hits harder than the cold. I want to hate him for it, but when his forehead presses against mine, when his breath ghosts across my lips, I can't remember which of us is supposed to be angry anymore.

He kisses me again—slower now, almost reverent—and I feel myself unravel, thread by thread. My fingers curl into his coat, dragging him closer until I can feel his heartbeat pounding against mine.

He whispers against my mouth, voice hoarse. "Forgive me."

"For what?"

"For this."

He kisses me again, like it's the last thing keeping him alive. My knees go weak. The snow catches my fall as he follows me down, his weight pinning me there. The cold bites at my skin, but the heat between us devours it. His mouth moves from my lips to my neck, down to my collarbone, his breath rough, uneven.

I can't tell if I'm shaking from rage or from the way he says my name like a prayer that hurts to speak.

"Adrian..."

He stills. His hand trembles where it grips my coat. "If you walk away now," he says softly, "I don't think my heart will survive it."

The words shouldn't undo me. They shouldn't feel like surrender. But they do.

I reach up, curl my fingers into his shirt, and pull him back to me. Our lips meet again—desperate, defiant, the taste of smoke and snow and something that feels far too much like need.

When he finally pulls back, his forehead rests against mine, breath ragged. "I can't let you go."

My pulse stutters. "Then don't."

The storm around us quiets, the snow glowing faintly from the heat still rolling off my skin. The world narrows to his heartbeat, my breath, the place where our hands are still locked together like a promise neither of us is ready to name.

And for the first time, I don't fight it. I let him hold me there in the dark, in the melting snow, caught between ruin and something that could almost be forgiveness.

Chapter 35

Octavia

Morning feels like a lie.

The kind that starts as mercy and ends as punishment.

Light filters through the curtains in thin, muted lines, the color of dirty gold. It makes dust look holy. The house is too still—no footsteps, no sound of the kettle, no rustle of Adrian's careful movements downstairs. Just me, the silence, and the steady ache between my ribs that won't decide if it's anger or grief.

I don't remember falling asleep. I remember snow melting beneath us. His breath against my mouth. The weight of him pinning me down, every breath of his an apology wrapped in possession. Forgive me. I remember saying then don't—and meaning it.

Now I wish I hadn't.

The sheets smell like him. That rich cedar, heady smoke, and the faint trace of something metallic—blood, maybe, or magic. I should strip the bed, wash it clean, burn the sheets if I have to. But my body won't move yet. It's caught in that fragile space between clarity and collapse, where every truth sounds like a threat.

I stare at the ceiling until the lines blur into something shapeless. My mind keeps replaying last night, looping through every word, every touch, every mistake. The way he said *I can't let you go*. The way my pulse answered, *then don't*.

God, what the hell is wrong with me?

I sit up slowly, rubbing my hands over my face. My palms smell faintly of smoke, and for a second I think I see faint light under the skin—like something burning quietly beneath the surface. *My flames.* The reminder makes me nauseous.

The air in the room is cold, heavy. I pull on the first clothes I find—sweats, soft and worn, the waistband stretched out. A hoodie that smells faintly like lavender detergent and borrowed time. I tie my hair up, then let it fall again, because nothing feels right. I look like myself and not at all like myself.

The mirror across the room catches me mid-movement, and for a moment, I don't recognize the reflection. My eyes look wrong—brighter, clearer. There's a faint shimmer around my skin that wasn't there before, a residue of light that flickers and fades when I blink.

Phoenix.

The word feels foreign and intimate at once.

He said the council would come again. He said I needed to train. He said he couldn't let me go. He said too many things, all of them true in the moment and unbearable in the morning.

I leave the bedroom before the thoughts can circle any closer. The hallway feels longer today, the air cooler. The house watches me the way it always does—listening, waiting. As if it is still deciding the truth of me. The floorboards creak in places that used to be quiet. My magic hums low in my veins, restless, searching for something to burn. The weight of the drastic turn my life has taken swirling around in my mind like gnats.

Downstairs, the fire's already lit. Of course it is. Adrian always leaves it that way, as if the hearth could substitute for warmth. There's a plate on the counter—eggs, toast, fruit. A peace offering as much as a command. A reminder that he knows me well enough to feed me before I remember I'm starving.

I ignore it.

Instead, I go to the window. The snow outside looks different today—flattened, muted, the pristine white trampled by the ghosts of last night's argument. The footprints we left are gone, but I can still feel the heat where he held me, still smell the sharp mix of frost and skin and something I shouldn't miss.

He's gone. Not far—I can feel that much. There's a thread between us now, invisible but undeniable, humming in the air like tension before lightning. I hate that I can feel him even when I don't want to.

"Get out of my head," I whisper, but the air doesn't listen.

I pace the length of the room twice before I cave. My phone's on the table beside the window, screen dark, battery at forty-three percent. One tap and I could call Jess. She'd answer. She always does.

Hey, guess what? You were right. He's hiding something. He might actually be dangerous. Maybe more than I realized.

I picture her reaction, the way her eyebrows will scrunch in disbelief, the worry, the quiet I told you so she'd never say out loud. The way she'd try to make sense of a world she's not supposed to know exists.

Then I picture the council's faces—cold, amused, arrogant—and I stop.

They'd kill her. I know that now. If not for what she knows, then for what she might one day figure out. And they'd make it look like an accident, a neatly folded tragedy that fits into a headline.

Still, my thumb hovers over her name. The photo attached is from last summer—Jess laughing, sunglasses perched on her head, sunlight catching the honey blonde in her hair. My chest tightens.

"I'm not calling," I tell myself. "I'm not dragging her into this."

But part of me wants to. Part of me wants to hear her voice again, to let Jess tell me this isn't as bad as it looks—that I'm not spiraling, not cursed, not whatever the hell the council made me feel like when they showed up at Adrian's door. She was there. She saw the way they looked at me. She might not know what I am, but she knows enough to be afraid for me. And that's worse.

The phone feels heavy in my hand. I scroll past her name twice before setting it back on the table. The sound it makes feels too loud, too final, like I've just shut a door I can't reopen.

The house creaks again. I swear I hear footsteps, but when I turn, the hall is empty. Shadows shift along the walls, slow and deliberate, like they're remembering what it felt like to be alive. Maybe it's him. Maybe it's me. Maybe it's the echo of everything we've already burned through.

I pull my knees to my chest and sit there until my heartbeat evens out. The fire pops once, a soft spark leaping into the air before disappearing up the chimney. The smell of cedar and smoke wraps around me, almost comforting, almost cruel. I close my eyes and try to pretend I'm anywhere else—Jess's apartment, maybe. The city. Noise and neon and people who don't look at me like I'm prophecy. A place where the only heat that ever mattered came from coffee cups and over-worked radiators. A place where no one knows what's under my skin.

It almost works—until I hear the door open.

The sound is soft, hesitant. But I feel it before I hear it.

Adrian.

I don't look up right away. If I do, I'll start something, and I'm not sure which of us will survive it this time.

He doesn't speak at first. The silence between us stretches taut, fragile as glass. Then the floor creaks behind me.

"You didn't eat."

His voice is quieter than usual. Too quiet.

"Wasn't hungry."

"Liar."

"Control freak."

That earns a low laugh. It's tired. Maybe mine is too.

He moves into my peripheral vision—barefoot, dressed in dark jeans and a black shirt rolled to the elbows. The veins in his forearms catch the light when he reaches for his mug. There's something maddeningly domestic about it, the kind of moment that would look normal to anyone else. Except the air around him still crackles faintly, power held on a leash too tight.

He sets his mug down and studies me. "You're angry."

"Observation of the year."

"Do you want to tell me why, or should I guess?"

"Why bother?" I stand, every movement sharp. "You already know everything, don't you? You read me like you read your damn ledgers."

He takes a step closer. "I don't read you. I watch you burn yourself down to make sense of what I already warned you about."

"Warned me? You've controlled everything since I got here! The council, the training, the letters, Jess—God, Adrian, I can't even breathe without you deciding if it's safe first."

He flinches, almost imperceptibly, and I hate that it makes me feel something other than triumph.

"I did what I had to," he says. "They would have torn you apart if I hadn't intervened."

"Then maybe I should've let them try."

He closes the distance between us before I can blink, one hand catching my wrist, not hard, just enough to stop me from turning away. "Don't say that."

"Why not?" I whisper. "Because you'd lose your weapon? Your experiment?"

His grip tightens—not cruel, but desperate. "Because I'd lose *you*."

The words break something open. I yank my arm free, stepping back until my shoulders hit the wall. "You don't have me."

He looks at me for a long moment, and in that silence, I can almost see the edges of what he's not saying—the violence, the guilt, the centuries of loyalty to something that doesn't deserve it.

My breath catches. The fire in me stirs, but it doesn't lash. It waits. It listens. I feel it stretch like a cat beneath my ribs, heat unfurling in ribbons down my arms. It's not wild anymore—it's aware. Watching him. Watching me.

"Octavia," he says, but his voice is softer this time, more warning than command.

"I'm fine." My tone comes out sharper than I intend. "You don't have to treat me like I'm going to explode."

He raises a brow. "Aren't you?"

Instead of answering, I lift my hand, palm up. A faint shimmer blooms across my skin—white-gold, steady as breath. The light doesn't roar this time. It pulses, matching the rhythm of my heart. The air tastes like ozone and candle smoke, and for a moment, the whole world hums with quiet recognition.

"I told you," I whisper. "I have control now."

Adrian doesn't move. The fire reflects in his eyes, turning them molten. "You shouldn't be able to hold it that cleanly."

"Maybe I'm done letting it hold me."

For a beat, he says nothing. Then, slowly, he steps closer—close enough that the heat from my palm brushes his shirt. "That's what scares them, you know. Not your power. Your restraint."

I let the flame die with a thought. The air cools again, and I wipe my hand against my thigh like I'm brushing away dust. "Then maybe they should stop underestimating me."

Something passes between us—something taut and dangerous. He studies me like a man cataloging a threat he doesn't want to neutralize.

"You've changed," he murmurs.

"No," I correct. "You just never bothered to see past what scared you."

The muscle in his jaw flexes. Silence stretches—too much history, not enough forgiveness.

"You think I'm the villain," he says.

"I think you stopped caring if you were."

His breath catches, and it sounds like a growl. "And you think that makes me what—one of them?"

"It makes you exactly like them." I hold his gaze. "You make choices for people who never got to choose."

The words land, hot and final. I can see the truth hit him, a flicker of something dangerous and unguarded beneath all that control.

"I don't need you making decisions for me."

"Then stop putting yourself in their sights," he says, low and sharp.

The quiet that follows is unbearable. I walk toward the kitchen just to breathe. Coffee and cedar—familiar and apologetic—greet me. My phone sits where I left it. Black screen, Jess's name glowing faintly. ***Are you okay?***

No. I can't tell her that. I delete the message.

When I turn back, he's in the doorway, unreadable. I hold my silence until it speaks for me. "I think I don't know who you are anymore."

He nods once, slow. "Then believe this much. I haven't lied to you."

"Not lately," I say. "That's not the same thing."

His mouth twitches—regret, warning. "You want answers before you understand the questions."

"I want the truth."

"You already have it. You just don't like the form."

The words hit harder than I expect. My pulse climbs; I don't look away. "Maybe that's the problem."

He exhales, weary, jaw tight. "You're not ready for what's next."

"Then make me ready."

"I can't."

The tiredness in his voice tells me everything he won't. I turn before he can read my face. "Then maybe I should go before I burn this place down."

He doesn't follow. He watches as I climb the stairs, the distance between us thickening like cold.

Upstairs, the air is still. I sit on the edge of the bed and stare at my hands. The faint shimmer beneath my skin hums, but the flames don't frighten me anymore. They wait for my instruction—faithful, patient, alive.

Maybe that's what terrifies me most... not the power, not him, but the part of me that's beginning to understand both.

Outside, snow falls again—soft, patient—pretending it can hide the wreckage underneath.

But the house still breathes him in the walls, the floorboards, the air. No matter how far I pull away, his presence hums beneath everything—steady, impossible to silence. And somewhere below, I swear I feel him too, pacing the quiet like a ghost that still knows my name.

CHAPTER 36

Snow makes a habit of pretending the world is manageable. By morning it has translated the garden into a single sentence, pared and pale, as if restraint could pass for mercy. The house announces the hour to itself, the boiler's even confession, the grate's soft bone-crack replies, the ticking that refuses theater. I do not summon her. I do not knock. Last night's distance still has edges and pressing on them would bleed the wrong truth.

The study is the only honest room I own. The cedar has learned to speak softly here. The carpet remembers the feet that paced it in better arguments than most men ever attempt. On the desk, the night's work stays in the order I prefer—ledger closed, vellum boxed, the diagram of circles face down because pictures like to boss the mind when it's tired. I hold the cup that forgot how to cool and listen for the sound only the bond returns to me. A second rhythm under the heart's, steady as a metronome that refuses flattery. It is there, fainter than I would like. She is awake, far and not far. The thread has thinned, not frayed. That distinction matters. I memorize it like a map.

Her steps in the corridor are barefoot and careful. When she appears in the doorway, she does not ask if I wanted her to come. She does not ask if she is welcome. She stands in the frame as if the house has always owed her ingress. Her hair is loose and unruly from sleep, curls refusing their own weight. She wears black sweats and a dark, ribbed top that bares a slice of midriff when she breathes. The simplicity makes my mouth meaner than prayer. Her eyes—green moss—flick to the window, then to my hands, then to the papers I haven't offered. She is cataloging exits and weapons and mercy. She is not wrong to do so.

"Morning," she says. The word selects neutrality and sharpens it.

"Morning." I do not put the cup down. I do not pretend I slept.

We could begin with doctrine. We could return to the council and their appetite trained to say duty. We could pick up the argument we set down last night like a knife we promise not to use. She walks past all of that and takes the same seat she chose before—left-hand, back to the wall, window in sight. I approve of the engineering. I do not say so.

"You're frustrated," I offer, not as an apology, not as provocation—just as an instrument named before tuning.

"Yes." Her gaze stays on the window. "At them. At you. At myself. It's... crowded."

I nod once. Crowded is honest. "You walked away."

"I did." Her mouth tilts, not in humor. "You let me."

"I did," I say, and the truth lands in the room without needing escort.

The air arranges itself around a silence that refuses to become a stalemate. She draws her knees up, ankles crossed, hands loose on her shins. The sweater she wore last night is gone, and the heat under her skin has worked its way to the surface in threads that have nothing to do with temperature. The mark at her neck—my bite nearly erased—answers the pulse I keep at the wrist.

She notices my awareness and does not punish me for it. Progress is sometimes the decision not to wound.

"You felt it," she says, finally turning to me. "The pull thinning."

"Yes." There is no good in pretending the bond is unbothered by distance. It is a physics problem, not poetry.

"Does it scare you?" There is genuine curiosity under the barb.

"No," I say. "It offends me." Then, because accuracy requires generosity, "And it worries me."

A breath that is almost a laugh and hates itself for it. "Good."

I set the cup down. Porcelain makes the small clean sound I like—a period, not a threat. "Come here."

"Why?" Challenge on a low flame.

"So I can stop pretending I'm not counting your heartbeats from across the room."

Her chin lifts, a bright, infuriating refusal to be handled. She rises anyway, crossing the rug with those precise steps that refuse ownership, and stops an arm's length away. The scent of her is worked into the house by now—warm skin and paper, lavender, and the ghost of cedar the walls will never release. I could take her wrist. I could press two fingers to the pulse and make a study of it until the study turns to sin. I do not touch her. I let the air do its work.

"You asked for truth," I say. "Have mine. The council's visit was engineered to frighten you into allowing their control. Your anger ruined their plan. I'm grateful for that, but it will also cost us. I intend to pay before they send the bill."

"*Us.*" She tastes the word for poison.

"Us," I repeat. "I will not edit the grammar to make you feel protected from inclusion."

Her eyes narrow, greedy for insult and finding none. "So what now?"

Now I should outline a day with clean edges. Training, containment, study, a walk in the snow to teach the body that cold is not argument. I should pour coffee and say something about discipline that would make her call me insufferable and later admit to herself she learned from it. Instead the thread at my wrist tightens, and every clause I planned fails its spine.

"You're pulling away," I say, and the admission costs me less pride than I expected. "I can feel it. I do not accept it."

Her mouth opens—ready with the quick knife she keeps under her tongue—then shuts again. The restraint is almost worse than the insult would have been. "You don't get to accept or deny how I feel."

"No," I agree. "I get to respond to it."

"How?" The question wears iron.

"Badly," I say. "Today I will do it badly."

Something loosens in her shoulders at that. Not forgiveness, but recognition. She moves closer, a single step that changes the room's math. Up close her eyes are a study in false calm, the green brighter when she is not convinced of her own safety. The bond hums stubbornly. I give it what it demands.

"Octavia."

"Adrian." A warning disguised as my name.

"Come here," I repeat, softer this time, and there's the moment—a small tilt of her head, the seam of her mouth parting, the decision trying to write itself as if I hadn't already composed it.

She steps into me. Not to be possessed. No, she wants to start a fire without matches. My hand rises of its own volition and stops a breath from her jaw. "Permission," I say, because theater is what men call consent when they're afraid of the answer, and I've been toeing that line for too long.

"Take it," she says, and the room drops a degree, and the study learns a new liturgy.

I touch her where the jaw meets the ear, two fingers and a thumb, not a hold, a mapping. Heat climbs the ladder of her throat into my hand. She exhales on it. The second rhythm at my wrist answers like a chord struck clean. I lower my mouth the distance of a decision, and she meets it before I finish choosing. The kiss has nothing to do with romance. It is accuracy—two flames deciding which one will lean and which will learn to stand still while burning.

She tastes like coffee stolen from my cup and something sweeter she refuses to name. When her hands find my waist, they anchor, not plead. I let the first kiss teach us both what we already know—that the distance is an idiot, that the night lied, that the house enjoys witnesses. The second kiss is more difficult. It is also more honest. I change the angle, she makes a sound I will not survive hearing from another mouth, and the study takes a step back to give us the room it pretends is not alive.

"Tell me to stop," I say, not because I intend to, but because a man should have to earn the risk he prefers.

"No," she says into my mouth, a word that chooses itself, "closer."

I oblige. Her back finds the edge of the desk, papers shifting without complaint. My hands span her waist. The heat under my palms confirms what her body already knows—she's been learning to bank the flame. It hums low, obedient, waiting for language. I give it one... *mine*. The word is an engineering note, not a collar.

Her fingers slide under my shirt and the breath I take has less to do with oxygen than with the shock of her skin to mine. She is not tentative. She explores with a scholar's discipline and a thief's entitlement. My composure—the city I've built in my bones—lists and warns me of collapse. I ignore it. I kiss her harder, then break for air I do not require.

"Say it," I tell her.

"Say what?" The challenge pretends to be innocence; the smile ruins the act.

"That you're here." I press my forehead to hers, teach the bond the rhythm I prefer. "With me. Not with your anger. Not with your fear. Just me."

She studies my mouth like it's a code she intends to crack and then—thank every god I do not believe in—decides to answer cleanly. "I'm here," she says, and the air around us learns to admit it.

I slide my hand to the inside of her thigh, just above the knee, and watch her eyes when the pressure changes from question to instruction. Her breath glances at my cheek, quick, unpretty, perfect. The second rhythm in my wrist pinches smartly, her pulse behind my palm answering like agreement. I lift her onto the desk in one smooth motion. The papers beneath her body yield like voluntary witnesses, rustling in approval. The bond flares—heat, light, the flavor of iron at the back of my tongue—not spectacle, evidence.

"Look at me," I say, and she does. Whatever we are doing to each other today, it will not be done with eyes closed.

The first sound she makes when I run my thumb along the line where fabric stops being useful is the sound that ruins men who rely on restraint. I am not ruined; I am reengineered. She opens for my hand because her body is impolite and her mind is tired of negotiating with it. I reward both. The pace is not punishment. It is devotion in a language that requires no altar. When her head tips back, I catch her by the nape and reorient the moment to my mouth. The second sound is worse for me. I ensure it happens again.

"Adrian," she breathes into my jaw, and I learn what certain names are for—invocation.

"Yes." My thumb slows, not to tease but to confirm she is the one in charge of the direction. Her body chooses yes without congressional review. The flames answer without spectacle—light behind skin, heat through cloth, the air tasting briefly of rain over hot stone. She laughs once, shocked at herself, then bites her lip to keep from apologizing for being alive. I will not allow that. I kiss the apology out of her mouth, then remind her how to forget it with my hand.

She folds into it. It is not a surrender, but a decision to be accurate. The desk shifts beneath us, a small consenting groan. The fire in the grate has the temerity to be jealous. When she breaks—shuddering, breath coming in beautiful, reckless fragments—she doesn't close her eyes. She watches me watch her. That is the rite. We do not lie to the witness.

"Again," I tell her, quiet enough to rearrange bone. "And *louder*."

"*Make* me," she says, voice raspy, wrecked and brand-new.

I do. The second crest is faster, built from the first's memory and my refusal to permit the body to underperform its design. When it hits, she says my name like a secret the council will never earn.

Light crawls under her skin—brief, veracious, a diagram made honest. The heat is clean, the air sweeter, the flame disciplined to a blade edge. She is learning control because rage is trying to recruit her and I will not allow it new members.

I step back only when her breathing remembers cadence. She pulls me back with a fist in my shirt because grace is expensive and she prefers cash. I go because I have never enjoyed saying no to truth.

"Your turn," she mutters, a threat disguised as mercy.

"Later." The word is a promise. It also keeps the room from forgetting its ceiling.

Her smile acknowledges both. "Coward."

"Architect," I correct, and lift her down as if the floor needed proof of gravity.

The distance of an arm's length feels like exile. I close half of it. She closes the rest. Her mouth finds mine again, slower now, the urgency traded for a meaner intimacy. The thread at my wrist settles into a line I trust. The part of me that passes for demon—the Noctevaris blood that has always preferred midnight to noon—purrs under the sternum as if the house has tuned itself to her pitch. It has.

When we finally stop kissing it is not for lack of want but because language has waited its turn like a good soldier and I am not immune to the pleasure of reward.

"You did not come here for this," I say, rougher than I like.

"I did," she counters, without shame. Then, softer, "And for what comes after."

"Which is?"

"You tell me the parts you didn't last night. And you don't put them in footnotes." A pause. "Then, you tell me why your restraint slipped just now. You don't get to pretend it didn't."

"I thought you preferred when it did."

She tips her head, green eyes narrowing. "I prefer accuracy. Start there."

I could retreat to doctrine, hide behind names she hasn't earned. I choose the mess instead. "Because the thread thinning felt like an insult I could not allow to stand." A breath, honest enough to be ugly. "Because when you walked away, I learned how much of my patience was performance. Because I do not want a world in which you discover what you are and then choose to be it without me."

Her expression changes by degrees, an eclipse in reverse. Heat, anger, comprehension, fury again because comprehension offends her—then a quieter thing I refuse to name. "There," she says. "Keep talking like that."

"I claimed you in front of them," I say. "Not as *property*. As jurisdiction. It will make enemies, but it will keep you alive while you learn how to choose which enemies to keep. I am head of a table that thinks it can convince a woman she wrote the letter that binds her. I intend to set the table on fire if it keeps pretending that trick is genius."

"Better," she murmurs. "Closer to truth."

"The killings," I say, and she goes very still. Good. If we are to be accurate, let it be full. "You want a line you can carve into me with. You want a denial you can hate me for or a confession you can leash me with. I will give you neither, not because I am protecting myself, but because I will not let you become a woman who needs purity in order to stay."

"That's manipulative," she says. No heat, all blade.

"Yes," I say. "And correct."

The anger returns, bright, exquisite. She does not spend it. She stores it. "Then show me the ledger. Teach me to read which acts belong to which hands. Let me decide if the ink on your fingers is yours."

I nod. The room relaxes as if the sentence the house wanted to hear finally entered it. "After breakfast," I say. "After training. After you hold flame in both hands again and set it down without insulting the air. Then the ledger."

"Okay." She says, sliding her palm over my chest, pressing just above where the second rhythm lives. For a second I forget myself.

"You feel that?" She asks.

"Yes."

"It's not going away," she says, equal parts warning and consolation.

"I do not want it to," I answer, and earn the smallest smile a man is permitted in a morning like this one.

I lift the jacket from the chair as she passes me—black wool, heavier than her top—and hold it out. She slides her arms through without a word. It's mine, but she takes it as if it had been waiting for her all along. She rolls her eyes at the gesture like a girl who'd burn a cathedral if the usher asked her to sit in the wrong pew. I lean and put my mouth to the fading crescents at her neck, tasting sleep and iron and the thing I do not dare name yet. She shivers the way precision enjoys shivering and doesn't step back.

"Breakfast," I say, because the body requires ordinary ritual if it's to perform the extraordinary without breaking.

"Then training," she returns, not a question. "Then the ledger."

"Yes."

"And later," she adds, mischief cutting through the morning like a thin blade, "your turn."

"Later," I confirm, and the demon in me bares its teeth in what passes for assent.

We leave the study as if it has earned a rest from us. The corridor gives our footsteps back in correct proportion. The kitchen receives us with copper that enjoys its own silence and the fragrance of ground beans that honors the cup it will become. I plate a breakfast boring enough to save gods—eggs with their yolks intact, toast that pretends to be modest because it is good at it. She eats like a student who has learned what appetite is for. I drink the second espresso because men who lie to themselves in the morning deserve worse afternoons.

We do not speak of the council. We do not speak of Jess. We do not speak of the way the world sharpens its knives when a woman refuses to hand them over. We speak of breath, of stance, of how flame is a grammar that hates adverbs. She laughs once into her coffee when I say it. I allow the offense because it puts color back where the night removed it.

In the hall we face the mat like contrarians at mass. "Begin," I say.

She fails beautifully, which is to say quickly and with attention. The first flare wants spectacle; she hands it patience. The second wants to be a scream; she gives it diction. On the third, I make the mistake of touching her wrist without warning—habit, not insult—and the spark that jumps to my fingers bites. I do not move. The heat climbs her forearm in a vein of light, obedient as a hound that wants to impress its cruelest trainer. She inhales. Holds. Sets it down. The floor does not scorch. I nod once, and she lets herself enjoy the line of my mouth that counts as approval.

"Again," she commands.

We do. The fourth time something older than the house slides under her skin and shows its feathers. It is brief—a geometry that finds a third dimension and doesn't apologize. I catch her before the aftershock unseats her and let her lean a weight I do not deserve. She steadies on my shirt with both hands, head bent, breath drawing order.

"*Phoenix*," I murmur, almost to the air, because names spoken to rooms sometimes coax them to be gentler.

"Maybe," she says, and her mouth finds a smile that puts a thumbprint on my ribs. "Later."

"Yes," I agree, and step back because I am not ready to be the version of myself who cannot.

By noon, the snow brightens. The house approves of what it has overheard. We eat again because the body will not serve an empire that refuses to feed it. We do not resume the argument, or tuck it away. It sits between us like a tool we will need later. After the meal, I take her to the study and set the ledger on the desk without ceremony. She looks at it like a woman looks at a door she intends to master. She opens it. She reads. She begins to annotate the world she was convinced could not be understood without magic.

The bond settles into its correct temperature. The thread at my wrist stops sulking and returns to discipline. She lifts her head once, eyes incandescent not with flame but with comprehension cruel enough to be holy, and says, "Teach me how to break their sentences."

"With pleasure," I say, and the demon, and the gentleman, and the rest of me that prefers accuracy to virtue agree for once.

Later will come. The ledger will bleed. My hands will learn a new grammar across her skin and the study will have to forgive us for what we do to its quiet. But now—now the morning has done it's honest work. The thread has thickened. The distance has been replaced with a tension I trust. The world outside pretends snow can keep it clean. Inside, we choose the more difficult salvation: *to be exact about what we want, and to take it without lying.*

"Again," she says, tapping the page.

"Again," I echo, and teach her where the ink reveals the hand that held the knife.

CHAPTER 37

Adrian

The study has moods of its own. It hums when the fire burns clean and sulks when the window fogs, and tonight it does both. The ledger lies open on the desk like a throat—ink pulsing faintly in its seams, the parchment breathing in a rhythm that is not entirely mortal. The scent of iron and oil rises from it, a priest's blend—sacrament and sin in equal measure. I have loved this book longer than I have loved my own reflection.

Octavia stands near the shelves, half in shadow, one hand resting on the carved spine of an atlas that predates any map worth trusting. Her presence warms the room enough to unmake the frost creeping across the corners of the windowpane. When she finally turns toward me, the fire answers her before I do.

"So this is it," she says. "The infamous ledger."

"Yes." My voice doesn't carry far; the paper doesn't like to share sound. "Every name the Society demanded. Every reason they invented."

"Yours?"

"Mine," I admit, closing my hand over the lower margin where the ink bleeds a little darker. "The pages record blood in the way scripture records miracles—through interpretation."

Her gaze fixes on the script. "You wrote this."

"I wrote what they wanted to see," I say. "They needed evidence of obedience, so I gave them beauty instead. A pattern they could mistake for penance."

I turn the page. The edges whisper like knives drawn slow. Names scroll down in red-brown loops, followed by symbols that look like musical notation for grief. "The Society calls it proof of devotion. Nytherion calls it tithe."

"Devotion," she repeats, the word tasting foul. "You kill for worship?"

"I kill to keep their god from waking hungry." I meet her eyes. "There is a difference."

The ledger shifts, almost imperceptibly, as though pleased to be mentioned. A faint tremor passes through the desk, and the fire lowers its crown. I let it. The dark is honest company.

"They demand offerings," I continue. "Always the same—young, gifted, touched by the flame. Each girl they chose was born under the wrong star, her power too raw, too bright. They feared her more than they pitied her, so they dressed the fear in ritual and called it mercy."

"And you did it."

"I carried out the sentence before the council could. They would have done worse—sacrifice without understanding, spectacle without silence. I made it quick. Clean. Every one of them died without fear." I look down at my hands, remembering the weight of each ending. "I told myself I was saving them from the Society's theater. That was the first lie I learned to live inside."

The room stills. Dust motes drift like ash in prayer. She steps closer but doesn't speak. The ledger listens.

"They told me Nytherion would bless me," I say quietly. "That service would earn control over what he gave me. But the Hollow Seraph does not bargain. He *takes*. He carved his wings into me when I was nineteen—shadow and bone and blood—then left me to find the rest of his hunger on my own. The council mistook that for favor."

Her eyes flicker. "And you believed them."

"I believed the absence of pain was forgiveness." I exhale a laugh too soft to be mirth. "But Nytherion's mark doesn't fade. When the hunger comes, I can smell it before it arrives—the static in the air, the metallic taste of thunder just before it strikes."

As if on cue, the light in the room shifts. My shadow lengthens, reaching the shelves, splitting into two, then four, tendrils rising like smoke given shape. From behind my ribs, something unfurls—subtle at first, then undeniable. The wings emerge half-formed, their feathers a weave of lightless silk and ash, edges flickering as if stitched from embers. My canines ache against the restraint of civility. The beast beneath my skin rolls once, restless.

"The Hollow Seraph," she whispers. "You're—"

"Vampire by blood. Noctevaris by inheritance. Bound to the Seraph by choice." The truth curls like steam between us. "That choice keeps the Society's monster fed so their mirrors stay clean."

"And the girls?"

"Each one a warning," I say. "Every century the Society chooses another child touched by the Flame. They tell themselves it is duty—to balance what the gods left unfinished. But it's fear. Always fear. They think Nytherion sleeps because they bleed enough to keep him dreaming."

She studies me, her pupils dilated by the flicker of my wings. "And what do you think?"

"I think the dream ended the moment you woke." I close the ledger gently, pressing my palm to the seal embossed in its cover. The sigil burns faintly—a pair of wings folded around a dying star. "You're not part of their pattern. You're the reason it breaks."

The shadows retract, reluctantly. The air smells of ozone and candlewax, heavy with the aftertaste of revelation. I reach for a quill that no longer writes ink but memory and trace the rim of the closed ledger. The pulse inside it slows, quieted by acknowledgment.

She takes a step closer, close enough that I can feel the hum of her flame beneath her skin. "And if the council finds out?"

"They will." I glance toward the window, where the snow has begun again, soft and deliberate. "They always do. They'll demand I prove my loyalty—blood for blood, devotion measured in ruin. That is what this ledger is for. It reminds them that I remember my place."

Her voice trembles, not from fear but fury. "And what place is that?"

"The one between their god and their guilt." I meet her eyes. "The knife's edge that cuts both ways."

The fire gutters, then steadies. The ledger's spine gleams faintly under its own pulse, alive in the way old magic pretends not to be. The shadows along the wall ripple once and settle.

"You could stop," she says.

"No." The answer leaves me before I can temper it. "If I stop, they'll find someone worse. Someone who enjoys it."

Her expression softens, but the sorrow in it is sharper than accusation. "And you don't?"

I give her the truth. "Once. I did."

The admission lands like confession in an empty church. She doesn't flinch. Her breath leaves a small bloom of heat between us.

"I can still feel them," I add, quieter now. "The ones I spared. The ones I couldn't. They sing when the ledger opens. That's what the council never understood—it was never about blood. It was about remembrance. Nytherion feeds on what memory leaves behind."

"Then what happens when there's nothing left to remember?"

"Then he wakes."

The words taste like iron. I look away, to the shelves, to the rows of quiet witnesses who have watched me rewrite the same lie for centuries. "That is why I stay, why I write their names, and why I choose which monsters live long enough to sign them."

The flames bend toward her as if seeking permission to rise. The ledger hums once in approval of the truth. I close it and turn the key in its lock, sealing the air with a faint hiss.

The house exhales. The fire resumes its ordinary language. The scent of parchment and smoke thickens until it could almost be mistaken for peace.

Almost.

She moves toward me, fingers reaching for me as if she can't stop herself. "It's your turn," she whispers, repeating the phrase from earlier.

A wicked smile spreads across my face, and I let it, admiring the way her hands roam over my body. She takes what she wants without asking for permission. That makes me proud.

First, she removes my shirt with careful ease, her fingers sliding down my chest and stomach with deliberate precision. I acknowledge her restraint, breathe in the lavender scent swirling between us—wholly like her—but there's something new beneath it, a hint of citrus. The blend shouldn't go well together, but it does. It curls around my body, smothering me in its intoxicating pull.

Her fingers glide lower, tracing the hard lines of my abdomen until they reach the belt at my waist. She tuts softly. "This won't do."

Her voice is breathless, raspy, laced with hunger. With agonizing delicacy, she unzips me, feeling for the hardness between my legs. I let her explore, her touch a slow study in possession, each delicate movement deliberate.

It's sinful. Wicked. Charged with something neither of us want to name. She strokes languidly, as if time bends for her alone, as if every second belongs to this.

Then, just when I think it can't get any better, her head dips—tongue swirling around the head of my cock with practiced ease. A groan escapes me, deep and involuntary, tearing free before I can stop it. Control slips its leash.

My fingers glide into her hair, wrapping around the strands as I pull her mouth deeper onto my cock. She takes it all like the good girl she is, choking just a little when the head grazes her throat.

The sound she makes—half moan, half defiance—vibrates through me. Her fist pumps along my length, her tongue swirling in frantic rhythm, slick and relentless. It's so good. So fucking good. Every bit of control I've ever had slips away, piece by piece, until there's nothing left but heat and want.

Her eyes never leave mine as she works me—no hesitation, no shame. She refuses to look away, refuses to hide from what we're doing here, in the middle of my study where the scent of old paper and cedar smoke clings to the air. I love that about her.

Love. The word strikes like lightning. I nearly flinch at the thought. There's no way this is love.

I force it down, refusing to let it sink its teeth into me. She senses the shift, speeds up, her mouth and hand moving in perfect, devastating sync. Her tongue traces the underside of my cock, teeth grazing the head in a fleeting drag of danger. It's her teeth—sharp, teasing, claiming—that break me open. I come hard, a sound tearing from my throat as her name burns the air between us.

"Look how undone you come for me," she purrs, her voice dark velvet, soaked in triumph.

But I'm not finished. I don't lose my hardness—only the last thin straps of restraint that beg to be torn apart. I grip her arms, pull her up roughly, spin her around until her chest hits the desk. Papers scatter. My breath catches on her skin. In one motion, I drag her pants and underwear down, the sound of fabric and breath colliding in the air.

She gasps, the word yes falling from her lips like prayer. I slide into her, slow at first, then all at once—sweet, molten heat wrapping around me like a vice. The sensation is unbearable, exquisite. I grab her hands, pin them behind her back with my hand, and start to move—harder, faster, until the rhythm becomes its own language.

She glows beneath me, golden light spilling from her skin, racing up her spine and out through her fingertips. "Adrian!" she cries, voice breaking, half light, half flame.

I don't stop. I can't. I drive her higher, deeper, until her sounds blur with the storm in my veins. My fingers slide between her legs, finding her clit, circling slowly, deliberately, until her body clenches around me like she's made to burn for this. Each thrust pulls another sound from her throat—raw, breathless, surrendering. The air shimmers with heat and the scent of her, of us, of ruin and devotion.

When she finally lets go, she screams my name over and over, her body quaking, every inch of her lit in flame. The sound tears through the room, raw and perfect, echoing off the shelves and walls until it feels like the house itself is breathing her name. I move faster, harder—punishing myself as much as her flesh—for the feelings devouring me as I watch her come undone in my arms.

My own release follows close behind, grunts and broken words spilling from my throat, sounding more like devotion than desire, more like prayer than sin. She's the flame written in blood I've been searching for—the one I was never meant to find.

I stay inside her for a moment longer, unwilling to surrender the connection, unwilling to accept the inevitable return of distance. When I finally pull out, it's slow, reluctant, reverent. Her body trembles against mine, heat still radiating between us, light still flickering across her skin in soft gold waves.

Our breaths sync—ragged, uneven, drawn from the same aching place. The glow around her softens but never fades. She turns, and I touch her face, thumb brushing the corner of her mouth, whispering, "My wicked ruin... what have you done to me?"

The question lingers, heavy and alive, suspended in the space between us. She doesn't answer. She only looks at me—wide-eyed, silent, disbelieving—with something deeper stirring beneath it all. Not fear. Not doubt. Something quieter, more dangerous. Something like contentment... and the first shadow of belonging.

CHAPTER 38

Morning always feels thinner after fire.

The air in the house has changed—emptier, lighter, like it knows we've taken something sacred from it and left silence in its place. I wake to the faint hiss of snow melting against the windowpane, the smell of roasted coffee drifting down the hall. The sheets beside me are still warm, but he's gone. It shouldn't ache, but it does.

For the first time in days, the world feels quiet enough to hear myself think. The flame inside me hums low, steady—a heartbeat, not a storm. It doesn't fight me now. It listens. My palms glow faintly when I stretch them toward the light, and for a moment, I just watch them shimmer. I've spent weeks fearing this thing in me, calling it a curse. But now... now it feels like breath. Like truth. Like I was always meant to hold it.

I find him in the study. The fire's lit, books open, a half-written note on the desk. He looks almost ordinary—barefoot, shirt sleeves rolled up, hair still damp from the shower. But there's something in his shoulders, a stillness that doesn't belong to him. When he lifts his gaze to me, the look that passes over his face is soft, and it breaks something small and stupid in my chest.

"Morning," I say. My voice sounds steadier than I feel.

"Morning." He nods to the cup waiting on the table. "I made yours how you like it."

I take it, fingers brushing his. The warmth seeps into my skin, steadying me. "Thank you."

We don't talk for a while. We never need to in the mornings. The snow outside falls in ribbons, thin and constant, and the house hums quietly, content. He leans back in his chair, watching the fire like it's the only thing brave enough to stare back at him. I sip my coffee, trying not to think about the way his voice sounded last night when he said my name.

Finally, he speaks. "You're ready."

I blink. "For what?"

"To go home."

The words hit like a cold blade slipped between ribs. "*What*?"

He turns to me, face unreadable but eyes full of something too human to hide. "You've learned control. The flame listens to you now. You can move through the world without burning it down."

"That's not what I asked."

He sighs, rubbing the bridge of his nose. "Octavia—"

"No," I cut in, setting the cup down hard enough that the liquid shivers. "Don't do that. Don't talk to me like this is some noble act. You're sending me away."

His voice softens, but the words don't. "I'm giving you back your freedom."

I laugh—a small, bitter sound. "Freedom? That's what this is?"

He stands, slow, deliberate, like he's approaching something fragile. "You don't want to be caged. You've made that clear. You deserve to live, to see the world again. You've been locked away here long enough."

I shake my head, but it's useless. The decision's already carved into his tone. "You said I wasn't safe."

"You're safer now than you've ever been." He comes closer, stopping just out of reach. "The council's eyes have shifted. If you leave, it'll take the heat off both of us."

I stare at him, the ache crawling its way up my throat. "So this is strategy."

"This is survival."

I swallow, the bitterness sharp on my tongue. "And what about you?"

He almost smiles, but it's the kind that doesn't reach the eyes. "I'll be fine."

"No, you won't," I whisper. "You never are when you start pretending you will be."

That earns me a flicker of a real smile, broken and beautiful. "You see too much."

"Maybe you taught me to."

He looks down, fingers flexing like he's fighting the instinct to reach for me. "This isn't the end, Octavia."

"Feels like it."

"It's the beginning." He steps closer, the air between us sparking faintly, that old pulse of heat alive again. "When you come back—and you will—I'll do it properly this time. I'll take you out. Wine. Dinner. Music. The things I should've given you before I ever touched you."

I can't breathe. "That's not what I want."

He exhales through his nose, a sound half sigh, half surrender. "You deserve to be wooed. Romanced. Not... whatever this was." His gaze drifts to the floor, then back to me. "You deserve to choose me without fire forcing your hand."

I take a step toward him, every nerve screaming. "And what if I already did?"

That stops him cold. His throat works once before he finds his voice. "Then let it be real when it happens again."

The firelight flickers across his face, making him look older, sadder, in a way that breaks my heart. I want to argue. I want to demand he take it back. But I know him too well. Once Adrian decides something is right, no force in the world—no council, no god, no flame—will sway him.

The room feels smaller. The smell of cedar and ash clings to everything. I move to the window, needing distance, seeking serenity. The snow outside has thickened, falling in silent waves, blanketing the world in white. It looks peaceful. It's not. Beneath that calm, everything burns.

"How long?" I ask quietly.

"As long as it takes for them to stop watching," he says. "A few weeks. Maybe a month."

"And then what? You show up at my door with a bottle of wine and pretend none of this happened?"

He almost laughs. "Something like that."

I turn, meeting his eyes. "You think you can just start over?"

"I think we have to." He walks toward me then, slow and sure, until he's close enough that I can feel the heat radiating off him. "I want you to see who I am without the council's shadow between us. Without blood and power and fire binding us together." His hand comes up, fingers brushing a strand of hair from my face. "I want you to see the man, not the monster."

My chest aches. "And what if I like both?"

He goes still. Then his mouth curves, soft, almost reverent. "Then I'm doomed."

A shaky breath escapes me before I can stop it. "You already were."

He laughs quietly, the sound breaking on something like relief. "Gods, you make it hard to let you go."

"Then don't."

He closes his eyes, leans his forehead to mine. "If I don't, I'll ruin you."

"You already did."

He huffs a broken laugh. "Fair enough."

The silence between us stretches. He breathes me in like a man memorizing a scent he doesn't want to forget. I memorize him too—the faint scar above his brow, the warmth of his breath against my lips, the sound of his heartbeat, steady even now.

Finally, he pulls back, brushing his thumb over my jaw. "Pack what you need. I'll take you myself."

"I can drive."

He shakes his head. "Humor me."

The hours that follow blur. We move through the motions—folding clothes, gathering books, the quiet choreography of pretending this is temporary. He helps me zip my bag without speaking. His hand lingers a moment too long, and I can feel the battle in him, the urge to stop this before it starts. But he doesn't.

By the time the car is loaded, the sun has begun to set. The sky burns in shades of gold and rose, the world reflecting my name back at me. I stand on the porch, staring out across the snow-covered field, and wonder how a place that once terrified me now feels like home.

Adrian comes up behind me, coat draped over one arm. "You're quiet."

I shrug. "Just thinking."

"Dangerous habit."

"Learned from the best."

He smirks faintly, helping me into the coat. His fingers brush the back of my neck—small, electric contact that steals the air from my lungs. "You'll be all right," he says softly. "You've learned control. You're stronger than you think."

I nod, though I don't feel it. "What if it all comes back?"

"Then you'll remember what to do."

"And if I forget?"

"Then I'll remind you." His voice drops to a whisper. "Always."

I want to tell him I don't believe in always. That we're too dangerous for promises like that. But I don't. I just nod again, because there's no version of goodbye that won't break me.

When I step outside, the cold bites through my boots—sharp, clean, the kind that tastes like iron in the air. The world is muffled in white. Adrian's already by the car, holding the door open for me. Neither of us speaks as I slide in. The seat is warm, the leather familiar, and the scent of cedar and smoke clings to it like a ghost that refuses to leave.

He drives in silence. The engine hums low, a quiet, steady pulse beneath the falling snow. The roads wind through the sleeping town, lamplight bending in the glass, painting his face in strokes of gold and shadow. Every now and then, he glances at me—quick, careful—but says nothing. I don't either. Words would only make the leaving heavier.

By the time we reach my street, the snow has turned to sleet. It taps against the windshield like impatient fingers. My apartment looks smaller than I remember—ordinary, warm light spilling from a window, wreaths on Antonio's doors already half-frozen. Normal. The kind of normal I don't remember how to fit into anymore.

He pulls up to the curb and puts the car in park. The heater hums, filling the silence between us. I wait for him to say something, to tell me this is a mistake, that I should stay. He doesn't. He just looks at me like he's memorizing every line of my face.

"This is where I leave you," he says quietly.

The words scrape something raw inside me. "You're really going to just drop me off like this?"

His gaze flicks to the building, then back to me. "I'd carry you inside if I thought you'd let me."

I swallow hard, fingers tightening around the strap of my bag. "I don't want you to go."

His smile is faint, aching. "You'll see me again, Octavia." He leans closer, voice dropping to a whisper that feels like a vow. "This isn't goodbye. It's just precaution."

Before I can answer, he opens his door and steps into the snow. The wind catches his coat, whipping it around him like wings. He circles to my side, opens my door, and holds out a hand. I take it, because I can't not. His touch burns even through the chill.

When my boots hit the ground, I can feel the heat of neighbors' eyes. Curtains twitch. Someone's front light flickers on. The woman across the street is standing in her window, pretending to water a dead plant while she stares. I can already imagine the gossip—who's the man in the expensive car, why is he dropping her off, why does she look like she's been somewhere she shouldn't have been?

Adrian doesn't seem to notice—or maybe he does, and simply doesn't care. He stands beside me on the steps, close enough that I can feel the pulse in his wrist. Snow catches in his hair, melting as fast as it lands.

"Inside," he murmurs. "Before you freeze."

I want to say something brave. Something final. Instead, I just nod. My throat feels too tight for anything else.

He brushes his thumb along my jaw—once, soft, quick—and then he's gone. Back in the car. Engine rumbling to life. Headlights cutting through the falling snow.

I stand there until the taillights fade down the street and disappear into the blur of winter. The cold seeps into my bones, but I can still feel him—his heat, his voice, the phantom press of his mouth against my skin. Quietly tethered.

Then my phone rings.

The sound startles me, sharp and sudden against the silence. I fumble it out of my pocket, hands shaking. Jess's name flashes across the screen. For a second, I just stare at it, pulse pounding in my ears. The normal world calling, demanding answers.

I swallow, draw in a breath that fogs the air, and swipe to answer.

"Finally you fucking answer, I've only been trying to reach you for the last week. Why won't you return my calls? I can only cover you so much, you know. Landon is getting anxious about why you're no longer popping by the office. And how is it that ALL your professors received the same cryptic message about you taking on a private course that required weeks of study for your dissertation? And what the fuck were those people talking about that day?"

"Jess..." I start, sliding a hand down my face. The cold bites at my fingertips, the screen slick against my palm.

"No! Octavia Adeline Hartwell, you answer me now. I'm tired of your excuses."

The sound of my full name on her lips yanks me back, to nights of bad decisions and good intentions. It almost undoes me. I push the door open with my shoulder and slip inside, letting the smell of the building swallow me—old wood polish, somebody's burnt pizza, the faint tang of snow melting on tile. The bell above Antonio's bodega downstairs chimes softly, a bright little sound beneath her voice.

I climb the stairs, boots creaking against worn carpet, the railing smooth and cold under my fingers. My heart thuds out a rhythm between her questions. "Hold on, Jess," I mutter into the phone, breath catching as I reach the next landing. "I'm going inside. Just—give me a second."

For the next hour, I give Jess everything I can—everything I dare—my voice low, urgent, carrying through the phone like a confession. Bits of the murders, the society, the strange coincidences, the connections between names she's only half-heard whispered in headlines. My words come out in broken pieces, like glass sliding across tile.

She goes quiet. Not the kind of quiet you get when someone's lost interest, but the kind of quiet that sharpens—journalist quiet, her kind of quiet. I can practically see her on the other end, one leg tucked under her, hair falling forward, pen in hand even if she swears she isn't writing.

I stop at my door, keys shaking in my fingers. "You can't tell anyone this, Jess," I whisper. "Our lives are at stake."

There's a beat of static, a breath, and then her voice, softer but no less relentless. "Octavia..."

"I'm serious." I press my forehead against the door, the paint cool against my skin. My pulse feels like it's trying to climb out of my throat. "Promise me."

Silence. Then, "I promise."

Something in me loosens, but it isn't relief. It's more like a knot giving up, the strands fraying instead of untangling.

I push the door open and step inside. The apartment smells like me and not-me—lavender detergent, coffee gone stale in the sink, snow still clinging to the sill. The radiator hisses like an animal refusing to be tamed. I shut the door behind me and lean against it, phone still pressed to my ear.

"You sound different," Jess says quietly.

I swallow. "Do I?"

"Yeah. Like... like you've been somewhere you can't come back from."

I close my eyes, letting her words land. Somewhere in the room, the heat of my own power hums under the surface, waiting. The snow outside presses itself against the glass, trying to listen in.

"Maybe I have," I whisper.

"Octavia—"

"I'm here," I say, and hang up before she can say anything else. My phone screen goes black.

The apartment feels too small, too bright. The ordinary things—my mug on the counter, my coat slung over a chair—look foreign, like they belong to someone else's life. I cross the room and sink onto the couch, pulling my knees to my chest. My palms are still warm from holding the phone, but inside, the flame stirs, coiling low and quiet.

For the first time, it doesn't scare me. For the first time, it feels like something I chose.

Outside, snow falls harder, catching in the streetlights like sifted salt. Neighbors move behind curtains, their shadows sliding across fabric, their whispers pressing at my door. My phone buzzes once on the table—Jess again, probably—but I don't reach for it.

I sit there in the dim light, feeling the world tilt. Adrian's absence is still a weight against my skin, the echo of his hands, his voice. I hate that it feels like a missing limb. I hate that part of me wants to call him back.

Instead, I breathe. I let the flame settle, a living thing tucked under my ribs, no longer begging to be fed.

And as the snow keeps falling, soft and patient, pretending it can hide everything underneath, I finally let myself believe I might be able to hold both truths—the life I had and the one waiting to burn through me.

I lean my forehead against the cold glass of the window, palms flat on either side of the frame. The heat of my skin fogs the pane and fades almost as quickly as it appears, leaving faint ghosts of my fingerprints. Below, the street glows in fractured amber, old lamplight bending around the snowflakes like a halo. Everything looks ordinary. Too ordinary.

Then I see it.

A figure at the far end of the block, half-hidden beneath the awning of the bodega across the street. Not moving. Just standing. Watching. It's tall but the posture is wrong—angles where there should be curves, shadows where the lamplight should cut clean. For a moment I think it's a trick of the snow, a parked shape or a slanted sign. But when a car rolls past, its headlights slide right through the figure without illuminating it.

The flame inside me stirs, a low hum under my ribs. My breath fogs the glass again, obscuring the view. By the time I wipe it clear with my sleeve, the figure is gone.

Just the street, the cars, the piles of shoveled snow. Nothing else. But the feeling doesn't leave. It lingers, thick and metallic, like the taste of a coin pressed to my tongue.

I back away from the window, pulse still racing from the shadow that shouldn't have been there. Inside, the apartment feels too small, too quiet, my heartbeat too loud. The scent of cedar from the candle on the counter mingles with the faint bite of city air that followed me in, vigorous and wrong. I sink onto the couch, pulling my knees up, trying to steady the tremor in my hands. The flame hums low in my chest, restless, like it knows what I saw but refuses to name it.

For a while, I just sit there, watching the candle flicker. The shadows on the wall stretch and twist in ways they shouldn't. Every creak of the building feels deliberate, every gust of wind outside like a breath pressed too close to the glass. I tell myself it's nothing—that I'm tired, that paranoia is the cost of surviving him. But the feeling doesn't fade.

When I finally crawl into bed, the sheets are cold against my skin, the silence heavier than it should be. The hum inside me sharpens, not pain exactly, but a warning that doesn't know where to land. I close my eyes and wait for sleep, but it hovers just out of reach, circling like a predator that already knows where I live.

CHAPTER 39

The Gazette looks smaller after everything. The brick front pinches in around the doorway like it's bracing for winter, the crooked brass handle still wobbly in that way Landon keeps promising to fix and never does. A handwritten sign is taped to the glass—BACK IN FIVE MIN—someone forgot the "UTES." I catch my reflection as I tug the door. Hair down and glossy because I didn't have the patience to braid it, black wool coat, gray sweater, dark jeans, boots that know every crack in this sidewalk, and a face trying too hard to pass for ordinary. I pull the door anyway and step into the hum I used to measure my days by.

Ink and burnt coffee. Printer heat. The faint, sharp sugar of cheap donuts. Phones ringing in syncopated little bursts like birds that never learned a proper song. The wall of clippings—election night, the river flood, the time a dog rescued a child from the creek and we all cried into our sleeves—hangs right where it always has, sun-faded along the edges where the afternoon light does its tender eating. I stand for a second and pretend the smell alone could graft me back into a version of myself whose life was made of deadlines and decent shoes.

"Look what the cat slept on and returned," Landon calls from his glass-paneled office, half smile, half warning. He's tall but built like he's been living on espresso and late nights—lean muscle wrapped in the kind of exhaustion you only earn from too many deadlines and too little sunlight. His tie is missing, his collar undone, the shadow of a beard crawling across his jaw. The sleeves of his white shirt are rolled to the elbows, ink smudged along one forearm where a leaky pen met too much caffeine and not enough patience. Two empty mugs hang from his fingers, a stack of mail tucked under his arm like an afterthought. He smells faintly of ink and roasted beans—burnout and bravado.

"Morning," I say, like that word isn't a lie in my mouth. "Funny coming from the man who's been on an extended coffee-break tour. Jess has basically been running the Gazette while you've been off chasing enlightenment."

His grin falters just enough to make it worth it. "Delegation builds character," he says, retreating toward his office again, where stacks of marked-up copy lean like tired sentinels around his desk. The glass door swings shut behind him, muting the sound of his sigh.

Jess straightens from her desk so fast her chair squeals. Blonde hair in a high knot, gray eyes that belong to someone who can talk her way into a locked building just by looking like she's supposed to be there. Winged liner, glitter at the inner corners because she refuses to stop being herself on principle. Her mouth opens—questions tumbling, I can hear them—but I lift a hand and send her the smallest shake of my head. Later. Please, later. Something in my face must land, because she swallows the words like pills and shifts to a different gear.

"You owe me so many coffees I could drown," she says lightly, tossing me a spare lanyard with my press badge. "Consider this the rope I throw you when you insist on cliff-diving without telling me where you're jumping."

I catch the lanyard. The plastic is warm from her hand. "I'll Venmo you actual money. Coffee's not enough."

"You can try," she says, and it's almost a smile. "Grab a headset. Landon wants to push a calendar piece on the holiday food drive and there's a city council rumor about new permit fees for street vendors. Also, your desk ate a mountain of mail."

"My desk eats everything."

"It missed you," she says, and if there's anything prickly beneath that, she hides it with so much care I feel my throat burn.

I slide into my chair like I never left. The seat gives with the same sigh. There's a sticky note on the monitor in my own handwriting—SAVE FINAL DRAFTS TO FOLDER / REMEMBER TO EAT—and the mundanity of it hits me with a kind of grief I wasn't expecting. I open a document. I type a sentence. The keys feel too loud and too far away. Words used to arrive easily. Now they come cautiously, as if the room might punish them for existing.

"Copy deadline moved up," Landon says, popping out like a meerkat, then softening when he sees me. "Not for you. You get today. Ease in, Hartwell."

"Ease in," I echo. The chair creaks. My fingers hover above the keyboard. I write a lede about canned goods and generosity and community like I believe it. I can make a sentence stand up and walk even when my chest is full of glass. That's one of the only useful things I know.

Jess appears and sets a paper cup within reach. "Hot," she warns.

"What's in it?"

"Caffeine and mercy." She leans on the edge of my desk, bends so her voice won't carry. "I'm not going to ask. I want to. You can see that I want to. But I'm not. At least... not today."

Something in me loosens and aches. "I'm here… barely," I say.

"I see that." She taps the rim of the paper cup with one fingernail. "Landon does too. He told me to tell you the council rumor can wait and we'll let the interns suffer through calling a list of donors who want to hear themselves congratulated. You get soft news for a day."

"Punishment masquerading as kindness," I mutter.

"Don't push me, I'll assign you a profile on the town's favorite cat."

"Sir Pounce is a menace."

"And yet he pulls numbers."

I do my work. Jess fields questions from a source about a zoning map. Landon swears at the printer and then swears at himself for swearing at the printer. The intern whose name I keep forgetting (Mason? Max?) answers the phone too brightly and then writes a message down like he's practicing calligraphy for a future where we all live in hand-lettered houses. The newsroom breathes. I breathe with it. Every once in a while something shifts—my blood, the air—and there's a faint rise of heat under my skin, a spark at the wrist like a tiny animal turning in its sleep. I keep my palms flat on the desk until it passes. The flame inside me obeys like a trained thing and I don't decide whether that makes me proud or terrified.

"Lunch," Jess says around noon. "Come on, we'll walk, I need a sandwich the size of my head."

"I'll pass," I say. "I want to get this filed. I'm not... fast."

"You're fast enough to out-write everyone in this room," she says, snatching her coat from the back of her chair. "But fine—*I'll* grab lunch. Try not to burn the place down while I'm gone. And if I'm not back in twenty, assume I've been abducted by the sandwich cartel."

I fake a laugh. She's polite enough to not call me out for it.

She goes, a scribble of scarf and relentless energy, the doorbell jingling once as the cold punches in and then backs out. I finalize the piece. I send it to copy. I answer a voicemail from a man who thinks a neighbor's wind chimes violate an ordinance. I stick a Post-it to my monitor that says in block letters: PICK UP BREAD. The domesticity of it lands like a dare. I picture the house I left, the study light slanting over the desk, the smell of cedar embedded in the woodgrain like memory. I picture him and then I force myself not to, because if I start, I will not stop.

Jess returns with a paper bag that leaks warmth. "Turkey with everything and a third of a jar of mustard, because I know who you are."

"I said—"

"You said you'd pass, which is cute code for '*I will pass out*,'" she says, dropping into the chair opposite me and unwrapping her own sandwich like a ritual. "*Eat.*"

I take a bite. It tastes like exactly what it is—mustard, salt, good bread, a kindness—and I have to swallow around the sudden pressure behind my eyes. Jess, because she's good at kindness without making it into charity, swings the conversation into weather complaints and an anecdote about a neighbor who decorates for Thanksgiving with more aggression than most people reserve for war.

I almost get through the day without breaking.

It happens at three, when the light goes thin and blue, the way it does in late November when the sky starts practicing being winter. I deliver a printed draft to Landon because he still loves marking paper, and as I put it on his desk, my eyes catch on the board behind him—the map of Blackmoor with red pins for crime scenes and blue pins for stolen bikes and a single gold pin for a feature that went oddly viral about a woman who teaches seniors how to use their smartphones. My vision tunnels on the constellation the pins make around Bellflower and two other streets that have become their own kind of gravity. The pins look like someone keeping score.

"You okay?" Landon asks, because he's not unkind even when he's pretending to be a cynic.

"Fine." The word is velvet over wire.

"Go early if you want," he says, not looking up as he draws a squiggle beside a paragraph that offended his religion. "Jess can file the afternoon blotter. Tell her I said it's good for her character."

"That'll end well," I say, and my voice almost knows how to sound like it used to.

I collect my bag. Jess looks up as if her eyes are on a string tied to my movement. "You heading out? I can walk you partway if you wait five."

"I'll be okay," I say. "I'm a big girl."

"Text when you're home," she says, then rolls her eyes when she hears herself. "God, I sound like a mother."

"You have the hair for it," I say, and she sticks her tongue out, glitter catching the light.

It's colder than it looks when I step outside. The air slides inside my coat and bites. The street has that late-afternoon brightness that feels thinner than sunlight—like the day is holding up a lamp and pretending it's a star. Traffic moves in polite lines. A bus exhale-hisses at the corner. Someone's playing awful holiday music from a phone speaker and the bells clang against the November light like they're not sure what month it is. I tug the coat closer at my throat and walk.

Normal. Sidewalk. Storefront window full of cinnamon-sprinkled things I don't want. A florist closing early, shaking snowwater off buckets. A kid in a puffer jacket stomping a slush puddle like he's paid to. I pass a woman talking into her scarf, a man carrying a package that looks like a painting, a dog that has decided it hates a particular bench and is informing the bench of this. My heart learns the beat of the city again, the one that says: *you belong.*

The hum flares beneath my skin. The flame sparking to life. It stays low, obedient. Every so often it twitches when I catch a shadow wrong or the smell of metal trips a memory, but I breathe and it remembers the rules we made. He taught me that—how to refuse the urge to make spectacle, how to keep the oxygen honest. The thought threads heat through me, not the dangerous kind. The part that feels like ache.

At the corner, the crosswalk sign still shows the man in mid-stride. I step off the curb with the other pedestrians. A white truck rolls past in the near lane, logo of a water filtration company blued across its side. The driver is talking, one hand on the wheel, carefree and unhurried. A bus approaches in the far lane, the sound big enough to fill a head with cotton. I wait on the median, nervous energy swirling inside me, though I can't say why. A woman stands to my left with a stroller, a baby sublimely unimpressed by weather and civilization. The baby drops a pink glove and the woman reaches to retrieve it with a laugh shaped like apology. The bus sighs past, wind pushing a scrap of newsprint into my boot. I step forward with the light.

Someone says, "Excuse me—ma'am?" Not the kind of voice that startles. The kind designed to be trusted. Reflex answers reflex, and I half-turn.

A man in a city-issue reflective jacket—orange stripes, patch that reads PUBLIC WORKS—holds up a phone and points at the back of it. "This yours? Picked it up by the Gazette door."

It's not. It's a black case like a hundred others, a small crack in the corner. I open my mouth to say so. Behind him, the bus brakes whisper. A second man steps up—also reflective jacket, clipboard—smiling that over-bright smile people use when they want to be invisible in plain sight. His shadow crosses mine just as the holiday bells clang from the bakery window. For one half beat my skin remembers every corridor beneath the university, every word breathed against my mouth, every warning and promise, and the flame inside me wakes like a startled bird.

"Not mine," I say, and aim my body toward the far curb.

Something sweet and wrong cuts the air—faint as a hospital hallway. The first man lifts the phone an inch higher, like a magician showing a card. The other drops his clipboard. It hits the slush with a smack that sounds like a bad joke. I pivot to avoid it and my boot slips half an inch on an invisible skin of ice. Not enough to fall. Enough to break a line.

A cloth finds my face from behind—cold, then not. The scent resolves into something chemical and sugary, the kind that makes thoughts flicker like lights on a dying grid. I jerk and the man with the "PUBLIC WORKS" patch makes a gentle shushing motion no one sees because the bus, because the stroller, because the bells. I try to do what he taught me—pull the heat inward, flood the lungs with air that belongs to me—but every breath brings more of the wrong sweetness, and the world does a slow, considered tilt. My fingers claw at the cloth and meet a hand that isn't careless. The second man's jacket whispers against mine, Velcro on wool. A voice—not mine, not his—says calm down in the low, affectionate tone people reserve for dogs and women. I hear myself think: *NO*.

On the other side of the bus, someone laughs too loudly. A horn taps. A pigeon lifts from the curb with a single beat. I catch the sky between buildings—a thin, flat blue like an eye that doesn't blink. The cloth presses harder against my mouth. The smell pushes through my head like fog that took a class in being precise. The flame tries to flare and I cage it because even now I know that lighting myself in the middle of the street will make a spectacle they can use. My knees soften. The world goes briefly translucent at the edges, all the outlines double as if memory and sight were having a small argument. The man with the clipboard hooks an arm around my waist with a neatness that says rehearsal. He lifts when I bend. I am walking and not walking.

We move and the bus windows reflect us—three figures stitched into daylight, but of course... nothing to see here. The door of a van by the curb slides open. Not a white van because the world is smarter than that—an unremarkable gray with a magnetic sign that reads DRAINAGE SER-VICES and a smear of real road salt along the panel to lie for it. Inside smells colder than out-side, a steel-clean chill, and something soft—laun-dry—or maybe I'm imagining the softness be-cause I want it. Someone's hand disappears my phone with a comfortingly deft theft. The cloth lets more sugar into my head. The day narrows to a tunnel with polite manners.

A passerby glances up, registers two men help-ing a third—workplace injury, winter slip, noth-ing here—and looks away. The van door murmurs shut. The street resumes its script... bells, a stroller wheel catching on a rut, the bus squealing as it stops. The last thing that lands is small and human—a faint tap as my badge, knocked loose from my pocket, skitters under the passenger seat so gently that no one hears it but me. Or maybe no one hears it at all and I only imagine that because the mind is greedy for order when the body is not allowed any.

Then the light folds.

The world—intelligently, efficiently—does not notice I am gone.

Chapter 40

There's an incessant, musty stench assaulting my nose—rot, damp earth, old iron. It's so strong I jolt awake, gagging on it. My eyes snap open, vision swimming as the world tilts in and out of focus. A slick weight clings to my tongue, chemical and bitter. Chloroform. An old and nasty trick that quickly calms its victims.

My pulse spikes. My brain stumbles over itself, clawing back fragments—the flash of movement, a hand across my mouth, the burn in my throat, the world collapsing to black. The men who blocked my path. The arms that held too tightly.

The Council.

Cold panic coils low in my stomach. Why?

Adrian said they'd let it go—that they'd let *us* go—so long as we were apart.

I sit up too fast, the room lurching around me. Stone walls crowd in close, rough and sweating with moisture. Moss creeps up from the corners, threading through cracks like veins. The floor is dirt, packed and uneven, and the air carries the metallic tang of rust—or blood.

To my right, a grated window lets in a thin shard of light—moonlight, maybe. It paints the far wall in silver and shadow. There's nothing else. No door that I can see, no furniture beyond a splintered chair and a basin darkened by time.

My heart hammers. Whoever brought me here knew what they were doing.

I flex my fingers, testing for restraints. Rope burns kiss my wrists, but the bindings are gone. My captors are confident enough not to chain me again—or arrogant enough to think I won't try to escape.

I will.

Because I have to.

Because somewhere beyond these walls, Adrian thinks distance can save me. And if the Council has decided otherwise, I'll burn my way through stone to prove them wrong.

Rot and damp and old iron sit on my tongue like punishment. I push to a sitting position, slowly, letting the room stop wobbling. The grated window admits a thin blade of light that cuts the cell on a diagonal—silver dust hanging, motes drifting, a drip somewhere keeping time. My wrists sting when I flex.

I move my jaw to work out the ache where a cloth was held too long, too hard. Chloroform lingering in the back of my throat, like a sour chemical ghost. I swallow it down and take inventory. Coat gone, boots still on, sweater stretched, and tights laddered on one shin where someone wasn't careful. My palms are gritty, but when I rub them together, heat wakes—low, obedient. *Hello.* The flame answers like a cat opening one eye. *Not yet*, it says. *Soon.*

Footsteps. Several sets clattering against stone. A key works in a lock I hadn't seen—stone gives up a seam and a door reveals itself, swollen with damp. Two figures enter first, black coats over crimson, hoods thrown back, masks on. One is a woman with hair like steel wool pinned in an uncompromising knot, the bridge of her nose thin and aristocratic behind a carved onyx half-mask shaped like a thorn branch. Shadebriar. The other is a boy, no older than me, jaw clenched so hard it whitens, mask a flat plate incised with winter roses. Nightbloom, or a cousin House that thinks itself poetic.

Behind them comes the smell of oil and chill air, and the man who fills the doorway like a verdict. Tall, grizzled at the temples, his mask a pane of hammered iron with a single vertical slit. Duskmere. His shoulders carry a weight that isn't armor. It's authority practiced until it feels like second nature. He doesn't look at me, not at first. He looks at the room the way people look at a stage just before a play.

"Miss Hartwell," he says finally, voice low in the stone. "Stand."

"I'm comfortable," I say, and I am, because comfort is sometimes a weapon.

Steel-wool lifts her chin. "Stand."

I do, only because it will annoy them less if they think compliance was purchased. The boy steps forward with a set of manacles—old iron, etched with sigils that are more decoration than function. Whoever cut them liked the look of authority. He hesitates when he meets my eyes. Up close, his are gray and uncertain, lashes dark with moisture from the damp air.

"Wrists," he says, trying for command.

I give them to him, turning so the rope-burns show. He flinches, then schools his face and clicks the cuffs shut. The metal is cold enough to sting, and the sigils nip at my skin like small teeth. I let my breath shorten, let my shoulders dip. I let them think I am smaller than I am.

"Walk," Iron Mask says.

The corridor outside is a throat cut into stone, lit by lamps that burn a greasy yellow. Water runs somewhere unseen. Old pipes rattle in the bones of the place. We pass doors that pretend to be walls, and walls that remember being doors. My steps echo, a half-beat off theirs. The air tastes like flint and earth. Somewhere above, the world continues, utterly oblivious to the wickedness just below their feet. The knowledge makes me angry enough to keep warm.

We descend a short flight and enter a round chamber that understands performance. Twelve seats rise on a shallow tier, evenly spaced in a perfect circle, each with a sigil set into the floor before it. No throne, because that would be too honest. Here they prefer choreography to crowns. The ceiling is a dome of soot-dark stone ribbed with iron, a skylight cut at the apex and shuttered from above so that daylight filters down in a dim, judgmental column. Candles line the lower walls, their flames breathing in unison.

The chairs are occupied. Robes deeper than blood, masks carved from bone, obsidian, and antique wood. The air smells like beeswax, old leather, and the smugness of ritual. I catalog insignia as if I'm taking attendance in one of Adrian's classes. Winterveil: a simple snowflake etched with ruthless geometry. Duskmere: a crescent that means silence more than it means night. Ashvale:

a brand that pretends ash is rebirth rather than residue. Ignisfold: bare, severe lines, the math of denial. Shadebriar is there with her thorn-mask. Thornehaven takes his seat and becomes the emblem he thinks himself. Nightbloom leans back as if performance is an art you can perfect through languor. Others I don't know—lesser Houses with the confidence of proximity.

There is one empty chair. The glassy cold that moves through me at the sight is not surprise. It's confirmation. They have done this without him.

"Octavia Adeline Embergrave," someone says, and the way my name moves through the room tells me Winterveil speaks. Old, careful, the words stacked like books. "You are called to answer."

"For what?" I ask.

"For existing inconveniently," says a voice that pretends to be kind. Nightbloom, amused.

A low murmur of rebuke that is not rebuke. Nightbloom only smiles behind their mask. Duskmere leans forward, elbows on knees. "For threatening equilibrium," he says. "For awakening what sleeps. For forcing our hand."

Ashvale makes a small noise of disapproval, then steels her tone. "We offer remedy," she recites, the capital letter audible. "For the safety of all—yourself included."

"Remedy," I say, as if tasting something bitter and considering the vintage.

Ignisfold's mask turns a fraction, candlelight breaking across the plane. "You will listen."

Duskmere gestures, and the boy tightens my chains to a ring bolted at the floor's center. The ring is old and knows what it's for. The manacles pull me one step forward and hold me there, neat as an exclamation point.

Winterveil again, ignoring my sarcasm the way archivists ignore floods. "We will ask. You will answer. We will help you choose safety."

"Will you," I say, and let my voice be mild.

The manipulation begins like a temperature change. Soft. Then softer. A pressure behind the eyes, the subtle cloth of something winding itself around the back of my skull. The air thickens with incense I didn't notice at first—lavender and something keener, medicinal, a cousin to chloroform's ghost. Words thread the smoke, old words stripped of context and repeated until they become pavlovian. *Peace. Shelter. Consent. Safety.* Words that are not my own.

Ashvale stands, hands raised as if in benediction, voice pitched to the precise frequency that hides command inside care. "Octavia," she says, soft enough that a child would lean in. "We can unburden you. The fire is not a friend. it is an appetite. Lay it down. Lay *you* down. We will keep you. We will keep them safe."

Shadebriar adds a low susurrus beneath her, a bass note you feel in bone. "Consent is mercy," he intones. "Surrender is wisdom."

Nightbloom's voice slips like silk. "It will feel good to stop."

The pressure wraps and tightens, not like hands, like gauze. Somewhere behind it, a rhythm taps—steady, older than Latin, too honest to be fooled. The flame inside me lifts its head, the succubus uncoils like a creature roused by a voice it refuses to obey. Heat crawls up my arms, purring. Hunger wakes—not for blood, not for flesh, but for agency. I think of the ledger on Adrian's desk, of the column in pencil, of his mouth when he said notes, not monuments. I think of the empty chair and the way he would have stood, if he had been allowed, in the gap and said, No.

The Council's veil thickens. Words slide like oil—trust, healing, chosen, safe. For a second, the world tilts, edges blur, my knees soften. I let my mouth part. I let my eyes unfocus. I let a tremor travel up my arms. I give them the picture they want. A girl persuaded by wisdom, a weapon folded into an heirloom.

Shadebriar's hands lower. His exhale is the kind people sigh when they've convinced themselves they're good. "There," he whispers. "Better."

My chains are loosened. The boy's fingers brush my wrist where the manacle sits. His skin is cold, and his reluctance is painfully human. He looks up, catches my gaze and flinches—and in that tiny movement, I find the exact weight of the mask he wears for them.

"Escort her," Duskmere says. "Gentle hands. We will begin the rite of concordance."

I let my head dip, let my shoulders soften, let docility arrange my body. They guide me—two, then four—down a different hall, this one lined with niches containing votive lamps that smell of tallow and a sweetness that makes my teeth ache. We pass a threshold marked with a sigil inlaid into the stone—a braided circle. Concord. Inside, a smaller round room waits—no seats, only a low dais and a shallow basin, its water black in the bad light. The air buzzes faintly, the way rooms buzz when too much ritual has been done in them. Honey. Milk. Iron. Old songs sung by tired throats.

They think I am malleable. They think I have agreed to be softened into someone more convenient. They think I credit them for their language.

The boy hesitates again. He means to step back. Instead, he turns me gently and positions me on the dais, as if I might bruise. His mouth forms a word behind the mask. Sorry, perhaps. Or run. It doesn't matter. I have already chosen.

I let my knees bend, as if I mean to kneel. I let my head bow, as if I mean to give them the back of my neck. Then I breathe, and I open.

The succubus moves first—quiet, precise, not seduction, sovereignty. I let the hum slide down my throat and out with my next exhale, a note pitched to the frequency of appetite. The air flexes. Where my breath touches the room, edges soften, attention blurs. Eyes on me dilate. The man to my left—Ignisfold's attendant, severe mouth, devout hands—sways. Ashvale's spine loosens, not in surrender, in relief, as if the thing she's been holding up is being held for her. Nightbloom laughs once, low, as if remembering a better party. The boy's fingers tighten on the chain, but he doesn't lift it. He looks like someone hearing his name in a language he learned in the womb.

I am not stealing minds. I am reminding them of their own hunger and asking it to look at me. As their focus tips toward me, even a fraction, my hands stop shaking. Heat slides into my veins with clean certainty. I open again—deeper this time—and draw.

Energy tastes like weather. Duskmere's man is fog and salt. Ignisfold is iron filings on the tongue. Shadebriar is atrium sun filtered through leaves, bitter where the plants are poisonous. I sip, not to drain, to unbalance—enough to make knees loose, enough to make hands slow, enough to lower the room's guard to its own pulse.

"Stop," someone says, as if naming it undoes it. The lamps gutter. The water in the basin trembles as if sound has weight.

Then I let the Phoenix answer.

It comes like memory that turns suddenly into fact. A long, effortless unfurling under the skin, bones remembering how to be lighter than air, tendons learning a new grammar. Heat blooms—not a roar, a crown. The golden threads I've hidden a hundred times braid themselves into something with lift. My shoulder blades ache and then do not. What lies beneath them wakes and opens, not feathers but the idea of feathers—incendiary and stunning. My breath becomes the bellows of a small, patient forge. The air in the room changes its mind about what it is for.

"Contain her!" Duskmere's voice slams through the hall behind us, the word contain hitting the door like a hammer on a plate. Doors move quickly for men like him.

The attendants lunge. I do not step back. I rise.

It is clumsy and exquisite. Lift is a fact. Control is a promise. My boots leave the dais, chains clatter, and the man who reaches for my ankle closes on light. I sweep the nearest lamp with a glance and it obeys, flame elongating like a bow, leaping to the next wick, and the next, and then to the honey on the walls and the milk in the bowls and the oil in the hinges. Fire is greedy when given permission. It eats politely at first, then stops pretending.

"Stop her!" Ashvale's voice breaks on the last word. The boy stares, transfixed, hands empty, chain dangling. His mask tilts, and I see the pale edge of his cheek. He is too young to have picked this religion of control. He will either leave it or be eaten by it. I cannot decide that for him. I can only be the reason he understands decision.

I breathe again and the flame crowns me. The succubus hum turns wicked with satisfaction. Energy pours into me—thin golden lines from everybody in the room, unwilling, astonished, *mine*. I sip and let go, sip and let go, leaving weakness in my wake, not ruin. I am not a monster in their design. I am the answer to their lies.

Stone resists fire longer than wood, but the old mortar is tired and the tapestries are eager. Smoke rises like a creature recalling its body. Sirens will not come here for the world above does not know this room exists. *Good*. It will burn cleaner.

The boy drops the chain. We look at each other, and whatever he would have said becomes a flinch as a crack opens in the ceiling—just a hairline at first, then a thin scream of light. Not daylight. Firelight, magnified by the dome. Someone shrieks. Someone prays. Ignisfold tries a word that might have worked last year. It does not work now.

I angle toward the door—toward Duskmere—and he sets his feet wide, mask fixed, hands bare. He believes himself a wall. The heat moves off me in a shimmer. He feels it and braces. I do not strike him. I pass him—close enough that the iron of his mask warms the air between us, close enough that he could have reached me if he believed he had a right. He does not. Not anymore.

The corridor is a throat full of smoke now, lamps flaring and failing one after another like a line of candles at the world's saddest birthday. I fly badly and beautifully, feet scuffing the wall, shoulder slamming a lintel, the new weight and new absence of weight teaching me on the job. Chains bang against stone and spark. Sparks like wishes. Wishes like orders. Doors remember their seams. I find air and push.

Up. Turn. Through.

The first stairwell is a chimney I have lit. I skirt it, find the second, and rise through heat that would have undone me yesterday. Not today, the new thing in me says, pleased. At the level where the air is cleaner, I land because landing is still important to the body's sense of self. Boots on stone. Hands on rail. The old world reasserting itself without insisting I belong to it.

Then one more door, iron-banded, swollen with damp. It does not want to move. I put my shoulder to it and it remembers me from another life. It opens a grudging inch, then two. Cold air pushes in like an apology. Snow-bright gray beyond, the color of sky just before it decides to keep its afternoon promise. I squeeze through, scrape my shoulder, rip my sleeve, and stumble into… daylight. Honest, indifferent, almost obscene.

Behind me, something deep collapses with a sound like a sigh turned into a scream. Smoke follows, dark, bitter, alive. Fire licks the edges of the hidden door and then takes an interest in the dried ivy that had disguised it from street-level curiosity. I put a hand to the wall to steady myself and feel the vibration of a system I have broken.

"Octavia."

My name lands not like a command, not like a plea—like a fact.

He stands twenty yards down the narrow service lane that fronts the back of the old municipal buildings—the ones Blackmoor pretends are utilities. Coat unbuttoned, tie dark, hair raked back like he'd been running one hand through it for the length of a bad hour. His face is clean of triumph or terror. Just... arrival. Behind him, the day keeps going—a delivery truck idling, a cyclist passing, a gull scissoring the air like a mean idea.

"You." The word cracks out of me with more gratitude than I want. I straighten. The chains hang heavy from my wrists, blackened and glowing where the sigils have failed. He scans me—hands, throat, eyes—and only when he sees that I am breathing and upright does something in him loosen enough for expression. It's small. It's enough.

He takes one step, then another, hesitant as if the street itself were listening for proof of who he is. On the third step the building behind me exhaled a new column of smoke, and flames licked at the lintel like a tongue. A siren far off decided to take an interest. He doesn't look back at the fire. He looks only at me.

"They acted without you," I say. It isn't a question.

"Yes." His voice is sanded. "They will regret it."

"I didn't pretend very long."

"I didn't want you to." He stops at arm's length, which for him is restraint and for me is mercy. The heat radiating off me strokes the front of his coat. The heat radiating off him answers it. For a second the world refocuses on only that exchange.

"You were coming to get me," I say.

"I was already inside," he says, and I see it then. The ash on his cuff, the singe at the hem, the scrape across his knuckles, the way his breathing is too even, the way a man breathes when he has been running stairs under smoke and will not let his lungs tell on him.

"*Adrian.*" I don't know whether I mean it as benediction or warning. Both.

He looks at the chains, then at my eyes. "Do you need them off," he asks, as if asking if I would like another cup of coffee.

"No," I say, and the word fills with a heat that is not fury. I lift my wrists, and the metal softens like wax in the right hands. The links fall open with a sound like a nest of insects dying. I step out of them and the street learns my weight again.

He reaches—slow enough to be stopped, sure enough to be believed—and touches a place just above my elbow where skin meets soot. It's nothing. It's everything. The bond hums between us like wire after lightning. Quietly tethered. Not caged.

Behind us, the hidden building is no longer shy about announcing its emergency. Smoke climbs the brick in loops. Windows that never admitted to being windows spit flame. The city will pretend this is an electrical fire. The Council will pretend it is a tragedy. The truth will live in the bones of anyone who breathed this air today.

"Walk," he says, so soft it could be a thought.

"Where," I ask.

"Away," he says. "And then toward."

It sounds like a riddle. It feels like a command I would have given myself, if I had lived long enough to know I could.

We turn together into the gray. My shoulders remember wings and then let them go, for now. My mouth tastes like iron tinged with honey and smoke. My hands smell like what I refuse to be remade into. Sirens gather their courage somewhere beyond the next block. The cold puts its clean teeth in my cheeks and calls it applause.

"Not the end," he says without looking at me.

"No," I answer, and don't look back. "The beginning."

EPILOGUE

The city sleeps the way guilt does—lightly, ready to wake at the first sound of sirens. From my study window, I can see the last coils of smoke rising from the place that used to be the Council's heart. The snow catches the soot before it lands, trying to turn it into something pure. It fails. So do I, but less often now.

Octavia is asleep upstairs. For the first time in too long, her breathing sounds like peace rather than preparation. Every so often, the flame under her skin flickers—a heartbeat the world doesn't deserve to witness. I tell myself that she's safe. That I've bought us time. That the gods—if they still bother with this ruined machine of a world—owe me one quiet night.

But I know better. I can already feel the next war moving.

The Council will call what we did treason. They'll call her a weapon. They'll call me worse.

Let them.

They taught me that love was leverage. That devotion was a ledger to be balanced in blood. They believed obedience could be bred like dogs. They were *wrong*. I've been their instrument, their wolf, their priest of restraint for centuries—but every structure has a breaking point, and mine is the woman upstairs with ash beneath her nails and stars in her eyes.

When I saw her wings unfold in that burning chamber—light made flesh, defiance made divine—I understood something no oath ever taught me: *I was never built to serve. I was built to end them.*

So I will.

I'll burn the Council for her, one House at a time, until every relic that called itself righteous is nothing but memory and molten glass. I'll pull down their archives, their bloodlines, their sacred mathematics, until the only record of their rule is the smoke that once spelled their names.

They made me the monster they feared, but she made me human enough to choose what to do with it.

Octavia thinks I set her free. She doesn't know that I freed myself the moment I chose her over them. And yet, she's right about one thing—it isn't an ending. It's the beginning of something the world has no word for.

We'll dismantle their empire from the inside out. Quietly at first. Then loudly enough that even their ghosts will cover their ears.

I look out over the sleeping city and think of her voice, her fire, the way she said my name like it was both threat and vow. My wicked ruin. My salvation. My reason to stop pretending restraint is virtue.

When morning comes, she'll wake to a world that thinks it still belongs to the Council.

By the time the next dawn breaks, it will belong to her.

And to me.

Together, we'll finish what the fire started.

About The Author

B is a devoted wife and dog mom who has always had a passion for writing. When the opportunity arose, she channeled all her energy into creating an immersive world that captivated readers from the very first page. B loves traveling, reading, photography, and videogaming with her husband. B actively shares her journey on social media, connecting with readers of Chasing The Flame, as well as Shadows & Starlight and Written In Blood.

ACKNOWLEDGEMENTS

To my incredible alpha readers, Kessa and Jackie—thank you for your sharp eyes, and late-night messages that somehow always arrived at the exact moment I needed to laugh or rethink everything. Your excitement made the shadows of this story a little brighter.

To my partners and co-owners at Golden Light Publishing House— Letta & Yvonne, thank you for every brainstorm that spiraled into chaos, for the random giggles that somehow led to breakthroughs, and for the countless late nights spent building something far bigger than ourselves. You've turned creation into communion.

To my family, who remind me there is life beyond the page, and to my husband, who loves me through every draft, every deadline, and every night I disappear into fictional worlds—thank you for your patience, your faith, and your unwavering belief that all of this is worth it. You are my anchor in every storm.

And finally—to every reader who picked up *Written in Blood* and chose to walk through the flames with Octavia and Adrian… thank you. You made this story real. You gave it breath.

Here's to the ones who crave stories that bleed.

With love,

B. Wills